Published by Golden Goat Guild

goldengoatguild.net

ISBN 978-0-578-60808-2 (paperback)
ISBN 978-0-578-60809-9 (hardcover)
FIC019000 FICTION / Literary

Printed in the United States of America

KING OF DOGS

BY

ANDREW EDWARDS

For you, my son

I fled him down the nights and down the days;
I fled him, down the arches of the years;
I fled him, down the labyrinthine ways;
Of my own mind; and in the midst of tears
I hid from him, and under running laughter.

Francis Thompson

Indeed, the art of tracking is a science that requires fundamentally the same intellectual abilities as modern physics.

Louis Liebenberg
The Art of Tracking: The Origin of Science

The decline of the West, which at first sight may appear, like the corresponding decline of the Classical Culture, a phenomenon limited in time and space, we now perceive to be a philosophical problem that, when comprehended in all its gravity, includes within itself every great question of Being.

Oswald Spengler
Decline of the West

1
The God

Just as the world of men turned the decisive corner heading into the long straightaway of its foretold end, an exemplary soldier named Jack died too early in a dilapidated government hospital as the January snow fell outside, and the country he had served collapsed in quiet increments. Much in the way its Soviet counterpart had fallen some decades prior, the American empire was long dead by the time jackals emerged in the first decades of the new millennium to devour the Republic's corpse. Only Grayson was there by Jack's bedside at the end. Between them were thirty years of friendship, two failed marriages, and one lost child. Two days and nights Grayson sat with Jack as the many monitoring machines twittered and glowed green. When Jack slept, Grayson stood at the big windowpanes watching the leafless white valley and the crumbling city of their childhood. When Jack was awake, Grayson got the young blonde nurse to feed him. Other times Grayson fed him himself.

As the windows grew dark on the second night, he watched the orange flicker of barrel fires in the interstices of the city grid reflect off the snow and the dark walls of buildings. When the nurse left, they talked of their time in the field and in the mountains, of hunting and of training to fight, with weapons and without. This was and had always been their shared cup. When home on leave or otherwise available, Jack taught to Grayson everything he'd learned in the Army, in Special Forces and in the theatres of war. And though Jack had said many times that Grayson was a natural warrior, Jack had also said Grayson was a born monk. And while both were true, Grayson joined neither military nor monastery. They recalled nights of campfires and whiskey spent beneath the great cedars that teetered on the northwest sky when they looked up, and they each spoke of waking fully refreshed in grey dawn with the spirit of the earth generously, unspeakably upon them. And at the last, in the late hours when the hospital was quiet, they spoke of dogs. With death attendant to the amberlit room, they spoke of loyalty. The inexhaustible adaptivity of dogs and mysteries lost to time that men only sense and cannot name. They spoke of those dogs gone but whom they hoped to meet again— the wolfhound and wirehaired pointer.

When Jack mentioned his younger brother Phil was still in the desert of Utah and with a child on the way, he brought himself up from the bed, out of the opiate stupor, as if to defy death one last time and said only, "Will you promise to go see about him?" And Grayson said, "Done. Let's write the address down now so we don't forget." This was Jack's last gift to Grayson. A righteous mission, which was Grayson's deepest wish. And so it came to pass in that moment that this particular history began. And because the promise was a true promise, or because the gift was given as the giver lay divided between the known and the unknown worlds, the many threads of time and of miles were drawn taut into a type of tapestry of being, a focusing, that has many names but is never entirely seen or understood, the domain of God alone. He who cannot be faced head on.

The next morning Grayson met the Orthodox priest in the ICU hallway. He pressed to the cloaked and bearded priest a stack of bills for the ceremony that Grayson would not attend. The priest embraced him. With the accordion folds of brow raised in a kind expression the priest said, "Saint Maximus taught that those who refuse to face their suffering know not what benefit it brings for the next world. This will not be a problem for you, I suspect." Grayson nodded. Outside he stood in a cold scentless wind on the concrete hospital steps and felt an odd lightness in his bones that he took to be the merciful pressure valve of time itself. He withstood the chill and worked for a moment at envisioning the forms of those countervailing forces, gratitude and sacrifice, which powered this fluid machine of sorrow called the world. In his years he'd gained fear and humility and could go days without food, but Grayson never could weep very well. And as he walked over the creaking snow to his truck with gunshots ringing plainly and unanswered in the neighboring residential blocks, instead of crying and instead of bargaining, he made calculations of funds and miles. Of time and degree. He breathed in steady counts of four. The sky roiled. By the time he reached the truck his next moves were lined out. A week later he was on the road. With no living family of his own there were no other goodbyes to be made.

The 84-highway going east out of Oregon transfigured itself from pavement to slipstream. The hours were surrendered to motion, to speed. Sorrow could be refined, distilled as fuel, and so it was—mile by mile, Grayson went faster on his way. In northern

Utah the dry snow sifted down so heavy he could see nothing, had to pull off on a desolated ranch road to wait it out. He stood in that white desert oblivion and observed a great herd of elk ambling over the parkland hills. With their dark brown briskets and heather-colored rear quarters that disappeared against the patchwork of tawny earth and snow drifts, they seemed halved and looked like a party of satyrs nimbling through the mist to some mysterious convocation. Their great alpha hierophant in the fore with his crown of sap-darkened antlers led them away in the ruffle of the canyons and again the landscape was blank but for the falling quiet snow.

In the Oregon he left behind, the cities were collapsing to the new religio-political-corporate order: pooled sewage and shanties juxtaposed with police escorts and gated communities. Yet Salt Lake, with its volunteer work crews shoveling snow and its eight open lanes of freeway, seemed little disturbed when he passed through. And then late in the night, having turned off the rural highway for gas far from any city, he stood beyond the cast light of the service station on an unmarred blanket of white and found the sky a cloudless monolith, brilliant with blue stars. It seemed to him a black parabolic screen observing him too as the muffled roar of a single Freightliner passed out on the highway. "Having no city here I seek another in the future," he said out loud to himself. Across the parking lot, a gypsy woman waylaid somehow on this back route staggered from a hovel of sheet plastic and cardboard near the green dumpster beside the station. As he approached the store, the gypsy with her half-shorn hair and garish makeup tried to sell him a thin cat she pulled from among her rags by its neck scruff. The cat beheld him with gentle yellow eyes, pleading. When he declined, the gypsy cursed him by spitting between the feline's calico hindlegs and she made bewitching stabs into the air with pronged fingernails where he had passed.

Grayson asked himself if even after all the books and lectures, after a decade's study and wandering, could he really account for the craziness of the world. As he entered the convenience store he wasn't sure of his answer. In these first decades of the new millennium, finished with social engineering and mere financial rapine, the oligarchs of the era turned to base thievery. They pillaged utilities, land and minerals. Water first: its ownership and its metering. And if American cities burned as the oligarch's corporate mercenaries secured trucking routes amid the early outcry, and if this sent economic and regional refugees of all colors and stations to antic motion, and if small wars waged scattershot here and there, and if in all this there was still no living God to be seen anywhere from seaboard to seaboard then the next logical step, by reason of the ancient paradigm become new: the oligarchs merely asked how might this activity too be mediated and metered? But in truth the cause of collapse and decline lay not in corrupt logic but in flawed hearts. Apathy and deceit are ancient enablers. Without trust there can be no social cohesion. If this is the end, it's a personal end. Yet, most persons simply ignored it all right up to their final moment of terror, loss, regret. And so, the few were left to fight, as ever.

In the early hours of the next day, Grayson reached Arches National Park on the north end of the one-road town of Moab, Utah in the southeast corner of the state at the edge of the Great Basin Desert. Smoking a rolled cigarette he crested the earthen bulwark beside the highway to see the rise of the sun feathered out long in yellow and blue plumes at the horizon. Under the horizon, miles of crimson red rock plateau and carved mesa pilings stretched forward like some asylum painter's bloodsoaked canvas. Through pagoda rocks and silica scrabble and ending at the tips of Grayson's boots, this was the vision set before him.

He put out his cigarette, went back down the embankment, changed into running shoes and jogged down the Forest Service trail with steam issuing at each breath. At the first switchback he stopped and adopted the yogic pose vrksasana to stretch. Standing on one foot with the other tucked in his crotch, he cast his eyes back out on the snow-powdered landscape. A bit over six feet tall, discipline and motion over decades had made him wiry and contained. He had the Anglo and Germanic admixture common to the settlers of the northwest quadrant, but it was coupled in the blood with something older yet that was voltaic. Women and children sensed it below the level of thought and it cast him outside the mass.

Later that day in the bright cold morning, Jack's brother Phil wept when he met Grayson on Main Street. Grayson had known him as long as he'd known Jack. Like his brother, Phil had grey eyes and a shock of pure blonde hair that he let grow, but he was much slighter in build and had little of Jack's predilection toward violence or mastery. Yet Phil did share an innate sense of honor and so recognized it in others. He said, "No doubt in my mind I'd be seeing you here soon."

They walked for a bit talking about the gap in time since they'd seen each other. Phil had grown to be a man and come to Moab for the desert—the road biking, the climbing. He'd met Sarah and, given the financial constraints of the times, had buckled down as well as he could. The child was intentional and yet surprising all the same. "The world is going to shit but strangely I'm thrilled. I'll be a father. Something real."

They decided to have breakfast in one of the cafés. The tourist business was slow. They sat alone at some French doors closed to the chill air looking out at the cacti in pots, the long-leaved succulents on adobe benches, and the cold creaking cottonwoods. Phil was not stupid, nor insensitive, and so as they ate he did not mention Grayson's more personal losses, but rather he asked vaguely about what he'd done and what he'd learned or been involved in since they'd last seen each other. Grayson told him of five years spent chasing poachers in South Africa and reading by lamplight in rude savannah camps. Hunting the hunters, as it were. He said, "Tracking forces empathy."

Phil laughed. "Empathy for you. Death for them."

And he told Phil of returning to Oregon when Jack's career had wound down and how they'd spent months training in the mountains outside Eugene and in the high desert south of Bend. When Jack was diagnosed, Grayson dragged him to the Russian Orthodox Church with its blue and gold onion domes, where the women were more beautiful for the scarves over their hair and where the theology had no holes. "We went to the Trappist monasteries out highway 99 too, where the monks brew beer. Nice place. Not Orthodox but more Jack's speed."

Phil's wife Sarah was native to Moab and would not leave until the child was born. Grayson had promised Jack he would retrieve Phil and get his family to Oregon in the midst of the country's dismantling. So if he had to wait for Sarah to deliver the child, so he could deliver on his promise-- then that's what he would do. Thus, in the second week he traded off the Toyota for cash and a shotgun and answered an advertisement on the Moab community bulletin board offering a room for rent. A middle-aged bachelor named Joe had placed the advertisement and rented him the room in the A-frame cabin across the single lot from a small house. For the next nine months Grayson worked with Phil a few days a week, doing odd jobs, landscaping and minor residential repairs. On the others, he trained his body and mind for war—running miles out into the desert in all directions to stop in some cool canyon and drill with his weapons or do bodyweight work or sit listening to the undisturbed environment to osmose the baseline against which he might detect any small change—threat or otherwise. Knives and footwear were tested against native woods for fire making and on slick trails to evaluate mobility and grip. By night he walked the street grids of Moab memorizing details and slipping through yards to test and maintain his stealth. Each week he visited a different bar, drank water and by listening to the gossip came to develop a sense of the local culture. On temperate evenings he would secrete himself into some marginal place—under a parked car on Main Street, or under the fence-line brush in someone's yard, and sleep in his clothes or pray till morning. To be a criminal of purpose: this was his mindset.

The cities of the nation had long been engaged with manifold chaos and were becoming landscapes of contradiction where tiny enclaves of exclusive wealth were rung round by burnt, wasted zones. Yet the old patriotic platitudes regarding democracy, opportunity and individual freedom wore on in every media. No better off than the cities, the rural sectors were beset with a plague of uncertainty, social disintegration, and low-intensity guerilla war. The civil, the business, and the extranational martial, now fully merged in cartels and cabals, sprawled over oceans and borders, eating states and then eating each other in fights over territory. If an area went untouched by direct kinetic conflict, there was still no avoiding confrontation with second and third order effects: epidemic human trafficking in the wake of mass, haphazard migrations and every associated degeneration and sickness, be it physical or of the spirit. Sophisticated and region-specific propaganda was ubiquitous. For the strong: lies to cripple. And the weak were sent programming to wallow in that weakness.

In the final months before the birth of the child, Grayson took Phil on short excursions out of town to acquire gear and gather intelligence. They went past the great desert surrounding Moab like a dry, foreboding moat to Grand Junction, where foreign criminal gangs clashed with local militias and then joined forces briefly against private military and executive protection squads who crushed the coalition and brought in outside labor crews hired to scavenge and cordon. Bodies swaddled in blood-soaked canvas tarpaulins and suspended on static lines from overpasses like strange chrysalides were still being removed. On a bluff outside Flagstaff, Grayson and Phil watched through binoculars as armed bandits-- men and women-- dropped a load of old washing machines onto the highway from a railcar trestle. When the eighteen-wheeler that was their target came to a halt against the wreckage, the raiders deployed Molotavs and a concrete saw to extricate from the trailer a shipment of generic cigarettes in large cardboard boxes.

In spring, the private military advance crews in their shiny black Suburbans crawled through Moab. Midsummer the advance detachments sent to gather their own intelligence returned, and Grayson recorded in a journal that the crews stayed a week at the Best Western and drove out south each day to reappear just after dark. The manager at the hotel told him when he inquired that the men had claimed to be oil workers in from Texas.

Then there was the influx of staging crews and heavy machines in the mountains. Local gossip had it that these too were oil workers but no one could explain why the crews were manned by Congolese and Zimbabwean black men who brought with them temporary housing modules but no recognizable drilling equipment. Nor could it be explained why the crews answered to a small handful of American white men who came and left at odd intervals in sleek up-armored SUVs. And Grayson logged all these changes in the community until, when the coming storm was so close, when the stakes legitimized the risk, standing in the summer garden at twilight listening to Joe relay his own experience as a miner, Grayson hazarded an inquiry as to the likelihood of Joe procuring some explosive materials. Joe cocked his head. He was tall and had ropey veins that stood out in his forearms. The long grey locks falling over his eyes as he smiled knowingly gave him the look of some aged roadie smuggler. The hallucinatory prolixity of the crickets and the wind propelled off the mountains and rattling cane at the driveway drowned the men's voices before the words could escape the garden. Thus, it seemed the deal originated in secret.

Later that week Joe drove him to the buy. When the old truck settled in the gravel outside the Navajos' singlewide trailer, Grayson scanned the parched side and front yards through the billowing dust of their wake for any sign of a set-up. As the sun shone through the swaying cottonwood leaves on one side, its rays portioned into golden dowels that went weaving with the sway of the limbs. Grayson produced from his pocket a fistful of bills which he held out for Joe but below the line of the dashboard so the passing of the money wouldn't be noticed by prying eyes. The trailing limbs of the cottonwood scribbled over the cab roof as Joe set the brake and cut the engine. They each caught the rustle of a curtain in the singlewide window but neither said anything. Joe treadled the squeaky clutch and eyed the money as the sun slats moved upon the cash like miniature searchlights.

"What's this?" Joe asked when the money was put in his palm.

"Your finder's fee for this business here, and last month's rent."

Joe pocketed the money and nodded. "You want me to walk you back there?" he asked pointing to the backyard of the house.

"I think you should probably introduce me to the dude."

As they spoke Grayson watched the back of the trailer where the prismatic mist of a sprinkler wafted through and the little hooded birds flitted up from the dusty privets and the oil-slicked drum barrels to hover against the trailer walls with straw in their beaks.

"Are you armed?" Joe asked.

"Of course I'm armed," said Grayson.

The neighborhood was situated just a few blocks off the main drag in Moab. The distant thrum of slow traffic underlay the close and alien buzz of the cicadas. As they crossed the shabby yard with the short dry grass shushing along their boots, Joe fiddled the truck keys and craned his neck toward the enshadowed trailer window. Wood smoke and burnt sugar hung on the air. In the back yard, the Navajos had strung a faded blue tarp between the trailer and a big saltbush. Under this limp cover were stationed five Indian men who sat or squatted around a little barbeque grilling chilies and toast. They wore hardened expressions and glanced at the white men with wild dark eyes. They diverted their glances and passed a bottle smeared in meat grease. Three other Navajo standing closer to the trailer shifted as Grayson and Joe stepped into the center of the dirt yard. From these three, the Navajo with close-shaved hair and sunglasses turned to Joe.

"The great white hope. The landlord."

Grayson took this man to be Roger, the leader. Joe and Roger shook hands and patted the shoulders of the other in vague ritual fashion. The two other Navajo beside Joe were younger and wore long black hair to their waists. They drifted from Roger toward the trailer and seemed to whisper to each other like women with one hand concealing their mouths.

"This is the guy?" Roger pointed to Grayson.

Introductions were made. Roger chuckled. Grayson tabulated the total men in the yard. There was nowhere to sit. The two younger Indians moved a bit to his rear and by reflex, as if in choreograph, Grayson angled his shoulders almost imperceptibly to keep them in his periphery. Joe and Roger exchanged a glance and the two nodded to indicate everything would proceed as planned. The unmistakable clack sound of an AK-type rifle chambering a round cut through the yard. Roger laughed again and some of the others chuckled along with him. Men under the tarp lit cigarettes and Joe stepped aside and stooped down with his head over the grill as if he might take a chili for himself but instead smiled and produced a pack of cigarettes from his jacket and offered it to the Navajos there who were already smoking.

Standing in the center of the yard Roger said, "Grayson you don't strike me as a man who wants to hang out or have a good time but rather as a man who has something he wants to achieve right now. Is that right?"

"No offense, Roger."

"Fuck it, man. None taken. A piece of business can just be a piece of business. Come over then and see the goodies."

Roger gestured toward a few ragged cardboard boxes and a grey plastic tub the size of a milk crate set atop a woodpile in one corner of the yard. As the men approached, an old and mangled Labrador and Rottweiler mix leered its milky cataract eyes and rose from its patch of earth by the cordwood to skulk off into the bushes between the trailers. Two more Navajos were standing grimly behind the woodpile, one of them holding the AK. Grayson tallied the Indians accordingly and reordered in his mind the likelihoods, the avenues of escape and the angles of attack. Roger tilted his chin to these men and they stepped back into the one sliver of golden sunlight in the yard and stood where the watered grass at the fence was tall and green. Roger lifted the lid off the top of the tub and said,

"Solidox. Good for making bombs, eh?"

Grayson remained self-contained, studying the contents of the tub as he brought out the wad of bills. He breathed deeply and slowly through his nose. Nothing on his face to read. He looked inside and surveyed the number of containers.

Roger took the money and asked, "You know I can get this stuff no problem but I don't know how to make it go 'boom.' How do they do that, man?"

Grayson tipped open the cardboard box. More of the canisters clacked a bit in the shifting and he said, "I don't know anything about that, Roger. These are for home improvements."

Roger laughed. A strong breeze swayed the leafy cottonwoods and the shaggy Bermuda grass, and as they were all men accustomed to the desert every one of them in the yard stopped to savor the cool air on their faces as they knew it might or might not come again that day. The dog had come back around the bushes and stood staring through the rusted fence wires to the empty field beyond as if out there was some threat the men neglected or perhaps could not see at all. The dog remained transfixed upon the field and with his glistening black nose sniffed the incoming draft. And then the wind was gone.

Roger said to Grayson, "You trust Joe. We trust him. It's all good. He said you'd build me some IEDs, dude. What do you say, man?"

Grayson stood over the box of canisters and just stared at him. The Navajos had all risen now and were milling about in the little yard. One of them picked up a bat from the bushes and feigned to hit the dog and the dog scurried off towards Joe's truck. Grayson rolled his shoulders and monitored the motion of the other men.

"Joe seems to have spoken out of turn. It ain't happening. I'll thank you kindly for these household cleaning products and that'll be that." Grayson nodded. "You understand."

"Those are some excessively combustible cleaning products, dude."

Grayson hefted the tub and carried it off through the shadows of the yard. The Navajos parted slow and without comment. At the truck he set the crate on the rusted and hay-strewn floor of the bed and stood to wait on the far side by the wheel well where the ballistic cover was best. After a while Joe emerged at the corner of the house chewing his lip and Grayson opened the door and sat in the passenger seat with the pistol under his thigh. Joe leaned into the cab on the driver's side.

"Listen man, you don't want to help them that's alright but I gotta tell you it'd be saving them a lot if you did."

"Stow that shit," Grayson said.

"What shit?" asked Joe.

"The guilt."

"We fucked those people," Joe said.

"The whole damn world is falling apart."

"Well, maybe the one thing led to the other."

Joe glanced over his shoulder to see if anyone was behind him and then shook his head up to the trees, as if hidden among the wickerwork of the swaying limbs there hovered some judge whose better wisdom he might beseech.

"Look, this situation we got now with not knowing if our military is even ours' anymore, whether they're fighting other folks' wars or whether they're righteously fighting foreign cartels or, hell, whether cartels run our military-- it's a clusterfuck, pure and simple. But to the Navajo it's about the land. Always was."

"They can have it."

"If militaries, private or otherwise, come here, they're coming for the headwaters, the river, to divert it off to California. You understand this is a mortal wound to the Navajo. It's no different than slitting their throats. That river is their blood."

"Bullshit. There are other rivers."

Roger emerged from the foliage at the corner of the trailer holding a hand against the sun to see them at the truck. Grayson sighed, stretched the muscles of both nimble hands like a piano player might and said to Joe,

"As you already know Phil is my only concern. He and his family."

"He's your charge. I get it."

"And Roger is not. Nor will he be. Now are you driving or should I walk?"

Joe tapped the window housing as if to close the discussion and shuffled back over the grass to speak with Roger. Grayson looked slantwise through the windshield as the heat riffled off the hood of the old Ford and watched Joe and the Navajo leader speak. Roger spoke more loudly and Joe threw his hands up. Joe moved like he was going to open the door to the trailer and Roger grabbed his arm hard enough to bring Joe to bended knee. Grayson could hear: *but she loves me Roger, she loves me and you damn well know it.* Navajos poured around each side of the trailer animated from their stupor by the histrionics. They reminded Grayson of great crows hopping to spilt grain. Grayson laid his hand over the pistol at his thigh, warm with the sun. He logged everything between the sprinkler misting the scant side yard and the quarrel taking shape in the front. The curtain in the trailer window was pinched open a few inches. The roving Navajos encircled Joe and Roger. The one with the baseball bat stood up by the door letting the bat dangle in one hand while his other spiraled loose as if he were winding the invisible lever on some translucent machine. And then the shouting stopped.

* * *

From the A-frame window on the second floor Grayson dripped sweat and gazed out across the patchwork yard and garden to Joe's separate place where the screened porch was dark and dotted with white morning moths clinging to the grids. His breath was metronomic. Wisps of clouds passed on the depthless blue sky beyond. He bent and found his own hand impressions flattened into the shag carpet and moved through chaturanga to updog and then proceeded with more pushups. If the world's troubles had at last come to Moab then there was no reliable harbinger by which to ascertain it and he figured further that that's exactly how cataclysms transpire. One second it's the unheeded whisper and the next it's down to blood. He moved to a makeshift pull-up bar in the doorway. His stainless Uno-Vac bottle stood on the window ledge glinting in the morning sun. A lone yellow jacket nosed around the lid. Books were stacked on the floor—Lossky and Neumann, St. John of Damascus and Zhuang Zhou, The Timaeus and The Book of the Dead. A Dopp kit, notebook and pencil, and his disassembled Glock were laid out on an empty blue pillowcase: his morning ritual. A yellow lacrosse ball and a votive candle had been set to one side.

After he'd showered he returned and sat by the window again with his eyes closed, breathing until the tires of Phil's work truck crinkled over the driveway stones outside and the yellow jacket departed the Uno-Vac and slipped through the cracked window. He reassembled the Glock and holstered it at his waist and rolled the other items away in the pillowcase and set it on the plain bed and hauled up an olive drab 80mm surplus canister and went out the bedroom door and down the stairs. On the deck, his roommate Ben was sprawled in a lawn chair wearing pink sunglasses and cargo shorts. An uncapped and half emptied handle of generic whiskey sat on the weathered deck boards beside Ben's dirty bare feet. Grayson stepped out and Ben shot his fist up in a mocking salute that recalled something of the anonymous and wool clad European partisan a century gone. In the knot of his fingers rested a smoking pipe. At nineteen, Ben's face was still whiskerless and like the hand holding the pipe was unlined by either care or work.

"Cheeba?" he offered.

"You go ahead," Grayson said and kept walking so he could slap hands with Phil who stood waiting in the driveway stamping his feet and smiling at the red yard chickens maneuvering in the cane and weeds. Like his brother Jack, Phil was built for work and had the aquiline look of his ancestry, of hunters. The fine dust rose and fell around his boots as if he were dancing the planks of an old theatre but his expression was all amiable business, embodying the lank openness of the natural.

Ben watched them go.

The neighbor's shepherd dog followed the truck for a hundred yards or so, as was its habit, and Phil watched it in the rear-view mirror. They drove along Murphy Lane without saying anything. Poor Lightnin' Hopkins played on the radio and they rolled the windows down for the relative cool. Both men tracked a rabbit bolting over the pavement in front of them. Phil let off the gas so it could clear the road. Between the men a plain trust and familiarity of the sort that doesn't require daily affirmation had built up.

Because the child was now safely born and the sun shone, and because Moab, Utah was encased as always by hundreds of miles of protective desert in all directions neither man spoke. They shared a preference, as many working men do, to allow goodness in whatever measure to continue unremarked. Each knew they'd leave that protective buffer soon enough. Phil tapped his hand on the wheel to the guitar rhythm. At the bend in the road before town proper, a few abandoned horses ranged free along the wrong side of a falling fence chewing weeds and then skittering as the truck passed. A bit further on a potbellied man on a mountain bike pedaled along in the opposite direction. Phil tapped the horn as they passed and the man, who went by 'Hostel Mike,' grinned in the interchange waving one hand off the handlebars.

"Sitting on the porch last night it occurred to me that there's almost no incentive in this modern scheme of things for loyalty. Nothing. Think about that," Phil said.

"I have. Deeply."

At Dave's Corner Market they parked the truck between a blue and white motorcycle over-laden with sunbrowned canvas saddlebags and another truck wherein a number of workers caked in red mud were huddled like mice in a weave of old blankets and cheap flannel sleeping bags. A swap meet, itinerant and impromptu, was ongoing in all corners of the lot. The participants were poorly outfitted travelers and tramps, refugees and peddlers. Multifarious shades of humanity wandered or lay strewn about the dry grass or installed before their barter goods that were set out on dusty blankets in the shade. A riotous white noise of babble rose from the crowd. Some of the worst addlebrained sat childlike against the store wall with their paranoid eyes shivering and others who mercy had lately visited were collapsed half naked and face down at the treeline. A few dogs that were tied up to bikes or to the trees whined while garbled reggae played from speakers sequestered somewhere in the crowd. Those in the truck eyed Grayson from under rag hoods when he got out. Then they looked away or pretended they were looking past him when he came parallel to the truck bed. Phil peered over at them with his eyebrows raised. A woman among them smiled and he nodded.

They bought good coffee inside and then stood at the window of the little store, Phil reading the bulletin board and Grayson alternating his attention between the truck where the box of explosives lay in the rear and the throng of peddlers dispersed about the intersection.

"We're kind of third world now aren't we?" Phil said.

"We're getting there," Grayson said.

Phil brought out a cup of coffee and two stacked cans of dog food. Grayson watched from the center of the lot as Phil went to the dog-owners in the shade and spoke a few words and handed them the food. A sleek black mutt with the space between its eyebrows wrinkled and raised in curiosity stood and came to Phil to be pet.

Grayson remarked, "You know they'll probably just eat that themselves."

"That's why I got them the gourmet organic stuff." Phil pointed for the dog to sit.

The woman who had smiled at Phil now slipped from the caravan. Flakes of red clay fell away from her tattooed calves. She cupped her hands as if she was making an offering to an altar. Grayson took a step sideways to put a space between himself and Phil and switched the coffee to his other hand, as he watched for her partners in the scheme.

All she got out was, "Do you wanna?"

"No thank you," Phil said.

They passed by. Inside her hands was a bauble, a token. She dragged the woven fingers down his back and skipped to catch up and muttered some lurid enticements to his ears. The travelers in the truck eyed him again. One smiled with his lips over his teeth. The others gawked blank and mute, pretending dumb wonder. Grayson and Phil took another stride, and as if maybe he were commenting on the weather Phil said,

"Front passenger side."

Grayson had already seen it and the pistol came out from under his shirt so fast and quiet—with so little adornment to the motion— that those crouched up in the truck bed shuddered. The woman with the bauble deviated into the crowd and dirt-streaked boys took her place. With another step Grayson had lined up with the rear quarter of their truck as cover. He held the black handgun pinned steady on a grimy ageless man with a filthy kitchen knife in one hand and in the other a heavy sap prepared out of a long black sock and a padlock. The weapon hung in his hand like an enormous drip of tar as his queer smile froze in failure. The crowd hushed. Others booed. Phil laughed. The man with the knife and sap lost his balance and stumbled in the river rock lining the sidewalk.

"You done fucked with him now," Phil said to the fallen thief.

The crowd stood watching. "You took his passably handsome and windswept drifter good looks for weakness didn't you?" Phil continued.

The thief's eyes were magnified behind thick glasses, giving him a demented look.

"Yes sire. Yes sire," he repeated as a foamy spittle dribbled from his mouth.

The thief slunk around the front of the truck all the while looking over his shoulder. Grayson brought the gun down along his leg. Phil smiled and sipped his coffee as the man loped over the road to the flood ditch where he fell again, and Phil called him back saying, "Don't you want to talk this over?" Grayson licked a stream of coffee off his hand and turned back to the storefront. Phil had the truck open and he was riding the starter. The girl who'd tried marking them now draped herself against the phone booth and bit her nails. The gypsies had already turned back to their separate hustles. From the far corners of the lot, raggedy and sunshocked children sprinted in bare feet among the drugged and dispossessed. As the truck pulled out on to the road, some of the children interpreted the scrape as being about a woman and others, who were older, said it was certainly a drug deal gone wrong. They agreed, finally, that the man who'd drawn the gun was a hero regardless and when the storytelling wound down, their parents did some halfhearted, rote scolding before turning again to their toil of making the day's sales.

"Dangerous neighborhood," Phil said as he turned down Mill Creek Road.

Grayson laughed and said, "Sure is a shame about that."

* * *

In the punishing noontime sun, they worked a yard on Spanish Valley Drive repairing a line of drip system and breaking at odd intervals to prepare and itemize various components of their bomb-making. On the tailgate were piles of red and green wire cut to a standard length beside a jumble of the riveted free-swinging halves of the enclosures. The 80mm surplus box with the solidox was open and Grayson wrapped rubber bands around the portioned wire and dropped the bundles inside with the burner phones and transmitters. Across the main road, two bison languished in the tall field grass somewhere between waking and sleeping, quivering their necks against the bullflies. Beyond the pastures and valley, the Manti La Sals ranged off to the south fringed in green, stripped of their winter white caps.

"Should we do this thing?" Phil asked, referring to the yard job.

"Lead the way," Grayson said.

Phil brought from the bed of the truck a six-foot length of three-quarter inch flexible tubing and two five-gallon buckets. One of these he emptied out onto the shaded concrete by the garage door and then set upside down as an improvised chair. He rolled two cigarettes and drank coffee from the Uno-Vac cup as Grayson sifted through the contents of the other bucket, collecting together the Oetiker rings and then the coil of dripline and the various barbs by which they would reconfigure the irrigation system.

"You need about ten of these?" he asked holding up the barbs.

"Yeah ten, twelve maybe."

"How much sleep did you get last night?" Grayson asked.

"Baby was up. Got about an hour and a half--tops," said Phil.

Grayson whistled. "I'd last about a week."

Across the road, one of the bison rose and made water looking straight ahead and then turned, eyeing the men, and snorting with enough force to sway the grass at his nose. The beast moved off closer to the fence with its patches of matted fur dangling like scapular trophies of war and flopped back down to proceed in watching them with one great brown disk of an eye that floated back until the white showed. Grayson wiped the dry corners of his mouth, stretched his neck and brought his hands together in front of him.

"Even though Sarah's not a hundred percent yet we might have to leave soon—maybe in a few weeks, though I'm hoping for a month," said Grayson.

Phil blinked and tapped his ash. "After forty-eight solid hours of labor and a C-section, I don't think she's ready, man."

Grayson was fixated on him, making measurements on the careful balance between advice and command, between instilling fear and conveying necessity. Phil drew his own handgun from the holster under his shirt and looked back to see if he was being watched from the window of the house. He set the gun on the concrete and rubbed his side where the frame had been digging at him.

"Fucker's uncomfortable," he said.

Grayson nodded at his friend and the gun. "Move your holster a few inches back."

Grayson tapped the ash into a neat pile on the flagstone. Phil watched him and looked off at the big red wall of the rim past the highway.

"You still wanna drink tonight?" he asked, picking some wet strands of tobacco from his lip.

"Well look—failed empire or not. You still only have a first-born once, right?"

"I don't know how you do it."

And that was all it took to rend the scar of time, that which isolates a man's interior functions from the material facts of his regret and his loss. The compressed vision of the events to which

Phil referred blasted through Grayson's skull as would an electrical surge through the brittle circuits in an old house. As soon as Phil saw it flash through the fine muscles around Grayson's eyes, he felt regret himself for having brought it up. Were the vision to be slowed and played yet again, frame by frame, it would be too much horrific detail for any man to absorb repeatedly. The mercy of time's immutable advance. But as is the way of such things, only three fractions of moments were needed to tell the tale entire, once again, and it was these that always came back unbidden and in the same order: he, Grayson, holding the tiny, lifeless pink bundle of his own perfect son as his wife lay weeping and decimated in the ICU bed pincushioned with tubes and wires. And as he looked between her there and the body of his son in his arms, seemingly from the other side of a vast psychic chasm, he wept too. Like the levee had broken, he was carried away completely.

He had driven her home from the hospital in the bright, cool light of an Oregon spring day with that brilliant sun refracting through the blue nimbus and over the dark green mountains to catch in the windshield. She sung their boy's lullaby through constant, depthless tears, through the pain of knowing she'd never held him alive and she'd never hold him again at all. And Grayson, realizing in that moment that no man could go where she'd gone or carry the weight or make it better, knew only to hold tight her warm wet hand upon the vehicle's console and bear witness. And then the worst: some months later, waking up in grey winter to her letter on the kitchen hutch. The last lines: *I'm so, so sorry.* That instance, its dark dawning of concentrated horror when he realized he'd never see her again, was far worse than the other moments, for it carried with it the emptiness of love's failure. It felt like a child's nightmare to the grown man. No matter how many times it played out in his mind, the final scene ended in a crushing flash.

"Sorry, man. I didn't think," Phil said.

"It's alright," he said to Phil who watched the fire of that triple vision pass away again weirdly under Grayson's blue, precision-guided eyes.

Grayson watched the near sky, the clouds moving. The green swaying tips of trees in the valley and the seedbearing cotton particulate cast out on the wind. Phil touched his gun lightly on the concrete as if it were a sacred item in a tabernacle. Or the object of coming sacrifices. Grayson looked back at him and saw him putting the dots of a grim picture together.

"When I made that promise to your brother there were no clauses on that, you understand. The deal is simple: no matter what. No matter what happens I'm not leaving you, your wife or your kid. No matter what."

Phil glanced up from wherever he was in his thoughts and nodded.

"I know," Phil said.

Grayson stubbed the cigarette and let certain histories pass away again. Phil waved his hand through a tranche of the floating cotton bits that had come through on the breeze. After a while Grayson stood and sipped his coffee as he looked over the valley. About nothing or everything he said, "It'll be alright."

The light over the desert valley shifted between enormous gatherings of clouds and cast the world in the filtered silver overlay of eclipse. Around them the desert plant life, the mausolea of red rocks and the insects and lizards extant in the crazings of the red rocks seemed themselves to diminish into an altered realm of shade, if only for that instant. A moment of blue midnight at midday. For in the desert each thing is augmented by its relationship to each other thing and this interchange is charged so that when one element alters, all others alter as well. Yet change only arrives in the desert via great force. Light and stone, time and motion, are at once linked oracles and familiars in a conspiracy of illusion.

Grayson fixated on the silver edges, the undulations and degrees of shifting light. And then, as the cloud's shade eased away like a scrim pulled back on some theatre of things and as the blasting sunlight returned to pummel the earth again, rock and man alike felt the instantaneous restoration of radiation and the cosmic order. Grayson thought about the decade of age between he and Phil, and then he thought of his temporary roommate Ben, even younger than Phil, who rented the other room from Joe. Ben survived on puny wire transfers from his mother, who herself survived on doles from the government. It seemed to him that the last twenty years in history had brought so much change so fast, yet all of it heading into uncharted or theoretical and baldly contradictory territories: abstract progress, undefined transformation, the primacy of the technological and technocratic and in the interchangeable and homogenous over both the traditional and the heroic. Yet the underlying essence of neither man nor of the world, nor of being itself, had not shifted one centimeter. Twenty years or twenty million years, the contingency of your existence, the contingency of existence itself upon some eternal ground was fixed, was it not? Only the surface, maybe only the perception of the surface, of things had rippled and he believed that if the essence of a thing was not lost then perhaps the thing was not lost at all. Misplaced, forgotten. But not lost. And this is why, despite appearances, Grayson was ultimately an optimist.

He mentioned something like this to Phil who nodded and smiled. They talked about young Ben's future and wondered how much of one he really had, being that he spoke of no father, no friends, no aspirations with women.

"Ben's trying to get me to eat mushrooms with him lately," Grayson said

"See, that's what I mean. Looks up to you," Phil answered.

"He's just never been in a fight."

"I think it's worse than that."

"How could it get worse than that," said Grayson and they laughed and didn't say anything further about the psychology of descending generations, or degeneration, nor of the operation of the work before them but just rose and divided it as if this exact job had been done countless times before. Grayson held a pair of white leather gloves out but Phil waved them away and knelt and dug his hands in the reject sand to find the severed end of the mainline before pulling it up from the sand to the point where it looped back on itself and he clipped it at the nexus.

"It's dry as a bone isn't it?" Grayson asked.

The black oval of the cut loop with the thin trails of driplines went sailing over the flagstones when he threw it and rattled against the truck bed walls and came to rest in the bed where it looked vaguely cyborgian and medical. Grayson handed him the new length and a handful of the Oetiker rings.

"Gimme a couple more."

One man crimped the rings down to seal the replacement loop and the other set to punch holes in it and foist the barbs and couple them to the little driplines. They then each took a small handful of the emitters in various configuration and applied them to the plants.

As they went along they spoke about uncertainty and faith, about tactics of survival. They spoke in their way about the deep madness of living in a world overbrimming with inherent meaning but where men and women blindly chased or accepted the empty pronouncements of the media or political propogandists. Phil claimed people believe meaning is invented but the truth is discovered, like Everest was discovered. It's just there when you look. Phil pointed to a succulent in the sand that resembled a mandala nested among smaller mandalas and smiled to make his point: meaning and mystery were everywhere abundant and obvious features of this world.

When the sand was shoveled back over the line to hide it, Grayson adjusted the timer on the system as Phil loaded the truck and went to wait behind the wheel and smoke. Grayson hooked the system to the tank outflow and watched the bison lounge as he walked back to the truck. They'd moved under a tree with their rears to each other and the flies were out so their tails snapped and fluttered back to rest, one on the other.

Grayson got in the cab.

"Returning to our prior topic of discussion, if we get hit before we can leave, we'll just adhere to the exit plan. The rally points, the contingencies. We'll finish these charges at the next opportunity and get them cached. Then, we just see. Might be I'm wrong. Could be months or could be never."

Phil let the truck idle a moment in gear. Grayson angled his head out the window looking beyond the house at the first dark clouds bringing an afternoon shower. Around them again the light grew rare and diffuse so that it appeared to dance on the surfaces of things—on the mineral sheets of rim wall across the valley that wobbled between pink and grey and the plant life in the neighborhood. Smoke bush and yucca, cacti and dwarf cedar seemed to become fluid in the corpuscle of an instant. Below, and surrounding the clatter of the pistons firing in the truck, the extraordinary silence of the desert cooled by degree, a process which was itself at once ephemeral and eternal, felt charged with an inscrutable ecstatic motility. Phil was fixated on the speedometer as if some answers lay within the arc of lines and numbers.

And though Grayson knew what he was thinking he only said, "It's going to rain."

"This time of year," Phil said. "It'll just be a shower."

When the truck didn't move, Grayson looked across the seat at his friend, his charge, and saw familiar darkness moving below the surface. Phil darted his eyes that way and then back along the windshield in silence.

After a moment Grayson said, "It'll be okay, man." And as he said it and as Phil nodded, Grayson reflected on what it meant to say such a thing in a world where an individual's control was in some large measure illusion. Or in a time when what faculties men did possess, and what assumptions of kindness they were expected to operate upon, had been diabolically twisted, cloaked in the fabric of lies, toward patently evil ends. It was the era of the soul's own desertification. Does it honor God to make a promise when all around you is falsity, Grayson wondered and then thought it did indeed, and as Phil put the truck in gear and gassed it, Grayson said again, "It'll be okay."

* * *

Grayson and Phil went early to the bar. They studied the selection of bottles behind the counter and found it much reduced from even a few months prior when they'd last drank together. The closure or diversion of highways, after events labeled euphemistically as terrorist plots, had steadily drawn down store goods nationwide, leaving shelves a patchwork of void spaces and angst. Yet the great wobbling machine of trade somehow trundled forth with enough liquor, sex, and drugs to stave outright rebellion. Women ravenous and of all ages, who would have found the notion inconceivable a year earlier, now draped themselves in the vinyl booths along one wall with their surplus or advantaged flesh well-displayed. In times dire and occasionally dry, the bar was nonetheless well-populated.

Mike, the portly dreadlocked man who had passed them that morning on his bicycle, now sat alone in his tie-dye shirt at a small table in the middle of the bar, with a clutch of bills in one hand and a long conical spliff in the other that he tapped over his empty shot glasses as if they were pieces of drum kit, snare and kick. The western sun going down over the rim vectored through the big front windows and cut a holy orange block out of the dim and smoky quadrant where Hostel Mike held his domain. The sharding light catching in the swells of the glasses wove out or cut away as he tapped so that he seemed the keeper and translator of some primitive signal language at the center of things. From the back booth near the pool tables where it was cooler in the shadows and they could observe the action at each entrance, Grayson watched Hostel

Mike just as he watched every moving body in the establishment: with respectful disinterest and a plan to kill them if necessary. In time Hostel Mike rose with his spliff and Budweiser to join them in the booth chuckling and saying straight away, "You fellows hearing what I'm hearing?"

"What are you hearing Mike?" Phil said, as he repositioned himself in the booth.

"Awww fuck just shit's going down, man. Like it ever has. But whatever." Mike demurred.

"Is it aliens?" Phil was smiling.

Mike smiled back. "You rascal. Don't go laughing at my beliefs, man. There's crazier shit going on in the world than you could ever know. Cosmic levels of spiritual war and every other fucking thing."

Mike put his hand out and Grayson shook it and having only met once before Grayson remained quiet, watching and listening as Mike and Phil discussed local gossip. Mike complained about what he called the sleepers--the millions of human beings who refused to acknowledge the decline of modern society. Grayson and Phil nodded and Mike went on describing the rumors of an impending maneuver on Moab to be made under the guise of domestic terrorism. Whether the operation was entirely private military, a coalition of private and foreign intelligence agencies, or any combination thereof was impossible to determine.

"False flags go back to Machiavelli at least," Mike said.

The bar began to fill with patrons. With their drinks, they overflowed to the patios front and side, mingling in the dying sun. Some consumed furiously as others sipped and glanced, turning away but never leaving. Others sought a perfect reflection of their own misplaced faith and false beliefs in the faces around them. The patrons outside were all pecked at by the transient hordes asking for smokes and change. Some few female transients joined the patrons by invitation. Barriers between life stations shifted with or without anyone noticing. This operation was mirrored at the level of the nation of course, but none there in the crowd realized it as all castes and creeds bore down blind on that semi-permeable membrane between having and not having. Someone fed the jukebox.

When Mike and Phil spoke about division among the local militias and about rumors of the state or corporate military contractors moving on Moab, both agreed that diverting the river to water-cool overheated California servers and feed orange groves was inevitable at some point. Grayson watched Mike tap the spliff and noted the twitch at the corner of Mike's wrinkled left eyelid and knew he was lying about something or lied constantly about everything. Grayson interjected and questioned Mike about the advance operations of the contractors, asking if among these rumors he'd heard details about their nationality or their equipment, their methods of psychological and guerilla warfare.

"We always called them Virginia Boys," Mike said and he went on at some length with certain theories involving a nexus of CIA and global power interests as Grayson watched the eyelid twitch and wondered where the lie was because all Mike had said thus far was true.

"Bad dudes, man. Gotta play both sides to win their game." Mike sighed and pushed out of the booth. Phil and Grayson watched him go across the foyer to where two men in new blue

Wranglers and Lucchese boots stood waiting with a woman to be let inside. The woman's countenance was distinctly out of place—she had the olive complexion and watchful or vaguely superior expression common to certain displaced eastern European women. Her sundress was ill-fit to her body. She wore no jewelry at all and seemed somehow split between being anxious and tired.

Phil said with reference to Hostel Mike, "That is a rare specimen there—the militant hippie. Native only to the western states. Extinction imminent."

"Hippies were never my preferred source for intelligence," Grayson replied.

"Or much else for that matter."

The waitress came over and they ordered four shots more of whiskey and another pitcher of beer and they paid her up front and she went off around the booth to get the liquor. They sat quiet watching the other patrons and rolling and smoking cigarettes until the waitress came back with the beer and shots an order above what they'd normally drink and which they hoisted to toast the newborn child who was yet unnamed but would be honored that night all the same. Just as the sun disappeared behind the rim, they drank the second shot and poured the beer and the albino known locally as Munson came striding through the back door tipping his hat. He sat down opposite to them at the pool tables where in the shadows he seemed luminous at the neck and forearms. Grayson and Phil got up to shoot pool.

The waitress came to Munson, and Phil and Grayson watched him speak to her in a familiar way. Taking off his old gentlemanly Stetson hat and setting it on the table to run a long thin hand through his pompadour hair that was slick with oil and the color of bleached eggshells he seemed a figure atomized and displaced from another era. As the waitress left him, he set a switchblade and keyring beside his hat and unclasped the chain at his waist from his oversized wallet and set that down too.

While they shot through a game, Grayson and Phil talked about Jack, his life and his passing, in some detail. Phil said he wished he had spent more time learning the arts of war from his brother, as Grayson had done. The regret would not leave. It was hard to accept that he couldn't fight his way out alone and that Grayson had been forced to watch over him. Harder still to believe a world with no brother was real.

"We haven't even gotten to the really hectic part yet," Phil said.

"The hectic part's the easy part," Grayson said. "Once you know who and what you're fighting, everything becomes much more straightforward. Uncertainty is what kills. Regret will kill you too, though."

Phil nodded his understanding.

They sat back down and Munson got up with his drink and his hat and sauntered over.

"Aww fellas I got the ass, I tell you what," Munson said. "Looks like Virginia Boys is early too. What'd you all say about it?"

The front and side doors were open for the breeze off the patios. Before Grayson or Phil could answer Munson's question the sounds of a scuffle and plastic chairs or tables snapping outside rang out. Then shouting, broken glass on the pavement. Grayson could see through the aperture to where the bodies of the fighters rolled in the barkdust and concrete and beyond them he saw the green waxy leaves were spinning in the trees. Individuals in the crowd outside were cheering or alternately spilling beer as they leapt out of the way. Grayson studied the leaves on the trees again, backlit on a purple sky and twirling above the mayhem like feathers of a diving bird. The music played. The fight ground on. Grayson noted the fists slamming and the soft rustling work of the twilight wind, again, in the trees but also on articles of clothing and hair and the accumulated organic duff between floorboards.

"I'm buying a bottle, boys. God save the Queen. God save that lying slut. Stay put," Munson gestured, "I'll be back and tell you another thing right quick."

Mike appeared beside them with a pitcher of beer in his hand, "Aliens. You are a wily one, Phil. Move on over there."

He sat down and the melee seemed to resolve. The snap sound of the cue ball against the pyramid shot through as someone began another game. Phil told an old joke that took Mike a moment to register and then he began to chuckle and it shook his whole body and the table vibrated with it, sloshing the beer in the pitcher. Grayson watched him closely. Mike had a scent about him that he couldn't place, and blotchy red skin as if he drank too much.

Munson came back around the booth and sat down and said, "You ever hear them say history is ended?"

They ignored Munson for the moment as Phil had become accustomed to Grayson's perpetual casing of the room, any room, and when the motion of his head ceased and the blue eyes fixed, Phil followed the gaze toward the front of the bar where three well-built men of middle age and obvious military bearing, one Latin and two English, stood holding full pints and staring into the crowd as great beads of perspiration dripped from the glasses. They were all dressed in new western shirts and Levi's that were too short to cover their expensive Lucchese boots. None carried a hint of beard or stubble.

Hostel Mike finally lit the spliff and said though his exhale, "Those are Virginia Boys. For certain."

Phil and Grayson exchanged a glance that Munson scrutinized. They all went quiet. Mike continued to smoke. He passed the joint to Munson who hit it and offered it to Grayson who waved it off, as did Phil. Through the cloud, Grayson looked out the window for the vehicle the men would have arrived in and then went back to the men themselves. They stood awkwardly at their table but the crowd didn't seem to take notice. They weren't advance men, they were enlisted officer types with long experience.

"Virginia Boys or not, every man best have him a getaway plan cause those fellas ain't playing." Munson said. He had the bottle he'd purchased in his lap. He snapped the switchblade open and scored the paper wrapper over the bottle cap and said, "Well fuck it, right? Anyway. So you fellas ever hear that, that history has ended?"

Munson looked to Grayson, waiting for his answer, and then raised his shot glass. So sunken and bruised was the crinkled sallow skin about his sinus bones that his eyes looked like animate blue marbles affixed at the base of darkly glazed teacups.

Hostel Mike pushed back up with his pitcher, "Munson you never fail to set my teeth on edge. You two should steer clear of his rambling mindless bullshit, I'm just saying." Mike lumbered off into the crowd.

Someone turned the volume on the jukebox up yet another notch and the wind pulsed through the open doors lifting up pressed paper coasters and beige napkins by the dozen, whirling them off like diminutive sails sundered from some beached bantam fleet. Several of the paper napkins caught in the airstream, and weirdly animated, flapped and rose to float over the bar before seesawing back to the floorboards. No one else noticed. Grayson took another measure of the men in the new Wranglers and boots. A soft, black canvas duffle bag lay on the floor at their feet that Grayson surmised was heavy with weapons and gear.

Grayson turned to speak in Phil's ear. "Let's go out the back. Right now."

"Munson?" Phil asked.

"Bring him if you want."

And so they did.

* * *

At sixty miles per hour the old truck was rattling hard over the dirt road. With the headlights off, Phil drove and held an antique Russian night vision monocular to his eye. As they passed a forest service sign on the side of the road, Phil swiveled and read out loud: *Ranger Station. One mile.* In the passenger seat, Grayson rode with a cigarette stuck in his mouth and the bottle of Johnnie Walker wedged in his crotch. Munson was in the open bed of the truck clinging to the underside lip of one wall and pressing his long, frail body against the wheel well as they rattled over the potholes. Chuck Berry played loud on the stereo. The dustcloud in their wake unspooled on the passing darkness.

"Are you worried?" Phil asked.

"I'm sort of gearing up to consider worrying but not just yet. We're wise to just bury the charges tonight so they can't be taken if there's a surprise search of some sort," Grayson replied.

Munson's sallow bony hand came through the cab window like a creature from a cave dwelling and tapped Grayson on the shoulder. Grayson took a swig off the bottle, spun the cap on with one hand and passed it back through the window to Munson. The albino was stuck in a deep lunge toward the cab with nowhere to go as the truck entered the last turn kicking gravel and creaking the sway bars. With one hand clutching the window frame and the other swung back with the sloshing bottle to serve as ballast, his thin jackets and scarf whipped and snapped in the wind as he turned his pale wincing face to the moonlight. For a moment, he looked every bit hell's embattled emissary.

They straightened out for the last quarter mile before the ranger station and Phil dialed back the volume. When the outline of the station came into view he slowed to a roll and snapped off the night vision. Grayson directed him toward a thicket of pines and Phil rolled the truck off the road into the sage where the sandy earth was crusted. Breaking under the slow movement of the tires the crust sounded like waves at low tide. They stopped the truck and got out and all three of the men dispersed to the bushes. The only sounds were the breeze in the scrub and the tinks of the engine cooling, then piss falling on gravel and sand. Silence returned as they walked back to the truck and Munson passed the whiskey to Phil. He wiped the glass and drank and passed it to Grayson who likewise drank but he did not wipe the glass. None spoke and it was for a moment as if they heeded some implied commandment to respect the desert with quiet prayer or contemplation before acting within its jurisdiction. Overhead, the imponderable dark, the stars were dying in their primordial moorings.

Munson finally broke the spell, "This shit's fixing up to be about dead fucking serious in a minute, ain't it?" Grayson and Phil both nodded in agreement.

"Believe it." Phil said.

Grayson handed the bottle back to Munson and went around the truck where he dropped the tailgate and pulled out two shovels that he leaned into the wedge of the bumper. He reached back in and dragged the long green 80mm ammo box across the plywood floor of the truck bed and hefted it up onto the tailgate.

"What's in the box, boys?" Munson asked.

Grayson walked back over to them and Phil said, "May as well tell him."

"Gold and silver and explosives."

Munson let out a low practiced whistle. They each drank again and then proceeded out as sojourners into the moonlit sage where they were observed by the tiny flammulated owls. With burning, blinking eyes and clenched talons, the small birds lay hidden in their shadowed perches amid the spindly pines lining the flat land around the ranger station. With the sage low to the earth swaying lightly in the breeze, and the men toting the shovels over their shoulders with the box suspended by creaking handles between them, and with the whiskey bottle gripped in Munson's off-hand where it bent the silvery moonlight through the gold liquid hue, the three looked and sounded like some imagined vagary of dead pirates traversing the ocean's floor to bury their treasure.

When the digging was done and they stood leaning on the shovels, the moon was clear of the threaded, passing clouds and lit the desert well enough to reveal silhouettes of mesas in the distance. The men passed the bottle and commented on the warmth of the air, the swoop of the night's flying creatures and which backroads by which to return to town.

Grayson lit up, "Munson, I apologize up front for my candor but it must be said, and I'm sure you realize, that if there is a problem with this box, ever, you and I will be out here again. But I'll be the only one wielding the shovel."

Munson sighed, "We're twenty miles outta town and even if I was that way, which I ain't and never have been, brother, I am just along for the proverbial ride."

"Good enough," Grayson said.

As they walked into the bushes, Munson kept talking, "Phil, man, how's that little lady doing?"

"Which one?" Phil asked.

"Oh damn man, that's right. Congratulations. What's her name?"

"I'm going to name her Jackie if Sara doesn't override me. After my brother."

They were silent on the return trip to town, sharing the bottle and observing the abstruse dark beyond the dull beam of the truck's yellow headlights. When the truck roared away from his rental and Grayson was left standing in the yard with the cane rustling and the wind carrying sage, he felt enveloped by the warm night air. He sat on a railroad tie and reasoned that as God is in everything—in the cat's eyes reflecting moonlight from amid the garden corn and in his fingers feeling the grime on his jeans—but further that as God is the source and grounding and structure for anything to be at all, then here in his knowing this set of relationships he suspected was, in part at least, the explanation for this sense of division within the unity. Like any man, he is tasked as both participant and observer.

And then he thought of his son and in the ache decided, as he had decided a million times before, that despite the gap he would go on no matter what. The act of going-on, of surviving, was his religion put over and against whatever else seemed true. The trick to survival was in realizing how utterly unnatural it was to give in, to cower or crumble. To complain and not act. A thousand generations of men, fathers and their sons, had faced austerity absolute in cataclysms, plague, extinctions, and exile. Murder and pain were implicit in the unity of things and while the saints had sufficiently, to his lights, reasoned out why it is so, Grayson reasoned that pain did not tell the truth but only pointed the way. The truth lies beyond the gates of pain.

In his dream, Grayson lay wedged under what felt like a great formless mountain that seemed infused with a sense of verging, as if motion itself had been contained somehow into an ideal of potentiality made sensual but not material, for he only felt and could not see the apparition. Visually, from the great blank of earth below him, rose a single ovoid point of light like a luminous egg that expanded toward him and was bound in distinct spiral tracks of surging jade-colored light. There was heat at his back, a profound cold at his front. The egg quivered with some apparent and totalizing power. It nucleated and grew into focus in the dream. Before him, it divided, like cells in a biological being, and an ordered luminescent plane stretched out as the one became two and these two positioned themselves in a shimmering black space that had not before then existed in the world of the dream. Maybe he was looking up at the floor of a sea valley that did not move. But why was it visible? The terms were unsettled, the cipher of the dream was unfixed and he knew only that he was too tired or too ill-equipped by nature to invoke an explanation.

Wet sand pressed up where the heat was and he felt the sand on his skin and saw in the opacity around the dream, more sand rising. He was neither above nor below anything, but rather contained at some center. He came to understand what he saw was an original referent within an original, underived matrix. And as the line unspooling between the quaking luminous orbs reached its terminus, a third orb appeared. Instantly, apportioned elements of the sand sprang to life moving, as if encoded, into particular geometrical patterns. Sparkling and roving spirals. An outer contingent worked upon the sand and the grains were twinkling over each other, falling into lines and grids. The floating pinpricks of clear crystal and ebony mineral drew into focus over him.

The depth of field changed. When he looked again it was some vast desert city and he stood on the precipice of a great mesa. The marvelous cluster of colored lights from skyscrapers and traffic arteries sat isolated in the bowl valley that was itself held in the circumscription of desert dark. There appeared to be no way into the city. And no way out. This was not his city. And as he thought about this rejection, he turned away as if he'd walk the mesa.

Grayson woke and roused himself from the ditch still drunk. Twilight. The weeds and globe mallows around him were lit up like seats in a theatre, moon and creeping sunlight sparkling off the silica in the sand. The motes of stars seemed within reach, like they hung in the near space about his head. Lying on his back he reached up to pluck one. Inside, he drank water from the kitchen in the dark. He left the door open for the breeze and walked the stairs to his room. At ten that morning, Grayson was woken by his roommate Ben who said the militias were fighting.

For a moment he laid there trying to get some saliva back to his tongue so he could talk. Ben said he didn't know who they were but they were certainly moving to commandeer the town and that already he'd seen helicopters carrying rockets.

"You got coffee there?" Grayson asked.

Ben held two aluminum cups of coffee that chimed together as he spoke the words. "Here you go." He handed one to Grayson who took it automatically and rummaged for his tobacco. There was cordite on the air. The coffee steaming in the cup. He rolled and lit the smoke.

There was dull gunfire in the distance. A car alarm whined down the canyon. Grayson's scalp felt somehow off kilter, set too far back. He pulled on his hair with flat hands and stared at the window. Ben appeared frozen in his spot at the door. Shorts, barefoot. Grayson scanned the room and rose, opening the side door to the jury-rigged terrace.

"Well let's take a look," he said.

The sky spread out clear. A single black pillar of smoke rose over the valley at the north end. Looking closer, there were actually two or three pillars, like leaf fires burning in autumn. He felt his heart pick up. Ben remained in the doorway watching the back of his head. Grayson drank the coffee in gulps and snorted and spat and pulled a long, focused drag on the cigarette. He turned around and lifted his chin to say move out of the way.

"Alright," he said.

"I'm trying to wake up if I can," said Ben.

"Shut up. Relax. Go make sure Joe knows. They'll draw out the militias first. People looking for a fight. There's time."

Despite his nineteen years, Ben was a boy. His hair long and unkempt. He seemed unaware of the confused expression of longing and entitlement on his face as he walked out. Grayson turned back and stood at the edge of the terrace listening to the gunfire, following the reecho within the city blocks. The air pulled dry in his nostrils. Brush smoke and juniper berries. The road out front was quiet. In his room, he picked out the binoculars from where they lay on the floor and went down the stairs to the kitchen where he finished the cup of coffee, grimaced and coughed. He poured more. He sipped it, grimaced again, and then went out with the cup sloshing and crossed the porch and the yard. He hiked up the bike trail with his arms crooked out for balance and at the top he looked back down at the A-frame and over to Joe's place where the cherry tree swayed and the chickens scratched roots behind the thin wire mesh lining the garden.

He set the mug on a rock ledge and fitted the binoculars to his face. There was a speckled falcon sitting on the clothesline at the edge of the yard, and he watched it through the glasses and adjusted the ocular piece. Brilliant yellow beak. *Untouchable*, he said to himself and moved the glasses to see out across the valley and the town.

Sweat beaded along the freckled white skin of his brow. Smoke from another fire on the south end of the highway reached into the skyline. Maybe a third large fire in the area of the town, or was it five now? He wasn't sure, as the smoke was spreading. A few pistol shots rang dull, closer than the rest. The light off the rim wall through the smoke was wrong somehow as if it were shifting. *Sober up*, he told himself. He went back down the hill to the A-frame and went in the kitchen door. Ben had lit a joint.

"You said to relax."

"The main thing was to shut up. What's with this coffee?" Over his shoulder he said, "Could vie for the title of worst coffee ever brewed."

Grayson went up the stairs to his room: desk and tubs, mattress and chair. He set the coffee down on the windowsill and went to unstack the plastic tubs and set them on the floor around the bed. Lime green, stickers still on the side. Two held dry food stocks. Two were gear. He heard Ben pacing, creaking the old floorboards downstairs and then a deep ripping sound as water ran through the pipes to the kitchen sink. Finally, a sputtering as it was turned off. All of this noise seemed odd somehow, precise, too close.

He brought out a black daypack and set to securing two brown side-bags into the military webbing. He strapped a bagged foliage colored poncho liner up under the base of the pack and he removed the knife from one of the side-bags, then stuffed it in his belt.

Gregorian chant dubbed over death metal music blasted and quit. Blasted and quit again from downstairs.

There was a good Remington 870 shotgun with a magazine extension and wood stocks behind the tubs that he slid out over the carpet. The state police logo rolled or stamped into the receiver was without words. There was just the beehive and a few of the bees flying. He set the gun upright with the buttstock on his thigh and depressed the ribbed node along the trigger housing and began breathing in deep, controlled breaths. Four seconds in, four second out. He broke the action and lowered it to see that the feed ramp moved freely. He dropped a shell into the chamber and ran the grip forward and paused to listen. Alcohol sweat was running down his neck and face now and the cicadas seemed preternaturally loud to his ears.

Out in the distance muffled gunfire was ceaseless and growing in intensity at each end of the town. The tight back and forth of an all-out gunfight. A mortar or a rocket went off. Seemed to be in town, but not too far into town. It sounded like an anvil dropped in a well. Dust powdered down from the rafters and fell soft like beige mist around him on the tub lids and in the folds of the backpack, down his collar. He spat some from his lips and stretched his breathing out to eight seconds in and out.

Ben blasted and cut the stereo again.

"What is he doing now?" Grayson said to himself.

When the magazine was full of shells he checked the safety and set the weapon next to the backpack. He located the Glock on the floor and holstered it along his hip and then removed it and press checked the slide back. Finding it loaded, he reholstered it and hoisted the pack on one shoulder and reached down for the stainless water bottle on the floor.

Ben was sitting on the couch staring at the stone fireplace. A well-worn .22 Ruger rifle lay next to his knee. He looked up at Grayson as he came down the stairs. Something distant and unstable, maybe crazed, moved in the boy's eyes. On the coffee table he had set out an orange rubber placemat, upon which was arrayed a tangle of dried blue and gray mushrooms.

"The Norse called it going berserk. Going to war on mushrooms made them fight like hell," said Ben.

"Is that right?"

Grayson stood at the base of the stairs with the mirror behind him and looked more closely at the table and the gun and his roommate. The clear plastic magazine of the Ruger, curled and slick with too much gun oil, glinted beyond the boy's arm. Sunlight lay chopped up in trapezoids that seemed in motion along the dirty couch and against the stock of the boy's rifle. The boy's eyes were alight with electric motion.

"You're hardcore then," Grayson said.

"So are you."

"We'll see."

"Yeah. You haven't felt it yet then? They act fast with the lemon juice."

Something inside clutched. His guts felt pressed up against his spine. His heart fluttered up a notch in pace.

"You gotta be shitting me," he said.

"The other half of this ounce was in that coffee."

Grayson's mouth dropped about a half inch, "You put a half ounce of hallucinogenic mushrooms in the fucking coffee?"

"Little more than a half. Zapped 'em first. With the lemons so it hits harder," Ben said.

"So it hits harder."

A low concussion shook the ground and clattered the fireplace tools against the lava rocks of the mantle. More dust sifted from the rafters. He stood with the shotgun hanging slantwise in his hand. The grip on his stomach relaxed a moment then redoubled along the string of his guts. Glancing to his right, the room swam.

"That was the waterline to the east side," Ben said. "Or maybe it was the sheriff's station. Oh, or maybe it was the gas station. Either way."

The gunfire began again. The shots ran together then came punctuated by something deeper. He felt like a battery being charged. Disparate elements of the world blended. There was a mechanical whining somewhere in the auditory gloss like a great alien clockwork at the center of things, a visceral winding in his blood.

"I heard Mike and Skins rigged that waterline last week. You hear that?" Ben asked.

"What happened to you shutting up?"

Grayson heard himself speak. He heard the kid speak too but the context slipped. The first wave of real nausea hit and the drug set him adrift from the pylons of normalcy: conjecture and routine. He was suddenly at the door sloughing the backpack down his arm and dropping the Remington along the jamb. Out in the yard, beyond the grey line of shade, the sun seemed nuclear, axial. He clutched the water bottle and went staggering out the door with the mushrooms hitting first gear in his guts and the alcohol seeping from his pores. Smell of coffee and cigarettes like cat shit around his face.

Think now because you won't be able to in a bit.

He groaned and lurched further into the gravel drive. The sun was blasting the rocks and the weeds were dead and brown. But in the dirt the black ants moved too fast, like the boy's eyes, as if they were more than alive—hyper-alive and militating against every-thing and nothing and running their white bundles of larvae from borehole to borehole. He stopped and knelt in the red dirt and retched. The world around him bowed in a wide arc and gelled. Dust kicked up in a plume. Bile splattered up to his knees. From the doorway Ben said, "Just let it go man. Just let it go. You're tripping, you just gotta trip and not fight it."

Sweat broke out double on his forehead, cold this time. The grip on his gut reasserted and he emptied the last watery contents out. He gasped, feeling both cold and hot. There was whiskey smell to the puke.

"There you go," said the boy.

His swollen fingers followed the seam of his jeans up to the base of the holster. There hadn't been an actual thought—just a reflex to draw and kill that fucking kid. An image of his mother in the old kitchen spun around in his mind's eye: she was so young and so was he, she put a poultice of baking soda and water on a bee sting and it cooled the skin. The world was right and true at that moment. Grayson snapped back to the here and now and mut-tered the simple prayer, *Lord Jesus Christ, son of God have mercy.* He steadied himself. Sweat pooled around his eyes and he wiped it away and cleared his throat and stood and spit the paste out onto his shirt as might some demented patient in a ward. He turned and looked at the boy in the doorway pulsing and grotesque and he spat again and wiped his chin of slime and tilted forward to brush past him back into the house on rubbery legs.

You really gotta make decisions now, he said to himself.

Another series of low explosions rang over the valley and he knew the clarity might not last. The puking was good, he felt more aware. He grasped the jamb to the kitchen door with both hands. He took a deep breath and exhaled and started counting with the next inhale.

You gotta get to Phil, he told himself

Some spring in his center tensed and he waited to see where it would go. It eased and he bolted to the open door of the bathroom already working his jeans down. He crashed onto the toilet where he sat there shitting with the door open. The boy was singing now and the gunfire nearing. His head hung down. There was a tea-colored classifieds section on the floor and he picked it up and tore it to wipe and he pulled up his jeans. Staggering into the main room again, the effects of the mushrooms went into full bloom: the blue shag carpet shivered and began to flow away to the walls. In the flow were uncoiling fragments of old architecture, pandemonium. Exquisite castles of liquid bone and skull carried off to the edges. He blinked, shook his head. Each breath seemed to elaborate the complexity and depth of the hallucination until as he breathed the room seemed itself to spirate in time, and he felt concentrated good and evil both pour through him and coil around him. In the visionary flux rose and crumbled imperial cities of light and detail so tremendous that his instinct ascribed it to something exterior to him. Yet he understood this was not the case, that somehow it was both he and the world that made what his eyes beheld.

Ben hit the stereo: old reggae. Grayson knelt and tore out a folded section from a book of maps laying on the floor and then another and stuffed these into his back pocket. He righted himself and sighed. After a while standing there he went out the door with his shirt full drenched in sweat to the sound of gathering gunfire and mortar impacts. Back outside everything was alive or dead and the dead things—the barbed wire, the tool shed, the rusted tractor blade in the tall weeds—had their own negative life. He picked up the water bottle from the ground and took a little drink. The boy was back in the doorway

"They're coming right now. What are we gonna do?"

"Did you find Joe like I said?"

"Joe's gone man. It's just you and me."

Grayson snorted. He crossed the drive again to the trail at the rear of the yard and went up. At the top of the hill the red dirt between the rocks swam. Behind him the desert beckoned him with pure silence. Testament to the vastness of its mystery. Across the yard he saw Joe was sneaking around behind his house and the outbuildings in the shade. A shovel leaned against one of the cottonwoods. He saw the limbs of the tree reaching into the light. Joe came back from behind the building with an M1 rifle and a drab surplus bandolier of clips. By the weight of it he figured the clips were already loaded. The fires multiplied over the valley. Fifteen or twenty of them now. The peregrine shrieked out over the slickrock behind him and the drug hit him again warping the wider view and causing the rocks around him to seem involved somehow. Silent witnesses or active agent, the boundaries between himself and the world slipped. He watched his landlord over by the shop rock the rifle under his arm and flip up the metal butt plate and look inside and clap the plate back down.

"What do they do now?" Grayson asked himself. They secure a center of operations somewhere and then section the rest out, he said. This thought repeated itself with other meaning. He cupped the light from his brow and tried to draw in on the southern rim but could not and to the north he saw amid the haze of house smoke an element of helicopters hanging impossibly over the park. There were two Apaches and a massive twin-rotor transport machine that dipped and lagged behind the two others like a drunken insect. The mushrooms hit second gear in his system. A hand went out for the water, or the gun, he couldn't decide.

"You have to wait," he said out loud to the stones. And as if they'd answered, he thought, *Yes, you have to wait a bit more.* They'll probably take the high school or the center of town and the hospital for a base and then get serious about breaking the neighborhoods through the day and evening. Looking back south he leaned forward to see around the escarpment. Some sound back to the north, and turning he saw a line of four up-armored Suburbans and two Humvees rounding the bend maybe three hundred yards from the A-frame. He grabbed the gun and the bottle and went bombing back down the trail. His legs felt bandy. The socks against his toes in the boots wicked up a gritty sweat. He went down in bounds. At the base, he crouched a moment and felt for the drugs to rush him again but they did not. The world as an entity to react to had folded away. Only the slipstream remained.

The blood beating in his ears melded in time and substance with the cicadas calling and became amplified hitting some resonant yet volatile frequency. He gripped the edges of his boots with both hands and ground some of the red dust into his palms. The engines of the armored trucks were roaring forth like gunships on a river. Less than a hundred yards to go. Weaving in the auditory wash he got up and crept toward the door where his pack and the shotgun lay half in, half out. Joe's rifle cracked just when Grayson reached the door of the A-frame. As if the cartridge had pierced the sounding chambers of some delicate instrument midworld to them, the eerie weave of acoustics stilled.

"Oh, Joe, what the fuck," he said to himself.

The mounted machine gun on the Humvee tore into Joe's shack even before the line of the vehicles on the road halted, and the big bullets went straight through and sang off the stone face of the cut hill behind the houses. Grayson heard Ben scream from somewhere off in the A-frame, and it was as if he'd never heard his voice before. At the doorway he knelt down and grabbed up the pack and the shotgun from along the jamb. It seemed to him that he was forgetting someone, but he was not. *You're gonna have to crawl.* Goddamn they came on fast. His eyes fell on the porch and he spun and crawled out to the edge of the boards and pulled and the weathered grey facade pieces came away from the old nails on one end. It was cool inside and reeked of dry compost as he scrambled into the leeway. Under his palms he felt chisel marks in the stone. One of the Humvees crunched the gravel as it turned up the drive. He saw the black rims of the lead vehicle through the cane skirting.

A second big gun opened fire on Joe's place. Linkage of the belt-fed weapon clattered off the side panels. No organic movement seemed possible in that view. He jammed deeper into the dark of the crawlspace and reached to draw the boards back down enough so the nails held. The truck guns blasted, mechanizing the world. Under the influence of the drugs, the immanent order of reality transfigured before him. The mild poison pyrolizing inside with the fear seemed to let off a third compound that was neither him nor the drug but some rare and discrete alloy of the two. The crawlspace around him contracted in embryonic shudders. He scraped further under the deck boards where dangling heaps of cobwebs stuck in his wet, brown hair and under his shirt collar. The tubular hollow thump of a 40mm grenade went out. He froze and the detonation was instant.

The A-frame foundation trembled against his back. Flakes of dried mud and the hollow bodies of long dead June bugs and crickets cascaded down from the underside of the deck. Resigned to that margin between the deck and the earth, he looked at the quavering slivers of dusted light through the floorboards. He blew the dead bugs away from his mouth. The mounted gun exploded again in a great modulated squall and boots hit the ground in multitude. Someone in the squad whistled. Movement along the far side of the vehicle. The boots stepped up on the deck passing through the slots of light and tilted dust into his eyes as they crossed over his head. A twined odor of wood smoke and gun gas poured forth with their passing. Wild bursts of thoughts blasted forward and were of no help. Over it all he felt a bone deep desire to run. *Just hold that one off.*

Ever so carefully he shifted and dug a knee into the stone ground. His hand went out slowly to rest on the shotgun where he found the triggerguard and steered the barrel straight with the facade. Ankle height. The firing ceased, and he tried not to breathe in the stillness. He thought he could hear the gun barrel on the truck expanding in the heat. He sucked in and could taste raw minerals of the cold ground and the stale cellulose of the old lumber, the rusty iron nails in the lumber. The 40mm thumped again. Everything shook and settled. In the corner of the crawlspace his eyes fell on the complete perfect skeleton of a cat. You crept under these boards to die, alone. The empty sockets stared at him. Four little fangs nested together in a smile. A single rifle shot and then two more rang from inside. Someone called out, "Fire."

He had a vivid mental image of Ben's face blown out across the floorboards. A breeze rippled through the porch planks carrying more smoke. A wall stud bowed and cracked in the house. Sound of old sheetrock crumbling. It occurred to him that he didn't feel alone. Perhaps it was the cat. But he thought not. A greater order unveiling itself in this moment had embraced him and he felt it expand in his actual heart. It was not fear, he knew that much. It was that which temporarily yielded to fear to pull it in and devour it whole in due time.

The rush of flames was above him somewhere—the kitchen from the sound of it. He turned back to run or fight. He got the bag and took the gun in hand and waited. The cat seemed to shift and watch him, the way certain paintings by old masters do. The contractor's vehicles were running again, moving. Heat came roiling out through the floorboards above and a blaze from within the main room flared louder. Blue flames licked out through the door, tentacles reaching at the blue sky beyond where the sun hammered through the scant haze.

There was no more time here. *Move.* He kicked the façade boards away and wriggled out, rose and loped crazily to the far wall of the barn, slipping between it and the blasted rock wall with which it was squared on that side and crumpled against the batten barn planks. He peered down the driveway to make sure it was clear. The heat pounding out across the yard drew the skin of his brow taught on his skull. Whatever had been in that crawlspace with him came along. He judged the distance from the fire was enough to keep him alive and he pushed back around the corner and sat shrouded in the wedge of shade between the rock and the wall listening to the inferno grow and the timbers shatter. At some point the drug shifted gears again, going higher, and he straightened his back to the wall of the barn and drank the remainder of his water. *You have to move again soon.*

A visceral expanding sensation in his spine like the stringing of some interior bow quaked over him as he thought of his mission, of Phil and his wife and child. He had promised Jack to keep them from harm and to transport them through the maelstrom made of the country's open highways and its cities. Phil was one easy mile from him now. The thousand miles back to Oregon he could deal with later. The gunfire throughout the valley was incessant. From one of the side-bags he retrieved another pistol magazine and shook it to feel the weight before he stuffed it into his back pocket. He dropped the other magazine out of the pistol and he shook it likewise. Contented, he sent it back into the mag well where it clicked home and then he angled the weapon inboard and pinched the slide back from the muzzle to confirm the round already chambered there. Finding it was chambered, he dropped the slide back and tapped the rear to reseat it upon the frame. Last, he lifted his shirt and holstered the gun bringing the shirt back over it as he stood looking away from the smoldering house toward skies that seemed to pull the smoke into coils by some uncanny vacuum. And the coils themselves, braided in yet smaller coils, were each alive in a frenzy of ever-diminishing geometric motion.

2
The Jealous God

After three hours of slow-going terror and sweat to cover a mile of war zone, Grayson reached the oak and cottonwood copse behind Phil's place and settled in the duff on his stomach. From here he worked to still his mind. Hallucinations stirred along the periphery of his vision, as the succulent arms of yuccas or the spiny lobes of cacti coalesced precariously into discrete cognizant beings that seemed willing to speak or listen should he choose to entertain them.

He ignored them. Phil's house was intact but nothing moved inside or out. Grayson forced himself to wait and watch. The swamp cooler on the bedroom window hummed. He watched in fascination and horror as a mole pushed dirt up at the edge of the yard and a red hill manifested from below. No sign of Phil, his wife, or child. Diesel noise of the Humvees shuttled up the side streets from the main drag.

He crawled to the creek and filled his water bottle and drank. Then he filled it again and sat in the shade watching the steely surface of the water slide past. The neighborhood was quiet. The fighting was much diminished and the nexus of gunfire and small, occasional explosions sounded as if the clashes between contractors and militias were waged farther into town and across the highway. It occurred to him that there might be no resistance and, instead of fighting, all the shooting was just pure assault. At dusk he went to the side door and tried it, but it was locked. He knocked twice. No one came. He went through. The house was dark. The smell of green chilies and bacon was in the air. He went room to room, calling. No one. No shoes at the door. Nothing out of place. Back outside, he crouched and studied the dust and gravel. Finally he looked to where the path led to the driveway and he got up and walked to the corner of the house and gazed out at a patch of windblown sand and mud that had overflowed at the edge of the driveway and where there were tracks of both man and machine. He stood there a moment in thought. The hood of Phil's truck was cold to his touch. Muted screams and the cries of the mourning, the anguished and dumbstruck echoed across the culdesacs of adjacent neighborhoods and the forsaken two lane before him.

It was well dark when he passed through the tunnel under South 400 E Street with the slow drag of the stream up to his waist and the pack and weapons brushing the top curvature of the tube. On the far side of the aperture, he emerged and crawled into the brush and lay prone, glancing between the road and the near line of homes. Above him the cocked yellow bowl of a half moon was out and there were no clouds. He ate a tin of sardines and filled his bottle again from the faucet outside the thrift store and drank. Working to quiet his mind as the mushrooms worked through his system, he resorted to counting breaths, letting his mind oscillate in a mad dialectic between exterior and interior and between the physical, wrecked histories before his eyes and the pervading sense of something or someone having found him at the heart. *Only God could find you in the heart*, he thought.

When he decided to call on Munson and enquire after Phil's whereabouts, he stowed his water and crept on through the neighborhood avoiding the pools of light by cutting a path north and west to South 300 and then South 200. Little throngs of transients shuttled loot in the shadows. Shouts of minor triumph in languages vaguely exotic to his ears and others in border Spanish that he could understand were punctuated by the occasional pistol fire exchanged between the tribes. Unseen by any of them, Grayson made his movements by way of contiguous shadows, in almost complete silence.

At the high school he found the forward base. A huge twin-rotor helo had set down next to the Apaches in the road. Canvas tents billowed in the currents over the sports fields and dark shapes of uniformed and plain clothes men and women crossed the lawn from the entrance and went through the chainlink fences toward the gymnasium. There were no guards bearing insignias of any sort. Grayson moved on and crossed into the adjoining neighborhood where the landscaping was comprised of mature junipers and manicured elms and the houses were small split-levels and ranch style. In motion, the edge of his fear was dulled. Breathing slowly kept the rocketing locomotive of his mind just barely on its slippery tracks. Bats whirled in the empty, smoky streets. He zigzagged north where the rim met the highest houses built into the bank and there he looked down on the empty, quiet highway. It was 10:24 pm. Thirty minutes later he went down the embankment and crossed the four lanes of blacktop. Picking up the pace, he wended between two light poles he had already picked out as beacons and wove on through the next neighborhood. These were small and dark and mostly empty double and singlewides. Caged sodium lights flashed.

At quarter to one he threw a rock at Munson's door, waited, threw another and finally a third. The albino man came around the side of the house with his eyes glistening in the moonlight and didn't say anything but just stood scanning the yard with a revolver at his side.

Grayson stood from behind the bushes and walked up and said, "For a nocturnal fellow your night vision isn't that good, is it?"

In the shop beside his trailer, Munson switched on a light but Grayson told him to shut it off and he did. Grayson filled his bottle from a sink in the corner and listened as Munson rambled alternately vatic and murderous for a few minutes, as he recounted his experience running thieves out of his yard that afternoon. Grayson brought him to focus. Munson told him the contractors had not hit the neighborhood. When Munson went quiet, Grayson explained that Phil, his wife, and child were not at their house. No sign of struggle.

"Phil likely went to the rendezvous. Your place is along the same line of travel so thought I'd make sure. Thanks for the water." Grayson picked his pack up off the floor and sighed.

"Ya'll going back into that shit?" Munson asked.

"I'm going to steal a motorbike first."

"I got six pieces of silver, two guns, ammo, and a metric shit-ton of tuna fish and peanut butter. Crackers too. Let me go with you."

"You got crackers? Well, sir, let me reconfigure my entire operation."

Munson sighed and stood up. A slit of moonlight fell in between the wallboards and he stepped into it unconsciously so it bisected his face. "You fixing to steal a bike out of Jake's shop? Jake wouldn't appreciate that, I imagine," said Munson.

"I'm not going over there to ask, I'm going over there to take."

Munson lit a cigarette. "I'll show you how to get into Jake's."

* * *

One block off Main Street, Gibson's Motorsports stood encircled in chain link and razor wire. Around the fence was a tangled row of scrub oak, blackberry vines, and wild salt bush that separated the lot from those neighboring. There was no wind and the streetlights cast down into a density of yellow smoke hanging over the road. The sound of a glass bottle shattering up the way pierced the silence. Shouts of a fight followed. Crouched at the edge of the fence and well hidden in the vegetation, Munson's alabaster skin still caught the little ambient light so that he seemed to glow in the hollow of limbs and vines like a luminous fish hovering in a deep ocean rock nook. Grayson emerged from the wall of shadowed bushes without a sound and grabbed Munson's shoulder, pulling him back into the weeds, out of sight of the road. They crept into the dim of the adjacent building.

When they stopped, Grayson said, "Bikes are on the inside, not in the yard. Fence is wired to an alarm. And we don't have bolt cutters. The other thing is there's a dog, at least one. I can hear him scratching, and there's a bowl right there at the door."

"Yeah, I know. We gotta kill the dog," Munson said.

Grayson glanced up the street to where the bottle had shattered to check for movement. "I don't kill dogs." His expression fell into a grim blank curtain of resolve.

Munson scoffed. "You're shitting me. You'll kill a person but you won't kill a damn dog?"

There were more heated voices from the alleys up there, but no eruption yet. After a quiet moment with his ear cocked to the road, Grayson cleared his throat.

"In the frigid north, before the domestication of dogs, men hunted and patrolled their territory in pairs or alone because the limited caloric resources couldn't support large tribes. Women needed to stay put with the kids. The necessarily small squad size limited men's travel. They couldn't haul much. It restricted when and how they could fight. They were pressed deep into tougher land. If you're the sort who believes in evolution, this would be maybe fourteen thousand years ago. And then the mystery arrives: these solo operators of the north all the sudden begin to domesticate wolves. Now they're going out to face the unknown with a true gang who will kill or die for their master, their alpha. They can haul, they can fight, they've got warmth in the blizzard. Dogs are an early warning measure, so security improves. This allows the northerners to survive and eventually thrive. Western man owes his existence to dogs. In my particular worldview it's neither contradiction nor exaggeration to say that dogs are a direct gift from God. That's why we don't kill dogs."

Munson considered this for a moment. He lit a cigarette. The voices up the road grew pitched. Munson squinted,

"To get a job done even? World's falling apart, folks getting killed for a damn jacket or some shit in the street and you won't kill a dog."

Grayson shook his head. The fight erupted down the street. More glass broke. Pistol shots and then quiet.

Munson said, "Dog don't know you killed him once it's done."

Grayson shook his head slower. "They're sacred, dude. Sacred means no exceptions."

"Well unless you got some steak bits to distract the motherfucker I don't know what to tell you but to kill him and get on with it, ya know."

"Gimme your wallet. We're going in the front fucking door and deal with it there."

With a few tries of Munson's library card, he had the door open in under a minute.

Munson rubbed his hands together over the wood grips of the revolver and said, "Now watch that beast."

Grayson opened the door an inch and the hinges squealed. They heard the claws skipping over the linoleum inside. Deep guttural growling closing the gap. He pulled the door back to the edge of the lock and wedged his toes up against the kickplate. He pivoted and set his shoulder up to the door to cushion the hit just as the dog slammed in from the other side.

Grayson said, "Go over there and grab a stick of that firewood and bring it back up here. Hurry up."

Munson came back with a wedge of the split wood and held it out in front of him as he hopped his weight back and forth from one foot to the other.

Grayson said, "Come up here. Listen. I'm going to wait a second until he backs off the door. Get right under here. No, on this side. Listen, when he backs up I'm going to open the door and he's going to fly out right there and you need to be fast."

Munson did a manic little dance back and forth, imagining the scenario. He practiced swinging the stick of wood a few times and then came around fast and positioned himself under Grayson's right arm with the stick cocked back by his shoulder.

"Don't hit him too hard. Hear me?"

"Now I gotta hit him just so? Damn, man."

The dog leapt at the door again and scratched at the floor like he would dig through to them. Grayson looked out onto Main for anyone watching. The dog began yipping and growling and he hit the door again. Black nails skittered on the floor a few steps and Grayson said, "Now." And he opened the door. Munson brought the stick down like a hammer right along the dog's ear and the dog hit the jamb and its legs went out like those of a flimsy card table and it fell into the doorway stone dead. Engines roared low from out in the desolated town. It was a muscled terrier mix of some sort with short brown hair and a studded collar. A single thread of blood drained out of its ear. One of its back legs twitched and kicked Munson's boot.

"Humvees coming. Pick him up you dumb shit," Grayson said.

They got the dog's body inside and hoisted it up on a line of torn leather waiting room chairs where its limbs hung over into the empty space and rolls of the brown furred skin slipped loose into the crevices of the cushions. Munson closed the door. The only light was from the polluted streetlamp coming in greasy through the wired security windows. Grayson cupped his head in his hand, sighed. Thick drops of blood dribbled from the dog's ear and wetly thumped the floor with slow uncanny regularity. Munson went across the little room to lean on the countertop. Though the strongest effects of the mushrooms had subsided, the residual unease and an overriding feeling of permeability between the world and his mind grew stronger for Grayson. In the dark, the luminous albino seemed to hover off the floor and the quiet dripping of the dog's blood came as perfectly calibrated as a metronome. In the oddness of this moment and the exhaustion, Grayson studied the outline of the limp carcass in the opaque grid light and, as is the feature of dark times, his eye began to see the porous nature of his reality.

Hallucination or otherwise, he observed the faint ticking of light particles encircling the body in a gossamer cocoon that kicked off soft sparks, as if he were witnessing the soul of the animal recollected in some way to a wider state. He shook his head to clear the vision and retreated to a grooved, quiet place in his mind. Rifle fire and the rumble of vehicles on the road brought Munson to the window where he bobbed and wove to angle his vision through the security grid. When Grayson remembered to breathe, he remembered also the sanctity of his promise and his mission and remembered that the one thing he knew about himself was that he always went the hard way out. *Good enough. Pray that God approves.* A searchlight wove over the building, reflected off the dog's anodized rabies tag and sent a little disc of light roving on the wall like a beacon. And then it was gone. Grayson dropped his hand away from his face and went back out the door and came in again with the shotgun in his hands. Munson watched him as he set the gun down and unslung his backpack.

"Get up and go find where he keeps the keys," he said. "And find a shovel."

* * *

On the BLM road with the white dust billowing up in the dark behind the motorbike and the orange cone of headlight cutting the dark ahead, he felt the last of the mushrooms' toehold on his mind slip away-- leaving an anxious, bitter aftertaste. With no visor or goggles, he kept his head tilted as if a daemon was perched on his shoulder, whispering extraordinary counsel in his ear. He switched off the motor and walked the bike over to the station and leaned it against the wall and switched off the headlight. He listened properly, closely to the desert. After a moment he called out for Phil and then Sara and Phil again. The desert was quiet but for the tremolo of crickets in the sage and a rustling breeze so light he hardly noticed it at all. He called again. He reminded himself to breathe. Sleep was coming. He rolled and lit a cigarette and a few drags in began to wearily unshoulder the pack and untie his bedroll. The stars and galaxies of stars hung like far off chandeliers as he passed out. And then, as if a vault door spun shut and then spun instantly back open, the sun was hot on his face and he woke.

* * *

Seven in the morning. A crow called down from the pines lining the ranger station. At the stationhouse, he drank and splashed cold water on his face and soaked his hat. Phil wasn't there, and he knew it bone-deep. Just the same, for a moment he stood looking for him in the sage and the tree shadows with the sparkling drops catching the sun and falling to the dust. When he was done he went back to his bedroll and picked up the shotgun and went to where the box was buried.

It was just a faint discoloration in the red dirt that betrayed the spot, the remnant of footprints of Munson and Phil and Grayson made two nights before from when they'd walked out to bury the 80mm box. He swept away the needles and debris he had sprinkled over it then to disguise the disturbance in the soil. The good smell of juniper and dirt was everywhere.

Turning around toward the road, he scanned for sign in the dust for tracks or disturbance of any sort that would tell him Phil had made the rendezvous. Grayson stepped off the spot and walked out fifty paces, examining the ground side to side and in front. At the end of his paces he spun and walked a wide arc all the way around the station cutting for sign until he arrived back exactly where he had started. No one else had been here. Not a print. Not a misplaced twig but what nature had done.

He set the shotgun against a juniper trunk. There were some hard, dry manzanita branches lying around and he chose one and started to dig. Ten minutes and he felt the surplus box and dug out the edges with his hands and yanked it out of the hole.

"Alright," he said.

When he had the shotgun and his pack all situated and the box tied to the bike, he went back and washed his hands and soaked some dried puke out of his lank brown hair. He squinted into the front window of the station to see through the blinds, but there was nothing to see and in his mind he was already halfway back to town. The bike started fine and then five minutes down the road it jerked and coughed and gave up and he rolled it off into the sagebrush a few yards and let it fall. He sighed as he crouched to inspect it and found there was a provisional plug, a peg carved out of a piece of varnished oak, that had been shoved into the hole where the drain plug should have been. A gritty windblown layer of oil extended back along the case where it had all seeped out and away. He plucked the peg out. Two globs of gelatinous oil dripped into the sand.

The box felt heavy. Yesterday's shock was catching up. By the time he had gotten the bike stashed away from the road and brushed the tire tracks away for a good hundred yards and lugged the box and the pack and the gun a half mile further down the road, he figured that was good enough and so he walked out again into the chaparral to bury it once more. He picked a shady spot where the road bent and sat down to break. He caught his breath and pulled the box over and unclasped the latch on top to check the seal. It was sound. He went to close it back up but changed his mind and kneeling he steadied the side of it against his stomach and took out the enclosures and the solidox from on top and set those on the ground and reached one arm back in and rummaged around, counting under his breath. The specie gold and silver inside was still cool. He put everything back and closed the lid and buried the box in a shallow pit and set off back toward the road where he crossed heading northwest and straight toward town.

* * *

It was two in the afternoon and Grayson was wrung out when he crested the low side of the eastern rim and looked down on Moab and across the valley to the opposite rim wall and then beyond to where the killing ground of red plateau ran to the horizon. There

King of Dogs

was no gunfire in the valley. But there was no bird song either. Having conserved his water this far he sat down on a shaded crag to finish the bottle. Most of the big columns of black smoke were gone leaving only small driftless spikes of white from house or shop fires and a general leaden fog that suspended itself ghost-like over the valley. At the north end of the highway off to his left, some four miles away, the small dark blur of a helicopter cir-cled on the otherwise brilliant blue of the empty upper sky as if it were overseeing the bridge out of town or the Colorado that ran through that end, perpendicular to town. Traipsing over the path and high-stepping the switchbacks so as not to disturb the rattlers who tended to coil among the rocks of these pinched places, he de-scended, listening all the while for the turbines to grow close. But they didn't and everything was quiet other than his boots scraping. Perhaps by some mercy of imploded plans or perhaps by sheer lack of permission, thoughts of failure or catastrophe had yet to mate-rialize with any great vividity across the rolling screen of his mind. The awareness of such outcomes was rather an omnipresent black void, uncategorized. Grayson told himself plainly that he would only proceed with the job. Yet he was aware again of his solitary status upon the unfolding stage of the world. The sense of carrying a passenger while hallucinating was gone and what remained now was a familiar emptiness, which he embraced if only because it meant he was alive and there was more suffering to come. The pain would be converted again to fuel.

"Bank on that," he said to himself.

At the midpoint in the trail, he was in the shadows and one of the Apaches came fast into the valley from behind him where its rotor noise had been shunted away. He crouched amid a cluster of boulders that stabbed up the wall at a switchback and clung there until the machine went through, and he knew that to the pilot's eyes in the cockpit he would be just another contour on the huge scrawl of rock and sand. And as he rose, he took the briefest of moments to linger, stretch his legs and back in a triangle pose, and to replace his shape upon the landscape in increments so as to allow the observant creatures, coyote or deer, to adjust and not be startled. The last bit of the trail he jogged and then he went into the scrabble and to the neighborhood and moved on like an alley cat going along the fences, wide-eyed and watching his back trail.

Munson was slouched in a cedar chaise chair in the screened-in room of his trailer wearing a tank top and sunglasses and a gray wide-brim fedora. His .44 revolver and two speed loaders sat next to him on a table made of old pallet wood and next to it was a bottle of Old Crow whiskey.

"Still no Phil?" Grayson asked.

"Negative. Guess you ain't seen him neither."

Grayson slung off the pack and sat on the porch steps outside the screen door. "Your hose work?" he asked.

Munson said it did and Grayson got back up with his water bottle and went to the hose to fill it. Two painted horses were at the edge of the driveway in the dusty road nibbling on weeds growing up from the ditch. Each of them brought their heads around when they heard the water running in the pipe and slapping onto the packed earth. Grayson sensed them, as they'd sensed him even before he'd opened the faucet, and he studied the immaculate brown glass globes of their eyes, and the sweeping skirts of their long black eyelashes. Beside the trailer was an inflatable child's pool, limp and pliable in the sun, that he inflated halfway. When he let the hose run into grass-stained plastic basin the horses knew and strolled over and sniffed him before they bent to drink. He came back to the porch steps flapping his hat on his leg and sat and drank the water from his bottle. He picked a thorn out of his boot.

From inside the screened room Munson said, "Well, sir, I can't help but notice you ain't following no strict recourse as implied. No rendezvous." Munson took a sip of the Old Crow and set it down slowly beside his gun and said, "Evidently, Phil done got on out with Mike before the Virginia boys even arrived and figured he'd hole up and wait for you."

Grayson turned around. Munson smiled wide. Grayson stood and stepped in the screen door in the shade and remained hovering over Munson there with his boots up on the sill. Blue veins below the translucent skin, smell of laundry softener from the house.

"After you lit out, Mike shows up, maybe four in the morning, and tells me this shit about how his militia buddies are fixing to counter strike and whatnot. I tell him that's insanity. I mention the business with the dog at the bike shop." Munson picked up the bottle and held it out for him. Grayson took it and wiped the glass and drank. He drank again and nodded for Munson to continue. "Anyhow, it comes around to Phil and the upshot is that he's cool, man," Munson said. Grayson handed the bottle back to him and wiped his mouth.

"Where?" Grayson asked. He was already shouldering his pack and gun.

"South end of town, the hostel. Take the rim trail. That's the way Mike came."

Across the street a cat nimbly tracing the apex of a clay tiled roof arched its back in the afternoon glower of the hanging sun.

Grayson said, "They'll clear the neighborhoods before long, one by one. You'll want to move."

"Squads cleared it this morning. I was off in them piney woods yonder. Believe that's whose horses those is. Neighbors got picked up or run off. I don't know." He handed the whiskey back and Grayson took it.

"About getting out," Grayson started.

Munson raised his hand and stopped him. "It's all good man. I got my ride. Mike worked a little a hippy magic for me, man. We're going to Texas, first light. You're on to Oregon. And so, Mr. Grayson, we all square."

* * *

Grayson went the long way back up the switchbacks and then along the rim trail parallel to the valley and then descended again and at five in the afternoon came to the highway's edge on the south end alone and wired on recoursed adrenaline. The helicopters were all gone from the sky. He crossed the highway in the open and ran into a willow thicket, feeling the raw spots under the pack straps. The temperature rose off the blacktop and pulsed out to the ditch where the stiff, twined smell of tar and roadkill hung about in the dead weeds. He crossed the frontage road and cut up the avenue toward the nearest house where in the yard he stopped and studied what remained of Moab's hostel.

Imprinted upon the fresh red earth were deep doubled bulldozer tracks arcing through the remains of the front garden. A heap of pale blue wallboards that had been yanked from the studs by the dozer blade sat jumbled with the viscous green stumps of spiny cacti flesh. In his intelligence gathering forays of the previous months, Grayson had found the hostel among the more interesting outlets for atmospherics and gossip as the clientele was often international and vocal in their travel observations. He recognized certain items amid two raggedy mounds of soot-laden household goods that were built up in the courtyard—a vintage arcade game machine from the foyer, shards of purple coffee mugs. Small fires smoldered within these piles and pewter bits of a board game and a deck of blue tarot cards with the edges singed were littered about the grass. Knots in the coals popped. Grayson knelt and thought. No hostel and no Hostel Mike. The message to meet Mike here before going to reconnoiter with Phil would have come before the hostel was leveled. Might need another plan.

Two elderly women wearing headscarves of scrap checkered linen emerged from the trees and went slowly poking through the debris searching for food or barter goods to fill the cloth satchels they carried at their elbows. Everything else in view was a dead zone. He got up and trotted down to the lot and then down the trail to an arbor grove of jimson vines where the air was so sweet and thick he held his breath. He kept jogging over to the houses on the other side and heard generators humming. At the first house he turned up the drive. A station wagon, boondocked some years, set rusting under blackberry vines and a heavy coat of rainpocked dust. On the off-side the trail was freshly trod with human footprints that rounded the bend following the tracks up to where the yard rose slightly and opened into another gravel lot hemmed with a dense row of yellow roses.

Grayson skirted the perimeter of the house among the scrub and bent down on the western side among the boughs of an enormous clump of sage and rabbitbrush. The engine of a car turned and died distant in the neighborhood. It turned again and caught. Exhaust popped in the muffler. He scanned a wide arc down the rise to the remnant hostel and the empty overgrown lots for some sign of dreadlocked Hostel Mike. He cocked his ear to the vehicle passing close to him on the highway. It went on without stopping.

In his mind, as in all minds, be they human or canine, there was a kind of model of space time, a grid, where people and places were to match up with their stated and implied intentions. The fact that Hostel Mike was not at the hostel when he'd said he would be, however, was not a huge surprise and Grayson took it in stride. It confirmed issues of character, in fact. Little could be expected of anyone at this point. The logical end state of an economic and social worldview that gave primacy to consumption and accepted fraud as the cost of business while discarding transcendent values altogether in favor of pure mechanical control over nature was, predictably, an epidemic of spiritual emptiness and a ruin of un-accountability. All is vanity, all is fraud and while vanity is sad and weak--fraud is far worse. Worse too than formal aggression, Grayson thought. Formalized physical aggression presumes terms of surrender. A man or collective could surrender rather than die. While fraud, in contradistinction, made killing a necessity of survival: for where there is no room for trust there can be no truce. And where there is no truce there is only war. And before Grayson, in the smoldering valley of Moab the chaotic axiom that killing will follow fraud was everywhere obvious.

A battered flagstone path joined the lot and wove around to the rear of the house. Dead quiet. No lawnmowers mowing. No dishes clattering. Just hot wind off the highway. And going through the shrubbery, he flipped off the safety on the Remington. Just as he did it and the sound of the lever clicked, he saw the girl. She was a bad case. Arab, half naked. She was sitting on a garden box with long, dirty hair in her face, eyes closed. A glass carboy sat between her legs and a white balloon over the mouth of the container stood erect and pressurized by the gases of whatever sat in the big jar.

"What in the hell have we got here," Grayson muttered, under his breath.

Lo-fi Arabic music played in the yard. He couldn't locate the precise origin. Black flies picked up off the girl rhythmically as she nodded to the muffled wailing and chanting. Gasoline in the air. He watched her motionless for a moment and then turned and went back on the path. On the other side of the house a series of old and faded two-liter soda bottles leaned against the stucco. Each was capped with the same balloons that were on the carboy the girl held. Some limp, others ready to burst. There was a murky tan liquid inside each of them. The whole scene looked like certain carnival games of yore. More flies collected and wove in small swarms

When Grayson saw the other slouched, evidently inebriated figure, he angled the shotgun away and checked back at the highway and then returned his attention and said, "Hey. Wake up." The figure was a young male with long filthy hair and stubby fingers that twitched drunkenly and of their own accord. The otherworldly, imported *ughniyah* music played from a phone set into an empty paint can by his knee. The young man's face was bloated and gaunt at the same time. In his far hand, he held another of the soda containers that was leaking from a hole on the side. In the near hand he had a damp stained rag clutched loosely against his chest. He looked at Grayson through beady, blood-soaked eyes. His head lolled on his spine. A yellow crust was built up around his mouth and nose. He said in a dry accented voice, "Hey yourself."

Grayson almost laughed.

The kid stared at him and then at the shotgun. Grayson took three steps forward with his hands around the wood stocks of the gun and hit a rich wall of sweat stench, stale sewage, and gas fumes.

"Is there anybody in there?" he asked, backing up a pace.

"Yeah I know."

"Yeah you know what?"

"I'm fucked up."

"I can see that. I'm asking if there's anyone around from the hostel. Do you know where Mike is?"

His face was a blank sheet.

Grayson sighed. "He lives right there in that hostel. Dreadlocks and about six foot two. Fat unsavory type of bastard, smokes a lot of weed."

The kid brought the rag up to his nose and took a deep drag and held it and exhaled. He was maybe twenty years old. "Dad left me this house. My father is dead, but I still hear him in my head," he said holding the container by his leg the way a child might do with a broken toy.

Grayson said more to himself than with any expectation of response, "So you're a Jungian of sorts. That's deep."

The kid fished a cigarette from off the paver stone. Stuck it in his lip and mimed a lighter as if asking for one. Grayson turned and wandered down the side yard to get a better view of the neighborhood. It was still quiet on the street. Somebody pulled a curtain shut. After a moment, he turned and hiked back up the yard. The girl shook her hair to clear the flies. The weird strobe effect of the Apache rotors thumping the air carried in from the direction of town like some fearsome heartbeat in the sky. From behind him the kid said, "I'll cut you up white man." The kid was holding a red plastic fruit knife. One hematic eye open, cigarette in his lip. Grayson pitched his lighter onto the boy's lap and walked off.

"Cut you, whitey."

The two elderly women in their rebozos had wandered on from the hostel. In the shade of a cottonwood he squatted and looked down the hill at the piles of loot junk where slanted sunlight caught in the green glass shards. The Apache tore through overhead. Grayson glanced up at the gray underbelly and went back to surveying the piles and checking different angles and elevations, as might a man measuring shots on a pool table. The two women made the sign of the cross—forehead to waist, right to left.

While coherent genuine worldviews are discovered and preserved, if only at great cost and sacrifice, it's true in the converse that the passably coherent, the fraudulent system of beliefs can be invented, marketed, re-branded and widely distributed at a fraction of the price. Performed properly, psychological warfare is difficult to distinguish from fraud. The one in private may in fact beget the other in public. Or be made to seem so. Each shares principles of presentation, misdirection, and substitution with other. Those wanting of reverent incertitude, those deaf and blind before the near-total mystery of being, and those whose lives are seared with terminal anxiety all share a pronounced distaste for the unraveling of contradictions. The psychological warrior need only extinguish those few with time and love for the truth and from there progress to seed the remnant population with various contradictory mandates, each by increments more self-destructive than the last until uncertainty itself is a virtue pedestalized. Human social and tribal realities of ostracism and inclusion are such that the herd will police itself. Vectors organic and contrived thereafter require minimal maintenance and only fine tuning. So constituted, man is a religious being and the key to his psychology is in where he places faith. As the seed contains the template of the tree, so the originating logic of a worldview can be deduced from that worldview's final form. Thus the psychological warrior's credo-- *deny, deflect, make counter accusations*-- is both the seed and the fruit of his operation and thus thrives an empire of distrust, unaccountability, and fraud.

Having made their peace or sufficiently filled their meager totes the two women teetered in their long skirts through the veil of vines and disappeared from the hostel grounds. Grayson stood and walked down the hill and from amongst the garbage fished out a full beer. He slid it into his back pocket and ducked off into the chaparral and walked on until he got to the creek where he sat down in the shade and sunk the bottle to cool it and wash it of soot and grime. Loamy smell of the desert creek wafted across the water. Bird tracks had dried in the mud. No hostel, no Hostel Mike.

He did not remember going to sleep. Just passed out with his head cradled in a mold of damp sand and in his dream, he stood at the mouth of a big corrugated runoff canal with cold blue water rushing by at his waist. A shrouded man sat on the bank to his left in a lotus pose. The edge of the current caught trailing threads of the man's beige cloak. The rushing throb sound of water in the tube and smacking stone dominated. Speaking was impossible.

Placed on a flat bloodstained stone set before the cloaked man, was a brass equal-arm scale and its correspondent set of burnished weights and these were banded by an indecipherable etched lettering that fascinated Grayson. Back up the canal it was dark. Downstream Grayson saw green northern lights merging into a dark forest and the shimmering surface water where the creek widened and met another branch. Slow and coiling like a helical ladder in the margin between earth and heaven, the fluid bands of green light billowed on a sky stratified pink and blue at sunset and for an interminable, recursive moment, he knew he was not alone and had never been.

Then the shrouded man put his hand out to receive the toll. Grayson placed a wet silver coin from his pocket in the bony grasp. In a flash of legerdemain, the coin was dry and rested on one scale. Two of the little brass plug weights teetered on the other as the arms rose and fell. Just as instantaneously the shrouded man flashed, as if the frame rate of vision were tinkered with, and Grayson saw the faceless man was now tensed into a pose vaguely yogic and it was clear he was in strange communication with the flat stone and the stone of the cut embankment and the metals on the swinging plates. It was geomancy, alchemy, or both.

Grayson went to retrieve another coin from his pocket. The man and the metals all flashed again, and the scales swung more heavily. The shrouded man oscillated on the rock as if he were sitting on a Lazy Susan. The torque grew. He levitated off the stone with the wet skirts of the cloak slopping out of the water and he hung there frozen in otherworldly suspension while everything in Grayson's periphery rushed or ran or pulsed and ascended and undulated so that the tollmaster was his only fixed reference. The thin hands did their trick, flashing as if segments of time were simply excised. In that lost time, the coins splashed into the water where a pale, pink fire was given off, lost or accepted by the gods of the place. Grayson looked back, and the shrouded man's hands had slashed into a third grimly taut pose seemingly saying: proceed.

He blinked in the dark until he made out the tree limbs overhead, fore laid on the sky like malformed fingers halting him, and he walked his own fingers out to feel for the surety of the shotgun before moving further. It was too cold near the water and he rubbed his hip where he'd slept on the Glock. There was small gunfire somewhere south. The creek water trickled over the rocks. The reeds along the bank shook in the breeze. He stood and forded the stream and stepped up the other bank to see the avenue. A few streetlamps were out but most were intact here. A garage door was open up the block and the light was on. He saw the burnt and shot-out husk of a silver sedan inside. The brown grass yard was festooned with half-melted plastic bubble wrap and the ashy parts of a bullet-riven barbeque. Cast offs of looting. The macabre humps of adult bodies were set in the road along the curb as if to sandbag some coming flood.

He thought he heard crying or wailing a few streets over. A stroller was turned over in the road, baby blanket and toys strewn around. A few feet to his left another car was wrapped around a telephone pole and there were curled flower shapes in the doors and quarter panels where fifty caliber rounds of mercenaries had punched through and kept going. Someone had carried the driver away but a good portion of him or her was still attached to the dashboard. Playing cards and crumpled paper wrappers from old burgers littered the hood and the sugary chemical tang of antifreeze that had splattered over the telephone pole was mixed with creosote from the pole. At last, he turned away.

Back at the creek he dipped into the cold up to his arm and brought up the beer and cracked it open. He drank half of it and exhaled and drank the rest. The crying continued. A woman somewhere bemoaning the day's evil. Soak it up. Get some. At dawn he got up and took a bag of cashews out of his pack and ate a few handfuls. The sky was purple over orange. His teeth chattered some as he washed his face in the creek. He got the shotgun and the empty bottle and crossed the water and the bank and came out on the street in the dim blue light of the war-torn neighborhood where the rats scurried, their beady eyes embroidering the shadows.

Minutes later, Grayson returned with the bottle full of gasoline and a sock was stuffed down the top and wrapped with a shoelace to keep it all in place. He started to trot to make time heading back the way he had come. Perhaps Hostel Mike would be up on the rim. If not he'd have to go back and look for him at Munson's place. Shouts from behind him saying, "There, see him? Honkey ass. Get that motherfucker, man."

The dim outlines of six men in the distance. Rocks went sailing into the dawn-lit sky. He kept trotting. At the highway he stopped in the weeds to look up and down and back at the remains of the hostel. The surveillance helicopter was in flight and moving somewhere behind the western rim wall. He sprinted over the highway and kept on through the few houses on that side of the valley until he was in the darker shadow of the rim weaving around the big pastel scrabble to the trailhead. The trail switched back for the first few hundred feet then came five hundred feet of incline. At the top of the climb dreadlocked Mike was waiting for him like a gnome among the rock piles wearing his sunglasses and a pursed smile.

"I saw you down there yesterday, man," Mike said and he laughed and wheezed through his graying goatee. Grayson didn't laugh but just crossed the distance between them squinting as if he focused on something more subtle, or more inclusive, than the mere physical reality before him.

Mike said, "I'm sorry. It's not funny" Then he laughed again till he coughed and when he recovered he said, "No it is funny. I saw you down there, man." He laughed again.

"Easy to watch. Tougher to be in the arena," Grayson said.

Mike stopped laughing.

They walked along the rim high above town to where Mike had a rudimental camp. A small coyote-colored tent was pitched under a great rise of boulders. A blackened firepit and a cache of split wood were stacked at one end of the hollow. At the other, a propane stove kit and a glass pipe stood atop a drab green 50mm surplus ammo can. Mike settled cross-legged near the tent in the dust.

Grayson asked about Phil.

"He's down there on the end," Mike said pointing toward the north end of the rim. "By the Bonderline house. The place is like a castle, man. Said you'd know it. Said you guys worked there or something."

"Sarah and the kid's with him?"

"Yeah I guess so. Unless he decided to cut weight," Mike laughed and wheezed and went on. "We didn't see any commotion. That's right by Munson's place, odd as it is," he chuckled. "His house being such a shit hole, you know. And then you got this mansion stuck right in the middle with all the trailers. Improbable Moab. Anyway already been through there. Yeah, they're there waiting on you, man. I'll walk down with you. See what ole lily white Munson's up to."

"You want to break your camp down?"

Mike waved his hand saying, "I'll come back when we're done and get it."

They got up and started down along the rim top. Grayson wedged the Molotov into the mesh on his pack, in place of a water bottle, and cinched it down.

"So what's your plan exactly if you don't mind my asking?" Mike asked, one hundred meters down the trail.

"It's not that I mind you asking it's just that I'm not going to tell you," Grayson said.

The sun was overpowering in the open. As they walked, Grayson studied the trail. Coming and going, the earth was almost shiny. While beside the trail, the dust had collected in little parallel running mounds of fine coral powder. Cresting out of the boulders, he got a good look into the verdant valley, which appeared so peaceful at a distance. In the other direction, running away from the rim, the rocky expanse of plateau flats and mounded outcroppings pulsed with a beautiful and foreboding glimmer. When they came to rest they were down a third of the way from the rim on a sizeable outcropping.

They stood a while at this provisional landing on the side of the trail. Mike poured sweat. They could see the huge Bonderline vacation house and its ornamented property that lay tucked beside the wetlands. Beyond lay the pastures and the river that intersected the valley. Grayson glassed with binoculars a good portion of the neighborhood back toward town where the watered oaks and alder stood in billowing green grids correspondent to the lay of the blocks. Adopting a seated twist with one knee tucked to his chest and his back against the relative cool of the shadowed rocks, he surveyed the view.

On the corner of Hale and River Sands at the irrigation canal, along the treeline, the cottonwoods grew thick on three sides of the Bonderline property. On the third was a straight view from the house toward the river and the bridge. Scaffolding of tilers or adobe applicators still clung to the sides of the exterior walls of the house but no men worked there and nothing moved, save in one of the quads of the pasture, a few rabbits that were eating clover, their ears twitching above the fringe of long green grass.

They proceeded the rest of the distance in silence. Grayson moved fast in the shadows and then paused at the switchbacks to let Mike catch up. Mike looked dour and shook his head as he picked forward over the little scree. At the base of the trail Mike stepped off to the right and Grayson to the left. Mike crouched down so he couldn't be seen from anywhere in the yard.

"Godspeed, amigo," he said.

Grayson took a step back onto the trail and looked him dead square in the eyes. The words came steady and direct.

"If there's any kind of problem here, Mike. I'll find you. I'll find you and I'll put a bullet right through your fucking heart. You hear me?"

Dreadlocked Mike who once lived at the hostel chuckled again and glanced down at the Bonderline property and then back to show he had grown serious.

"Yeah, man, I hear you."

Grayson was still staring at him, reflected twice in the sunglasses.

"Godspeed, man, Godspeed."

* * *

At a jog he went down the hill and out across the scrabble and small boulders into the reeds and green grass of the wetlands. With sweat in his eyes, he couldn't see through the overgrown foliage around him. Frantic starlings harried a crow as it cawed once and rose jet black on celestial blue out of the treetops. Two or three steps more and Grayson paused to listen and then move on. This was his method. A couple steps and listen. Twenty minutes of this and he came out of the grass on the south side where the marsh dried up, where Bonderline's property ended and the pasture reaching up to the road began.

Splashing out of the pools he stumbled a bit but caught himself and went jogging along the fence up to the back line of the property to where the line of canal trees ended. At that corner he turned back north and ran a few yards over the rutted meadow perpendicular to the canal with his head snapping around to each far side of the property and in among the little orchard trees.

The yellow pioneer's oak in the far corner was his mark. Beside it was a concrete retaining wall and dense bulwarks of sage, tamarisk and knee-high grass, succulents and lilies with white flowers the size of goblets living on the largesse of the river spillage. All of it straight ahead of him as he passed in line with the stone-built keeper's quarters to his left. Maybe Phil would wait for him there.

As he got to the spur of tamarisk outstretched from the canal about midway, he felt the rifle shot tug at his pack and heard the projectile whistle past his left ear all in a piece. The roar echoed back down off the rim. Face down in the thicket another shot whined over his head. The impact of the bullet loosed a slab of the rim rock that fell and cracked in the rubble below. Then there was a moment of relative silence. Mosquitoes flew around his ears. He felt the heat and breathed with more difficulty. His already searching hand came back dry, no blood there but just a hole in the top of the pack. Lucky once, likely not twice. He was rolling over and feeling farther up the arm when another shot tore up the earth at his side and ripped at the tall grass. He pitched forward and pulled himself toward the canal and when he came into the open ground before the dip of the bank a torment of gunfire was unleashed from somewhere near the mansion and went chipping through the stand of cottonwoods he had just passed by.

It was a 5.56, he figured. Maybe thirty caliber, but absolutely semi-auto. They had magnified optics to see him in the shade and the high ground. Bad odds. The shots cut through the top of the bank. In the canal, clods of mud and bits of exploded tree roots rained on him and the rounds kept pounding away at the same spots as if to cleave it from the earth. He pushed back against the mud bank to right himself and began crawling on hands and knees in the ditch water and paddling in the deep areas. At a curve in the canal he stopped and lay in the water on his back with his hand in the moist roots to brace up. The shots died down. Brown water lapped in his ear turned under the surface. They were moving. Or they're watching and calling on a radio.

He pushed down and around the bend to a spot where the trees were thick and a density of brush crowded in among the trunks. It was cool and dark there in the canal. He stood to look over the lip of the dirt bank and around the trees. A stout bearded man in desert BDUs and matte black, insectoid sunglasses was advancing down from the house with a black rifle crooked up. Grayson got up and ran angling for the western edge of the keeper's quarters.

Just as Grayson came to the rear corner of the cottage the cornerstone nearest to his chest exploded where the other shooter had led the shot too much. Tiny shards of rock and lead nicked his face and neck. Behind the cover of the stone wall, two more rounds chipped at the line six inches below each other. Blood streamed down one side of his face as he got back up. Through the back window he caught a shadow of movement. He leveled the Remington to his shoulder just as the advance man rounded the corner and Grayson fired and kept walking around the corner, working the pump action of the gun. The man tried to get up. Grayson slipped and going down he caught the muzzle of the 870 under the man's armpit and fired. The meaty top portion of that shoulder and bicep disappeared. The man went rigid and rolled and Grayson worked the forearm again and put one more round of the number four buck into the man's head and neck and the holes in the tan camouflage jacket turned bright red in the sun.

Grayson was heaving, gauging his heartbeat by the blood in his ears. The floodwaters of survival rose in his body. At the edges of his vision a black halo started to cloud out the light. *Shake it off.* It was cool on the stone wall in the shade where he leaned for a moment breathing and counting and exhaling until the cloud passed and the adrenaline stabilized in his blood. He had the dead man's rifle pulled around to him. There was a high quality 1-6 power scope mounted to the top rail of the rifle. Jacked up to six-power he sighted up the rim and the trail for Mike. He moved it back down to three. At a glance he had known everything about it he needed to know: standard direct impingement running mid-length on a sixteen-inch custom stainless recon barrel in a one-piece upper receiver. Damn fine weapon. *Thank you.* There was some dust on it but otherwise it looked new. Something moved in the rocks up there and he went back up to six-power.

Mike.

He dropped the magazine into his hand to check the weight and the rounds in the metal box. Heavy enough. Hollow point boat tail, seventy-seven grain. Could be sixty-nine. Shiny brass, either way. He figured most likely a hundred yard zero. The reticle was an unfamiliar mish-mash. Hash marks everywhere, not a mil dot. *It's maybe three fifty to that knob. Take back what, twenty-five for the angle. Nominal drop. Put it on his head and see where it lands.*

He flipped the safety down and planted his feet and pumped his diaphragm to issue the air from his nose like a deer blowing. The rifle bucked lightly. Good smell of the gas in his face. He watched the round blossom dust on the rock maybe two inches from his point of aim. *That'll work.* There was no movement up there. Mike was somewhere on the trail, likely hugging the earth and waiting.

Two more rounds came in from the area of the mansion and went through the window to Grayson's left. Chunks of glazing and glass and splinters of the frame blasted out into the grass. He gave it another thirty seconds with the reticle floating just over the area where dreadlocked Mike would have to stand to get out of the crag. Another round landed on the stone wall at his back. *Treacherous son of a bitch aren't you?* he said to himself.

The dead man wore a nutria brown, old stock South African chest rig that held five more magazines. There was another half-full magazine in a Kydex pouch on his belt. He unwound the straps of the chest rig and pulled it away from under the weight of the man and took the magazine from the belt and stuck it into the empty pouch on the rig. There were neither patches nor insignias anywhere. The man's boots were well-worn but everything else was fairly new. Tobacco-stained teeth showed where the upper lip was pulled back. His glazed hazel eyes were cast straight up to see the next world. Time to go. A limb cracked somewhere behind and he turned to look upon the horses he had seen at Munson's place now stamping around in the wetlands. They were gunshy and heated up not knowing the right way out of the field. He noticed how the animals were painted like negatives of each other. One was brown with pretty white patches and the other white with the brown patches and both moving as a tethered unstable unity, swishing their tails wildly through the cottonwood duff floating on the breeze. A part of Grayson wanted to gather the horses and shelter them somewhere, however the impulse hadn't even coalesced before its impossibility sank in and he shut the door. He was moving again. There was a small clearing of rubble that he had to cross to get to cover again. When he crossed it, with the rifle and chest rig in one hand and the shotgun in the other, the second shooter put a round just behind him, perhaps compensating for leading too much before. Grayson stepped it up a notch and ran to the first big boulder. The temperature climbed.

Olive thorns dug in along his legs. He ran on another fifty yards to the lip of the portal where the primeval water had bored through the great menhir of the western rim, where now a man could pass through if he knew the spot. He climbed. The sun cut through the worn slot and like some outland postulant he wove the twisted course skyward with his arms teetering for balance and his feet finding rubbery purchase amid stone fragments and the hot rock under his hands pulled away here and there in crisps and the horses neighed to each other, snorted, and splashed in the marsh behind him. In a crevasse between the rim wall and some big stones he stopped and shoved the chest rig into a hollow. He set the shotgun down and wrestled the broken remains of the Molotov out of the side bag. Only now had he noticed the faint gas fumes. He released the magazine from the rifle and tossed it back with the rig and ejected the chambered round into the sand and popped the rear take-down pin so the upper receiver levered open. He took the bolt and the charging handle out and put them in his pocket and closed the receivers together and snapped the pin back. He closed the dust covers on the scope and the ejection port and set the weapon in the hollow with the rig and started off west into the wide open labyrinthine snarl of slick rock hoping to wend his way north, intersect Potash Road, and follow it back to the ranger station.

* * *

Way out in the desert, the smoke was diffuse. An acrid chemical and sweet juniper perfume blew through his rest spot. With the binoculars to his face, he puzzled over the bewilderment of the Ranger station smoldering in the distance. Crows crossed the azure sky, one behind the other, toward the pines beyond the arroyos and the spina bifida of mesa shapes on the flatland. Among a stand of scrub oak dusted in talc and sparse yellow grass he sat cross-legged with his back to a lone boulder. The glasses dropped into his lap revealing a triangle of pinched brow flesh articulated over his dirt-stained nose. Through the mirage, he could only make out the blackened shape of the station and a large dark mound a few yards out in the lot. After a moment, he brought the glasses back up and surveyed the road locating the spot he'd thought he had buried the 80mm box the second time. There were tracks from a truck where it had backed up over the sage. Another course of tire tracks lay at an angle, showing where the same vehicle departed. The handle-bars of Grayson's stolen and discarded motor bike poked out of the dead grass.

His mind was working hard to reconcile his expectations with what he saw through the glasses. Hard to work it as things were. *You're going to need to access that water at some point*, he thought. He wanted to get up. He forced himself to stay put. The sun was almost right overhead, irradiating the terrain. He pushed over farther into the shade of the rock and ate the rest of the cashews, drank the last dribbles of his water, and viewed the wide arc of land set before him once more. A half hour, forty-five minutes, and finally an hour passed, and he got up and went to look at the hole in the ground where the box had been. The tracks of three, maybe four men lay plainly in the sandy ground.

A story was there in the dust, one replete with betrayal and de-sire. If you could read those things, and Grayson could. Fingers on his left hand twirled as if sketching or taking notes on an invisible tablet. There were crescent slits in the crusted desert surface where they had stood their shovels straight and leaned on them. Two pinched and tarred cigarette butts lay in the base of the hole where they had flipped them as they finished. Perhaps there were others in the loose dirt. He checked and found one more. A rectangular outline of the 80mm box was impressed where it settled deeper on one side, and on the other, the sand had slid away where they had opened it, rocked and closed it, and finally taken it back to the truck.

All this was clear in his mind somehow. He squatted down in the grey-blue sage with the butt of his shotgun in the ground for a rest and looked again to see if he had missed anything. "Man," he muttered.

He rose and went through the chaparral and transplanted pines around to the far side of the ranger station parking area where a layer of soot radiated out from the burnt hulk of the station in a black band on the ground. The extant smoke off the mound was not tremendous but everywhere there seemed to hang a thin caustic fog of burnt polyester and flesh. He cleared his throat and spat. Now he wasn't so keen on looking further. From this angle it was hard to tell whether the mound was all bodies or not. Maybe there were only a few. He hoped that was all. The plasticized remains of a few cheap packing blankets were seemingly lacquered onto that side. While on the other, the blankets and nylon scraps were intact and tucked in among random slabs and crisps of hairy human meat. The white curvature of a skull shone through flaps of a paisley sundress. The bone was dry already in the sun. Two chrome spokes of an office chair were stabbed up through the hardened shell of the mound and there was a pool of baby blue plastic in the gravel where the chair backs had melted away. Early fear quaked through him as he envisioned what he knew he must do. The apprehension stemmed not from the work but rather from what the work might reveal.

Grayson unslung the pack slow and set it against one of the little pines and positioned the Remington beside it and opened one of the side-bags to bring out a pair of worn leather climbing gloves. Rolling his sleeves up as he went forward, staying in the shade as he could, he angled his head away from the smell. Around the other side he could see that maybe half the mound was just junk from the station--invoices, printers, defunct keyboards and such. There was a backpack he could make out. His hand went out in the mirage to feel the temperature. Still plenty warm. He coughed as he put on the gloves.

Back near the bodies on that side he pulled on an edge of the shell and it broke off bringing blue threads of an old tarp along with what appeared to be a man's foot encased in his melted yellow running shoe. He stopped and took out a bandana and tied it around his nose and mouth and went on breaking off pieces of the shell until there was a three- foot section that he could see through to the inside. It was just a black mass, shapes of limbs in the shadows and steam.

When he had the outer shell off, or mostly off, it became apparent that the whole disaster of flesh was further melded together with hardened clothing and odd pieces of luggage and pools of purplish plastic that had yesterday been toys perhaps. More chairs maybe. He wished it all to be chairs. He pulled on an area that looked like a hip or a shoulder expecting the thing to pull away from the pile but it didn't budge. "Fuck," he said.

Turning away from the heat and gases he brought the bandana down to get some air. And retch a few times. The sun hammered down. Water ran from his eyes. Snot from his nose. Pacing and shielding his face from the heat pulse with a gloved hand he sought a place to get a grip as he bobbed up over the top peering into the miasma and then down around the base of the thing in the manner of a bobcat or lynx seeking mice absconded in a woodpile. Where to begin? Turning away he spat and pulled the bandana back up against the hot graveolence. One of the crows watched him from up amid the pines and gurgled.

Grayson stepped away to try and breathe again. He watched his backtrail. Nothing down there on the road. Just the grey vein of the gravel snaking into the red rock hills. A line he'd read somewhere came to him: *The evident way is not the way.* Returned to the mound and muttering the cryptic line like a mantra, he stared at a few baked and ghoulish masks that stared back at him alternately in anguish and surprise with eyes like marshmallows blistered in a campfire and others just viscous slop running from empty loose-lidded sockets. Get cracking. His shoulders shrugged taking a large breath and he drew the big bush blade from his side and stepped into the mirage and proceeded hacking at a space where two bodies were joined in a sticky black embrace, like beetles in molasses.

It took ten solid minutes of chopping and prying with the blade to make any space to work. To get a whole body free. Sweat was pouring off his head and around his ears and when he bent over to gag it streamed together in a single rivulet trickling into the gravel. He turned back and took another swing and something popped and a thick jet of yellow and black gruel sopped his shirt.

"The Christ," he muttered.

By the end of the second round he was soaked from boots to his chest in an olive-colored cocktail of foul fluids and stray bits of entrails and meat draped from him as if he'd been sent down the sluice tube at a slaughterhouse. Slime dripped from the blade and the angry sun pulsed forward the day's portion. In a provisional triage he had the bodies separated into general categories. Enough to tell how big they were and to some extent how old. Index of leg and arm. Another of torso and skull. There was gray hair on one and blonde on another. None of these categories suggested Phil or Sarah. He gazed into the order made of the carnage and whipped the running red slick from his hands. He walked away to the pines and the shade and stuck the blade in a tree and sat down to rest. He glanced about the empty terrain in raw disgust as if some mineral segment of the desert might by magic agitate from the immobile dust a golem deigning to question his methods or the ferocity of his vows.

When he'd caught his breath, he left his weapons where they lay and wandered into the chaparral and stood looking into the horizon with his hands on his hips. The crows called and dipped from tree to tree. He stood there until the sun looked like it would finally go down. With exhaustion came the whisper of defeat and following close behind that malevolent voice came a very familiar intimation of the unbearable gravity in the memory of his son. His mind flashed on the tiny, perfect pink fingers. The new white hospital blanket. Grayson shook his head, wiped his eyes, and blew out through his mouth like a horse. True defeat and true loss, like terror, feel like being emptied of an electrical charge. Early that night in his camp he fell asleep instantly as the first stars were already infringed on the opposite dark wall and Venus and the moon and Cassiopeia oversaw his rest among the horned lizards and speckled birds in their crannies. The desert hares and the night-walking miner's cats for their part forayed in their patches of desert but avoided the area of the ranger station. Or perhaps the coals of the little fire at his camp granted him exception somehow--neither resident nor trespasser but a middling thing admitted under rude or ancient codes.

In the morning he was hungry and looked around in his bag for something that didn't require him to boil water. He ate a fruit rollup. He went about packing his gear away. His clothes hung stiff with dried blood and matter. At the station he stood in the shade and drank a full bottle of water and refilled the bottle and stowed it away. With his wiry athlete's frame, sharp features, and the insouciant lithesome habits of movement that come from decades of testing oneself against the world and against other strong men, he was, despite discomfort or suffering, physically at home in material space. He moved through it with great purpose yet carried neither the weight of self-doubt nor its inverse pride. While this grace was perhaps due in part to being tested and found bona fide, it was more owed to having kept his own counsel. By nature, he sought to know the truth. Charges of arrogance, not entirely without merit, had been leveled at him since childhood but his genuine indifference to the label only reinforced upon him the air and outward expression of impenetrability.

"Alright, Phil. Enough fucking around," he said out loud.

The great sweep of the alien desert capped in blue sky absorbed him for a moment.

The chevron impressions from the thieves' truck tires went straight down the road and the road went north and northeast toward a rise of rock across the hardpan. He had no map of this area, but he thought he knew in a general sense where the road wound out. To get the feel of the tracks, or perhaps to recur somehow to the time of their leaving, he squatted with the sun on one side so the shadows fell right and brought his eyes level with the immediate terrain. He needed to envisage the way an animal or man might move upon its surface. He spent ten minutes there mentally harvesting the past and sifting it through the hazards of conjecture and carrying on an inner dialogue, a tracker's dialectic between logic and intuition. The vast quiet immanence of the crimson and beige sediment, the stark defiance of the leafless trees like wispy sketches or runes of life upon the blurred horizon, transported some deep liquid element of his anima back to the red soil of the South African veldt where he'd become a tracker. Where the primordial hunter had become again in him.

When he had the design in mind he went to work down the trail to test the theory against whatever traces of man or beast the hourless past had granted him. As he tracked forward he kept to the middle or the edge of the path out of habit to avoid disturbing the shadings and dents and minute alterations he followed. His eyes flashed into the bushes and shrubs at intervals, alert to any small thing that might have fallen from the thieves' truck or been thrown. As if by dint of the mutual and occult contract between hunters and their hunting ground, between the first big outcropping and the station, Grayson found the roach of a joint, and four faded brown socks. These socks were his own from just a few days before into which he had deposited Phil's inheritance of gold and silver. Inside the roach, the tarred remnant of marihuana was high quality Indica that he ground up between his fingers and ceded back to the tracks. The flower aroma passed in the slow breeze. He inferred that the thieves had opened the box and kept the explosive components but dumped the gold and silver pieces out from the socks to see it all together and feel its weight and texture. That was a guess, and it was a good one. Maybe they had divvied it up amongst themselves in the truck, as thieves new to working together will not trust enough to wait. Or maybe they just counted it out and skimmed what they thought wouldn't be missed by someone else. *You should probably consider who this someone else might be, what were the possibilities exactly in terms of some network. As opposed to some bit of opportunism.*

Go back on the tracks to make sure they didn't go off in the trees. See that they didn't drop one or two of them off to ambush you. The footprints of common soldiers boots wound out. *You can see the tracks coming back and the big lugs of the soles grinding up the precious, pink biotic crust. Broken green limbs on the sage going grey. They were a bit sloppy in their tactics. Or drunk and high perhaps.*

He looked upon a little dark area out there where someone had pissed and the crust reformed and they'd walked back to the road. No ambush today. They didn't even post any particular security. *Dilettantes.* Or they just weren't concerned about threats at all.

He ambled along the spur road watching the tire tracks now. With his head down, his fingers twirling at the edge of the walnut shotgun stocks—utterly alone in that place--he looked like the sun-sick devotee of a nomadic earth cult. Stopping here at a featureless patch of the road, he bent to analyze a minute trace of disturbance in the inscrutable shifting dust. A pebble dislodged from its earthen socket. A tuft of anonymous fur, coyote or cat. He wheeled to the rear and pointed with sun browned fingers, envisioning a trajectory and a motive.

This is the essence of tracking man or beast: to sift multitu-dinous possibilities and project an imagined actor into the past, upon some particular terrain, and extrapolate from whatever mi-nor residue that actor has left upon the earth his intentions, his condition. The tracking hunter reconstructs the past from dust, logic and interior vision. It is an uncertain enterprise. To track is to be a time traveler. It is also to be a type of prophet, insofar as the tracker's crowning achievement is to arrive at his quarry's destina-tion first because the tracker has so absorbed the quarry's thoughts that he predicts and determines the final meeting. The tracker is ultimately a redactor of meat and bone. He imbibes uncertainty. He is time's heretic. He is the madman forging divine warrants.

At the rock outcropping the road did what Grayson had hoped it would not--split in two directions. He walked around so he could have the sun between himself and the tracks again and read: another vehicle, sedan or a wagon, waited and they all met driver side to driver side. He saw the place where the subtle wiry track of the lighter weight car continued but also rolled over itself when the car took the road back to town, turning severe in a way that is only possible when the driver stops and starts again with the wheel wound round his hands. The heavy truck then proceeded out into the desert and did not return this way.

They've got you got backed up against a decision again.

No footprints at all. No one had got out. An empty soda can likely tossed to the roadside by the passenger of the waiting car now rested in the boughs of a sage clump and tilted in the breeze. No one traded the box off. It stayed with the truck. No shell cas-ings either.

Then they're certainly working in concert, Grayson thought.

In the shade of the outcropping Grayson sat to think, sometimes out loud and other times silently, just following a line of speculation. The crow cackled in its tree. There was dried blood in the beehive rollmark on the shotgun that he picked and wiped off absently. As the wind came through, it rattled the sage branches softly so it sounded like rice running in a silo. Carrion birds spiraled way up on the thermals. He thought about eating something but the water bottle was half full now and the beans took at least that much to rehydrate so he had another fruit rollup and sat munching and took a sip of water just to wash it down. Halfway into rolling a cigarette he looked up again and finally noticed the cairn of rocks.

Look, right there in the crotch of those roads.

He had not seen it from the road, half-hidden in tall brown grass. Maybe he'd noticed it but had not thought it out. He tried to remember but his head was hurting. *Water will be another consideration here real soon if you keep going off this way.* Looking down at the cairn it was difficult to tell how old the cairn was--not years, maybe not even months. The wind blows the dust daily but the rain washes it away only so often. The sand of an old flood was crusted up around the base rocks and any vanished human prints were replaced here by divots of a coyote's pads and there by the scrawled signatures of marching ants that were stitched upon the overlapped emblems of crow's feet.

It could mean anything. Hippies did shit like this all the time.

His mind moved to assaying the area for water. He knew roughly where the river wound through the terrace-lands. But how close to the road? Grayson started talking to himself.

Say you find this vehicle, so what? You get the coins and the demo-
-you still gotta get back to town to get Phil. Maybe you find Phil in
their trunk. You got your ass hanging out here, and his.

The whole desert, apportioned half to the empty blue sky and half to the empty red basin, seemed itself to confront him now with his situation. Mute perhaps, but not indifferent, the subtle geologic message transmitted from the landscape to the particular consistency of his desires, physicality and beliefs—to his raw receiving soul, was more panentheistic conspiracy than some dead material challenge. The static moment evoked in him his own responsibility and involvement. The separation of context and character was an illusion. He was a man with no vehicle and little water scraping around in the middle of a hinterland, puzzling together bits of inference and trash. He had a vision of himself going to the river: saw himself stepping between the bank reeds and into the cold deliverance of the Colorado and felt the pure extinction of this moment as his head and shoulders went slow under the surface. The rush of the water in his ears washed away all fear and despair, all the gore and toil. These tracks will be here another day, he decided.

Phil is waiting somewhere and that's where you need to be.

He picked up his feet and marched.

And as he marched and fell into the purity of the motion his mind stilled and expanded into a familiar sequence of thoughts: that man was constituted as a hunter, and that in the very observation-postulation-testing operation that a tracking hunter makes when he comes upon tracks in the mud, here in analogue were set like gems in the firmament of existence itself the essential epistemological components of man's logical, narrative, and scientific processes. Tracking is thus not only the supernal rudiment to all man's survival and the fundamental superstructure of his experience of being but also the fountainhead of his highest achievements. If in the mud from which it is said both predator and prey have arisen, were inlaid the preconditions and encoding for the very structures of thought, then did it also follow that there in that maker's clay were also inlaid the primeval constituents for love? And he thought it was so. For the essence of love is sacrifice. And perhaps if it is only through the hunting of a thing that we overtake it and gain possession such that we might later give it away, then woven into the living matrix of stone and shrub, and the flux of blood and time, the whole contingent order of being--there must be the threads of a strictly necessary integrant of pursuit: a relationship of hunted and hunter.

On the material plane, the steppes and tundra, man seems the sole creature dealing in multiple moments. He is death's own rhetorician arguing backward and forward over moments, segmenting time to make his provisional case. And it seemed to Grayson self-evident that if the material was contingent upon the spiritual and the etheric and that if the energies and essence of God were ontologically prior to everything he might know—to the red sand disappearing underfoot and the bones in the foot, and to terror, and to whatever sacrifices he might make to quell that terror, then it must be that in time and outside time, God hunts man just as surely as man hunts God. Chasing, eluding. And this is the way of things until one finds the other again on this or some other glittering globe.

Eight hours and some twelve-odd miles later, he was back on the south edge of the rim staring down at the town in the twilight from the same spot where he met up with Mike who'd then walked him into an ambush. Long-gone Mike. Two hours later in the valley he stopped at the first house he came to where there was no visible damage or sign of anyone still residing within. All the rest were ransacked, shot to pieces, or gave off in their windows the small glow of candlelight. By these standards, he figured he stood a reasonable chance of pilfering some real food without any hassle. He kicked open the back door and went inside. It was cool, and also civilized with the good scents of lemon cleaning solution and laundry soap hanging in the air. The deep and uninvited wave of longing for a woman, the desire for a totalizing spirit complementary to his own, hit him so hard he nearly staggered.

He showered and slept and woke up naked in the strange dim house clutching the holstered pistol under the pillow and breathing deep with his eyes closed to reorient himself to his waking circumstances. A can of tuna sat half- eaten on the counter and he finished it with a fork he found and rose and went to the kitchen to make coffee. On the counter he unrolled the blue pillowcase with his peculiar cobbled tabernacle. There was the lacrosse ball and notebook, the sharpening iron in its sheath, the leather gris gris bag containing the secret amulets heretical and orthodox. He added the big blade and small pocketknife and the Glock that he disassembled to complete the solitary place setting.

It was dark outside. He checked the back and the front doors and found them the same way he had left them. He made four eggs, bacon, and toast and sat eating it all on the couch and went back and made two more eggs and another slice of bread. He washed, sharpened, and oiled the knives and wiped down the Glock slide and barrel and reposited each to its station on the portable altar. On the sideboard was a photograph of an older couple somewhere at the beach. The man was portly and wore a tourist's sombrero. The woman, in sunglasses and with slumped shoulders and her blonde hair pinned back in her flushed ears, looked tired. He sat looking into it awhile and then took and held the frame in his hand.

"Thank you," he said.

* * *

The whorehouse was a local monopoly. It originated as one of the small older ranch homes on the southeast part of town. At some point a singlewide had been joined to one side with metal flashing, pier blocks, and foil tape. From the economically strategic point of view, perhaps the one redeeming feature of the whorehouse itself was its location at a crossroads and in between lampposts. Parked in the yard of the whorehouse was a 1987 Chrysler Caravan with faux wood panels. Two or three other vehicles were parked down the road under oaks and alders that stood at the curb. Two lights were on in the singlewide and another in the main house glowed behind waterstained curtains.

It had been dark little more than an hour when he saw Munson pedaling up the road on his bike under the shadows of the trees, the bike tires hissing on the pavement. There was an outline of the bottle in his hand clutched to the handlebars. Grayson watched him skip off the bike short of the driveway and walk the bike and the bottle up to the gate and reach between the boards and pull the latch and go inside the yard. The madam, just a silhouette holding a cigarette in the orange backlight, came to the front door when he knocked.

They stood there speaking for a moment between the screen door. Munson slapped his hip pocket to jingle the chain on his wallet. He paid, and Grayson could see that she motioned for the albino to go on over to the trailer. The crickets were calling but stopped as Munson went around stepping on trash or in the gravel. The bottle tinked off his wallet chain. Grayson waited. A door slammed. Five minutes he sat and watched nothing happen. Scenes flashed on a television behind the curtains where the lady sat transfixed. Stray dogs emerged in the light at the far end of the street sniffing in the yard and collecting on one another in various configurations. One yipped and snarled and the group of six or eight dispersed like molecules in a whorl and gravitated back together on the run to recapitulate in the reckless dark.

The backpack and his water bottle were next to Grayson. The shotgun was between his legs with the muzzle in the grass, when he got up in a squat and eased the forearm back. He stayed the feed ramp just enough so that he could confirm there was a shell chambered. There were six more rounds in his front shirt pocket.

The door was quiet on its hinges as he eased it open. He had expected otherwise. There was a long hallway with four hollow doors on each side that were hung in a crude framework of bare two by fours. A single bulb hung centered in a frosted globe. The walls were cabinet-grade plywood painted white. A strip of sky-blue industrial carpet cut raggedly from a scrap lay down the narrow walkway and at the end of the hall was hung a gray steel door with a deadbolt and at the base was a wooden chair and under it a small pile of women's clothing.

One step up into the trailer and as he went he brought the butt of the shotgun over his shoulder, so his hand lay along his chin with the trigger finger indexed straight along the side of the receiver. In this way the overall length of the gun was brought down by about a foot. The crickets were hitting a rhythm in the darkness behind him. From within the first door on his left came the clank of a belt buckle and something soft being pulled across the floor, like clothing or a blanket. Grayson took a step so he was square to the jamb. Then, the hallway erupted.

Four holes punched through the door and the rounds carried through the opposite door and through the exterior wall. Grayson had hopped off the ledge and turned back as two more shots deafened and cut through the trailer. Glass broke somewhere in the street. He stepped back quickly. There was a cantaloupe sized area of the door that had splintered away. The light went on inside the room. Munson's white ass cheeks flashed through the space and Grayson shoved the barrel of the shotgun through the splinters and leaned to one side to see over the barrel and through the hole and the gun bucked. Munson screamed and slammed into the nightstand.

Other bodies moved behind the other doors.

He'd shot him in the pelvis, both so he wouldn't go anywhere and so also that he would still be able to talk for a while. The girl was thin, with long brown hair and wide exotic eyes. She was hyperventilating between little shrieks that barely came through the warbling ring in Grayson's ears. The albino had his jeans against his body like a towel trying to stop the bleeding. His expression was blank, horrified. His right hip oozed heavily from a ragged red and white mash. The girl sat in a corner chair, frozen with her mouth open and splattered with blood. The bottle remained upright in the nook beside the nightstand and there were two pieces of silver set on a full pack of Viceroy cigarettes.

Grayson looked at Munson. He still had the speed loader in his bloody white fingers but the .44 was across the room on the floor with the cylinder open and the spent cases still in the wheel. Grayson looked at the girl. The girl looked at the silver and the cigarettes. "Go on," he said. "You earned it."

She did not move, breath wheezing between her fingers.

He pulled Munson up into the corner and Munson howled again.

"There's a hospital," he said but Munson was still wailing, and then moaning.

He brought the shotgun up and set the hot muzzle on the notch between Munson's collar bones where it would sting. Munson shook his head to make it stop. Grayson pulled him in harder before speaking.

"Listen. Here. Look at me."

Munson nodded and smacked his lips dryly.

Grayson controlled his breath through his nose now. He said, "Okay listen. Here's where you decide. There's a hospital they got set up in the high school. Clinic or some shit. I can put you in that minivan out there, right now, and drop you off and you'll probably live. Sound good?"

Munson brought his eyes around straight to Grayson. The sound of the throaty, robust breathing Grayson continued exercising seemed to unnerve Munson further. His pale eyes shimmered and darted and came to land on Grayson. "You tell me what's going on here and you live to fuck again."

Munson was blinking fast and mashing his lips together.

"I'm listening. There's a hospital."

"That's right and you can go there and I'm sure they will get you all stitched up and we call it even. Or, you can keep thinking about all that blood that's running out on the floor and how she and I are the last people you'll ever see. And meanwhile you're not telling me where the fuck is Phil, where the fuck is my box, and what precisely Mike told you was going to be your take in this sellout."

Munson was listening. With everything he had. His corn-flour white hair had fallen from the pompadour and the greased strands of it quivered in time to the heart hammering through his thin colorless chest. There was a weird moment of silence. Just Grayson running breath like a mule. Munson went half limp as if he might pass out but he caught himself and the girl yelled, "Jesus, Munson. Tell him what he wants to know."

Munson said, "Mike told me he knew some dudes that could get me out man. They got the box. Those dudes in the bar that night, you saw 'em."

"The Virginia boys."

"The Virginia boys yeah, I think so."

"Where's Phil?"

Munson looked away. "Dude, I don't know. Just get me to the damn clinic, man."

Grayson pressed the shotgun into the man's trachea until the cartilage popped and breath squeezed out. He said. "Where's Phil and his family?"

Munson said, "Mike said they got him man, but I don't know. That's just what Mike said, man. He might have gotten away. They might've shot him. Who knows. I mean I didn't see any of this shit myself, you know."

"Why would Mike say that then? Who got him?"

"I don't know. Let's go to the hospital, dude."

One of Munson's stockinged feet slipped in the growing red pool on the chipboard floor. Grayson yanked him back up and leaned him harder into the wall. "What did he say to you?"

"Said they's rounding up people out of the neighborhoods. Said they'd got Phil. Man, he just said he knew you guys had something cooking and he could use it is all."

"And you sold him the rest. Sold him the box. Sold him the owner."

Munson was quiet. Then he said, "Come on Grayson. I swear to Christ on my mother's hallowed grave. That's it, that's all I got. I just wanted out. That clinic, man."

He hoisted Munson up and looked over at the girl and said, "Go get the keys to that shitbox vehicle outside."

* * *

The madam stood silhouetted behind the screen door like some diminished antebellum warden watching them pull away in the light of trash fires licking up in barrels on the street. The vagrant and refugee keepers of the fires cheered and called out in the night for revolution. For core division. For murder. Some chickens in a coop off to the side of the front yard murmured in seeming disgust or disappointment of it all.

Munson was dead before they reached the end of the block. Grayson turned the Caravan and went the back way toward the cemetery hill. He kept the lights off and rolled through the stop signs with the muffler chugging out into the quiet street. No other vehicles were on the road. The van reeked of hand lotion and cinnamon. He dropped the window down. A tangle of contradictory thoughts passed through his mind, all orbiting the necessity of answering gunfire in kind. He let out a long sigh. Would he have let Munson live had he not fired first—he wasn't entirely sure one way or the other and saw no sliver of time in which to luxuriate in further consideration. Treachery is no light offense.

At the end of the block he caught in the rear view someone crossing the road when they figured he couldn't see them. He put his foot lightly on the brake. The red glow went out around the back of the van and over the litter and loot-strewn street. It was a woman in a long skirt with pale skin. A child held her hand and stood close. No weapons he could see, no backpacks or loot bags.

He punched the gas and drove around the block to see if they'd pass through the lamp light behind the tiled house roofs. When they did pass through, he didn't recognize them. "Was Phil's child factored into your thinking Munson?" he said out loud. The woman and child, their outlines hemmed in light like figures in a dream, trailed into another yard and Grayson wove the van forward through the blocks until he got to Phil's house and parked across the street. A symbol like a doubled check-mark was spray-painted on the garage door. A picked-over mound of household items was gathered up in the yard—clothing and speakers, coffeemakers, and rolled cellophane. Same in the houses next door on either side.

"You say they got picked up," he said to Munson's body. "Picked up."

He pressed the button to bring the passenger side window down and it went about a third of the way and stuck. "Piece a shit," he said. A slushing wet sound of blood on vinyl issued from the rear. He turned to watch Munson's body slide off the seat into a jumble against the sliding door. He tossed the spiced scent tree out on the sidewalk.

"Then what Munson? They just round 'em up and talk to them. Bullshit. That lady's walking around with a kid but Phil got picked up? No. No god damn way. They hollow out the center and cordon it off. They beat down the early resistance to make their point. Then they systematically isolate the useful and deploy them against their own. Phil would be useful but grabbing him first makes no sense. You're suggesting, excuse me you *were* suggesting, as well that they accomplished this in the space of a few hours. Improbable. Impossible without deep advance work and a target folder."

Alone now, the boy turned up the road toward Grayson. He had a foldup military shovel over his shoulder and wore shorts and a t-shirt and red sneakers. His hair was floppy on his head and his face was clean. For his part, with his hands and his shirt and his face smeared with a dark mixture of dirt, soot and blood, Grayson observed. The shotgun was on the seat next to him, dead man in the rear. When the kid passed he looked at Grayson and said in a small confident voice, "Hi."

Grayson smiled. "How you doin, bud?"

"Fine thanks," he said. The kid kicked the scent tree and walked on.

Grayson watched him in the side view mirror go down the road. The familiar pang of incompleteness that was the reverberation of his broken vision for his own son who never grew to walk or speak shot through Grayson's soul. As ever, he let it pass with no more decoration or self-pity than what was inherent to the undisputed facts. He looked back in the direction of the woman who had been holding the boy's hand. *She must have sent him off alone.*

"Now this kid's strolling around fine, Munson. But you say not Phil. Fuck that." *Phil wouldn't have gotten nabbed so easy. Not like that. Meet at his house, get 'em out. Leave 'em. Back for a suitable vehicle. Get the box, back to pick her up. On our way. Simple, flexible fucking plan.*

Target folder.

He sighed. Munson's bottle of Old Grandad whiskey was on the passenger seat with his wallet and chain. Grayson took up the bottle, unscrewed the cap and sniffed and took a good slug. He took another.

"Backup plan was simple enough: wife, vehicle, and straight to the box. Contingency to the backup plan: just get to the plateau on the rim or to the ranger station, either of which was entirely doable. Wait a minimum two days. Maximum three," he said to no one.

One of the helicopters was coming up from somewhere but he couldn't place which side. He pushed back in the seat. The turbine noise grew near. A spotlight blasted down into the street ahead and skittered along washing everything out as it jumped over the houses and the cars, never stopping as if the mission was more communication than interdiction. He took another drink of the whiskey. When he turned the key, the passenger window rose ghostlike on its own. He snorted and backed the van up to turn around in the road. A block down, the cemetery gate was open. He pulled in alongside the wrought iron fence and turned the engine off and sighed again.

"Regarding your question about the end of history, Munson. No, it didn't end. That's the empty, wishful projection of technocrats. Little more. But now, your history? Ends right here. And that's the thing about history, or histories wholesale. It's all personal. Which tells you a lot about the characters who thought they could end it with a pronouncement, I think."

He took a final snort from the bottle and capped it and tossed it back with Munson. He got out with the gear and gun, leaving the van door ajar, and ran a block in the shadows of the willowy trees lining the street. Thinking sub rosa, on the level of the tracker, the killer, of time's prophetic madman: *target folder.*

Two more blocks down, he saw the boy with the shovel pass out of the intersection looking all around. A man and a woman were waiting there for him. The woman touched his shoulder. Grayson watched their reunion from the ash-powdered grass of one of the dark houses. An orange cat watched him in turn from the steps of the houses, whipping its tail and blinking in the refracted moonlight. Father, mother, and child all moved together through the lonesome intersection, gone into further shadows. Grayson, with blood on his hands and whiskey in his veins, followed.

* * *

The family slipped from the street into an alleyway where the trellis on either side was wreathed in wisteria and emanating low white light from between the delicate leaves. Grayson crossed the pavement and stooped at the corner and watched the triad of two parents and child engage two rotund guards with rifles, all of them standing in noirish angular light bands. At the end of the alleyway stood a small adobe house with a roughhewn portico bookended right and left in ornate gardens of cacti and succulents. Smoke tree and San Pedro. The guards' rifles were bone stock and brand new Colt 6920s in cheap black nylon slings. Heavy countenance, no agility. Grayson waited a moment for the family to move past the guards and then he stood into the footlights carrying the shotgun crooked out far from his right side like a candle bearer so as to calm the uninitiated doormen. Just the same, they visibly stiffened as he approached.

Moab's one-time purveyor of motor bikes, Jake Gibson, joined the two guards as they queried Grayson there outside the adobe house saying: smells like alcohol, and why hadn't they seen him before. In observing these territorial expressions, he adjusted his demeanor so as to allow the the amateur guards to relax and sketched his contingencies—multiple escape routes and excuses, lines of cover and cover stories all tailored to the contextual flux. It was not good enough simply to show up. To expect as much was to, by default, accept the physical disempowerment of living in a machine age—a pathos that these men before him had come to accept, and which had made their weakness visible a mile off. The verbal and the social are prelude to the inherently physical. A thousand calculations internal and external. "Have a drink," Grayson said, thinking it might further calm them down. "That guy's alright," Gibson said as he approached. Grayson stepped between the men out there on the sidewalk.

"Thanks."

"No sweat. You're Phil's buddy, right?"

"That's right."

Gibson gestured toward a separate garage on the side of the house where a door stood open and the asymmetrical flicker of many gathered candles shone through and fell in the garden. "Just head right inside. We'll get started in a minute."

Grayson nodded and went forward down the pavestones with the long ungula of yucca and swordplant passing over his boots and jeans. The boy still had the shovel over his shoulder and was standing inside the door in the fashion of a sentry. He did not say hello, but he smiled. Grayson passed him into dimness. The meeting was comprised mostly of women though he made out several couples with their children standing or sitting where they could. They murmured as he took a place against the near wall and set the shotgun with the muzzle down, letting his hand hang close to the stock.

A lady well on the far side of fifty in a purple cotton blouse and expensive jeans rolled up at the ankles touched him on the shoulder. Purple glasses frames and thin graying hair cut around a sharp angled face that had seen some sun but not too much of it at labor.

"Hi, I'm Nancy," She said

He stuck out his red right hand and said, "Grayson."

She shook it without looking and said, "I just wanted to tell you there are finger sandwiches right over here if you're hungry. You look hungry."

"Thank you very much."

"There's also berry iced tea in the cooler. It's just from a mix. But best we can do. We had pretzels but then everyone ate them and they're all gone. I'm sorry."

"That's fine. Thank you very much."

When Gibson and the guards came back they joined their wives and children and took seats on the floor. A younger man who looked like he might have just showered and shaved that afternoon cleared his throat and said,

"I guess we all know why we're here so I'm just gonna jump right in and you can interrupt me if you've got anything to add."

No one spoke up, and so the young man went on. Grayson took a stack of the triangle sandwiches. Delicious.

"First thing is, it turns out there is another group of us on the north side by the employment department building, that area, that's gotten together, and we're going to try and make contact tomorrow. Mr. Gibson is coordinating. There doesn't seem to be any particular time that these outsiders, mercenaries or whatever they are, come around, but the thought is to stick with nighttime for meetings with other town groups. If we find more, that is. So, just wanted to keep you up to date on that."

The young man speaking paused to arrange himself a place on a small green carpet where a pregnant woman sat in a half lotus posture. One of her hands went to his knee as he sat down, and he overlaid it with one of his own. Another woman about the same age, seated on a short stack of packing boxes to their left said, "Who are these people?"

"Yeah that's what I want to know," said yet a third woman in a slight valley drawl. She was athletic and youngish. Tank top, freckled all over. There were two children beside her. A man in white jeans with his mouth partly open stood to her rear. The woman went on in her drawl saying, "I mean are they like a government or something? Are they military contractors? I don't know. There's been nothing official about this whole thing. It's just really weird and unacceptable." The woman looked to Nancy.

Some people muttered approval, and Nancy added, "To say the least."

A man in the rear said, "Look at the hardware. They're serious."

Silence. Grayson wolfed down another stack of the sandwiches. The man conducting things from the little prayer carpet said louder, "At this point I don't think anyone knows any more than you do. They're not telling us anything yet. Some folks were speculating, maybe a strong militia. Maybe some kind of international crisis group, NGO. No one is sure. Maybe it's our military gone rogue."

Another man in the rear spoke up. He was bearded with a shaved head and glasses. He proclaimed, "I guarantee you they're government proxies. Shadow government proxies here to claim the river and divert it to California at the behest of oligarchs."

Grayson shifted his weight against the wall, turned to see the man in the rear. The man in the rear went on.

"One: no one else has that kind of equipment. Two: this is exactly what'd you'd expect if you'd been paying attention. Full scale, multi-stage, fully-controlled and highly-orchestrated balkanization. Starting with financial distress and resource bleed-off coupled on the timeline with dynamic and targeted psy-war on the cultural, racial, ethnic, gender and intergenerational levels along with a general agitation and eventually an increase, in terms of sheer numbers--mind you--of the underclasses to eventually be brought in from their separate client groups under one aegis or coalition of the dispossessed. They succeeded in squeezing the middle to death. And as for the US military, we haven't had one that served anything but international interests for nigh onto a century. What is now called the US military is a jobs program. The few good men that served of late were likely targeted and terminated quietly over the last decade in preparation for this little resource coup we're undergoing now."

Nancy waved her hand and flipped her hair. She sighed. She said, "Oh here we go with the conspiracy theories. Christ almighty, that's the last thing we need. Is there any way that we can just not go there right now, please?"

The man in the rear continued, "Of course, it will all be airbrushed with psy-ops and lies. A decade from now this will either be forgotten--jettisoned entirely via the proverbial memory hole--or twisted and trumped into some mighty nationalistic achievement."

"By whom? Begun by whom?" asked Nancy. She didn't expect an answer.

"Well, that'd be the multi-trillion dollar question wouldn't it."

"Aliens, right?"

"You're simplifying a complex and entrenched web of networked interests, sophisticated mafias, and working groups in order to gloss over your discomfort. I get it. Suffice it to say it's not likely there's even one man out there with a gun knows who he's pulling the trigger for with any certainty."

Nancy threw the man in the rear a little grimace as if maybe she'd say something more, but she didn't and turned quickly back and nodded at the man in the front to continue but she couldn't help it and added as an afterthought, "I mean there are children here."

The younger man went on, "In terms of our goal here tonight we've got four more people than last night. So at least we're making headway on that. I think that's fantastic."

Some murmured approval. The disjointed candlelight wavered.

The athletic woman nodded, placed her hands in prayer and said, "Welcome. Namaste." She smiled at Grayson, but he looked away and bent to the cooler. He took out the jug of iced tea and almost drank it straight from the source. The kid with the shovel handed Grayson a short stack of red and white plastic cups. "Thanks buddy," he said, and the kid stepped back with his parents who were yet to speak.

The man up front pulled a small backpack from around behind him and said, "If you'll give me just a second. I should have had this list pulled up already. Just gimme a minute."

The athletic woman tapped her husband on the knee to get his attention. His mouth was still open a little bit but snapped shut when he bent down for her to speak in his ear. He stood and looked across at Grayson, looked back at his wife and shook his head and shrugged. Grayson said, "Does anyone here know Philip or Sarah Hixson?"

A few of the people looked around and some shook their heads.

"They've got a child. A newborn. They lived just up the road here in the first house across from the cemetery. She's got short brown hair, hazel eyes, and he's blonde and blue about six feet. He's a landscaper. She used to work at the library, while back."

Silence. Jake Gibson said, "No one's seen him, man." Voices in the back echoed Gibson. Grayson stepped back and said, "Alright thanks."

Thoughts of getting his gear and leaving crossed his mind. Instead he waited.

Nancy brought both hands by her face and said, "What this is really all about, but no one wants to see it, is that they're powering us all down. Can't you see that? Why there has to be any violence involved though is beyond me. It's not like all the sudden violence is going to solve anything. But I guess no one told that to those militia maniacs. It's as if we went to sleep in Utah and woke up in Gaza or Yemen or some unholy thing."

The man in the rear was about to contradict her, but a tall blonde who was evidently his wife nudged him to be quiet. Nancy said, "What we need to be focused on right now is building up community one, and figuring out how we're going to be sustainable, two. I mean we could be on our own, folks. We need to share resources and empower ourselves. And fast. A phone tree as a starter."

There were four more triangles of tuna fish sandwich on the plastic camp plate. He'd been eyeing them. The kid watched him and nodded for him to eat them. Munson's blood was still streaked over Grayson's face and neck. The kid studied broken bits of pine needle stuck in the darkening blood on his hand, up his arm. He caught the mother's eye and held the sandwiches out giving her a last shot. Mediterranean, bird-like in her expression with cropped black hair and around her neck hung together a small sterling cross and a dull brass lotus flower pendant. Smiling broadly, she waved her hand and said, "No you go right ahead."

Jake Gibson said to the man who had just booted up his laptop, "Have you got the internet on that thing still?"

The man kept looking at the screen and said, "Unfortunately, no. But I cached as much stuff as I could, so I can justify hauling it around, I guess. As long as I can keep it powered."

Nancy said, "Wouldn't it be nice if we could just pull up the news and find out what the heck is really going on. I mean I'm sure it'll be back up at some point. At some point when the actual government gets here."

She looked over at the man in the rear, but the man's wife was telling him something. His face had grown red. The kid with the shovel heard it first: low hum in the cement beneath his feet. A hush went through the room and the guard at the door stepped in and closed the door behind him.

Someone said, "Get the light."

Someone else said, "No just get the door and be quiet."

Through the garage walls the precision cycling of the Humvee diesels was unmistakable. Everyone froze in the wavering dome of amber light like novitiates in a night vestry awaiting omens. They heard the queer whirring of the heavy tires rounding the street corner too tight. And then another just the same. Grayson counted what he figured was five vehicles in total. The line of them moved on down the roadway and the aggregated engine noise receded into other neighborhoods. His hand relaxed on the shotgun. The kid watched him let it back down, and then the kid looked at the blood on his face again and back to his mom.

"We just need to talk to them," said Nancy.

Jake Gibson said, "I think a few folks tried that already and it didn't work out. They're piled out there now for all to see. You could go ask 'em what they got out of it."

"Well fine," she said. "You go join the militia too then."

Jake Gibson chuckled. "I am the militia, lady. Maybe you didn't know there ain't just one. They ain't all the same."

"I've gathered as much."

"And this shit isn't as simple as picking a side. No one knows who is on what side. I'm here to help. To provide some semblance of order."

When everyone but the kid with the shovel and his parents and the man in front had cleared out of the garage, Grayson stood against the wall until the door closed and stepped forward with his gear and gestured to the man with the laptop still inputting his spread sheet. Grayson introduced himself and inquired about maps.

"Oh yeah. I got maps. I got satellite, local, maps of Utah, maps of Montana. Except California. There's no way I'd go there."

"These the kind you can zoom in on?"

"Oh sure.'

"How about one of the area near Potasche Road, you know that old ranger station?"

The man went back to clicking and soon found one and Grayson took the pages torn from the roommate Ben's library books out of his pack and overlaid the two, so the blue light of the screen shone through and he traced some lines with a felt pen. The parents and the boy slipped out behind them. After thanking the man and stowing the maps, Grayson downed another cup of tea and exited, shutting the door behind him with care for the latch noise.

Outside at the edge of the portico where the pale moonlight was cut short on the curling bark of the vigas, the young couple and the kid with the shovel were standing and waiting for him. She was holding the boy's hand. When it seemed like Grayson would come over to them she turned with the boy and spoke something to him and they walked down a bit into the alley with the wiry tendrils of the wisteria enjoining them to go slow. Then they stood together in the cut light of the ground lamps.

He went over the pavers nodding at the man to follow him out into the alley. The man had a new haircut and wore an old western shirt over mountaineering pants. On his jaw was a few days of beard but no more. In the folds of the shirt Grayson saw the outline of a pistol concealed at his waist. "Talk to me," said Grayson.

"My name is Alejandro. I'm the doctor who delivered your friend's child just a few weeks ago. Good-looking kid. Very tough delivery." he said.

"But you don't know where he is," Grayson said.

"No. Of course, I couldn't say for sure as there're people running around all over day and night and then it's quiet for hours and it's just a lot to keep straight. But I would have remembered had I actually seen them."

Grayson nodded. Alejandro continued, "Look, I'm not stupid. We need to get out of this town post-haste. I've lived through lesser versions of similar events in my own country. Okay, I know there are always ways. There are always men, perhaps such as yourself, who can guide others through the wire. So to speak. Are you such a man, can you get us out of here?" Alejandro motioned over to his wife and the kid. They each looked that way. Crimson and yellow wildflowers and penstemons lined the alleyway between the footlamps on either side and the mother and child were among them until her hand came away from the stalks with a June bug clattering its wings. The boy stanchioned the shovel tip into the pine tassels and bark wafers collated at the boundary of the pavement to lean into her long swinging hair as she rose and both whispered, and he laughed quietly. Grayson had not had a chance to reply. "My wife thinks we can make it out on foot. Like her mother she's one to stop the galloping horse and storm the burning building. Bless her. I'm somewhat more familiar with the limits of the human body and I've seen those slot canyons up close. Serious shit."

"Go south. Avoid the canyonlands."

"They came from the south. My theory is they're going to place checkpoints at either end of town and allow traffic at some controlled point. Commerce must be allowed to flow at some point, yes? But when, I don't know. I do know that my son's medical needs will force my hand if this goes on indefinitely. If you take my meaning." Grayson was staring over toward the mother and the child and he kept doing so for a long moment. He looked back at the doctor.

"I can't do it," he said.

"I've got about six thousand dollars in cash."

"It wouldn't matter if you had six million, man. My priorities and my promises are elsewhere. To Phil and Sarah and that kid. It's not that I wouldn't do it if things were set out different," he said, and it was the truth.

"He can't get through those canyons," the doctor said. "My son cannot."

"I'm sorry. I just can't do it for you," said Grayson.

Grayson looked away. In some ways he respected the doctor's directness more than the tentative circularity of the territorial approach made by the guards earlier. If a man will fight then he is at least something, if perhaps only a nuisance. If he can fight and gain skill then he can be dangerous. And if he is the rare man who can fight, think and has some joy in violence then he is extremely dangerous indeed. However, a man's gameness to fight can shift. One day he may fight viciously and the next lose stomach in a similar contest. His measure in these terms can never be known outside of the game—the decisive moment when he goes or stays. For it is only at the border that one finds out if they will cross it, and with what measures of control or abandon. A theoretical line means nothing until it means everything and, paradoxically, when it means everything it's sometimes too late to think one's way through it—those decisions must be made prior, in dreams or daydreams.

The doctor looked off too and after a moment said, "I understand. We'll figure out something." He put out his hand and Grayson shook it and the man added, "It's different when you have kids."

Grayson moved the pack on his shoulders and said, "How's it different?"

"It just is, man."

"No. No it's not any different at all."

One hour later he walked out of the house where he had showered and made his liturgy. With his backpack resupplied and his belly sloshing with water he cut through the side streets and green spaces turning here to elude a gang of refugees armed with aluminum baseball bats and tire irons and there to bypass a clique of the accomplished homeless who made their cook fires down in the ground as did the bygone Lakota to conceal their operations. Some of the newly transient he saw huddled alone in doorways and many more lay dead in ditches. Along the flat stretch of black asphalt highway, piles of their unnumbered bodies burned blue-green under the orange as if they were boding derrick fires on the surface of some antipodean and negated sea. Two more hours and he was on the plateau at the south edge of the rim looking at the place where Mike had made his camp among the fissures. He folded the sheets of his maps in hand, letting them whack against his knuckles in the wind coming down over the round red boulders.

3
The Human

When he got to the ranger station the third and final time, it was mid-morning and the sun was high in the east. He stood in the road and oriented himself to the map, the map to the terrain. Where the rock cairn lay he drew pencil lines of the split road in both directions. He rough-calculated the distance at forty winding miles. He wondered again if he might have been better off just stealing another vehicle, but then he imagined the Apache helos homing in on his dust trail out here in the bushland. He concluded that what time was lost was just lost, and that a limited signature was the wiser path.

He expected the journey would take two days, if all went well— three, if the furrowed lines on his sketch were slots necessitating a slower pace or if there were other problems on the road. He thought that if Phil had left the house, if he'd been pushed up the ridge by the first assault, and then spurred further by the child's needs or Sarah's insistence or the helicopters whirring or some suggestion from Mike or any number of other factors--if one of those possible outcomes had led Phil to eventually wind up at the ranger station rendezvous point waiting for Grayson at the exact wrong time such that he'd been abducted there, which seemed possible given the tracks, the missing gold, and the treachery of Munson and Hostel Mike--then for Grayson it was evident this and every other figurative stone had to be turned.

It was 87 degrees at 10:45 am. He slept until six and then set out and walked through the early evening. When it was full dark he stopped for ten minutes to sit on the gravel embankment below the dirt road. All night he went on, listening to his feet over the dirt and the pebbles. The owls hooed and once a coyote padded in the needles, and shortly after, came the small cries of something dying out along the cooling rocks.

At eight the next morning he walked off the road into the scrub toward a jumbled archipelago of rocks and sat down in the shade and started a small fire of manzanita to cook the dry beans. Little caches of cleaved pinecone were deposited among the folds in the rock where squirrels had stored them and with these he stoked the flames for the sap. He took his boots and socks off to let them air-dry and when he was done eating and the fire was snuffed out he put his boots back on and laid down on the poncho liner and moved a stone that he could use for a pillow. He watched a blue and yellow collared lizard chase ants among the rocks until he fell asleep.

In his dream, Grayson and his father are cresting a two-lane road in Sonora somewhere along the ocean. His father is driving, the suntanned skin on his knuckles crinkles and grows taut as his hands manipulate the wheel. As Grayson is staring past him to the sea on their left, he vaguely recalls that his father is not alive anymore. They park the car and step onto a pathway. It is lined with beach grass and trees with huge oval leaves growing up in twists. The path splits with the trees into high and low forks. Grayson watches as his father points him to the low path. Grayson does not go but the father nods again for him to walk and the father turns away and disappears over the bluff. So, he takes the path. It spills out and widens into a bank beside a blonde sandy slough. The water is clear and at the lapping hem, dragonflies rise up above cattails. The dragonflies hold momentarily to the furrow of the sand shelf and then whirl off together in tranches to the great blue plain of the sea. He tries to track the water, or portions of it, as it dumps in from off to his left where now it is importing the stalks and insects and the visual web of the whole cycle from some cloaked originating source. His father is at his side, smiling past him, and he follows his father's steel blue eyes. In his ear, his father says something but now he is looking at what his father is looking at: a piglet seated in the sand. Pink and docile, doglike on its haunches. The piglet has been waiting for Grayson. His father's hand falls gently on his shoulder and he says, *Go on toss it in. It'll live.* Grayson kneels and lifts the piglet in his arms. It does not struggle and he feels the soft skin and he hears the father's voice again in his ear as he and the pig stare through the water to the grey rocks at its base where the sun refracts in heliotrope shards then shimmers away and is gone. The father says: *Go ahead, he'll live. He has to run.*

Let him run.

Grayson woke and lay a long time watching the same blue collared lizard who between forays into the labyrinth of rock fissures seemed to be satisfied in watching him right back.

When the sun moved and it was too hot to sleep, he picked up his gear and relocated himself in the jumble for better shade and sat to eat a tin of sardines. He gazed out at the red spires and the banded paint dunes. A division of yellow jackets buzzed around the empty tin. He slept again until early evening. The first bats were out and streaming over his head in twirling black squads. The aggregate of their leathery wings shuffled up there while below them rabbits sat at the edges of their warrens, listening, ready to gamble again against the ghostly stealth of the speckled bobcat.

That night Grayson did nineteen miles. Just before dawn he came to rest in a grove of dwarfling scrub oaks clustered up on a bluff overlooking an ancient brown gorge. A rural compound could be discerned in the white blue glow of the unrisen sun. A semi-enclosed pole barn standing opposite two small brick and board ranch houses and a maroon sheet metal shop made up the west portion of the property. Old apple and pear trees heavy with fruit stood in the yard but nothing else grew in the way of culti-vated landscape. The spindly antennae of a ham radio were erected upon the asphalt tiles of the shop roof. In his surveillance he saw one hundred yards to the east were built six one-room cabins of split timber and batten board all fixed among a grove of cotton-woods. A child's bucket and shovel, faded blue, and a dolly girl in a tattered peach dress lay reposited in rainpocked dust behind one of the cabins. Outside the wood barn an old Kyocera dozer with tracks caked in dried red clay was parked on one side near two pallets of black plastic rain barrels still in the shrink wrap and at the other side was parked a long, white Econoline van. "Zion Bible Camp" was stenciled in fading turquoise upon the dustcaked rear window. The entire operation was fenced and gated.

He rolled a smoke and glassed the compound. The sun rose and the shadows bent. The outside lights at the barn and the two at the gate flickered out and he guessed the time as six-thirty or so. *It's go now or likely wait the whole day.* A light went on behind curtains in one of the little houses. He set the binoculars down on the pack beside the shotgun and drew the Glock to confirm that it was chambered. He skulked around the bluff and went over quick to avoid skylighting himself.

The old gorge widened and grew shallow where the grove of cottonwoods rose up. Grayson descaled the short wall there and dropped down catlike into the switchgrass. Apples in the trees drummed hollow against each other in the morning wind. Robin birds whistled. He crept westward along the wall. His shadow slid black over the washed stone until he came to the pole barn and looked in through one of two plastic-cased windows. From the window on the opposite wall, the light fell on a sagging plywood stall beset with old dead hay. A rusted-out tank desk stood in the dirt in one corner and a length of sisal twine and a screwdriver sat on the surface in a thick cake of dust. Beside the desk on the floor was deposited an egg-shaped pile of deer hair lined up with a pulley rigged into the rafters. A dank animal stench lay imprinted on the earth around him such that he knew a good bit of killing had been done here over the years.

At the back of the first house he peered in the window and found it entirely dark inside. A pop can that stood next to the slider was peppered at the rim in cigarette ash. A foul sweet smell of the mixture passed up to him in the rising dew coming off the mown weeds. A woman's cosmetic bag lay open inside on the kitchen table on a stack of magazines. He returned to the front and crossed the driveway back to the pole barn and slipped around the side to where the Econoline was parked. The passenger door was unlocked. In the glovebox were the usual registration documents and a nylon dog collar. A few dusty prints lay in the vinyl floor coverings. No 80mm surplus box. No gold, silver or explosives. And no Phil.

He came back and stood in the thin strip of dirt that separated the twin houses. Listening. Watching the sheet of sunlight slip down the gorge wall. He went toward the house with the lit window and opened the front screen door. The shiny brass knocker caught the sunlight coming over the gorge wall. Coffee was on inside and water ran in the pipes. He knocked and a moment later a figure passed behind the frosted glass and the door opened about halfway. A man's voice said, "Come on in. Be ready in a few minutes."

Thinking about this for a moment Grayson didn't move but just pushed the door open over wide oak flooring. The man who'd spoken turned down a short hallway without looking back. Just swinging his arms. Large man, thick black hair. Navajo. His voice came down the hall.

"Coffee's in the kitchen," he said.

Grayson stepped inside and cleared the corners of the front room and the kitchen. Water ran in a bathroom. The stainless pot sat steaming on the glasstop range. The house was immaculate. New carpet in the front room and oak cabinetry in the kitchen. A half- eaten plate of eggs and bacon and a slim manila folder lay on the antique craftsman kitchen table. He looked around the corner back down the hall where the bathroom light shone and the Navajo man's whistling could be heard.

This man lives alone, Grayson realized.

Grayson stepped back into the kitchen. Orange and purple dragonflies hovered beyond the glass over the sink. He heard the man's footsteps coming back down the hall and the sound of him brushing his teeth.

The man said, "I didn't hear you guys come through the gate."

Grayson readied himself, fixing the placement of the backdoor in his mind if he needed an exit. If this gets out of hand. Whoever he is expecting is likely to walk in momentarily. Grayson stepped around into the nook and squared up between the table and a breakfast counter as the Navajo turned the corner from the hallway with the brush in his mouth. The Navajo stopped in his tracks with one eyebrow raised. His ponytail was slicked back over a thick neck. His eyes cast down and discovered the sheathed knife stuffed into Grayson's waistband. His eyes rose to waver at Grayson's chest and did not rise further, as if the man thought the truth were in there somewhere behind a veil of fabric and flesh. Or as if he didn't care to make eye contact. The Navajo wore a white bathrobe open over his barrel tattooed chest and Wranglers with no socks. A thick silver necklace embedded with a brace of blue rock beads hung over the tattoo.

The florescent lights over the stove hummed.

Making eye contact now, the Navajo asked, "Where's Bob at?"

Maybe a split second too long in waiting Grayson said, "He's coming."

The Navajo's hand fell away from the toothbrush. The tell was that he shifted his weight from left to right and instantly Grayson caught it and rushed him. They collided between the breakfast bar and a pantry cabinet in a wreck of power and muscle. Green foam bubbled and spewed from the Navajo's mouth. As they pivoted in the clinch, the coffee maker slid from the counter and the glass carafe shattered. Hot coffee and shards shot out across the floor. The Navajo grunted and swung at Grayson's hands guarded at his head. The punch deflected off and the Navajo's big brown fist carrying forward plunged through the thin oak of the cabinet. Grayson felt the seriousness of the man: no reticence or fear, and he was strong but he was unprepared and there was no deeper cunning beyond the strength. Grayson pivoted again, drove short left hooks into the Navajo's kidney and spun him that way so the man's arm drove further inside the cabinet. Grayson snaked his own arm through for a choke. Their feet slipped in the coffee and glass. Grayson viced down on the windpipe, hauling him over to their left and into the entryway hall where they went down like two maddened bull elk locked at the horns. Glass jars of pickled purple corn and one of dried rice fell from the pantry and shattered. The Navajo's free hand slapped around blindly trying to take the knife from Grayson's waist. Grayson rolled him and freed the Glock from his holster bringing it level to the Navajo's head just as front door opened. He cinched the Navajo's neck into his elbow crook and grasping the other arm that held the warm steel of the pistol at the Navajo's temple to form a neat package. At that moment, they each gazed up to where three unfamiliar men stood backlit in the doorway.

Joe rushed past the three men and into the hallway. "Whoa whoa whoa," he yelled. Grayson felt the big Navajo ease up a bit. Two of the other men at the door were identical twins. These two departed the doorway, heading back out to the yard. The remaining man was shorter and pudgy with a wispy bald head who stood where he was on the porch rubbing his hands as if unsure what to do with himself. Joe swinging his long grey hair out of his eyes stopped shy of their feet.

"What in the fuck is this?" he asked.

Grayson let the choke loose and the Navajo rolled and coughed. The two men who appeared to be twins returned from the yard and each carried long bird hunting shotguns with black plastic stocks entirely ill-suited for the event. The soft, pudgy man who had remained in the doorway stopped the twins with a paternal hand on either of their chests and spoke in placating, demure tones.

The Navajo asked, "You know this motherfucker?"

"Yes, I do," Joe said.

Grayson watched the men at the door with the shotguns turn their weapons skyward and sling them over their shoulders. Each was overweight and plainly dumb. The Navajo massaged his throat and Joe patted him on the shoulder hard. The Navajo's eyes were vast, nearly all black, and freakish as if he were high. He was. But on what, Grayson could not say.

"Grayson, what on earth are you doing," Joe asked.

Grayson said, "We may have had a misunderstanding."

"Bullshit. You came like a bitch to rob me. That I understand," said the Navajo.

Joe pulled the Navajo up and said, "Let me see what he's got to say, Johnny. Bob give me a hand."

The man who'd simply watched from the doorway, Bob, responded now and stepped into the hallway. Grayson drifted into the front room a few steps where there was a clear angle to the back door if needed. On the surface of a pinewood sideboard positioned between the kitchen and the living room a small, tidy altar was arranged around a modeled-clay figurine of Santa Muerte and a coiled a rosary. Dead flowers and yellow candles, a cloudy shot glass, and few grey business cards were placed near the figurine and all of it rested upon an orange crocheted rug roughly the size of a placemat.

Johnny, the Navajo, said, "Is this the fucking guy?'

Joe stared at Johnny. "The guy who the tribe helped out. Yeah," he said.

"Right, right, right. Damn. You don't reciprocate. Then you break into my home and destroy my kitchen? You fucked up. Hard. It'll come back to you."

Grayson still held the Glock along his leg. The bird's beak grip of the big blade hung off on his left side where it had been stuffed back in his beltline. His expression was calm, observational.

Joe said, "Let me talk to you outside, Johnny."

"We got that thing," Johnny said.

Joe nodded and said, "I know. We'll get there."

Grayson said, "A truck came through here up on this BLM road on the hill. Came all the way from the old ranger station on Potasche in the last couple nights."

All three men listened. The other two with the shotguns remained in the doorway.

He went on. "I'm looking for that truck. Do you drive a full-size truck?"

"No buddy. I drive a Jeep. Plenty of trucks come and go on that road."

"Lately, I imagine not so many," Grayson said.

"Where's Phil?" Joe asked.

"Well, Joe that's the fucking issue, isn't it? That's why we're standing here in this fellow's kitchen guns drawn and holding up everyone's day. The rest of it can wash away."

"Let me talk to him, Grayson. Just hold on a second here."

Johnny stripped off the bathrobe and deposited it in a neat folded pile on the marble topped console table. Bare-chested now, he shook out both arms hard enough that the muscles underlaying tattooed murals of Japanese elm and dogwood with crimson leaves rippled and his fingers slapped each other bone on bone.

Joe gestured and Johnny strode out the door on bare bleeding feet. Grayson sat at the kitchen table two feet from the back door with the Glock set crosswise on the table and his trigger finger outstretched. He unlatched and cracked the door letting the bolt rest on the strike plate and a current of air whistle through. The quiet man named Bob came around the corner smoothing a few long thin hairs over his freckled dome. Nodding as he advanced, his strange smile showed gums too long and teeth too squat and square—like baby teeth. He wore a new pale green polo shirt tucked into a pair of stonewashed jeans over white sneakers. Around his right wrist was tied a rainbow bracelet of braided thread, like something a child would make at day camp.

"Do you mind?" he asked, nodding to one of the chairs at the table. "Quite a way to start the morning." He chuckled and the fat around his neck shook as he collapsed into the chair. "I'm Bob. Everyone calls me Brother Bob. I'm a Man of God. Those are my deacons at the door. Nathan and Doug."

"That your van out by the barn?"

"Oh, yes. Well, yes and no. Johnny and I used to share partnership in a Bible camp. Yes. Ran it right here for many years, in fact. It was a wonderful, wonderful thing. Glory be."

Bob's eyes seemed over-pressured somehow. He did his best to look very grave, and his best was rather good. Practiced. Grayson watched him closely. The house felt false, like something pieced together from a magazine. The sense of artificiality extended to these men around Grayson. Everyone conspires but these fellows, while not exactly polished, were experienced.

"I'm after a man named Phil Hixson. You know him?"

On the table, the manila folder and the half-eaten breakfast sat undisturbed. A pale and ringless hand lay over the area of Bob's neck where his chin should have been and with his eyes still moving he said, "I'm sorry I do not." He met Grayson's gaze. "There are so many missing now. It's hard to fathom."

Bob was about to say something more when Joe stepped into the kitchen from the front room. He had a cigarette between his fingers and the smoke unrolled thick in the light slashing through from the curtain edge.

"I got him cooled down," he said.

"Oh good. Usually that takes at least an hour." Bob said. "Then we're off?"

Bob clapped his little hands softly and rose and passed Joe in the front room waving the smoke out of his face. Joe sat down in the chair, pinched look on his face. Sheaves of grey hair pinned behind his ears like a college girl. He tapped his smoke on the plate and the delicate crinoline shape of the ash tumbled and collapsed in the white coagulated grease.

"Look, we're late to a tribe thing. Johnny's making a call though right now to a friend who might have a line for you on Phil. If anyone knows where Phil would be it's gonna be this guy, alright. Denny something or other. He's old pals with Bob and Johnny. Some kind of retired government man. Solid. Solid if he's with Johnny. So he's probably got like back channels that he can use to help. Okay?"

Johnny came through the front door and turned down the hallway without looking in the direction of the kitchen. The front door was still open. Shadows of the two men with the shotguns stretched against the wallpapered foyer wall.

"Joe, what are you nervous about?" Grayson asked.

"Aww. This meeting we're going to. Tribe thing, man. Drama, right?"

"You should get your own tribe."

"Look who's talking, right?"

"I'm getting back there, Joe. Bit by bit."

Johnny came back to the kitchen and kicked at some of the pickled corn on the floor with the tip of a black ostrich-skin boot. Joe turned in the chair and the two exchanged a glance indicating each was ready to leave. Johnny gestured at Grayson.

"Unless you're going to clean the kitchen, you wait outside. My guy will be here straight away. He doesn't fuck around."

Johnny stepped forward and took up the manila folder from the table. "I'll take that." His eyes fell on the ash in his breakfast. He snorted in disgust. He looked at Grayson and waved the folder. "If you ever come in my house without knocking again, I'm gonna lay you down. I'm gonna lay you right down."

"Be more careful who you open the door for," Grayson said.

* * *

In the shade of the gorge wall, Grayson sat in the orange mallows with his eyes closed counting forty deep breaths. Some speckled house sparrows bathed in the copper dust of the driveway and fence lizards emerged from their stone battlements to take the sun and snap at scouting red ants. Forty breaths was close to enough to five minutes that he rose and crossed through the heat and rounded Johnny's house. The door was blown open wide. He closed it behind himself and went to the bureau in the front room where, at a slotted wooden mail caddy, he rifled through envelopes looking at the addresses and the names and separating out two provisional stacks. When he exhausted the mail, he set the envelopes back in the sorter—save two that he folded away in his rear pocket as he walked down the hall. He pushed open the bedroom doors and stood a moment in front of the long mirror at the terminus of the hall scanning the two rooms. Seeing nothing extraordinary, he spun on his toes and went back out of the house, turning the lock as he did.

As he closed the door, an attractive woman in a long flannel shirt waved to him from the shaded backyard of the second house. She tapped her cigarette on the pop can ash tray rested on a stack of split cedar firewood and swept long dyed-blonde hair over her shoulder. He considered making some excuse but just returned the wave and kept moving, rounding the house through the blasting sun on the drive and into the shadows of the gorge again. He kept to the wall until the barn gave cover and there he broke into a trot over the fallen rocks and around the long stretch to the cabins and cottonwoods where the wall broke up and he could climb hand over hand onto the bluff. Then he took up the trot again along the deer trail rounding the bluff where he was in the full sun and could see like a monstrous dead grapevine the dirt BLM road he'd come in on just hours before. Earlier it seemed full of dread but now held little mystery.

He could see black arcs of county road pavement rising and falling into the south back to the valley. As he crested the trail and came out on the smooth sandblasted slab below the scrub oaks where his glasses and shotgun and rucksack waited, he held one hand to blade away the sun. He saw through the heat whiffles rising off the pavement a dark blue truck moving fast maybe a mile out.

Grayson waited in the shade of the dwarf oaks and rolled a smoke. From his left, the ring of tires on the good pavement echoed through the gorge. The eruption of the new diesel cranking perfect like an enormous sewing machine overwhelmed the otherwise tranquil quarter. Careful with the glint, he drank from the water bottle and stowed it back. Through the binoculars, he watched the midnight blue F350 pull up and idle at the gate. The man stretched his hairy tattooed forearm out the window and entered the code and the slow swing of the gate began.

The truck wove through and disappeared behind some old sagging trees and then again behind the gorge wall and reappeared directly below him and eased to a stop between the houses. The reverse lights sparked and the man maneuvered the truck around so that it faced back toward the gate. The truck jolted with the setting of the parking brake. When it did Grayson heard, and saw, the green 80mm surplus box jump a bit in the clean, rubberized bed. There was no real need, but he studied the wheelbase and the tire tread and the 80mm case laying there, and he calculated the odds of these several facts being coincidences and roughed that likelihood as zero. Silence when the engine cut.

The man, Denny, stepped down from the truck with his arms swinging like an old silverback and glanced around the yard. He appeared to be listening, taking the feel for his environment perhaps. *This here is your courier,* Grayson thought.

The front door to the other house opened and the blonde stepped out with her hair in one hand and said something which brought Denny around the truck. Her legs were bare beneath the flannel shirt and she held the hem in place with one hand as she pranced down to meet him. Up on the rise, Grayson couldn't make out any of their conversation. She gestured and looked around the yard. *Yeah, I just ran off didn't I.*

He went back to studying the truck. It was new the year before. Full luxury package. The window-tint concealed the interior. A light coat of dust particles lay on the side panels like spores suspended upon the surface of dark water. A rectangular gold decal emblazoned with the same Bible camp logo he'd seen stenciled on the Econoline van was stuck to the glass behind the cab. He heard her giggle and brought the glasses back on them. The man had his hand between her legs under the flannel shirt, and she stood wide-stanced with her bare feet tiptoed in the dust and gravel and her hands on his shoulders. It lasted all of a minute. The man stood oddly distanced while he performed the act and held his hand out from his clothes when he was done as to keep her starch from his clothing. With the other hand he drew the keys from his pocket. She flipped her hair as a further invitation. He was already turned back to the truck and a moment later it started and he rolled forward and out the gate and dropped the pedal hard on the blacktop.

The knowledge of what Grayson would do in the next fifteen or twenty minutes was certain in his own mind. He'd gather his gear and descend once again over the bluff, but this time he would cut the phone line outside the house and take the Jeep keys from the woman inside. Beyond that approaching quarter of an hour he knew there were potentialities, risks, and inertias in play but they were no longer contained in anything recognizable. *It feels like a departure somehow.* He considered his own lack of sleep against the urgency of the scenario. He had no backup. No choice but to go hard now. The binoculars lay upside-down in his lap and he stared backwards into the large objective lens, swallowed to affix his gaze, and he kept staring--as if maybe in the refractive light of the apparatus there was the power not only to close space and magnify the given light of the world but also some hidden, reciprocal power to project the light forward into the oracular dark of time and thereby close distance to the future as well. But he knew well there was no such power in machines nor in men.

As if he'd been electrocuted, a shiver went through him. It was not fear, as he'd lost enough in this life already to have dispatched base fear from his psyche. It was terror, the mortal terror that lies below fear in the dark recesses of being. And having met terror before, he knew faith was the only suit to wear in meeting it again. Grayson knew that this man Denny had his box, the explanation for which was difficult, if not impossible, to grasp. Grayson knew his own heart and knew he would stop at nothing to fulfill his promise. He assumed God too would know this of him. Thus he concluded that God wanted him to confront Denny and very likely kill him. *The evident way is not the way.*

As he gassed the Jeep out of the fiberglass carpark alongside the woman's house, he took from his pocket the two folded envelopes and glanced at the addresses of each. The gate opened on an infrared, so he eased off the clutch and let the engine idle as he stuffed one of the envelopes back in his pocket and slid the other under his thigh.

"Let's go see why Denny has that box," he said out loud. He glanced at the address.

Zion Bible Camp c/o Dennis W Wills 89 Bender, Moab UT.

As he turned onto the county road and dropped the shifter into second and then third and lay heavy on the gas because now he was out in the open, it occurred to Grayson that whether Denny had or had not shown up with his 80mm surplus box today and whether Denny did or did not run into Phil on the night he'd stolen that box, from the moment he himself had chosen to unlock that back door of Johnny's house today he was always going to this address. It felt like déjà vu. Like returning to something or slipping into an abyss, leaving behind the last natural light. He was always going to see Denny. And he knew that whatever wider ordering entity played men on earth, it had the quality of occasionally doubling down for you. A set of moments wired into a loop. Under particular pressures this was how life seemed to unfold, as it had in the hospital. As it had when his wife had disappeared in the night.

The same shiver shot through him again. The sun was blinding on the empty road. He speculated that perhaps something beyond his or anyone else's will was operant again in his life or in all lives. Something to approach only at oblique angles.

As the hot wind blew in through the open windows on the Jeep and he redlined the engine, he determined that every decision forward would have to be made with the knowledge that his soul was at stake. Beyond terror resides God, and the only way to fulfill the promise he'd made to Jack was to pass through terror.

* * *

No Apache interdicted him on the BLM road nor did the mercenary shack guards a mile back toward town notice as he crossed the 191 highway and descended the embankment and drove over the frontage fields among the trundling white sheep. He ditched the Jeep in an enormous hedgerow of blackberries grown in its decades along the watering canal to the height of a touring bus and twice as wide. Some of the sheep took their shade beneath tamarisks and cottonwoods growing beside the arterial canal running perpendicular to the highway. With bland eyes, the sheep watched him don gloves and pull some of the thorny vines over the Jeep and slip away with his pack and the shotgun to the cooling dark that encased the whole network of canals nestled in the shadows and fed from foothills of those mountains just to the south of town.

Grayson moved a mile or so through a skewed patchwork of houses and diminutive farm plots keeping to the canal groves and eating blackberries by the handful that he washed in the cold stream. It was another stepwise mile or so through the yards to get to the place. No need to cross that two-lane in daylight. He built a hide back in the grove behind the drive-in theatre and stared through the ivy and some old cabled oaks upon the desuetude of the tattered screen and the call boxes. These were now full of bird and rat nests, while the teller stand was just a sagging hovel.

A motley refugee gang of men woke him just before dark as they dashed over the two-lane ajangle with loot and blades. One of their number lagged behind pushing a caterwauling shopping cart, singing something in an indecipherable gibberish while all of them screamed little cries of defiance and bravado. With the last of the daylight turning blue through the grove, he listened to the crickets join to create their cumulative Wurlitzer and went about checking his weapons and ordering gear. When darkness fell, he was already moving across the two lanes and up into the neighborhoods that looked down on the valley.

The F350 set in the driveway facing out to the street. Sniper fire and small explosions went off some few miles away in town at no particular interval. The air was still plenty warm under a perfect purple sky where the zodiac was yet to coalesce out of the deep ether and a red moon roved over the La Sals. He made his reconnaissance from a bank of cacti and landscape stone in someone's yard about a hundred meters out. It was a two-acre plot with some willows that grew there from the run-off with well-established tamarisk and apple trees that towered over a luxurious triangular plane of trimmed lawn as fine as any golf course he had seen. A light in the house shone through the open windows. A pair of dish satellites and antennae stood silhouetted against the sky.

The right side of the house facing the foothills was steep, dropping abruptly into a slip of paved side yard where you might park a boat or another vehicle. The hobbyist's orchard and a section where long garden boxes overflowed with tomatoes and beans on lines melded into more tamarisks of the neighboring house. There were no lights anywhere else on the dim street. He could have just walked right up the street in dark but the slope on the right side made him nervous. You wouldn't want to get pinned down with nowhere to go but up. Laying there prone in the dirt, he let his head hang in hand and calculated the noise he might make going through the grass and the leaves on the other side. He considered further unknowns: a security system, guard dogs, that Denny might not be alone. But going up the hill or down and around where it was desert cliff to view the backyard was out of the question. At least the blacktop was quiet.

Grayson went straight in. At the edge of the driveway he paused behind the grill of the truck to listen. The hood was warm. The automated light in the garage blinked out. He waited a moment. Wind in the hills. He looked back in the truck bed—the surplus box was gone—and at the base of the headache rack a line of climbing rope lay half-coiled. Another length of the same rope was coiled and cinched with a zip-tie and stuffed down in a halved, empty plastic bleach bottle. A thin roll of black trash bags was wedged into a tie down. Going forward the smell of two-stroke gas and ammonia wafted from the garage and he pivoted and went along the front edge of the house where everything was manicured away from the wall and the dark earth was soft and still from the day's watering.

At the window he peered between the blind slats into an office, where a few filing cabinets stood beside an executive desk. A green gun safe stood in the corner with the door ajar. An overhead fan twirled oak blades in the room beyond and bony twists of a pronghorn skewered out from a European mount on the wall beside other mounts of goat and bighorn. A television was on somewhere out of view flashing reflections into the back windows.

More flbreeze swirled in the canyon. Dry and living leaves shook together on limbs over the garden and with pains to avoid even a pebble where he stepped, he crept forward that way around the side where it was dark to the back yard and a grape trellis was crowned in the cast light of the house. He stood thinking, listening. Someone laughed on the television and he turned and went back silently along the front with the shotgun low and to his shoulder, crossing the front walkway and crouching in the grass. He merely noticed the passenger side window of the truck was open and immediately after saw through the dim of the interior cab the gray flash-hider at the end of Denny's short-barreled rifle. It hovered like some taloned thing at the back of a cave. His eyes travelled to the holographic red glare off the lens in the optic and lastly to the big square head. Denny's teeth emerged in the shadow, smiling.

"Son, you can't out-creep a creeper," he said and chuckled low.

Grayson froze and slowly righted himself.

"Just set that bitch down on the driveway. That's right. Now go ahead and stand on up. Yep. That's right. Now take two steps to your left. If you wanna run you go right ahead."

Grayson stood still.

Denny went on, "I'll just put four or five of these green-tips through your spine as you go and let you crawl out in the weeds if that's what you'd like." He chuckled again as he got out of the truck. "Take two more steps to your left," he said.

Down the street it was dark and quiet. No one else was out here.

Denny said, "Go on in through the garage."

Grayson saw Denny's eyes in the light for the first time. Even at a glance a child could have seen that inside the man lived the ill twins, malice and indulgence, and Grayson knew that back in the recesses of this man's psyche these two impulses would never truck with negotiation. Inside, Denny walked behind to the edge of the kitchen where he told him to turn around. He took a set of chromed handcuffs from out of his front pocket and tossed them over.

"That ain't jewelry, honey," he said. A two-way radio crackled from near the sink.

Grayson snapped the cuffs around his wrists.

"Pull on 'em so I can see. Hold 'em up," Denny said. "Alright, now here's how we handle that pistol. You reach over with your left hand. Thought I'd missed that one didn't ya? Left hand. Take it out. Drop it on the cushions there. Sit in the couch, other side. We're gonna be here a while."

Grayson read the man again in this light, noting the trident tattoo he had seen earlier that day and another of a pin-up girl that appeared to be reaching down the density of his forearm. Above his wrist a hexagram was inked in thick green lines. Two meaty fingers were choked in gold signets. On his face was a salt -and-pepper horseshoe mustache finely-trimmed. He wore jeans over hiking boots and a guayabera shirt that was opened over a gold Cuban chain clasped with a diamond crusted medallion nearly the size of halved tennis ball. He carried the short rifle level on a single point sling that he kept tense around his arm. He turned away and opened a drawer beside the kitchen island.

The furniture was tasteful: a leather couch and chairs. There were some antiques. He smelled lemon cleaner and could hear Denny breathing even from across the room. On one wall were hung six dirty blonde mountain lion pelts with the claws retained and splayed. Below six beetle-cleaned and boiled skulls of mountain lion gazed out from custom mahogany pedestals. Suspended on another wall was a theatre-grade television playing a sitcom and below it on a long teak buffet sat two more sets of handcuffs and a framed photo wherein a younger Denny and a bald woman in a muumuu dress roughly the same age sat at the foot of a Japanese garden waterfall arm in arm, smiling.

Grayson felt cold in his solar plexus and stomach, as if some interior warmth were receding. He had a notion that this man, this house, the moment itself—were disjoined in a fundamental way from all things good and right. To negotiate with the feeling, he tensed and relaxed certain muscles in his low back and hips. He breathed in a steady eight count, but the feeling remained.

Denny chuckled at the sitcom as he wiped his hands of something on a towel and took up the radio, a high-end and duty-grade device. He clicked once and said, "Axis four this is axis six, over." In the television's reflection Grayson could see Denny looking at him, at the back of head, and absently passing a hand over his belly. The response came over the radio, "Axis six axis four-send it, over."

"Bob, I got him here. Over," Denny said.

The reply: "Copy that Denny. I'll proceed. Wait for confirmation from axis tower, over."

When he was done speaking he clipped the radio to his belt and opened the refrigerator and brought out a sandwich on a plate. There was a foil bag of rippled chips and a side of pepperoncini on the plate and he carried the plate and slung the rifle as he passed the pelts and the skulls and sat down on the loveseat across from Grayson and flipped channels. He stopped and turned the volume up on a movie.

"You seen this?" he asked.

Grayson looked at the screen and looked back but didn't speak.

"*Goonies*," said Denny. He finished his sandwich and set the plate on the side table and muted the movie. He wiped his mouth and said, "I'm Denny."

"Like the restaurant."

Denny chuckled. "That's good. Never heard it before. And you are?"

"Where's Phil?"

"Is that your boyfriend?"

"You're the Navy guy."

Denny laughed and bit into the sandwich.

"He was out there at the ranger station when you stole my box." Grayson said.

"You sure about that?"

Grayson just breathed and Denny added, "You never been handcuffed before I suppose. You'd relax your wrists more if you'd had it done to you before. It's hard to forget 'cause it cuts the circulation off and pinches the nerves. Here I'll show you."

Denny got up from the couch. He took the plate around to the sink and walked into the office. The door to the gun safe squelched as it opened and closed and Denny came back out with a disc in a clear plastic case. He ejected the occupying disc from the machine and slid the new one into the slot and walked back to the couch. A generic menu appeared on the screen with two boxes marked A and B. Denny pushed the button on the remote.

"I don't think you've seen this one either," Denny said.

On the screen a boy of maybe twelve years was kneeling on a stained mattress without sheets set on a gray concrete floor. The boy was naked with his hands handcuffed behind his back. A red bungee cord was coiled around the boy's arms so tightly that they were turned blue below the elbows and it looked like he'd dipped them in a paint bucket. The picture was grainy as if it had been transferred from videotape at some point. Abstract patches of red and black stood out on the boy's otherwise white back and sides. The marks were fresh, but not that fresh. This had been a marathon. Inside, a heart was slamming against the little rib cage to get out. You could see it pattering below his sternum. His interior legs were caked in his own dried blood. Conjoined with the sheer malevolence of the images Grayson sensed a total lack of trepidation. As if the adult actors knew with certainty there was no way to get caught. Denny's voice in the speaker. It said, *Get up*. Another figure flashed into the frame like something from a storybook. Huge and hairy, slathered in grease. Denny's tattooed forearm crossed the foreground of the image to adjust a pulley chain away from the figures on-screen. Crude directorial statements from somewhere off screen. Hyperventilation and a godawful crushing of bones. And then he heard brother Bob's pallid voice in the speaker, *Bring another.*

Denny turned the volume up a few notches but did not look over at Grayson who was already surveying Denny, cataloging the weaknesses he could identify. Both of them in their own separate worlds. Grayson felt a savage, primordial rage stir in him like magma welling up through forgotten stone fissures, and he turned inward, clawing back to cold ratiocination. This went on for some time until the headlights of a truck hovered through the front windows and grew bright in the driveway and shut off. Denny hit the remote to switch the television off and stood up.

"Everybody outta the pool."

There was a knock on the door leading into the garage. A tall and muscled man with blue eyes stepped into the kitchen light wearing a camouflage plate carrier with full kit over plain tactical clothes and boots. There was an Mk12 precision rifle in one curled tawny hand with a brown sling dangling.

He looked at Grayson and then at Denny and said, "This him?"

Grayson was still manacled as they drove through the night silent until the highway. They turned heading further from town. Bob was in the passenger seat fondling a plastic water bottle between his thighs. The man with the Mk12 rifle drove and listened to radio chatter in his earpiece. The headlights of Denny's truck following them shone constantly through the cab windows. A steel grate like those found in police vehicles separated Grayson from the front seats. The floor was bare and his cuffed hands were cuffed again to an eye bolt driven through a custom-fabricated scaffolding behind the seat. In the bed, two animal cages were bolted down and shrouded under a fitted blanket. The edges of the blanket turned up in the wind flashing black wet noses and lips. He could hear their tags clink and their claws gripping between the cage wires and scratching the metal truck bed as the truck turned. When they turned off the highway Grayson could see the dark rise of the La Sals on the starry skyline. They wound through the foothills still having said nothing until Bob turned to the man driving.

"Are you fellas about done?"

The driver glanced at Bob and turned back to the road.

"Getting there," the driver replied. The driver's long blunt nose hung over a short mustache and beard. His hair was recently trimmed and lines of print were tattooed around his neck in a bastardized Arabic font stretched up from under his collar.

The truck started to climb, and the driver transferred to four-wheel drive. He rolled the window down. Evergreens and sage swept through the cab. They downshifted and climbed higher going through the switchbacks slowly. In the moonlight Grayson could make out old slash piles in the clear cuts beside the logging road. They stopped beside a glowing gate shack on the side of the terraced road. Over the idling engine there were footsteps in the rocks.

A voice outside the window said, "All good?"

"All good," the driver echoed.

"Proceed," the disembodied voice said, and the driver let off the brake and they rolled, and the driver gassed the truck. They climbed again until the road leveled out and spilled into a large landing area rounded in tall dark trees where the driver reversed to combat-park the truck. The engine cut. Through the windshield Grayson saw particles of road dust silently vortexing in the head-lamp light. The driver grunted something to the dogs in the cages as he and Bob got out but the dogs made no noise in return.

Before dawn, four black men mumbling in broken English and French came and hauled Grayson out in the dark. He was still in his shackles and purple bruises had begun to well up on his wrists. The wind blew through the ring of evergreens and they went quiet letting him stand and wobble a moment in order to in-spire some trepidation. Knowing approximately what was coming Grayson filled his nose and lungs with the piney air. There was a snapping sound of metal batons opening and one of them clicked on a small flashlight.

"He jus' a little one isn't he," one of the dark figures said. And they laughed the soft laugh of men under yoke but momentarily granted some small mastership. "No, he good size. We keep him." The light flashed over the men and back to his face. Long spidery arms and green fatigues rolled up to the elbow.

"Warm him up. Sor say don't break him," one of them cautioned.

"I got it, man," said another.

Grayson heard the sounds of Velcro separating and something unsheathed from a pouch. Hushed laughter. The tethered steel barbs stuck in his back somewhere and he seized up chomping his tongue and pitched over in dust. The man pulled the trigger on the Taser again and he couldn't help but bite harder. Warm blood and drool flowed in the dust and someone said, "That's good, now hit that bitch." He felt the stinging whacks along his sides and shoulders and legs all at once. He heard one of them say, "Roll him, roll him now. Yeah, it's football you know."

* * *

He woke up to sunlight and an American voice saying, "Jesus, he shit himself."

Another American voice, "You want gloves?"

His eye was crusted part way shut and something in his leg didn't feel right as they stood him up. The truck with the cages was still parked across the clearing beside Denny's, and Denny and Brother Bob stood there holding white Styrofoam cups steaming in the morning cool. A length of old smooth chain was wrapped around one of the great pines and the two Americans clipped his handcuffs to the runner and one told him to sit down. He oriented himself. You're looking west and north. He watched insects zip through the pale, sheeted dawn light coming over the rim. Long boughs overhead swayed and knocked hollow and over the valley a set of dense and brilliant clouds, spaced even, roved east on the wind like annular war ships.

Grayson muttered a prayer and spoke to himself and said, "If you gotta go." And he dropped his head loose and closed his eyes to breathe. He counted to twenty-six and then heard voices coming through the trees somewhere. Just a few at first and then many. Likely they're not bringing your last meal. Past the clearing and the trees, the mountain sloped out almost level and there was a field of brown tallish grass. He cast his eyes on the bare stones that punched up through the mountain slope at the edge of the road and they seemed holy and simple. The sky continued to rearrange itself for him upon the margin in the trees where the road came through. Several of the black mercenaries grabbed him up and un-clipped the chain and pushed him across the lot and through the trees to the meadow. Below him over the valley, dark water birds with long necks rocketed into formation.

Over his shoulder he glimpsed a legion of mercenaries, di-verse of color and uniform, gathering at the edge of the meadow. Denny and Bob donned sunglasses and stood away from the mer-cenaries with their coffee looking much like men at the racetrack or the golf course. The sniper Sor, who had driven Grayson to this place, was trailing just behind the two men that were holding his arms. Grayson cleared his throat and spat into the grass. The men held his upper arms loosely and one let go completely to light a cigarette as they walked. He heard the steel on plastic sound of a handgun being unholstered and then the snap and clack of the slide as the man chambered a round. Halfway across the field the sniper's radio clicked. Denny's voice went out over the meadow saying, "Hold up."

The sniper walked off from them and stood listening to squawks over the radio. The man on his left said to the man on his right, "We get whores now." Both men chuckled. Grayson moved against the stiffening crust of shit and piss on his clothes to break it up and looked up the parabolic chain of mountains. The sniper came back up the meadow and spoke.

"Mission change, boys. Bring him back. Bring him with you." The sniper walked past them.

"So what, now we're not gonna smoke this dude?" The man on Grayson's right said in broken English.

"Just bring him," the sniper said.

They walked him back over the field toward the mercenaries who parted and called to him saying how it was his lucky day, and some said he wouldn't get any whores, and others said they'd make him their whore. When they were past the mercenaries his guards turned him onto a trail that skirted a spur on the hillside and they went on through some small oaks into another forest of pines.

"Is this the desert master," one of the guards asked with a chuckle.

"Is that what you guys are calling him?" Sor the sniper said.

The man smiled and replied in his French accent, "Yes. Word has come."

"Word has come, huh?"

"From the captains, we hear the story. And we say to each other, if he is still alive, then he is the desert master."

"Sounds like some kooky shit to me. What do you say about that?" Sor said.

"I don't know kooky shit.'"

Through the trees, Grayson could see yellow heavy machines, bulldozers and backhoes. The brown dirt around them was churned up fresh from their recent work and beyond the machines was parked a contingent of some forty-odd Humvees and deuce-and-a-half trucks painted beige. Where the dozers had terraced into the mountainside and made level ground on the mountain slope, there were set down on temporary foundations of pier block and four by four beams perhaps ten aluminum-clad work trailers. Among these were spaced out a matching number of portable powerplants configured onto their own orange trailers. A commercial tanker for the powerplants was parked below in another area of terracing that held more Humvees. A pad had been formed adjacent to these provisional parking lots where a Chinook helicopter and one of the Apaches had been set down.

Workmen in faded green coveralls and red hard hats loitered in the shade watching two of their compatriots run conduit and cable to one of the plants.

At the first of the trailers, Sor took Grayson's arm from the lanky African guard and continued walking him up the newly built porch steps before knocking. As Grayson weighed the odds of an escape his eyes fell on a designated marksman tucked back in the trees with his scoped rifle swaddled in burlap strips. He found another marksmen a hundred yards apart with the same rifle watching a separate sector and angle on the mountainside spur. The door opened and the man inside squinted into the light.

"The goat?" asked the man. He was a clinician of some sort with jet black locks and unnaturally large ears that were pulled flat to his head in a sanitary lace hairnet. He had the sallow look of someone whose life had been spent indoors. His eyebrows were raised in query.

"Finally. Got our goat," Sor said. The clinician told them to come inside. Florescent lights and the smell of coffee and sweet creamer overpowered the trailer. There was a couch on one wall and a folding desk and chair before a partition in the center. Voices carried behind the partition. In the corner there were two false, portable walls of newly hung and textured sheetrock set into a two by four frame. A ring light and a collapsible fabric light reflector on stands were positioned in the corner.

"You fucked him up a little bit," the clinician said and chuckling stood looking him over in the florescent lights. "Well, let's note he bumped his head getting into the truck."

The clinician went behind the partition and came back with cotton balls and alcohol. With a glance at Sor and the cuffs to confirm Grayson was controlled, he began dabbing away the crust over Grayson's eye. When the clinician was done, he went back behind the partition and returned with a handful of wet blue paper towels that he used to wash the dirt off of Grayson's face and a kit to draw his blood. "That'll do," he said when he was done with the washing.

Sor pulled Grayson's arm, "Over here. Don't fuck around."

The clinician wrapped the length of green rubber around his bicep and tied it and inserted the valve into his vein and drew two vials.

"Why do you guys take two?" Sor asked.

"Usually it's in case we lose one but with him we might need both. I should actually take three but as long as we have the body it'll be fine," the man said. He went back into the rear with the vials and returned to the corner where he slid the light and reflector away from the wall and snapped the switch on the ring light. Sor pulled Grayson's arm again and stood him in the false corner and the administrator produced a small digital camera from inside his desk that he spun into the tripod and set before him.

"Look straight ahead." The clinician nodded to Sor and snapped the photos. "And we're good. Just make sure we get the body at some point."

The African contractors were waiting for them outside. The Africans were both young and tall. Their heads were cleanly shaved and one had daubed a few nicks with tiny bits of toilet paper. Two other European mercenaries stood off from them also waiting, chatting quietly. When Sor saw them he spoke again. "Gentlemen."

The Europeans were both bearded and wore the same Multicam uniforms Grayson had seen mostly on other whites but also several of the black mercenaries. The uniforms were modified, shorn of any insignia and worn with the sleeves rolled to the elbows and the lower pockets had moved up to the shoulders, angled toward the pectorals for easier access by hand to the pocket's contents. The men had stripped-down chest rigs of good quality with three magazines in the center and blowout kits and radios at either side. Each carried a sidearm in a drop leg holster and their rifles were set up in the recon style identical to the one Grayson had taken off the man he'd killed in the marshlands.

"You want, I take him," offered one of the Africans.

"Yes, I want," Sor said.

"Put him on the chain up there. No diversions, no side trips."

The Africans both smoked store-bought generic cigarettes as they walked him. He thought again about escape but remembered the marksmen on the ridges. The rotors on the Apache parked on the lower terrace lit up the hillside, first with a low torqueing hum, then a piercing whine as they built speed and cut the static space. The Africans laughed and made jokes in French. Grayson didn't understand French.

As he walked and listened, it occurred to Grayson that he hadn't thought of his former wife in a long, long time. Yet now, in this place, peculiar and mundane images from that dream he'd dreamed with her, the nightmare, flashed through his mind: exhausted, walking on the quieting maroon carpet of the hospital headed to the cafeteria as she slept in the ICU, and standing out front in the spring sun watching crows on the green lawn. The disintegration of social and commercial schemes had only began to appear back then: transactions processed, a pantomime of trust and care still allowed for the genuine articles to manifest on occasion. In the garden area of the hospital as his wife recovered, as he sat hollowed of hope with the plastic box containing his son's ashes, he watched gray squirrels emerge from the open crook of a hemlock in the yard. In some way, here now, a shackled prisoner in a quiet war, he felt sheltered from that worse nightmare, and those worse creatures that knew his private interior pathways and ran amok in the vacancy.

By the time they crested the trail and stepped into the lot, the whole hillside was enveloped in a monstrous deafening wash of turbulence and noise. A cloud of thin dust passed through as the guards clipped him back into the chain. He pushed back up against the tree and tried to lean and then crossed his legs underneath him. All three of them, two captors and captive, turned to see the Apache lift up off the hillside like a waking dragon with its symbiotic gunners perched in the open bays. The gunners were dangling their legs out over the earth and already roving their Dillon guns in the swivels. Green signal lights burst once in the passing dust cloud. The Apache hovered and pivoted to churn the dust into brief spirals and whip inexplicable blue tracers of spark light at its rotor tips. The mighty pines in the circumference seemed to swoon as the machine went forth. Grayson felt the tree against his back shake to the roots.

* * *

In the afternoon one of the mercenaries kicked Grayson's feet and he woke. The man filled out his uniform better than the others filled theirs. He wore knock-off Aviators and had a touch of grey in his patchy beard and at his temples. He held a milk crate that he used for a seat and took a pack of cigarettes from his shirt pocket. He lit the smoke with a worn brass Zippo and clove smoke wafted over.

"Desert Master," the mercenary said smiling.

His English was pretty good, laced with French or an accent Grayson didn't recognize.

"I just want to get a look at you. The men are with the whores from this little town, but I don't do this anymore. I've had my fill.

And so, I thought to myself, I'll get a look at this goat. But you look more like a rabbit."

"What do you mean by 'goat?'" Grayson asked.

"Oh, I see. I had assumed the Desert Master knew all things but he doesn't know he is the scapegoat for this operation." The man chuckled with subdued but genuine mirth. "Did you know that in my home of Zimbabwe the whores will squeeze your ding dong so hard that you will just get up and leave the whorehouse? Did you know that? You didn't know that either, I suppose, but it is true and is why I am here now. Talking to the goat, who looks like a rabbit, I say."

Grayson spat in the dirt off to his side and rearranged himself against the tree so the cuffs didn't hurt so much. "Why is a Zimbabwean mercenary, burned out on whores, sitting on a milkcrate high in the La Sal mountains of Moab, Utah? What series of events would bring about such a thing?" Grayson asked.

The old mercenary gave a knowing smile and tapped his ash. "I've been many places. You really want to know? I'll tell you. Spoils of war. Same as any man I suppose. But in this case the mighty western man and his Empire have fallen. I am given an opportunity to clean up, to take my piece, so I do. Simply put."

"As an American let me confirm there's no such thing as America," said Grayson.

"Yes, of course. Look at you. Literally fallen. Here I am. There are tens and hundreds of thousands and eventually millions like me coming over the shores, over the bridges and on the trains into America to take what is lying in wait." The old mercenary said this and let his head recline slightly. He smoked the clove.

"Let me tell you something," Grayson said.

'Okay tell me, goat."

"You're not gonna get shit. They're gonna drop your ass off at a bus stop with whatever you've got on you and that'll be what you go ahead with. There's not going to be any fucking spoils of war for you or any one of those dumbshits. You're just the second rat to the trap that gets the cheese. There's another trap set with new cheese for your children. It's a long con."

"But I have a plan for this too. If I need it and you may be right. I have given it a good deal of thought. There are many ways forward if it came to that but I don't think it will, and I will tell you why. You see in Africa there was nothing and so we went to France or Italy or wherever we could get into a company, usually. And what we find there is that America wants us too. Americans, of course, do not want us. Why would they? That would be insane to give this away. Look at it."

He swept his arm over the valley with theatrical embellishment and continued saying, "But America I came to understand is not Americans. Do you know what I mean by this?"

"America is an abstraction. A brand name." Grayson couldn't help himself.

"Yes. Desert Master sees it too. It's an incredible thing. Even in France or England there are still Frenchmen and Englishmen but in America men believe they live in an ever-expanding place where no homeland is required. Even these men here, mostly dumb niggers from the bush, feeble minded though they may be, know perfectly well that nothing on earth expands forever. They know you need to guard your home. Of course, that's why they are here though."

"When you say 'scapegoat' what exactly did you mean?"

He sucked on the cigarette with thin eyes and said, "For the television."

"For the television." Grayson smirked with understanding.

"Yes, for the people. The public opinion. Didn't you know? You did all this, bruh. Desert Master is a dangerous insurgent leader. You agitated this militia and armed that one and set fire to the town. Extrajudicial forces were required to quell the unrest. On and on. They even got a recording of you buying explosive materials, man. They make up the rest, and it's a good show. That's how this works. Town to town, man."

Grayson laughed and the Zimbabwean mercenary lit another cigarette and laughed his way too. The creases in his forehead and cheeks deepened as he smiled. Grayson thought of Jack once telling him that most modern warfare is stage-managed, that the results shown on television are a sanitized and distorted version of the truth the soldier makes in the arena of war.

The old mercenary said, "It's some funny shit, huh. Best to not worry. The Desert Master knows this I am sure. When you're already dead why worry then? Am I right?"

"If that were true, I'd have not worried the past decade."

"Well. For the most part these boys are, as I've said, dumb niggers. I would not mix with them myself outside of war and even now I liaise for the Boss Man and bide my time, as they say. But this is the thing that an American, even the Desert Master, doesn't likely know: even though most of my workmates here are just drones, there is another caste of fellow in this company who can hunt men the way hyenas hunt the antelope calf. Genius beasts, these men. They run like the wind on the track and see things regular men do not see. They have supernatural sight, savage instincts. One or two of them learned from former Koevoet operatives. All tracked as children on the farm. The stuff of legend. How do you confront such men?"

Grayson cast his eyes down in thought. The Zimbabwean stubbed out the cigarette on his milk crate and placed the butt in the cargo pocket of his pants. Grayson said, "Before the time of the early Church Fathers, there were wandering monks out seeking God in the hinterlands. One of these monks asks a savvy hermit how he could be saved. The hermit stands and throws off his clothes, his staff and to the monk the hermit says: 'Thus, ought the saved man to be. Stripped naked of everything and crucified by temptation and combat with the world.' And that's how I think you confront everything."

The lines on the old mercenary's face went slack for a moment and then he pursed his lips in consideration. Grayson spat again into the needle duff. The mercenary glanced away--at the shock of a foreign land, some workers beneath a tree drinking coffee from paper cups. The mercenary slipped the Zippo from his pocket to light another cigarette and said through the smoke, "Very good. The world is combat. But now, so I may place proper bets tonight, you see, tell me what military schools you attended. I have not been given access to your file. No one has. But certainly, you have a military background. Where did you get your training?"

"DVDs and books mostly."

The Zimbabwean gaped at him in mock disbelief, teasing. He pursed his lips around the cigarette and put his hand to his ear as if to say 'come again?' He slapped his knee and began to laugh. He laughed so loud it echoed in the trees and brought the workers' heads up toward them. "Yes. Yes, this is the answer. Desert Riddler. Truly, Desert Master. A natural. It will be a fine contest."

4
The Animal

In the mid-morning some black guards unwrapped the chain from the tree and looped it back through the cuffs with a padlock. They stood and walked Grayson over the lot inspecting him as they went and commenting on his gait and proposing probable tales of ancestry as if they were breeders at a track or cattlemen at an auction. The sky was overcast from one end of the valley to the other, but it was warm nonetheless and a charged alkaline taste hung in the air. His shirt clung to his back still wet with dew and sweat. As they walked, the guards prodded the purple, yellowing bruises and cuts from the handcuffs on his wrists. One gave a playful kick to his hip and whistled. They spoke in French but from the modulation and excitement in their voices, he could tell they had bet against him in whatever was coming. He could smell creek water and wildflowers carried on the currents rising from the valley and he thought about how sweet the water would taste and that its mere presence in the desert was a mystery that he didn't understand.

They swung the chain and steered him to the edge of the lot where some dustcaked Humvees were parked. One of the Africans ran the chain through both of the tow hooks in the undercarriage to account for the slack and then snapped the padlock shut and shook it as he smiled to the others. Another of them tested it and then they walked off to the shade to smoke.

Across from him on this side of the lot, Denny sat on the rear bumper of his truck staring at him through his sunglasses. He stared back for a long time until Denny took a fancy pocketknife from the area of his waist and began to clean his fingernails. A half hour passed in the clearing with the camp noises of birds above and men going into the bushes and utensils being washed in tin cups at water stations. He counted forty breaths and stretched his back, side to side, to work out his hip. Guards moved slowly between posts and those off-duty began to collect themselves on the lot and others stood on the hillside in the leaden light. A stout white mercenary in full kit jogged up the trail with his rifle in one hand. Denny turned when he heard the footsteps and the jostle of gear and Grayson watched him as he rounded the tailgate smiling at Denny who also smiled. The mercenary kept coming straight at him unbuttoning his battle dress pants with one hand as he went. He came to a stop at Grayson's boots with his business out and stood pissing on down in the dust between his legs and on his boots.

"The coffee is terrible here, bruh," he said.

He was South African by the accent, his ice blue eyes that had seen the desert and the jungle. The men lined up to watch, laughed, and yelled that the Desert master could live off of piss and that it only fueled him and that he ate scorpions which also powered him.

"Then I'm just giving 'im a boost."

As the laughter died, a steady line of some thirty armed and outfitted mercenaries marched up the trail and over the road passing him into the skirt of the field, and the South African joined them. They were plainly of another class: elite, highly trained, and experienced. Four whites were among them, the rest dark African or mixed race. Vehicles moved along the road below. Some of guards and workers not of this caste sang lines in their native tongue. A rhythm beat out on hands and knees. Others traded last-minute bets of cash with a bookmaker who called the odds in French and again in English.

The last of the mercenaries bounded over the road as the first of the vehicles emerged into view. The man trotted like a nimble mule, even with the handicap of his full load-out and came to rest at the edge of the field in shadow among the others. Together they seemed something from a bygone era where men were warriors unambiguous and life was paid for in life in every ledger.

Grayson studied each man one by one and noted how certain of them fell together and others stood alone, or seemingly alone. A few looked hung-over. Most were bearded and wearing baseball or boonie hats except the darkest Africans whose faces were hairless and shone slick even in the dull light. They were all heavily armed, wired for sound, and none were at all new to the carrying of weapons. A few looked back at him and spoke about him among themselves. Some laughed but most looked dire and dull and blood-grim.

Another vehicle came up the hill. The men standing at the edges of the road stepped away to let it pass and when he saw it and noticed who was driving, he looked closer. The extended Econoline van arrived into the clearing and went slowly over one side of it in order that the crowd could make way.

The wild barking of dogs that only hunt and only ever ride in vehicles when they go hunting rang from the rear compartment where someone had pulled the bench seats and set down four steel cages. Some of the men smiled and walked over to the van to look through the window and coo or bellow for new odds depending on how they had laid their bets or what they saw in each dog's demeanor. The two dumb brothers who had wielded shotguns in the doorway of the Navajo Johnny's house stepped from the van. A white South African had approached Denny, and they walked around toward the dogs and the van. And as if he'd been waiting for this precise transitory juncture, one of the African cooks in his hairnet and emerald culinary blouse, half-slunk and half-knelt beside the tire of the Humvee and began some queer incantation or curse to gods no one in that place could name. In one of the chef's spindly caramel hands was a desiccated chicken's foot that he gyrated over Grayson's outline as he went on with the conjuring in a low, demure tone indicating his ways were subject to reproach if discovered by the others.

The dogs in Sor's truck had started whining when they heard the others in the van. They would soon be getting to work. Grayson saw Sor was already dropping the tailgate and making room to release them. Sor was talking to the dogs and they quieted down. There was a beat-up diamondplate box along the edge of the bed that squeaked when he opened the lid. Collars and harnesses and small dog-sized saddle bags hit the tailgate near the rifles that the men laid there.

Grayson sat watching this unfold. He rotated his wrists as much as he could in the cuffs and flexed his ankles. As Grayson turned back to the conjurer, the man blew a great handful of something like ashes from his palm that powered his face and neck then the man came down with two thin slashing fingers to dab a kind of maroon paste or paint across Grayson's cheeks. By the time the shimmer of dust had cleared, the chef had disappeared in the crowd.

More cars came up the road: a Suburban and a Mercedes utility vehicle. Executives in casual slacks and blue sportscoats got out with their personal guards who were themselves a different caste from those on the field. These men were all white Americans or Europeans wearing casual clothes and carrying fully automatic SAWs and folding stock HKs. The singing from the guards had continued even as the executives stepped out and assessed their investments—material, manpower and everything else such martyrs call out as being the whole world.

Cold water bottles were procured. Cameras clicked. The South African who had pissed on Grayson's legs spoke with one of these executives as they examined him. Grayson watched the South African shake hands with the executive and then walk over to Denny and the two dumb shotgunners. He realized by the way the shotgunners mimed Denny's hand gestures and by their similar carriage that they were Denny's sons. The South African pointed to Grayson telling them something about the proposed events of the day he imagined and then slapped Denny on the shoulder and walked across the lot to Sor who had the first dog out and was clipping the harness along its shoulders.

Both dogs were dark splotched Malinois with black noses and lips that drew back when Sor spoke certain words to them. The white and yellow teeth flared. The perfect pink tongue welled up in the cracks of the sharp teeth. They were both sleek and well built. Perfectly suited to this one task. Their coats were covered in a light road dust that billowed around them as they quivered in the bed. A child would know to fear them at a glance. Sor got the harnesses buckled onto each Malinois dog and handed one of them to a lieutenant at the tailgate. Denny and his sons' dogs were all a shepherd and coonhound mix. They had short brown and gray and white fur that was smooth on their skin up to the hackles that stood out in quills on all four of their backs. Denny was straddling one of them to look in its mouth. His sons stood to his side anchoring the other three hounds already harnessed and leaning on the leashes.

Some people in the crowd of guards and mercenaries and workers started bawling and shrieking short war cries until a warbling glossolalia echoed in the trees. Denny's dogs yelped and whined. One of the sons went along slapping them on their flanks. Sor yelled commands to his dogs over the voices and then turned and yelled commands at the lieutenants. The executives and their guards strolled out with a retinue of assistants into the fullness of the clearing with the manicured air of royals going to a picnic. The South African pulled Grayson up by the chain and said, "Walk." An element of the tracking team also went ahead out into the meadow. Their rifles were slung over their shoulders. The whites were sunburnt and the blacks carried gossamers of salty dust on their necks. All wore the same camouflage that disappeared against the backdrop of brown grass. The rim was bright off to their right where the sun was coming through a keyhole of clouds. Over their heads, the same light slotted and wove as the incoming faction of clouds bunched and grew and morphed.

The man yanked the chain and Grayson stopped. He felt him maneuvering the chain back through the loop. The cuffs twisted in the man's hands digging the edges into the already purple abrasions.

"Who has his knife?" the man called out.

"Rod, incoming," someone said. A squat mercenary trundled down the meadow with his knife in the leather sheath and the long lanyard wrapped around the handle.

The South African named Rod called out to the men standing in front of him, "Train your guns on this brak, boys."

The men unslung their rifles and snapped the lens covers away from the optics and racked the charging handles and switched down the safeties. They squatted and knelt in the grass and put on their sunglasses and held the guns on him lazily, using their knees for support.

Denny handed his dog off to one of the sons and went across the meadow with the rings on his fingers glinting in the caught light as he swung his arms. Rod saw him coming and turned and waited with his chin up in a gesture of reception still holding the cuff chain on Grayson's wrists. When Denny got there he slipped the Al Mar knife from his pocket and flipped it open. "Hold him one. Let me get my scent swatch," he said. He used one hand to stretch the fabric over Grayson's shoulders and brought the knife across in three quick swipes. Three lines of blood oozed. "Hold the fuck still," he said. Denny sawed at the flap of cloth and ripped it away. "Got him. Carry on."

Rod unlocked the cuffs and dropped them with the chain. Grayson rolled his wrists and wiped them on his shirt and felt the shoulder to see how deep Denny had cut.

"You want this blade or not, shithead?" Rod said holding the bush blade out. He took it and wedged it down in pants.

The gunmen out in front redoubled their grips and realigned dirty, steady index fingers till they leveled with him along the receivers of the painted guns.

"I'm going to take that knife when you're dead," Rod said in his ear.

Denny held the swatch in the air to indicate to Sor that he had it and Sor waved him away. When Denny got the smell into the hounds' noses they bayed almost in unison and it went calling down the canyon wall. Sor's dogs went rigid with anticipation. He patted their sides until the muscles went slack again. There was a bowl of water set out for them and they each kept going to it and slapping, chopping at the water and returning to watch the men with the water and saliva streaming off their muzzles. Grayson watched them carefully where he knelt checking his laces and Rod walked away just a few steps leaving him standing on the edge of the mountain. The cameras clicked away. Men in the round were strapping and zipping down their gear and checking magazines and med kits and testing or doublechecking night-vision devices, handguns, and food and water rations. Rod, sipping his water, looked up to the executives who had taken a spot at the treeline. He held his thumb up in the air and the men in suits responded in kind and turned to walk the few paces back to Grayson. They looked at each other directly in the eye for the first time.

"Well what're you waiting for? Run, bitch." Rod said to Grayson.

And he ran. The men cheered and quickened their last preparations.

The engines of three Humvees fired up. Sounds of the gears grinding and wheels pivoting in the gravel came down the meadow loud in his ears. Someone fired a single shot. Of course, Grayson flinched and there was laughter among the tracking squads and chastising over fire control and howls of anger from the men who had laid their money on the line to see a chase to the death and win or lose wanted the satisfaction at least of seeing how the event unfolded. The executives watched his back through binoculars. The bookmaker yelled, "All shut. All shut."

Grayson kept running toward the edge of the meadow where he had no idea what was beyond. It looked like it just fell away. The excitement of the men sent the dogs almost to their breaking point. Even Sor's dogs cracked and began howling and their master had to clap his hands. The African guards and the Mexican and Guatemalan workmen ran across the lot to look down through the trees. Grayson could hear the rhythm of their song building even as he gained distance over the field. The first bolt of the heat-lightning flashed in the sky. No thunder yet. He was sprinting now. And counting his breaths. Stretch them out. Let it do its own work.

The men began collecting into their teams. He heard the doors of the waiting Humvees open and the clatter of men mounting up and stowing weapons and the scything sound of the grass rushing past his old boots and the surface crust breaking. Others on foot went at a jog over the meadow, laughing darkly and slapping each other. One of Denny's sons had brought Denny's truck to the edge of the clearing and loaded the dogs into the bed.

At the edge of the meadow he saw that the embankment did indeed fall away. The vertigo at seeing a thousand foot of descent veered him hard left, wobbling. The deep gorge just kept expanding on his right—a great temple of silence where anything could go to die if it wanted. Past the chasm dotted with greenery and shadows of smaller voids he could see the swoop of the foothills meeting the red plane of the desert. Risking vertigo, he snatched a glimpse beyond all that was near, far out to the coriolis where the earth arched as if to uphold the stratosphere. He craned his head back and down and kept sprinting into the hot wind swelling up out of the gorge and whipping at his shirt and over his rolling shoulders.

More distant laughter was slammed away as the Apache swung around the trees over the lot and circled once for the pilot to get the lay of the things. It then turned and dove hard to the landing pad to pick up the executives. *Oh yeah*, he thought. *There's that too.* The meadow flowers wore out underfoot. Green became brown. He turned uphill and stole one last glance at his pursuers. The men were trundling forth and behind them in the wake of the Apache articulating spools of dust rose from the mountainside like wraiths of miners or scouts, Indians or railroaders. Way in the background the sky was roiling black and synaptic streamers of lightning bounced among the cloud banks.

Smells of pines and rock dust hit him. He wheeled and leapt off into the gorge and hit the loose scrabble under the meadow's edge and slid down to an area of boulders, small fir and alder and high-stepped along the incline for about fifty feet. A network of deer trails was woven over the surface of the spur beyond the boulder line, and he crossed the boulders on hands and knees expecting them to shift, but they held. He slid again in the next layer of scrabble down to where the rock gave way to dirt in a small clear cut, a splotch of mange among the evergreens. On the packed ground he just ran flat-out and didn't look back, though he could hear Sor's dogs nearing the drop-off and the first teams of mercenaries moving through the rock tailings.

The helicopter lifted off from the mountain. It floated over the canyon and emerged on the sky just as he entered the tree line. He slowed to listen to the high squeal of the turbine, the strange hallucinatory beat of the blades and then he stopped to shake out his legs and back muscles. A rain shadow was passing and a straight line of darkness slid down over the mountainside as if a curtain were being drawn on the land. The first drops fell on his face. Blinking against the drizzle, he could see the figures inside the cockpit with their headsets and sunglasses and he knew they were calling the description of things to the men on the ground. *There, now you know what you're facing,*

He sprang into the cool of the forest where it was dry again and jogged until the trail bent sharp up the hill. He hopped off and went bushwhacking through the needles and limbs heading south and straight down to yet another strand of the spiderwebbed trail system. Loose slabs and flakes of the mountain crashed back there as the dogs and the rear guard of trackers began to negotiate the drop off. Full bore another minute.

Let your breath catch your feet. Now stride for two more.

Then everything around was quiet again in the grove save the murmur of crows observing from the dark weave of limbs overhead. His flanks were seizing up and relaxing with each breath around the sore spots where the guards had deployed their batons on him.

They'll be looking for your sign in the trailheads right now. And then they'll split and run the various likely lines or leapfrog ahead with other teams to cut you off. Just keep moving.

If he could get to the desert and continue just simply to advance even if he had to walk in the wide open, the dogs would at least tire at some point.

The helicopter climbed away higher on the mountain to do the overwatch. He went down in bounds sliding through the debris and catching himself on the downside with the one leg that was already burning. The duff was greener. It didn't snap and scratch. He caught woodsmoke on the air. The sky between the treetops lit up, re-darkened. Where the draw of the canyon met the tree line he stopped and turned to look back again. Up the hill the first team was trudging forward on a trail he didn't think he had taken. That was good. A man among them was lagging behind amid the grey slash piles. Rain was coming down in the pocket now. The man lagging walked between the piles and over the boulders with a scoped rifle very much like the Mk12. When Grayson saw him bring the rifle to his shoulder he dove and tucked tight to the nearest tree and pulled himself around to a patch of blackberries. A half minute passed as he caught his breath and uncoiled a tether of thorns wound into his forearm. He watched the man with the rifle squat among the stumps scanning for him with the railed forearm of the gun depressed against the bark to steady the optic as he panned and then clicked the headset to speak. The sky flashed blue again. Flashed off the man's scope lens as vertical cords of lighting descended out from where the storm was unfurling up the back side of the mountain.

Sor's team was above this one in the sparse trees. Grayson could see the posture of the dogs pulling and yipping as they seemed to find his trail while Sor heeled and commanded them. With a whirling motion of his arm his team gathered around. The ground was cool in the vine thicket and he let it drain the heat away from his chest and belly. Let his heart catch up.

They'd be studying up on the type of your sign, Grayson thought. *They'll make notes on the length of your stride and the width of your running prints and discussing how a duff mound doesn't just peel itself back and pile up like carpet scrap. And they'll probably take some nice photos along with the measurements to show off back in the team room.*

The whining of the Malinois persisted. The men were talking about the storm. He could see it but couldn't hear any words. One of them took out a notepad and Grayson said under his breath "For your memoirs no doubt." Two others in the team were looking down the hill and pointing in his direction. Grayson rolled over on his back. Looking up he saw the sky was full dark with clouds now. He could hear the rain in the green needles and he was gearing up for another burst when he heard something else that brought his head around. A crashing and snapping of branches and brush and it seemed almost on top of him, and some instinct forced him to roll up and stand. That can't be one of the dogs. The blade came out. The noise was rocketing through the underbrush with unnatural speed, but he heard the rhythm of four legs bearing down on the duff and on the rocks beneath.

He caught a glimpse of flame in the brush. A gray haze swept back in the limbs like vapor off a steam train. The thing grunted spastically and shrieked. That's not a dog, he thought. The sheath dropped in the weeds and the rain dropped and beaded on the oiled grey blade. The beast was circling in a thicket. There was an explosion of tree branches against flesh, then more thrashing, and the thing blasted out through the thicket and he saw that it was a huge black boar with its shaggy hide aflame. Two dingy white tusks worked up and down. He crouched looking for what it would do. The hog saw him move and planted its hooved feet to change direction. A billow of smoke puffed sideways and hung and the instant acrid stench of searing hair and flesh hit him and the pig went tearing past, lost in its own mayhem. He watched it barrel on down the hill with weird blue flames spirating over its bristly body, screaming all the way. In its wake a cloud of char dispersed.

He stooped and sheathed the knife and wiped the gathering of sweat out of his eyes and threw a last look at his pursuers. Back up the mountain there, Sor spoke into the radio calm and steady. The other team had crossed the clear cut. They were all staring right at his position. Some looked through binoculars and others through riflescopes at where the pig had passed by. Grayson turned and ran all out for five minutes.

At a logging road he stopped in the ditch. The road was clear both ways. Heavy rain fell on the road dust and he drew deep the smell of the mixture. He stepped out with his hands on his hips, sucking wind. An engine chugged along somewhere below and he crossed the road and looked down and saw Denny's truck in the switchbacks with the four hounds leashed in the bed. He watched the switchbacks ahead of him and the truck to see if it was the same road.

It was the same road.

The hounds were slipping and scratching against the incline and fighting each other not to be pinned against the tailgate. He held his breath to try and hear better. One of Denny's boys had his arm hung out the window. The diesel engine growled low. Breathe. He breathed and tried to hold it again and listen. A big limb snapped somewhere on his back trail. A hundred yards away maybe. In the woods it's always farther than it sounds. Plus the humidity. Close though. And then he heard the helicopter also moving down the slope. He spun around on his heels over the ditch and pulled the weeds back upright from where he had stamped them down and then scrubbed out the prints in the road with his foot. He tucked the knife back into his waistband and walked twenty yards down the dirt road on tiptoe and stopped and kicked the roadway up where the ditch began.

He stomped his way back over the road to the upside making sure to drag his feet and leave as much sign as he could while intending to make it appear he was headed up the slope, as if they'd run him out of the brush. He trailed a few green leaves upon the rocks to oversell the trick and then went back into the trees--straight toward the tracking teams and the Malinois dogs who were coming likewise, right at him. Twenty yards into the bush he watched the truck roll into view and slow at the spot where his tracks crossed the road. The hounds went quiet. Just whimpering over the engine idling. Come on, look at it. When the truck stopped and the open-door chime rang the dogs exploded again and he knew they'd taken the bait.

"That's right," he said.

With as much control as he could manage he crept along parallel to the road toward his actual backtrail and when he saw it there on the ground—just a varied shade in the upturned leaves and needles, a line of pebbles darker than their neighbors—he blew hard from his mouth and turned up the hill highstepping flat out. He heard the teams up there, their gear clacking and steel harness links tinkling just over the rise.

It was going to be tight.

A few more paces and he began looking for a place to step off, a downed tree or some stones to dance over. The idea was to slip off the track and let the two groups meet in the middle and then detrain the whole mess amid the shouting and the barking. With any luck, some shooting, and they'd take out a few of their own. The smell of burnt pig and hair was everywhere. At a small boulder, he stretched, mindful to touch nothing. The toe of his boot caught and he vaulted off the line and leapt over to the next rock. He'd felt his sole slip on the lichens on the rock.

That's how they'll get back on you.

More stones on the other side. He took two surgical steps over the duff and then up onto a windfallen and barkless tree laid straight up the slope where he went forward like a tightrope walker to the trunk end and leapt off onto more stones. He went another ten yards and got back behind a little crag to watch. Sor's teams were already below the rise. Whether they could see Denny and his hounds coming through the bush below them, he didn't know but he could hear both parties moving on the forest floor. This meant he was within range of both rifle and shotgun. He cocked his head, straining to hear. Someone fired and a dog yelped. He got lower behind the crag.

In the salt bush maybe two feet away, a rabbit sat sideways with one chestnut eye on him. He could see the light brown ticking at the tips of its hide hairs and the black color below the ticking, the white nails clutching the spinning earth. The blood pounded in his neck as he watched the animal watch him. The rabbit quivered as if its tiny atomic heart was too great a thing to bear. He could see it beating below its pelt. And indeed, he thought it was perhaps not a mere heart at all but a subtler more exquisite and imponderable thing precisely composed to re-time the volatile world to the mystery of the something holier. Its nose was working sideways, whiskers swept back in line with its flattened ears.

"Now when I run. You run too," he whispered. The rabbit sniffed at the changing air.

The dogs went to barking now. He heard men yelling "cease fire," and he got up in the melee and ran for his life. He went bounding around the side of the spur to the first trail and fixed himself like a pinball in a side race against the slope burning through the open ground for the next tree line with his footfalls clapping dull on cobbles punched up through the dirt. The helicopter hung stable over Denny and Sor, their packs and teams. With luck he'd have about ten minutes while they argued over which of them was responsible. The trunks of trees dull and brown and wired with old yellow sap passed in a blur.

Quiet again. No more tricks. You just run and run and make the distance, he told himself.

Clouds churned above him. He could smell the lightning and desert dust saturating and charging unseen circuits of silica and iron, blood and ether. The psychosphere. Tails of the knife's lanyard snapped at the back of his hand every other step till it stung. He disappeared to himself in an ancient alkahest of terror and adrenaline, and a half hour later he was grinding up the last climb, the thunder bellowing down.

Through the trees he could see the low pass between the slope he had come around and where the chain of mountains climbed and went on climbing some distance to the south. It was green in the draw and was green down the other side to the slots beyond. Then it was just red desert stretched to the horizon. A few shots broke the air over his head. The mercenaries were only toying with him, he hoped. He didn't look back. He counted breaths to forty and started again. At the crest there was the pitched sound of the turbine working as it struggled in the fluctuating drafts. He still didn't look back. The helicopter came down level to where he was running. It cantilevered against the pouring rain and the wind. The sliding door was open and Rod was inside sighting a scoped rifle clipped into a web of elastic stabilizers. He squeezed off a round and three more in short succession. The echoes were dull in the canyon, barometer still falling. Let it fall. The bullets snapped at the trees and spalled into lead starfish on the rocks.

Grayson kept going. At the top he clawed the ground. With his hands and toes gripping, he pushed until he flopped over to the other side. He lay feeling his heart hammering through his ribs into the rock beneath him as if it meant to imprint there a glyph of his trial: the hunter being hunted. The helo waiting was drowned in the thunder.

Out of the foothills and into the flats, Grayson let momentum carry him toward a patch of red slickrock canyon and chute perhaps a quarter mile wide and a half mile long. The lowland pines diminished, replaced with sage bolls swaying in the storm like ocean seaweed in a bottom current. Nothing else living moved. At the edge of the canyon where it got treacherous fast, he let the momentum fall away and went jogging along the perimeter until he came to a crimson mushroom of rock the size of a semi-truck. Smoothed and left suspended by immemorial floods on a crumbling twist of stalk he slowed to walk in and take the shade of its umbrage.

The great stone seemed to preside over the little canyon and as he passed within he saw winding slots and stone bridges encasing a grand bowl of smooth pink where the old boundless water had flowed and left a Martian amphitheater now collecting the rain and swelling the sound of the rain drops. A fence lizard came out on a boulder near his arm, cocking his scaly head to look up at the man and the sky and the sheer impossibility, the absolute size of the world stretched out to the edges of the known. The lizard just blinked and tested the air with his tongue and watched the man go past the cavity and merge into the chaparral.

Behind him the green rise of the mountain was nearly black under the kneaded clouds. Light mist fell on him and steam whirled off his shirt and waist where he was plastered with sweat, old blood, and rainwater. Loose leaves of the sage like feathers or grasshopper wings stuck to his legs. The dank musk wafted as he passed. The area around him shimmered in the play between the sun and clouds. Bits of the sand twinkled. The yucca and cacti seemed somehow reanimated, receptive. It occurred to him that he was quite high on his body's chemical cocktail.

He saw everything. He saw the very particles of everything.

Keep running, he thought.

The soft lines of the stormfront stretched down-gray on black to the north. Looking south he saw girthy veins of lightning that shot out crosswise to the earth and then sent blue, fractalated feelers down to the rim walls above the town and also into the mountains. Fires smoldered in the trees along the chain. He saw orange flames creeping in the undergrowth. The thunder cracked and roared. Seconds later, he could hear the men at the base of the mountain and the dogs howling.

Antelope sprang together now, way in the distance moving off a bare red shelf toward the next low area where they'd feed again before the storm pushed them off. After a while in the chaparral, his legs worked hard with a new wind. He fixated on the sound of his breath dragging in and out, his boots shushing in the sand. Actual thoughts swam away, drifted through. Just moving out into nothing and nowhere, and he had no other ideas but to keep going into that negated future. To make the distance and assume deliverance was out there in the forward dark of time.

He thought about the correlation between the presence of rain and the shifting ability of both men and dogs to track anything. Man, goat, hog—all take the easy route when possible. Locked on to his quarry, the tracker asks himself what he would do in that quarry's place: for water, for rest, to travel the straightest line. If he knows the thing well enough the tracker can out-guess that thing. As Grayson came around the patch of slickrock and saw the limping tracks of the monster hog in the sand, these thoughts of likely routes and least resistance and patterns lost or secreted, invented or inherited, took residence in his foremind. On the ground were cloven hollows in sets of four pressed deep in the top layer where it was wet. Over these sets was a consistent sweeping impression as if a blanket had been dragged over them.

At the farthest edge of the slickrock patch where the desert proper began and before him lay only the miasmatic rise and fall of sand and grey clouds merging he came upon the hulking red marbled carcass of the boar where it had given out. It looked like a fallen meteor. Its black nose was pushed up in the sand where it had slid and collapsed. Vapors rising in the cooling air. Its eyes were closed, peaceful. The thing that had looked like a blanket dragging over its tracks was its burnt leather hide, which had been all but stripped, attached only at the raw rear haunches. It wore an adornment of green or gold leaves from the mountain and thatches of pine needles like medals and service ribbons. There were already ants investigating splayed globules of the exposed fatty flesh. He didn't believe in omens, as such, but he stood there a moment contemplating all the same. He thought of the hunting of men. How some of the hunted fell and others slipped from their pursuers. Into villages of peasants, farmers, and tinkers.

Grayson had nowhere to disappear. When his mind was ordered, consequences refreshed, and when the smell got to him, he strode away to the entrance of the actual desert where his postulations would be hammered out and he ran on with nothing but his knife.

Behind him, the trackers were coming down from the pass. The Malinois were led like extensions of the men. By command they would trot, run, or walk just until the leashes tightened up.

They would pull a bit when they caught Grayson's scent on a back draft and their master would mutter something, not even a proper word, and they'd slacken the leash and go on at the man's pace. Had Sor let them loose they would close the distance in minutes and tear him apart. But it appeared Sor preferred the wild hunt.

When the team reached the carcass of the pig and the dogs had to be reared, Grayson was on the first rise looking back and watching them gather around. The dogs' barking came across the flatland in hungry piercing squawks. He thought he'd watch the team for a moment longer to see just how good they were. If they were tiring at all and if the hog might hold their interest any length of time. It did not. A motion was made and in a second or two the tracking team was fanned out ahead of Sor and moving. Not really even studying the ground as there was no need but just trucking steadily forward on the trail evident in the wet sand. They advanced in the formation of an inverted arrow: flanks farthest up the track, tracker and a team leader back at the peak of the arrowhead, a security element trailing in the rear. Sor and the dogs comprised the rear security, and they all militated through the boulders and up the tables of rock and through the mist. Where Grayson had changed direction, the flanks would pick up his prints in a track trap of sand or in a little wash and they would signal and the formation would rearrange on the line and roll forward as if the whole thing was just a march, an exercise.

Oh, they're good at this, alright. In that moment, bent at the waist with his hands down on his knees and his head cocked up to see down upon them, he tried to think about how this would play it out if it were reversed. If he was hunting himself how would he do it exactly? He cast his eyes out into the empty basin where there was nothing but impartial land upon which they would hunt him. Whether in the islands of rock jumble or the open land the contest was not going to last long. He decided he didn't really want to think about how it would play out. The options weren't good. When he spun back, the teams had seemed to halve the distance. He could make out their faces, the machined lines of their rifles.

As he ran, he felt the wind push at his back. Let it push. The storm was catching him. Which meant it had probably already caught them. Over his shoulder, he guessed the distance gap somewhere between a half mile and a mile. When it rains they'll shelter. They're still hungover some of them.

They'll rest until it passes and then try and catch you with the dogs if the tracks are washed away.

Grayson ran on but his breath was getting dry and ragged and his head screamed for water. On through the drizzle and just chipping away at it going up the hills. He tripped twice and once dropped the knife skittering across a plate of slick rock and slipped again it its retrieval. He got up and drove on. Somewhere in his mind he knew that the next place to catch the river was twenty, maybe thirty, miles away. He'd have to cross the geological schism that was the Arches park. Or he could try skirting the park to the south. Either way, the distance would probably kill him.

On he went, counting breaths to forty, forgetting and reminding himself to start again. The rain started coming down hard. He slogged on until the pellets of water came down in slops and little creeks formed in the washes. The heavy shower trailed hunter and hunted alike for fifteen solid minutes. When he felt it let up a bit he was all but walking and hauled five or six extra pounds of water weight and the whole divided world— grey slate above and red rock below— stretched out in a long pulsing vertigo to his eyes and quickened in the margin between observer and observed as the saturated air hovered in strange half-light, neither falling nor rising. On the low side of a smallish plateau, he stopped and turned and walked back to see if anywhere he might see the trackers. Nothing but the same great division. If you're gonna dig down now would be the time. He went back down the side slicking the water off his face and arms and kept running. Twenty minutes more and he collapsed into a sandy wet bank heaving breath. The distance gap was just shy of two miles.

He got up and walked toward the west where there was a rock shelf he could crawl under. The pants and shirt stuck to him in every place. The back of his tongue felt like something that had been beaten raw with a mallet and salted. The rain was running off the ledge in a rivulet, and he got over to it and put two fingers there so the rivulet caught and trickled down his purple hand off into his mouth. Five minutes this went on with him frozen there on his knees like some bizarre backland ritualist, improvising mudra to the sky, running the water into his face until finally his hips got to shaking so badly he thought he'd cramp up and he whipped the water off his hand and fell back. The sky thundered out on the hardpan where the storm had moved.

Lightning coursed in the foreground, ripped through the sheets of rain. White cords of it sought the ground, where they would hit, pooling for a blue instant before snapping away, leaving a strange charged place on the hardpan that his eyes wouldn't focus on clearly as if the place, momentarily, did not quite exist. He watched it all, still heaving. Smells of scorched earth and cactus carried through. The water settled in his stomach and he sat up.

In his pocket he had the Bic lighter and a single drip emitter from the day he and Phil had put the irrigation system back together. The emitter, a black and green plastic nipple—for a minute he was somewhere else, twirling this reminder between his fingers, but staring at a spot in the air between his nose and the mushy sand at his feet.

He shook his head to get out of the past. There was a faded brown bandana in his back pocket that he let soak up the water at the rivulet and he sat working away what was left of the caked blood and crust around his face and ears and along the side of his distorted hand. That's enough, get up, he thought and he got up and wrapped the paracord lanyard around his wrist and walked across the wash and up the little plateau to look back along his trail. Light rain was collecting in the places where he'd broken the surface crust but already it was also smoothing the edges. If this kept up there'd be very little indication he had crossed through here.

Dogs don't need to see to track, though.

Through the lessening rain he saw no movement. The horseshoe shape of the storm was driving one dire curved arm down from the mountainside and out across the first foothills and the reciprocal arm banked the north and extended east and beyond him toward Castle Valley.

As he went, he imagined his trackers. Imagined the Malinois dogs sitting next to each other under the tarp looking out into the storm—probably imagining him likewise. He saw in his mind how the leader Sor had the small tarp in a hasty Whelan configuration as he rested his back against his rucksack. The warmth of the dogs were around him. The feeling of space to operate. The knowledge that your quarry is close. Food, water. Tobacco. He imagined the other men were likewise set up in a nest of rocks beneath their little survival tarps. Some of them eating, other smoking. And yet others just resting their eyes. All with their rifles cradled in their laps or against their legs out of the rain like bouquets of dark flowers that must be delivered on time.

Yep, that's probably about right, he figured and kept moving.

He chased the rear of the falling rain clouds until they veered south. Then the sense of moisture on the air simply stopped. The wind picked up. He kept on toward the outer edge of the park. The sand was already starting to dry. Older, rounded slots emerged out of the wet slickrock hills. Just running. Like an old goat or an old man. The mercenaries were now running too.

They'll probably lose you on that rocky rise. They'll slow and stop, do a lost track drill and find those boot heel impressions you made under the ledge. It'll be a flanker who finds it. He'll hold the hand signal, go to studying the ground and others will stand security and watch the horizon. Then he'll find the line, call the play and they'll roll on.

In his mind, he could hear the dogs' nails scratch along the boulders. He saw a man slip and catch up as they went leap-frogging ahead on the line, one forging forward on the tracks and signaling those in the rear to keep pace. That's how you close the distance. At a red trough of slickrock smooth as bloodgutters, Grayson went off the trail and didn't look back and just dove headlong down the rock face as if it were a playground slide. His hands went out to stop him and raked over sharp edges. At the base he pushed off hard and rolled out onto the sandy wash and got up and ran and stepped onto the first trail he came to and bore down. The trail took him off south for a hundred burning yards to an outcropping. He climbed some boulders, hopped off to another trail and kept going. Ten minutes later, he came to an overlook and a parking lot. Green trash can kicked over in the corner, Forest Service placard fogged out. In the garbage were tracks of coyote and vulture fresh in the drying sand. There was no sensation in his feet and he was wobbling with every step, heaving. He got behind those tracks and started up again, lagging through the sand and up the rise. Looking back out over the lot and past the slickrock into the chaparral, he saw the trackers jogging in the heat riffles and the dying fog, hunting a vision of his death.

Little glass beads formed on Grayson's eyebrows and lashes. Their velocity seemed illogical, too great. Impossible.

The rise dropped back again into another sandstone and slickrock valley of slot canyons at least twice the size of any he'd seen yet. It looked like a great heap of petrified intestines. There were dark shadows where the coral half tubes wove away innumerable into old depths or broke up into smaller slots and tunnels and chutes going who knew where. No design and no exit. Above the slots were pagodas and tufts, spires and pinecone shapes of red rock. The shapes were drying in the sun. The temperature rose. All of a sudden a desert again. He went slipping down the side of the valley and ran over the terracing to the first cavity. Some twenty feet to the base. The insects were out again.

Behind him the trackers grinded out a dark cadence as they ran. His personal death ballad. Or they were laughing, he couldn't know. He started down the nearest slot, spine and feet wedged. He dropped the last couple feet down into a fetid green puddle. A damp odor of algae and bird droppings. With great care he stepped through the water. A shoal of larvae woke in the ripples.

Don't splash, he told himself. He heard the trackers come to the rise one by one and he heard Sor speak to the dogs. They were smacking their mouths, whining and grumbling.

Someone said, "MacIntosh, hold one."

Grayson was moving through the first bottleneck, crawling.

This man MacIntosh said, "Hurry up, they're going in."

All this talk was warped, as in a hydrophone. The slots were labyrinthine. He crept forward. Dark and then light, dry and then puddled. Mosquitoes rose around his legs. A single band of light wreathed the tops of the slots, stark and plain as they coiled and curved, shrank and grew with no discernable pattern. The voices of the mercenaries carried over and through the slotted tubes of rock twisting in and through the maze like air through a pipe organ.

Then he heard the actual scratching of the dog's nails on the rock when they were released. It was unmistakable. They did not bark. He spilled out of the bottleneck and started running again. Slamming into tight corners. He heard them crying his blood, bedeviling him. Negotiating with how to get down into the first tubes. He heard them skidding down the side of a wall and splashing. There was cheering from the men. He rounded a bend out of a deep chute.

One of the trackers yelled, "You hear him in there?"

They were calling back and forth. His feet mashed the sand as he ran. The sound amplified and distorted through the coiled tunnels. It felt as if he were in a hide drum or the chambers of his own heart as there was no demarcation between his feet running and the blood slamming in his ears. And then he heard the dogs go down the next coil and into the water and they went splashing through the curves one behind the other like frenzied sharks thrashing at the bottom of a deep well. He ran and hit a dead end. He traced his hand over the sandpaper wall and it crumbled. At his feet were the scattered, bleached bones of a hornless antelope or white tail, the teeth were intact in the skull half buried and one hollow socket spilled with red sand. Going back, he made the other turn and ran forward to a place where the ancient sea water would have dropped down lower to an aquatic floor, a wide gully weaving north and south. The walls up the sides were some twenty feet, maybe forty on the other. Smooth face, almost nothing to climb. All rounded off and laced with white fossil chips of fish and bird.

There was a moment of silence. The air here was cool. The blood throbbed in his neck. Flighty chemicals of panic seeped, unmistakable—the metallic taste of it in the back of his throat.

The dogs barked and it warbled through the crinkled trench. They were just a slot or two over. He stuffed the knife in his waistband and scrambled up a boulder looking for somewhere to start climbing. The dogs came around the last turn slavering and they saw him and their eyes shined. His hands and feet were operating on their own. His stomach went void, featherweight as if there were nothing to him at all. The black blur of the dogs overrode all until he was only his fingers scratching for a hold. He felt the blood of abrasions emerge over his wrist gritty and warm and wet. In periphery he saw their sleek bodies closing and he thought: *protect your neck.* The first dog bounded up the boulder and leapt snapping at him. It brushed his boot, came down awkward on the boulder and slid away. The second Malinois was right behind. Clear drool poured from one corner of its jaws. It was everything he could do to get his other hand up into something like a grip, anything. He dangled from a crumbling little shelf. They were barking and flaring their teeth and snarling. The second dog slipped off the boulder and landed on the first. He got his feet anchored and pulled. At the top he flopped over holding the purple forearm to his chest and rubbing it absently. Sweat in his eyes. The dogs were quiet below. Just the sound of their panting. He had his back to the ledge and his legs splayed and for a moment he saw the sky above the rock spindles as if he were looking up from a grave.

When he rolled over he heard from far off, the man named MacIntosh call out over the maze of slots: "Got him, eyes on."

Jesus. Over his shoulder Grayson could just see the man with the rifle trained on him. Two hundred yards, two fifty maybe. His head went back down among the rocks. Feeling both immense gratitude and diluted rage he wondered absently if anyone in all of history had rested on this precise ledge as he was doing now. Déjà vu washed over him as if in reply. The relevance and ordering sense of time ceased. There was only himself and a slip of sky above the red canyon. From those two hundred yards off, the rifle trained on him roared and the interior spell, the intimation of something sacred, was erased instantly and he slunk away along the ledge laughing very softly for reasons unknown even to him. He came out on the narrow ridge in the open. He was running, with no clue where he'd end up.

* * *

Grayson ran along the trail, picking over crags and yardangs. The ridge rose. He climbed. And the dogs followed him with their eyes until he disappeared leaving the trail for the next mesa. They whined for him through the breeze that was stirring after the storm. The temperature dropped fast as the evening approached. Out to the west, the dark clouds made strata above a bright strip of yellow light along a horizon sawtoothed by a distant mountain range. The mercenaries would be stuck going over the wall or through the slots. Either way it wouldn't buy much time. The dogs had lingered down in the gully looking at the area of space where they'd last seen him, as if he might reappear. They sniffed the ground, and after a while they went on ahead in the gully to where it spilled out and turned right, going east. They knew full well that this was Grayson's direction of travel and pursuing him was the job with which they were tasked. They ran and ran through the twilight and into the dark for their master until at some point they split-- with one going off onto the hardpan chasing gusts, the scent of man. The other kept to the mesa.

Grayson drove on rambling over the rock and sand keeping to the huge slab where he could until there was no light. An hour slog and he turned down the lip and walked on to the first overhang and crawled under the shelf and flashed the lighter once to see how deep it was and if any creature had already taken up residence.

Deep enough. He pulled a few small boulders to one side to build a half-ass wind break. This was the far side of the park, the outer edge, he realized. The flatland stretched out to the horizon, going toward Arizona. He watched the day wink out. His head and hand were aching. There was hardly any feeling at all in the rest of him. It took an effort just to swallow. He figured he had a day more without water and then he'd die. If it got much colder he'd have to think hard about a fire. He imagined the dogs out there walking zigzags in the night, searching for him. Though he knew doubtless they would kill him if they could, for the dogs, he felt no animosity.

And what could you say about those dogs' minds with their master so far away and their mission unaccomplished? Grayson thought they couldn't know anything of self-pity, or perhaps even of self, and that their one long moment, days upon days, was lived with no notion of death and with no sliver of their great giving hearts available to the fear of death's arrival. They would simply go forward through pain and distance yet at each step love their pack—man or beast. When he heard the coyotes, crying, loping alone out there miles off, he knew they heard it too and he shivered. And while he vacillated between water and fire and sleep, one of the dogs sat resting lopsided with a single hind leg stretched on some slickrock not five hundred yards from the ledge he lay under. The other was distant and roving. But this one stayed to finish the job and alone in the dark with his rear end in the sand he let his tongue hang out wide and when he sorted a particular scent out of the matrix he would blink and swallow to categorize it and go on panting. The wind shifted and he caught Grayson's particular odor and took off along the edge knowing only the mission and nearness of its promise.

Grayson built up the wind break with more rocks and tucked his legs up tighter. He quaked against the ledge. The wind whistled through the break and went slack and he heard the sand churning. He raised his head up just as the Malinois got to the ledge. It growled and lunged down. All he saw was the shaggy and shadowed outline of its shoulders coming at him. The noise in the dog's throat was worse. He scrambled his legs to push back under the ledge and kick at the beast at the same time. The teeth glowed yellow in the moonlight, pink tongue licking away the slather. It dug at the sand to make room for itself and pushed deeper into the crevasse. It barking and Grayson yelling, their twined voices were caught against the ledge and whipped away in the wind coming down. Grayson's spine was pushed up against the rock. It was as far back as he could get. He snapped his heel out hard against its jaw and it squirmed and backed out.

The dog was mad now. It tried higher up the ledge with no luck and came right back. The knife had fallen somewhere. He felt around for it but came up dry. The Malinois bowed up and dove halfway back under the ledge trying to steer over to grab his knee in its jaws and got stuck against the underside of the ledge, growling and trying to wriggle out. It lunged in at an awkward angle and got ahold of his side and sank its teeth through the skin pulling it away from his ribs. A black wave swept over him. Unreal force. He groaned and twisted away and screamed to come back and got his hand on the high side of its head in the thick black hair but it wriggled out again. It probed from the other side, trying short forays into the cavity, popping its mouth and scratching the sand. Grayson pushed himself back. Pulled his legs in tight to give it space. He waited a second for it to try digging again. Ears flatted back and its gums showed over the teeth as it slashed in at him. Grayson came down with his far hand on the pack of muscle at its shoulders and the jaws snapped up and bashed the ledge hard enough to break one of the incisor teeth away. He got one hand behind its head pulling on the loose skin. Its nails scratched on the ceiling to find a hold. And he pressed the snout down and away with his other hand and hauled it up on its back between his legs as if it were a child or lover snatched up from a rushing river. It snarled and bucked every way. He planted his feet and pulled it onto his chest and roped his purple forearm over its throat as he brought it close. Sweet breath steamed in the tight space as he closed the windpipe. The dog tried to yank its lower body away, claws slipping away in the sand and on the craggy ledge.

The smell of fear and sweat and damp rock all over. The dog wheezed and Grayson clamped a bit more and pulled it closer until he could feel the notches of its spine in his own breastbone. It got its legs under itself and tried pressing away. In the dog's ear he groaned the word--*Sleep*.

The dog went limp and the chest rose and fell under his arm. Against his chin. The scent of the fur, rain soaked and dried. Grayson lay there a moment longer collecting himself. The windbreak was broken away. He crawled out over the rocks and found the knife where it was pushed out to the front of the overhang and half buried. He picked it up and shook the sand off and unsheathed it and shook the sheath and wiped the blade on his arm. There was sand in his ears and nose and down his pants. He brushed himself off and dropped back on one knee. His entire body quaked. The lighter flicked and he held it away to let the light glow and held the knife in the off-hand low to the ground. Little puffs of air in the sand and dust at the black nostrils.

"Fourteen thousand years of friendship and this is how you treat me." Upright again, it was cold and dark. He sheathed the knife and walked out about a hundred yards into the flat scrubland and sat on a rock breathing hard and looking back at the ledge. And it was as if the two, man and beast, had arranged perhaps in some other realm, and by strange means, to collide and change positions of this night. A few minutes passed and he heard it scratch and clamber out and he watched shadows of the Malinois skitter a bit as it gained its equilibrium. Then he watched it take off back toward the gully and disappear.

The breeze picked up. He stuck the sheathed knife back in his waistband. Big Dipper, North Star, he pivoted and set out east. When his natural night vision got settled in, he found a deer trail and walked it toward a yet further mesa. The mesa he knew would drop onto the highway at some point. The highway he knew would take him to Castle Valley. After that he didn't know. At each drop or rise in the chaparral the mesa appeared farther away.

Hallucinations were just fine with him, and they came austere and direct: off to his left, in the mad light of the moon refracting in the silica and shimmering on the thorns of silver cholla and prickly pear it seemed something horned--drauger or magus--was matching him step for step, playing with him, making mincing slashes in the blue air with the pronged horns. As Grayson trundled forward delirious and parched, the trail beneath his feet stretched and wobbled in scintillating shadows. He kept his eyes fixed on the trail and at some point the landscape began to glow with a green fire that grew contiguous, quickening between the grey tufts of sedge grass and the starveling pines. The trail undulated and flared out to the looping twists of manzanita trunks and became so bright that he stopped and submitted to stare at one of these small wind-twisted trees burning with secret light. After a while he marched on and swung both arms in a kind of locomotive unison that forced propulsion to his mindless feet.

This rhythm came to feel essential, critical even. *Orion's Belt, Cassiopeia, move on.* His legs felt absent, almost external-- as if some vestibular circuit between his awareness, his spine, and the crystal mineral ground was overtaking or merging with his will.

Vague bits of what he recognized as his authentic being, his true depths, floated in like sleeping cranes or egrets adrift on the waved surface of his mind. But they were nothing on the order of proper thoughts and seemed rather to be signals transmitted over great distance. And once received in consciousness, these missives required translation from an older language to his own. The visual feast calmed and left just the compulsion to make the coordinated motion of his feet and breath and the swinging hands continue to exist. Stillness is not death, he thought. But keep moving nonetheless. Let the engine run whatever be the price. You pay on both roads. Either in the day by the day's measures or by the night with its oddities and irreducibility, its broken vows and quarklight.

* * *

In the morning, Grayson was draped twenty feet up on an island of solid slickrock that stood out in the open sand of the desert like the offal of a shipwreck. The sun was still close to the horizon and there were tiny tracks of mice in his rain-splotched bed of dust where they had come to sniff him in the early morning and gone hungry back into their holes. A residue of scum and debris stretched over the ground below the rock where a flood had passed the day before. The stench of rotted plant matter wafted in the breeze, and he felt he would puke but didn't know if he could move to do it and so just retched over the side. Dry heaves carried on until he was wrung out and he lay and breathed rank air and shivered for ten minutes against his nest of stone.

A hundred yards down the rock island he found the limp carcass of a fawn. It was balled up in a cup of moist twigs and branches as if laid in a basket and set out for him. One of the forelegs hung wrong when he picked it up and he saw it was attached only by a little string of tendon that was all washed and the bone stood out white. He carried it in one arm to the shade cast by the rocks and went back to find tinder and dry fuel. When he returned, he shaved the tinder with the knife into a good pile and prepared the dry branches of manzanita and some of oak in categories of size and dryness. He ran the blade up along the spine to take the straps and scored the skin around the back quarters and pulled the hooves to snap the hips out the sockets. When he had the straps laid in a bed of coals he walked back out along the rock seeking water that might be pooled in the shade of the ledge. When he found some he stripped his shirt, wound it around a few times and went hands and knees soaking the water out of the scoop with the twisted end and twisting it again into his mouth. He came back and flipped the venison. As he waited he arranged some flat rocks into the coals to cook the thighs and then went back up the rock island to see if the trackers were on him yet but there was nothing moving save the crows crossing toward the valley in pairs and cawing before they dipped out of sight beyond the chaparral. Helical tracks of Mojave or Diamondback were woven over the sand that way.

He listened for the Apache helo or other vehicles but there was nothing of the sort. Just the unnerving, indiscriminate winding sound of the desert waking. The insects whirring, the dew evaporating out of cracked rock, all under the sun's blistering ritual assault on the basin in every quarter. When he'd eaten the straps and the thighs and licked his knife clean he tested the rock to see it had cooled and then licked it too of grease. Then he stood and kicked out the coals and buried the carcass in wet sand and started walking over the rise, shaking his head to the real and breathing in counts of forty.

By midmorning he was famished and thirsty all over again and crossing a last bit of scrubland at the foot of a rising mesa that he figured lay somewhere inside the park. Halfway up the mesa he heard dogs barking like they were in a big soup can. Near enough. At the top he looked out expecting to see the river ahead yet there was none but rising mesa and the running slide of red monolith. To his right this great derangement of patchwork cliff and valley and post pile crumbled gully wove on for tens of impenetrable miles. To his left in the distance were the La Sals from where he'd come.

Looking at the terrain strategically he thought, "Now to this, your grave and gravestone."

The mercenaries were less than a half mile out just coming off the edge of the park. They were in the shade of a crescent rock wall and jogging. They had let the dogs run ahead. The Africans' faces were shining in sweat and showed no sign of wear. They all kept coming and he watched them cross the flats to the base of the mesa where his tracks wore out. When the trackers were twenty meters or so from his mesa, Grayson crouched. They looked at where he had gone up and laughed. In moments they dispersed squads on both downward sides of the mesa and set up for a break. If he wasn't pinned before, he was now. There was nowhere to go. 102 degrees, no water.

Even the ridge where Grayson was tucked in rose and fell everywhere in square crumbling columns where bat and bird guano ran down the interior sides collecting in crusted patties at the floor around his feet. There was an alley in the middle of the ridge, the column walls of which would provide relative cover from their gunfire on three sides—four in some places.

He could see through the cracks in the columns as in a parapet. He looked down from between two pillars and spotted the team on that side was set out from the mesa wall under a couple of tarps erected against the sun. In terms of attitude they looked like men recovering from a practice session of soccer, drinking water and joking. Stretching their legs. The gear and their weapons were piled at their feet. The dogs drank from collapsible rubber bowls as Sor inspected their feet. The men ate granola bars and sucked peanut butter and florescent cheese from green foil tubes between jokes. Brief radio transmissions relayed the conditions of their chase to the base back in the mountains.

Grayson rolled over and pulled through a tight space to where there was a reciprocal crack to look through on that side. The other team was almost directly below him, nearer to the wall. In a moment he could smell their sweat and make out the clamshell patterns of their boot soles in the cup of dust where they sat. Some of them were fanning away the mosquitoes. One had pinched in his fingers a small wayward cicada and was holding it in the light for inspection. The man named MacIntosh was off to the right watching the valley through his scope and smoking a cigarette that he wedged into the heat vents on the forearm of the rifle. If he went east, Grayson would be running in the open. The men on the first side would just take turns until one of them hit him. They could leave him for the coyotes and mice or come up the hill at leisure to exercise the dogs on his corpse. If he went west, he would have to drop right down practically on top of MacIntosh and the others and that would bring the end even faster.

Grayson relaxed onto his back and breathed as one would in a jail cell or upon an operating table. He ate the last of the deer meat from his pocket--lint and all--and wiped some of the grease into the leather sheath and some into his cracked lips and looked at the sky. No rain today. He thought about how he might take a few of his killers with him. He thought about where Phil might be, what he'd say. Disembodied voices from below spoke, and he listened.

One of them said, "We had these hajis in Bamyan province one time. Way out from the FOB. The whole fucking place was mountain after mountain. This was '08 or '09 maybe. Four days of running and hiking up and down, up and down 'till we finally run them to ground."

"You have dogs?" asked the other man.

"No but it was a real tracking team—salty Green Berets, some intel dudes and the indigs. The dogs would have died at that altitude anyway, I swear to God. Four days. No resupply, no air support. Just that team and the hajis leaving fuck-all for tracks. That was a truly wild hunt."

A moment passed and then he heard: "What happened, did you get 'em?"

"Finally. They ran out on some promontory just like this dude here and got stuck. We found them frozen solid about twelve, maybe thirteen thousand feet up. Those fuckers were curled up together like babies in a crib. Three more days of boogie back to the FOB."

A radio squawked. The men hushed. Grayson heard rustling of gear, garbled noise.

"Those dogs are done run out," one of them said when he was off the radio.

"Ran all night didn't they? Crazy sumbitches."

"So did he," one of them said in reference to Grayson.

Several minutes passed in silence. Grayson rolled back over and snaked his way down to where there was another opening in the rock wall. When he got there and looked down the line of boulders, he realized it was climbable. It would have been an exit. But now it was wide open to the rifles on that side. He rolled back over and folded his hands over his chest. The thought that he had done exactly what everyone always does occurred to him: as the tracker you just let them run, you keep the pressure on, and they'll make their own mistakes.

"And you surely made a mistake," Grayson said in a quiet voice.

He heard them talking again on the north side. He crawled back through the alley of columns until he could see and hear and he cocked his head and heard one of them say "You won't need it."

The other voice said, "Fuck that. If I assault I carry mags. It's the principle of the thing."

So here they come.

"Save something for the TV," the first man said. "The helo is gonna pick his body up. Seriously though, hit him center mass or in the hips. That way they can show his face and it'll match his driver's license."

"Copy that."

Through the other side Grayson saw the dogs still panting under one of the tarps. A few men sat beside them. Four others had already moved. The crags where Grayson had come up an hour before, and where they would come up now, terminated at a boulder the size of a sedan. It obscured his seeing them for the moment.

And vice versa. Unless he stuck his head out. The crag wasn't technical climbing but it was hands-on in a few places. He listened and watched, lying on his stomach. One of the Americans was scouting for him up there through binoculars. An African who had traded his battle dress shirt for a tank top and had long vertical scars of pink keloid on his shoulders and biceps had his hands held like a visor over his face. Grayson thought he heard this man ask in a soft voice if anyone had seen the goat yet. The angle and direction the African faced as he watched his teammates ascend indicated the men were still near the base of the mesa. This was not the case. Sor and MacIntosh and the three other men climbing were about halfway up the route but Grayson still couldn't see them. By their voices and the scrabble of their boots over the rock it was clear they were coming.

The channel where he was tucked in went down behind him in a straight line. In front, it curved on a smooth column before the slick rock crag started and went down to the north. *This is where they'd come up*, he thought. He crept to the big boulder and pulled himself up and stooped and unsheathed the knife and tucked the sheath in his back pocket. He switched the knife in his hand and picked up a fist size rock from the ground and threw it down the straight away. It hit the wall and fell back in the channel and he threw another and bounced it out over the side. A few seconds passed and the man they called Felton came over the radio to the men climbing,

"South end. Fifty meters from the top of that climb you're on." The voice was African, full of bass and with good English. Grayson heard both the report on one side and the report come through the speaker with a short lag on the other.

Sor was on the rock face with the rifle slung over his back. He clicked the radio just to confirm he had heard Felton and went on. Felton could see them on the rock and must have watched him click the radio. Grayson heard over the radio, "I'm gonna put one right over his head. Keep him down. Click to confirm. I got whores waiting in the next town."

MacIntosh was right behind Sor and could see Sor was at an awkward place for the radio so he clicked the radio for him and looked back at Felton. Felton was down in the prone position under the tarp with his hat turned around on his head to find the right eye relief as he sighted his rifle over his backpack. There was a sprig of sage clenched in his teeth like a toothpick that he pinched out and used in a forwarding gesture to indicate the assault team should proceed.

The sun was full on the men climbing and blasting off the rock face. MacIntosh waited at a landing and let Sor go through a tight series of vertical switchbacks. "Incoming," MacIntosh said.

Felton fired and the round pocked the lip of the ridge right over Grayson's head. The bullet ricocheted like a penny whistle over the mesa. He heard Sor or maybe MacIntosh yell, "Whoa." One of the men below on the other side clicked a radio.

The men below on the rock face laughed. Grayson heard MacIntosh yell. And when he heard it, realized he had it all backwards. They were coming up the other route. Grayson went back down the channel crouching, scrambling as low as he could. He heard the men that were close underneath say,

"Movement, movement twenty-five meters."

But he'd closed it to ten. Sor was breathing hard at the last push coming up on his hands and walking his feet with his legs straight and at the top he stood up straight and spun around to look back at MacIntosh. He took a step to balance, and the way it happened--the weight of the blade and the angle and momentum, it was as if Sor just sat back into the tip of the bush blade and Grayson pivoted and drove it to the hilt. Sor gasped as if his voice didn't work. Grayson brought his hand around over Sor's mouth and yanked and rode the blade deeper and pulled Sor around the column and out of sight of the men. The rifle was hung below where the knife went in and the handle was caught on the scope and the sling and he just rode it around as Sor flailed and hot blood sopped out onto the gravel and dust.

MacIntosh didn't see what happened. None of them did. MacIntosh looked up the hill at the space where Sor had been and said, "Yo?"

Behind the column, Sor was twisting around trying to reach back or push away and Grayson planted his feet, leaned him into the column as he twisted the knife down and pressed out towards both of their right hips. A purple slab of organ meat slid out of the wound. Sor found his voice and screamed through the hand over his mouth. Grayson pulled his arm tighter. MacIntosh was going up the boulders yelling, "Sor, Sor. What the fuck?'

Sheets of bright red blood pumped out over Sor's belt. They both slipped in the slickened stones and fell. He withdrew the knife and Sor rolled over in the dust with his head jacked up wrong against the boulder and Grayson's weight full on him. Sor's right hand was slapping at his thigh and hip reaching for his handgun. Grayson drove his free hand into the long gash on Sor's midsection. Wrist deep. And he swam it around through bulbs of pulsating organs until he felt ribs and muscle and took hold for leverage and torqued as he brought the knife up and slammed it down again below the pectoral. The mercenaries cried back and forth over the radios asking for "eyes on" and calling "man down." Up in the melee it was all white noise to Grayson. Sor bucked and each time he did the blade cut deeper. Grayson reefed on the knife but it was stuck in his ribs. Sor screamed and kept trying to get to the sidearm. He pushed Sor's hand from the holster but it came back. The knife wasn't coming out. MacIntosh was still yelling and scrambling up the rock face and trying to bring his rifle around all at once and the men below MacIntosh in the climb had their rifles sighted at the top of the climb scanning for a shot. Grayson dropped his weight at an angle on the handle of the blade and Sor's hand went to his chest and he wilted. Grayson snapped away the retention strap on the holster, pulled and had to bring the handgun so close to his own face that when the gun roared the muzzle blast burned his forehead and shards of Sor's teeth splashed back in his ear.

He half-stood and half- crouched over Sor's body crumpled in the channel. Cognizant of his margin for error Grayson held his breath to listen. Dogs whining and the wind vacuum in the channel. Scrabbling in the scree. MacIntosh crested the hill sucking air and Grayson stepped around the column and blew the man's brains back out into void where they rained down on the men below.

There was a wet smack and the sound of his femur breaking as MacIntosh's body impacted seconds later. His rifle snapped at the buffer tube and polymer pieces and springs and detents went off in all directions in the jumble. The dogs on the far side of the camp where they were tied up were near spastic and mad with unknowing, whining and quivering and looking at the men in the round who paid them no mind. Down below, a man was pinned in the rocks under MacIntosh's body and one of the Africans ran up and yanked the body aside to free the pinned man and then stepped forward and fired a string of rounds up the route. Felton had brought his rifle over and leveled it again on the backpack and began dropping most of a full magazine into the top of the climb and the first column. In the torrent Grayson pulled Sor's body over his shoulder and got down behind it as further cover. Blood was pooled everywhere and the pool was pulsing out to the edges where already it was being sucked down into the dust making a gritty paste. Bullets from Felton's side kept chipping away the stone one on top of another.

He cut the sling on Sor's Mk12 and brought it around. It looked fine. The scope was coated in blood but when he popped the lens covers the lenses were clear. He dropped the magazine and pulled the charging handle back enough to see the chambered round and rode the handle quietly back down. Shards and grit of the soft rock rained in the channel. Grayson looked up at the sky. A blank umbrella of bright, pacific blue. He crawled along to a crack between the rocks and set the rifle up being careful not to show the front lens. The whole desert went quiet for a moment. Behind the rifle, he slid his left hand over the front lens of the scope to limit the glare and inched it forward and sighted through his parted fingers to where Felton and another man were set up behind their packs and guns with their heads down. It occurred to Grayson that due to the angles of the ridge if he cleaned his pursuers out of one side or the other he could run again. Wait until they start firing so they can't place you. A few of the Africans had come over to pull away MacIntosh's body. He listened to hear if they were going back down the mesa or others were coming to help.

"This is motherfuck. Papsotnot." he heard one of them say.

And another, 'Yes, motherfuck. Moffie fuck soutpiel. Pull that arm. He dead as shit.' Grayson picked up a guano-laden rock and rolled to one side to lob it down on the men there at the base.

A moment later he heard in the accent, "Cover, cover. Voetsek, man."

The guns on that side tore up the columns and in the cover fire his rifle bucked lightly and the round snapped at Felton's shoulder. Even keel he squeezed off seven more rounds catching the impact through the scope each time and walking the rounds up the sides of both men as they tried to roll away. He let the trigger reset and watched them a moment writhing and scrambling for their med kits, then he angled the gun around and went to work at the rest picking them out in the rocks where they'd crawled or were crawling toward.

When he had spent the magazine, he snaked back down to Sor's body and went through his pockets. They kept calling for Felton on the radio. Sporadic fire on both sides. Gun smoke hung in the channel. A man answered on that side saying, "Djou ma se poes. Give a evac. Over."

They came back asking about Felton and the Afrikaner said, "Jou maaifoedie. Evac" and they stopped calling. Grayson tried the knife but it wouldn't budge.

"God dammit," he said and sat back down.

From Sor's pockets he pulled a granola bar and one spare rifle magazine. Two spares for the 1911. For a few minutes he sat there slack against the wall staring at the equipment and eating the granola bar with the crumbles spilling out on his chest. He picked these out of the folds of his shirt and ate them as the mercenaries went about reloading and tending the wounded. Plastic packaging unraveled and gunmetal bit into rock. Cries emanated when tourniquets went tight. He went back to Sor's body and steeled himself to get the knife out. He parted the warm flesh with his fingers and squinted in the blasting sun to see what was going on and he found that the blade was slid sideways between the sagging ribs. He sat back and finished the granola bar with his head against the rock column. *That knife's gotta give*, he thought. He got his foot on the slippery hump of the rib cage and dug in and heaved as he pressed down with the foot until the breastbone snapped and the ribcage bowed inward and up like pages of a magazine open on a table. A bubbly red sigh issued from the man's lips, and with a twist the knife popped free and he fell back into the column.

Getting the rifle down into a shooting position on the side where the dogs were was tougher, the angle was awkward. Given the juxtaposition of the mesa and the bowl, the vision of these men would be eclipsed once he started over the parallel ridge. But it seemed wise nonetheless to put some further reticence to them. With care only to avoid hitting the dogs, he emptied one full magazine out into the bowl. As his gunfire echoed he snapped the pins to get at the bolt and then went racing down the channel and out onto the ridge with Sor's pistol in one hand and his blooded knife in the other and a thoroughgoing sense of having stolen something back that had once been robbed of him. Or having awoken from a series of dread nightmares into some equitable minute. The spare magazines, the scope in its mount, and the charging handle and bolt carrier group were all bundled in a bloody satchel made from Sor's BDU shirt. The rifle was just too heavy for what he had to do, which was run flat out for as long as it took to find water and refuge. An African, one of the few men left with limbs to operate a rifle, went chipping at the rocks behind him for a few hundred yards. Grayson ran on.

5
The Hungry Ghost

He dreamed of the heedless French Quarter at night where he stood in the middle of the dimpled pavement as it rained, and a faceless throng passed him by in gibbering quartets and couples. The odor of urine and whiskey rose with the steam as it ran to the drain grates. A skilled band played ragtime somewhere nearby. The clarinet soared. Where is Phil? Looking up past the Creole houses, the sky burned dull orange as if the ocean was aflame. And then the dream jumped: he was on the mezzanine terrace looking down and across the street and through the open wood shutters of a bar backlit neon green. A long-bearded man sitting at the nearest booth transferred some elixir from a beaker to a flask that caught the neon light as he held it up to his face. The man knew he was being watched and turned to find him through the windowless frame.

The dream jumped again: who he thought was the same man was now standing outside the bar under the eave wearing the black cassock of a Russian Orthodox priest, and he was flanked by two more priests also in black but with red and gold vestments. The priest on the left raised his hand in a rhetorician's sign. Three fingers curled and the index straight up. *Wait one.* The clarinet tore through a minor anthology of melody fragments and then tightened and restored to the head. He thought maybe Phil could be in the audience, listening. A brunette stepped out on the adjacent balcony in white high heels. The rain was warm on his face. A featureless man stepped out on the other. In his hand was a white ballroom mask on a dowel. The priest in vestments still held the sign. The other priests spoke, but he couldn't hear their litany over the drums and hum. As the balconies across the street also filled with seemingly hatched onlookers, an awareness of the gears, the ontological clockworks, that had been extant in the firmament of the dream the whole time dawned on him. The gears churned and settled and a pendulous action transferred into the world of the dream with each, pulsing the vision as if it were all a gelatinous mirage set upon the gambrel of a great clocktower. Syncopated with the gears, the onlookers stationed in the balconies donned and passed and received the masks. The drums beat the time and the sky glowered orange as the rain fell down as it had in the desert, as it does at sea.

Before the dream, as he had approached the outlying neighborhoods in Castle Valley, he'd gone slow to avoid getting shot by fearful residents mistaking him for a threat. Then when he'd heard nothing but squirrels scratching in the olives and loose fence wire pulling in the wind. He had stumbled down to the first of the mauve and coriander colored adobe houses and tapped a single pane of glass from the backdoor with the handle of his knife and popped the lock. As he woke now, the shades were pulled and the windows beside the couch where he laid were open. The dim blue light of the moon and the clean alkaline breeze entered through the screen. He got up and went down the hallway and came back with a dog's tennis ball and an armful of pantry goods that he set down on the floor beside the bloody bundle made of Sor's shirt. In the kitchen he found a can opener and utensils, which he brought back with a green kitchen towel that smelled and felt clean. He opened the blinds on two sides, so the moonlight shone through to the floor and on the opposite wall in pale bands. He sat eating tuna fish and beans and drinking warm bottled water. When he was full, he laid out the towel on the floor and inventoried the bundle. On the towel he set the knife and the dull grey 1911 beside the lighter and the slobber slicked tennis ball and started unloading the spare magazines to inspect the rounds one by one and shake the dust from the springs.

Satisfied with the ammunition, he broke the pistol down inspecting the rails and wear and testing the trigger break to familiarize himself with its character. He itemized everything on the towel and reassembled the pistol. Then he set the ball out in the middle of the floor and laid down with it between his shoulders rolling out knots along his spine. It occurred to him based on the décor that these people would not likely have weapons, but they would have other gear he might need. And it occurred to him whatever his next moves would be, they would be moves made under great scrutiny. Even if he were to simply leave—Moab, Utah, Phil and his family, the country even—some part of him sensed he'd be hunted again because operations such as those taking place in America now, like those that took place in the Soviet Union in the century prior, are run ultimately by organizations that never relent, never clear accounts until the price is paid. But it never occurred to him to leave. For he knew perfectly well there in the hallucinatory dark of desert's moonlight, just as he had known in the false halogen light of the hospital when he'd made the promise, that you're either in or out. And when you're in don't even think about stopping. A promise is more than a hypothetical agreement. Dogs know this fact. A promise is a type of challenge to the darkness of the world. A promise is a source of light that burns in eternity if made good while those broken are inverted, swallowed in the expanding nothingness.

And so with the knots worked out of his muscles, he finished the last of a can of baked beans in barbeque sauce, prayed for good long spell, and then he reloaded the 1911 and got up to run again and kill whoever he had to kill or maim whoever he had to maim to get Phil and his family out of Moab.

He checked the garage before leaving and found a deep green Jeep Cherokee. No oil stains on the floors. The door squeaked but the inside was clean. When he had the back seats unhooked and set down flat, he went back inside and started loading cans and boxes of food from the pantry into milk crates, hauling them around the hall and out into the back of the Jeep. Upstairs he found two sleeping bags. Outside the bedroom was a chiffonier to match the grain and hue of the wood floor. There were photo albums on the surface that looked like they'd been powdered, and faint lines of a finger lay under the new dust. He caught his own face in the mirror. He looked just long enough to see who he was and who he was not then went on down the hall with the sleeping bags. The big garage door was automatic, but he popped the release and slid the lock and went outside through the regular side door with the pistol in his hand to watch the street for a minute before raising the big door up. The house was up on the wall in a little canyon with maybe a half mile to the river and the highway that mirrored it forty odd miles back to Moab. Opalescent winged ducks glided along above the river chattering in flight. The bats were slashing around the driveway and the street in expectation of the streetlights and the insects they brought with them. The constant low growl and wash of the river wearing away the rocks backstopped everything.

When he had the vehicle on the street he left the engine off and kept it in neutral until the stop sign at the highway. Past the river running green and fast, the cut gorge wall glowed pink and white where the minerals were banded, and past the wall an arcade of stars waited up there, bright and cold. Or they were already dead and what men saw in the iterant blinking was not the wait of starlight but its homecoming. Who could know?

* * *

As twilight fell, he pulled the Jeep off at the old hotel and restaurant on the east side of the highway and parked it in the back where the ivy grew over the brick and the fence and it might be missed by any looters. What few of them might remain. The hotel sat about a mile outside of town proper and had already been ransacked several times over. A few moldering bodies lay half-naked in the garden out front. Green shards of broken wine bottles were piled inches thick in places and charred ends of the wine box slats were scattered here and there in ash where cookfires had been made on the browning lawns. Grayson shouldered the requisitioned daypack with his diminished kit, pocketed the Jeep keys and went out to the highway with the pistol in his hand.

The river pounding the bedrock far below resonated in the cup of the gorge. The wind with the smell of the cane and marshland washed out the rank of carcasses. He went on wraithlike, scouting for a place to climb into the slope to bypass the guards stationed at the edge of town.

At a place on the east rim a few hundred yards into Moab proper, he stopped and shook off the pack to rummage out the scope from Sor's rifle. The sun burned away running clouds and the town was quiet. Through the scope he looked back over the roof and treelines skirting the highway at the changing of the guard. One of the aluminum work trailers was positioned over most of the southbound lane and abutted by concrete dividers. A Humvee was parked in the other lane facing back to town. It looked like they ran the radio through the vehicle as Africans were going from the trailer to the open door of the truck and sitting and smoking or talking into the handset during the exchange.

By 9am he crossed the highway at a dead run and kept going into the neighborhood where he had bought the solidox from the Navajo militia with Joe. Certain that the old Zimbabwean was correct about the deal having been recorded, he deliberated on how it had been accomplished as he strode on. The city park lawn was dead and brown and peppered with trash and downed limbs from the surrounding oaks. A few minutes later, he passed Munson's trailer. Two pairs of his black jeans and a cream-colored Levi's western shirt were still hung drifting on the clothesline. The sound of his boots in the pavement grit sent a coyote darting out from some mature azaleas lining the sidewalk. As it ran down the center of the street, amid the abandoned and burnt out vehicles, it carried in its mouth a Styrofoam flat of old ground beef that was green, yellow, oozing.

Grayson went on wading through the marshlands behind the mansion and clambered up over the rise at the portal and saw no tracks in the dust save those of hare and deer. The recon-style rifle was still in the hollow where he had left it along with the chest rig. In the half-light of the canyon he dusted and broke the recon gun down and inserted the bolt carrier group and the charging handle from Sor's MK12. He checked it for function and set it against the rock and went through the chest rig inspecting the magazines and the blowout kit. Tucked into a rear pouch of the rig was a half can of Copenhagen chewing tobacco and a folded glossy photograph of a young woman at a tropical outdoor bar, both of which he tossed into the hollow. He waited there for a while thinking and watching curve bill birds feed from sconce protrusions in the portal wall. When they flew off, he donned the rig and the pack and racked the rifle to charge it. Then he went back down the scramble and through the reedland to listen again for anything moving in the neighborhood.

In the preparatory months of work and training before Phil's child was born, Grayson and Phil would take lunch at a bakery where the owner swept the floors herself to make sure it was spotless and made the organic roast beef sandwiches to ensure they were perfect. A few blocks off Main Street, in the trees and the quiet neighborhood, they would sit outside among the flowering vines and feel luxurious with the sandwiches and a cup of coffee. Now abandoned and ransacked, Grayson approached this bakery with caution and went in the open back door in search of the phonebook. Addresses. Names.

Fifty-pound bags of flour had been cut and dumped from the kitchen through to the little sitting area and fragments of seafoam china platters lay among tracks of coyote and raccoon in the spilled white dust. Few of human. An egg-shaped wad of shrink-wrap the size of a heavy medicine ball had been placed on one of the bistro tables and when he looked through the layers at the dark center he saw the tortured and lifeless face of a tabby cat swaddled within.

He crossed the alley strewn with milk crates half melted from pallet fires that had blackened the cinderblock walls. Halfway across the loading pad of the next bombarded restaurant he paused and listened and then snapped the safety down on the rifle. A rat maybe. Squirrels. The back door was ajar, and he went through to the area of the walk-in freezer with the rifle shouldered to clear the corners. Written on a whiteboard over the sink: *Today's Special-Pork Tacos.* Down the hall he could see the hostess station and a stack of phonebooks on one of the shelves.

A backpack and .22 rifle lay awkward on the checkerboard hallway floor and a hushed voice from the dining room said, "Hold his damn head." There was a scuffling sound of boot leather and limbs on the floor, and he heard hot muted screaming as through a mouth held closed.

He double-checked back out in the alley and again down the hall at the pack and the gun. *I know that rifle,* he thought. Stone silent he stepped down the hall and peered through the cook's windowpass where at the base of one of the vinyl booths two grizzled transient men in careworn mismatched rags were clinched to a third smaller man with his pants down around his knees. The assailant nearest the naked man's head was sleeved in tattoos and he had the naked man wrapped full around in both arms and as the victim bucked and thrashed the second assailant kept trying—without success-- to hold his hips down and thrust into his clenched buttocks.

"Quit squirming, fucker."

This one who spoke was shirtless and a surgical scar as thick and pink as a nightcrawler ran straight from his xyphoid to his navel. He was trying to pin the victim's legs with his knees while grabbing around in the booth for something. In the hallway, Grayson glanced down at the grey poly cutting board and over the burners in the kitchen and then back to the dining area. The grimy tattooed assailant leaned back from the booth with a wire basket of oil and vinegar cruets in hand and proceeded to dispense the oil in a long golden stream over himself and along the cleft of the man's buttocks. When he was done he went to hammering the man's kidneys with a greasy fist and muttering, "Just relax."

The other man was reaching over with one hand trying to grab and spread the oiled white flesh as Grayson rounded the half-wall and the plastic ficus set there with an eight-inch bone cleaver in one hand and a cylindrical steel sharpener in the other. The man managed to say "Hey" just as Grayson skewered him through the right eye. He had driven the sharpener clean through to the back of the man's skull where it thumped hollow. In one fluid muscular motion, Grayson uncoiled and pivoted and slung the cleaver down on the nape of the other man's neck splitting it crosswise so the jet force of the arterial spray pushed his head over onto one shoulder. Grayson simply carried the momentum through as if bowing on a stage.

He stepped nimbly away from the red geyser as it splattered over the booth and wall. The headless man pitched forward flesh-to-flesh crushing Ben whose hands and elbows and naked body slipped in the blood and oil as he struggled to get up. He gasped and flailed, and Grayson kicked the body over and pulled Ben out of the slop by his heel as you might a baby from a bathtub.

He stood looking at the scene a moment and shaking his head in revulsion. Ben began blubbering. And because he was quite certain the youth had not been penetrated Grayson said, "You'll be alright. Clean up. I'll find some water."

Grayson let the cleaver clatter on the floor. He went out the back door again with the rifle to check the alley and let Ben get his pants on and collect his mind. When he came back Ben was cleaning himself with stiff dirty towels from the kitchen. Grayson shared his water bottle, sat down in a booth with the phonebooks and started thumbing through them for Bob's address. Ben sat down in the booth and cast his eyes over the gore in the diner. Grayson surveyed him for shock, asking him a few basic where-withal questions, looking for coherence. He thought Ben seemed fine, if embarrassed. Ben claimed he'd have killed the attackers if Grayson hadn't arrived and he went on to say he'd already killed one person in the previous weeks.

Grayson soothed him, "Of course you would have."

Ben's face was white.

Grayson weighed his options and said, "Let's get some air. Go sit in the back."

Ben glanced absently to the door. Grayson fished the Cherokee keys from his pocket and slid them over the table. 'It's at the old hotel. You're going to go there and try not to get seen and try not to let anybody run off with it. There's some food in the back of the bar but not much. Don't make a fire unless it's a tiny one. There're sleeping bags in the back you can use. What have you got in the pack?"

Grayson rose from the table and Ben followed. They sat in the dry gravel of the back lot where the tall brown weeds were grown up against several railroad ties laid down to mark off a parking area. He encouraged Ben to drink the water. "You want a cigarette?"

Ben nodded blank, slackjawed. Grayson said, "You very nearly ended your brief sojourn on earth right there." He gestured back through the open doorway to the slick red gloss and mangled bodies.

Ben winced a bit but it was if the thought of his death came from far off and even the wince was uncertain. It seemed that he might cry but perhaps could not bridge the gap between the actuality of the events playing out and what he was, in any genuine fashion, prepared to confront. *Adrift* is the word that came to Grayson's mind. Beyond the alleyway stray bits of paper trash carried along the neighborhood street in the breeze, weaving, tumbling, and floating amid the torched husks of a few cars. A small spotted dog trotted past on the sidewalk. Ben waited to see if it was followed but it was not. Grayson lit the cigarette, took a long drag and passed it over. He readjusted the rifle against the railroad tie so it could be raised quickly if necessary and let the kid smoke as he thumbed through the phonebook.

Five minutes passed and Ben, still with the slackened expression of shock and now scratching the thin hairs on his chin in a compulsive rhythm said, "This world is an asshole."

"Drink some more water. When's the last time you ate?"

Ben didn't answer. From his pack, Grayson assembled a small butane camp stove and for the next twenty minutes occupied himself with hydrating and cooking some powdered beans in a stainless steel cup. He considered lying to Ben, telling him that the world of men he referenced was not malicious. But it struck Grayson as a platitude so absurd not even this undisciplined kid would accept it—perhaps especially now. As well, given the suggestibility of Ben's probable condition, anything but the unvarnished truth seemed in some sense a cruel mistreatment. When the beans were ready, he set the cup on the railroad tie to cool and told the boy to eat—no discussion—and as Ben ate, Grayson rolled another smoke.

"Some people would tell you that you put yourself in that situation. You did. But they likely won't account for those other two putting themselves there the same. There're more people than you might think who'll without a second thought send you into the next world. Where, I'm gonna point out, the rules might be no different. Or they might be substantially less forgiving. They might be worse."

Ben was half done with the beans and shoveling them into his mouth. He said, "So what are you supposed to do? I didn't go in there to mess with those guys. The place was empty. I went in for food like any of the rest of us dipshits starving out here. They followed me in to fucking rape me? Jesus H Christ. If I'm out here starving and I find some girl starving too that doesn't mean I'm gonna rape her while I'm busy trying to eat. I was just hiding out in the park and thought of this restaurant. Thought that place was damn good, I wonder if they still have something stashed away. I'll check it out. They followed me in? Why? I didn't hear shit. So they fucking stalked me. Sweet Jesus they almost fucked me. God damn they almost fucked and killed me. I can't fathom it, man. What the hell would I do then?"

Tears of shame, frustration and fear welled up in the kid's eyes.

"I mean, what the fuck do you do then? You can't win in this life."

Grayson let him be for about five minutes. Watching the sway in the high limbs of the neighborhood trees bent with the weight of leaves that had turned partway orange he rolled another two cigarettes. With his thoughts set finally he said, "Look over here." He gestured for Ben to look at him. He paused when Ben met his eyes. What Ben saw there was a fearsome wordless form of human care—a staggering marriage of ferocity and kindness that he'd never seen before and would never see again. Grayson said, "What you do is simple and eternal. What you do is you fuck them up."

Ben vacillated--both grateful and terrified. He swallowed hard and returned to eating his beans. Wind whistled in the industrial hinges of the open back door of the café. Flies buzzed near the overhand. The sky was flawless blue above. When he was finished eating, Ben's eyes welled up again and he said, "This whole thing is so far past out of control, man."

Grayson listened, smoked. Ben lit the cigarette he'd been given and trailed it in a gesture traced between the open back door of the café and the direction of the city park as if he were retracing his steps, or silently retelling the story to himself. "Everyone always says it's about love. That's what they always say when people talk about heavy shit. The ultimate point of life or the way you're supposed to be living. I don't see why, if that's not true, that there's much point to anything at all. Especially now. Fuck it."

Grayson shifted the recon gun. "A skilled producer of a thing, a craftsman, if he can do so without compromising his creation, will oftentimes make a template of a certain process or some stage in the creation that he can continue to reuse in other applications. He can resize or retrofit how he pleases. He can use it as a sort of echo if he wants. In aesthetic terms you'd call it a theme."

"What are you talking about?" Ben asked.

"You ever see a frog's egg?"

"I don't know."

"You ever see a baby in utero?"

'Yeah in the sack. In pictures I've seen it.'

Grayson said, "Okay. Now imagine a planet and its atmosphere. Same thing. Patterns repeat at different levels. Branches of an oak tree in winter, branches of a mammal's nervous system. Same thing. So it should stand to some reason that if coming into this life is precarious and full of blood and pain and then life proceeds, you grow up and it seems totally without any discernable merit and it pretty much gets more variations of harder from there—if those two things are true--then likely it's going to be at least as tough to survive in the next plane as this one. Being that it's referenced as a higher plane, I conclude it's harder to survive. So if a man wanted to do the wise thing, he would spend his life in preparation for suffering and predation. Just in case."

Ben cast his eyes down at the packed gravel and the infinitude of miniature crevasses and hairline apertures between the stones. He fixated upon a battalion of tiny black sugar ants weaving black threads of their bodies among the tiny rocks and scaling their sheer faces and cigarette butts--the whole descaled landscape before them--with total commitment and a replete lack of what might be thought of as emotion or feeling. Grayson returned to flipping the pages in the phonebook, scouring.

A moment later Ben asked, "What do you mean harder to survive? How could it get any harder than this shit?"

King of Dogs

"Lonelier. Scarier. More dangerous. The stakes are intrinsically greater and maybe there's no one there to walk you through it, or to point out the learning curve. Maybe here, now, is your one shot at that kind of care and repetition. Because in the next life you're on your own. Who could know what terrible, merciless shit the future holds?"

Ben shuddered and looked away and quietly wept. A moment passed. The afternoon light seem shifted, filtering the world now in antique hues. Trash blew on the sidewalk. The tiny tireless ants on their mission wove elastic lines through the gravel that looked like mineral-rich shards of oyster shells in the uncommon light and the sound of the breeze sucked through hollow places in things— fences and walls.

When recollected to himself Ben wiped his eyes and said, "Thanks."

Grayson stood and slung his weapon.

* * *

The bluish glass panes in the big rollup doors from when the building had been a service station were papered out. A swamp cooler ran against the wall beside the entrance door. Loud condensation dripped into the sand. Two blocks up on Main on a side street to the north, Grayson could hear the overtone of the Humvees and shouts of the African guards out hunting him. Some spoke now in low Spanish. Gunfire and return fire. Hot breeze rolled through the old pioneer oaks and at the side entrance he slipped inside and crossed over the oil blackened cement. Fructose and pumice soap in the air. Bob's hands were flat out on the desk. He had a toady look about him and went to shuffling some papers when he saw

Grayson standing in the office doorway. Bob brought his mouth softly shut so his neck flesh ballooned out. A ghetto blaster stereo on a side table played inspirational music. Grayson motioned with the 1911 before he ventured to order Bob.

"Shut that bullshit off."

Bob nodded and snapped the button on the tape player and only the sound of the cooler through the ductwork could be heard. Grayson pointed to a clock on the wall. The red second hand wasn't moving, and the time was stuck at four twenty-one. "You got a watch, Bob?"

Bob raised his left arm flatwise. The watch was a gold leather-banded automatic.

"Take it off and hand it to me," Grayson said.

Bob unclasped and set the watch at the front of the desk where Grayson swiped it up and checked the time and said, "We've got seven minutes and change until the next interval window in patrols outside opens and I leave. You're going to answer my questions."

Bob pursed his lips as if swallowing was difficult and nodded. Little crocheted crosses and yarn were piled up in a brown paper bag beside a pair of handcuffs and a Smith and Wesson model 19 revolver on a side table less than a foot from Bob's hands.

"The dopey looking twins you brought to Navajo Johnny's house, who you referred to as deacons, they share something in their looks with this friend of yours, Denny. They're his sons, aren't they?"

"They are, yes. Nate and Douglas. They're slow but special. They were just tagging along that day at Johnny's."

"Where were you fellows headed to? A meeting you said."

Bob shifted in the rolling chair and his eyes fell over to the revolver and Grayson said, "You can get there sooner if you really want to."

Bob looked back at him through glassy eyes. Beads of sweat were breaking out on his splotchy scalp. "Get where?"

"You know."

Grayson stood and picked up the revolver from the desk and opened the mini-fridge that stood along the wall and brought back a bottle of water and sat down again. As Bob watched him empty the shells from the wheel of the gun into his palm he slid the papers off the desk casually and set them on a table behind the desk without looking. Grayson set the revolver on the fridge and pocketed the shells.

"We were talking about the meeting."

A muscular tic at the corner of Bob's left eye began to fire. He swallowed hard and readjusted himself in the rolling chair. He looked concerned but the obsequiousness evidenced in their prior encounter was absent. "It was just a meeting with Johnny's guys. To go over what he thought they should be doing. With reference to the militia and what not."

"With reference to the militia and whatnot." Grayson repeated as he tipped the bottle and drank down half of it and set it back in his lap. "Do you want me to beat it out of you, Bob? It's preferable that you just spill it all and we keep everything nice and tidy. Or if you want to be beaten half to death first then that is what we will do. What do you say?"

"No. I understand."

"So you and Denny and the Navajo Johnny. And old Joe. You've got a little something worked out. You're the local connection and Denny's tied to these contractors? You guys are tied to Denny? Talk. I want the whole picture of relationships including whatever exists with the child abuse illustrated, and I want it right fucking now."

"I never knew Joe well. He never had anything to do with the Bible camp or anything else. The camp was mine and Johnny's project. Joe just idolizes Indians. Indian women mostly and I believe that's how he came to know Johnny, actually. As you've probably guessed, Joe set you up. That was all Joe. One hundred percent. Johnny told him he was looking for someone to put a lot of heat on. A drifter type but plausible as an insurgent leader. And Joe came back to him later saying he knew the perfect guy—you."

"I see."

"I never had anything whatsoever to do with any of it. Not a bit of it."

"What does setting me up have to do with my friend, Phil. Where is Phil? Where is Phil's wife Sarah? Where's the baby?"

"I don't know those things. I don't know anything about this Phil or Sarah. I'm just business partners with Johnny. I'm a pastor. I run a fucking bible camp. Maybe you saw the old van at Johnny's. That property was the site of our camp. Was very beautiful at one time. As for Johnny and Denny, they're old old friends who served together. When Denny retired a few years back, he returned home here to Moab and laid it all out: how the collapse would unfold, how to survive, and how we could all profit by getting in on a piece of the river being diverted. You see, Johnny and Denny are side-gig types of guys, always hustling. Me, not so much."

With two pinched fingers, as if drawing a perfectly straight line on a chalkboard Grayson gestured for Bob to be silent. Grayson said, "You've got three and a half minutes. Assuming Johnny had gotten wind of some gold and silver riding along with my IED fixings from certain locals, let's say, could Johnny have sold my box and, thus my friend's wellbeing, to either his militia fuckups or some of the mercenaries?"

"You mean the private contractors? Yes, it's possible. I don't think anyone in the slightest expected little old Moab Utah to present such an obstacle to these guys. The organizations who run the contractors I mean. They're international, untouchable. Plugged in heavy. Global logistics, intelligence, you name it. But as to something ad hoc, this box of yours—I cannot be certain either way."

"So no one expected any problems, and thus Johnny might well just have figured fuck everyone, I'll sell this, that, and the other thing down the river, one after the other. And being as every familial, ethnic, communal, or auxiliary interest is about to be mercilessly crushed anyway as they've been right here, for example, and then it will all be papered over or covered up or just generally come out in the wash, then who's to complain? That sort of thing? We'll come back to it. Three minutes forty seconds."

Bob wiped a stream of sweat from around his ear with the collar of his polo. Grayson finished the second half of the bottle and tossed the empty over Bob's head and resituated the rifle where it rested muzzle-up against his leg.

"Where's Roger, Navajo militia leader?" Grayson asked.

"Dead."

"How do you know?"

"One of the first things the contractors did was sweep out all the organized parties. Any formal militias and such. Just blew them to hell. Day one, maneuver one. Some fought, obviously. Others just got hit. But they didn't get them all routed out quite so immediately."

"Yep. And Johnny knew that?"

"You mean sold his own people out? Yes. Yes, he did."

"And so, your meeting."

"We watched the helicopters hit them from out on a ridge out near the golf course. The executives, the contractors I mean, and Denny were all in attendance."

"I guess you played a round then to celebrate."

"I don't play. But Denny and the others. Nine holes. Johnny wanted us to watch. We watched the helicopters swing over the mesa. The Indians just froze. Good lord, what a thing. Watched them swing over like these giant black dragons and they spit fire leaving nothing but a series of smoking craters where Johnny's tribe had been standing a moment before. I gather it was to make the point that we were past any sort of, I don't know, old ties or old rules of tribes or alliances and such. I suppose that our boat was docked with the contractors so to speak. It did accomplish that. Maybe that's why Johnny took liberties, as you're saying, with gold or other projects. I don't know but we threw in whole hog with these guys—Denny's international contacts."

The whir of the fridge and the swamp cooler, the ticking of the air in a grate somewhere were the only sounds for a moment. Bob looked away at his desk, the wall. Grayson said, "If you're gonna go to heaven what are you so scared of?"

Bob blinked. "Aww, Christ." Bob's hands fidgeted in manic fashion, like little pink birds at the ends of his arms. "To kill is a sin. You don't have the right. What right do you have to condemn or execute judgement? Only God can judge, only He can decide my fate."

"Man, you got this all fucked up, Bob."

Bob hung his head in his hands and went to kneading his bald reddening scalp with vigor.

Grayson said, "Speaking of side gigs, you know Denny was weird enough to share some of his movie collection with me."

Bob froze. Taking small sips of air, he looked as if he were boiling inside. "I never touched them. This is absurd. You're making baseless accusations. Who do you think you are to look down on me or to pass judgement much less act as the executioner? You've no fucking badge that I can see. You're not a soldier, you're not a cop, you're not even a lawyer, and you're going presume to know the truth of something extremely complex and then kill on assumptions? That's pride, mister. That's pride and that's arrogance that you'll never get away with."

Grayson laughed. "Your church is a fraud, a heresy. Your conception of God as some bearded man in the sky is juvenile, no more insightful or meaningful than the way atheists see the world. Less so, actually."

As if he were preparing to embark on a carnival ride, Bob had taken grip of the arm rests on his chair. It appeared he was, while very angry, possessed of enough cognizance to observe the fact that violence was the primary option on the table at present. Being the party less proficient with that option, he struggled to conduct himself and wet his lips to speak.

"Sir, I am of the so-called baby boomer generation which no-question makes me your elder. You've heard the commandment to respect your elders, I assume?" Grayson was unfazed. Bob straightened in his chair gripping the cloth elbow pads so hard his knuckles splotched white. He continued, "I've learned a great deal about my own faults. Lord knows. Lord knows. But I've also been a keen student as to the multitudinous faults of humanity. You understand, sir? We are flawed, sinful creatures but we are also extremely complicated. Life is, in case you hadn't heard, very, very complicated and without a serious, careful education in theology at a recognized school and probably a good deal of law to boot—well, I don't think there's anyone on earth who would believe for a minute that you—somehow above all others—would be the single one with the truth in your pocket."

And then as Grayson leaned forward in his own chair, his eyes shone in the way the eyes of wolves will shine in cold winter nights when moonlight reflects on the white snow and the wolves are very hungry, searching, and the scent of nearby prey wafts through the dark trees. That was the light in Grayson's eyes. "To kill is a sin, yes. And atonement followed by repentance is the true way to face the inevitably of your sins."

Bob almost stood from the desk but caught himself. "So don't do it then. I've got more life to live, goddammit. People to care for. And do you, do you really care to risk that kind of judgement on your soul?"

Grayson forced himself to think of the mission, of Phil, the overview. He'd gotten what he could out of Bob and the interval in which he could move through the guards approached. "Hand me the stack of envelopes and notepad you tried to hide."

Bob blinked, trying to remember and then turned and brought the papers up from the side table with them cradled in both hands like an offering. Grayson motioned for him to set them at the very front of the desk and Bob did so. With the lupine light shining again and knowing that because Bob could never repeat what he was about to say it should be said with full transparency. And it was.

He said, "Rest assured, old man, that after God took my child I wandered the earth east to west like an exile--fully saturated in an anguish of the sort that drives men into traffic and jumping from rooftops and by saturated in it I mean I never turned from how it felt. Many, many nights I watched the traffic pass from atop a trestle bridge. Watching until it was a long red blur one way and a white blur the other and if God wanted to push me, He could. Or whoever. Voluntarily homeless, eating by grace and luck, and I took comfort in neither women nor whiskey for several years to make sure I was purged and sober and prepared to determine the rest of my life on my terms. That is, to be accountable to that thing that surrounds us that is so obviously greater than ourselves. That can take and give and twist time back on itself. That which can create existence itself. It's in this room and in our cells and in the fabric of reality before our eyes right now, always. This is all really happening. Now, I've seen your work and I'm not naïve: you're the second or third tier in a pedophile ring. Above you, as in any cartel, are the untouchable and untraceable who consume your goods themselves or use the kids as bait to blackmail others in their class. Denny is your conduit. You were probably all molested right here as boys growing up—these things often being generational in their origin."

Grayson let that linger. Bob cast his eyes away and a tension somewhere in his body seemed to deflate so that his shoulders slumped heavily. "Denny is also the conduit through to the private armies—Virginia Boy, shadow government, black budget operator-- a fact which you so generously confirmed a moment ago. You fellows with your snuff videos and kidnap pipelines are the stuff of nightmares and conspiracy theories. You're legend, Bob. It's all in a hundred books and whispered from Tallahassee to Tacoma. So in answer to your questions concerning my execution of judgement, I'll say that after ten years of consideration and study with priest and sage, after listening for God in every green forest and in all the red deserts, I trust--that is--I have faith, in the order of these things. Me being here. You being there. And as to the question of whether I'll be granted the requisite time to properly atone for killing you or anyone else that I'm going to kill—that's a judicial, divine grey area which while gravely serious is ultimately one of acceptable risk."

"I was molested as a kid. Does that matter to you?"

"That is some tortured logic."

Bob whined, "The stuff with kids never seemed real. Unless when we were doing it. But not after. Besides, I didn't kill your fucking kid. That's got nothing to do with me. It's just circumstances—me here, you there like you said."

Bob's face twisted in hot teary folds of sagging flesh. Then he voided himself. Grayson heard it and the smell of hot, horrified shit hit the room fast in swamp cooler's wind. Bob shifted in the chair, his head went to the side like he was looking for something over there.

"You're a legend, Bob. You're a myth. And I'm the one made to end the myth. You pimp yourself as a man of God. I simply seek Him."

Outside in the alley and the street, where a small grid of power was contained to the municipal buildings and a couple of gas stations, there was ample ambient noise of coolers and pumps and piped water to muffle the reports of the pistol shot that killed Bob. Grayson walked out of the building, shutting the door behind him. Limbs of the mighty cottonwoods swayed in the breeze. The first tint of twilight was coming and silhouetted batteries of flies swarmed on the palette of the sky like nucleating matter. In the long shadows he slipped through a place in the perimeter where the African guards manned their posts but the coals of the American cigarettes they smoked flared and stole their night vision. They jokingly referred to Grayson as the Desert Master. They murmured of tulpas and said there was no cause to worry, for the Desert Master wouldn't come into town anyway and why would he when the desert gave so freely to him as if he were its child or its hero.

* * *

In the lot of a bombed-out drive-in restaurant he sat in the bark dust margin between a concrete retaining wall and some high bushes eating green beans from the can and some foil packages of peanut butter. As he listened to the deuce-and-a-half trucks roar down Main from out of the La Sals to change guards and relay rumors of his passage, he thought about what he told Ben about the afterlife. In all the years he had never before told anyone of his speculation. God would forgive if he was wrong. While if he was right, perhaps then God would have mercy. For a moment he watched bats twist over the mulberry sky in phantom cursive southbound to the floodlit perimeter. He set his trash up in the limb work of the hedge and by method silently reorganized his meager kit and arranged himself in the space to run or fight as necessary. With Bob's phone in hand and his ledger opened in the dry ground, he sat straight back and cross-legged, breathing deeply as if here was the place prayers might be heard or meditations might resonate. From the ledger and addresses logged in the phone's contacts, he deduced Johnny's likely whereabouts. "Conveniently located," he whispered to himself.

When the night was settled in, he moved fast on the avenues, on the side streets, so he could take his time closing on the address. Humvees hampered his speed, if only with their presence on the roadway, as the Africans didn't want to get out of their trucks. He just listened for their engines and waited to let them pass. Stray bands of road-hardened refugees and children still found pockets in which to eat or sleep. He caught sight of their miniscule pot fires flickering as he ran. In the slips between shadows, invisible urchins set out snare traps of salvaged wiring harnesses for rats or felines. Other kids picked grasshoppers from the lawns and dropped them into coffee cans to use later in bets or barter. They had already figured out how to improvise slingshots and fire gravel at the roaming dog packs to keep them at bay. They knew that the ways out of Moab across the great basin of desert in every direction meant unprovisioned travel, and so they toughed it out in the new ruins.

In the little industrial park lot south of the hostel, he hid and scrutinized Denny's boys, the twin brothers, for the better part of an hour. In their matching haircuts and slovenly t-shirts, they hardly moved but to piss in the bushes and check the levels on

King of Dogs

the power plant trailer. Each twin carried the same long Mossberg shotgun. Nate on the east side and Doug duplicated on the west. A yellow and black backhoe was parked in the dim fringe of the yard. Just past eleven-thirty, he took two ghostlike steps from the shadows and drove the bush blade through the area of Nate's esophagus with a furious and complete precision. He let the shotgun clatter on the blacktop. Loud enough to bring the brother. Grayson stepped to the back corner of the building and crouched with his chin and forehead to the cool sheet metal wall and waited for footfalls. *Could be he's moving slow. Could be he's coming the other way.* And then came boots of the twin scuffling over the aggregate concrete as he rounded into the conical amber cast light of the second floor window. Doug froze there with the encircling gnats and night beetles shimmering overhead. With a slack jaw, he squinted into the shadows. Tobacco grains were in his teeth and the brown stain leeched out on his stubble. Stretching out for the upright shotgun barrel with blood-slicked left hand to catch it Grayson whispered, "Hey."

Doug gasped, and Grayson yanked the barrel to slingshot the bladed right hand parallel to the earth and slipped it through the same few inches of neck meat and gristle as he had done with his twin. Doug looked confused and then enraged. As if some third party had pushed them they went down together in a clinched lather of blood. The shotgun fell away. Doug pressed his neck together with one doughy hand and snicked out a little blade with other and sunk it into Grayson's side. Wincing and then scowling, one hand slipping over Doug's mouth to shut it in the slather, he bucked and stabbed the bush blade into the reciprocal torso but much deeper. For a moment, they seemed frozen, locked into strange mirror of total contract. He felt Doug's heart hammer as he stared into those mean dumb eyes, glassy with terror.

In the shadows Grayson wiped his hand of blood to get a clean start and dabbed his wound. Lucky, he told himself. It felt like it had slipped up between the ribs and skin, maybe between the ribs at one place. He spat and crossed the lot and came back with the rifle knocking the safety off. He eased open the door. A bell rang from sensors in the jamb. He stepped inside and paused in the dehumanizing florescent light of the foyer. Cigar smoke was on the air. The totalized hum of electricity cycling in the walls wavered with the cycle of the air conditioner. The foyer door was open to the shop. Nothing moving. Stone still, ear cocked to listen. He was washed in blood and drips of it from the blade's handle at his waist fell in the short teal carpet. He looked maniacal, like some fiend wandering past hell's gate. Still counting under his breath, he took two more steps and the baying of hounds exploded from the shop.

Going fast through the shop door, he glanced left where there was just a gloss of green I-beam pillars, cornmeal insulation. He swiveled and put nine deafening rounds into the hips and heads of two men in tannish plate carriers as they were rising from a card table with their weapons akimbo. His ears shut down. Dull, muted barking of Denny's hounds in their kennels emanated from along a far wall. Panning left, his eyes fell over a grey concrete and green steel blur to stairs and an office loft. He figured he probably had less than two minutes before the Humvees arrived. Halfway up the stairs midstride he saw Johnny's long swinging hair through the balcony on one side. *You.* One of the executives from the mountaintop who had stood wide-legged in the short grass, drinking Pellegrino, and analyzing him from behind sunglasses now wore those same glasses and chinos but stood half- crouched at the top of the stairs, wildly pulling the trigger on something small like a sub-gun.

Muzzle fire. Gold glint off his pinky ring. Grayson fired straight into the oncoming blast. The man dropped in his chinos. Still more coming. Johnny fired a shotgun from across the office and got down behind a tanker desk working the arm and firing through the foot space. Brick kilos of heroin or coke split on the floor. One exploded from the scattershot. A small Styrofoam cooler lay tipped over and Grayson caught a glimpse of its contents: human hearts, paired kidneys and other organs vacuum-wrapped and labeled with printed white stickies like steaks from a butcher. One was full of very small, pink and greyish glands. In the back of his mind, less than a full thought, Grayson registered the trafficking of organs. Yet another lucrative side gig common to warzones worldwide. Amid mingling clouds of dope and cigar and gun smoke sifting through the loft, Grayson fired through the tanker desk until he'd emptied the rifle. As he came around the desk unsheathing the knife he felt a hot spot where one of the buckshot had gone in his thigh. Johnny was writhing in the margin between the desk and the wall. He had no shoes on and his long yellow toenails dug at the parquet flooring. Grayson stepped a crushing boot down on the pistol in Johnny's hand and hammered the blade down pinning him at the spine clean through to the varnished wood like a scarab on a mounting flat. Kneeling on Johnny's back Grayson got to his ear and whispered,

"You are about to come squarely before your failings as a human man, and they will unfold through infinity like mirrors upon mirrors. There's no bottom to it and it's too late to ask for a guide."

Johnny coughed a froth of lung matter out on the floor and shivered as he expired. Grayson stood and chastised himself silently for killing him before he could get any information out of him. Grayson said out loud, "Move."

* * *

From his overwatch position, advantaged among the cobble of the east rim where the rock face sloped back toward the river, Grayson watched the mule deer nibble in the fields and water birds rising up from the gorge drafts over the Colorado and descending into the copse of cottonwoods that embroidered the wetlands. Well in the shade of tamarisk and surrounded by yucca on the ground he washed and dressed the knife wound with some packets of solution and gauze pads from the med kit. He heated with his lighter a piece of wire bent like an egg-dying spoon and dug out two number four buckshot from his thigh and washed the crater out with water and more solution. Letting it weep for a while, he ate a cold can of chili with the knife. Shorn of multiform vanity, a man must only concern himself with observation and acceptance if he wishes to go on when most men give up. Observation so that he can respond to what the world presents and acceptance of the inevitability of it bringing more suffering and eventually death. This was the secret to Grayson's endurance: the worst had already happened. All that was left of psychic weight was to prepare to smile at death.

Without the integrity of his promise to Jack complete, however, Grayson felt an interior psychic ravenousness beginning to take hold—an amplified sense of running late that he worked to soothe with reason. If that didn't work, prayer would be next. Had the worst already happened or would letting Jack down in fact be worse in some sense than anything else he'd experienced in losing his family? Should he have forced Phil and Sarah to move despite her discomfort after delivery? He felt like an animal caught alone on the tundra where the blasting wind swallows all voices and the world's mandate to perform or die draws into focus. *God would provide,* he thought. *Try to relax. If you're still moving, you're not dead, and if you're not dead then you're not done with your mission.* It was no use to hope to go back in time. Stop trying.

Through the riflescope he observed a small cadre of white guards debrief the black Africans at the guard shack. By physiognomy and the tall leather boots into which their fatigues were tucked and the way in which their hair was shorn equal to their beards, he figured the whites were Eastern European, former Special Forces. Mercenaries long on experience in the Caucasus and the Middle East. One of the Europeans wore spectacles and smoked a cigarette that he lit with his hands cupped to the wind. The man unfolded a grid map onto the hood of their beige Suburban, and he and one of the Africans went to work with a yellow marker. Then the European queried him and poured coffee from a steel Thermos to drink as he pondered the answers given.

Now they're serious, Grayson thought.

When he got back to Ben at the old hotel, he found him sleeping in the rear compartment of the Cherokee with the backdoor and tailgate open. Ben was not snoring and, aside from his dirt and tear-stained face, looked just fine. Without disturbing him he took one of the sleeping bags from the Jeep and rolled it out upwind of the gardens in a mulch bed and slept. When he got up again having slept a few hours, orange and purple swatches of lit clouds tumbled on the skyline. Grayson smelled tobacco burning. Ben was seated in front of the hotel at a table on the flagstone portico with a bottle of wine open as if waiting to see the menu. When he saw Grayson, he pointed to the sign.

"I never went here when it was open, but I wish I had. It's nice."

"Where'd you get those goodies?"

"Restaurants I worked in always had an employee stash spot. You know where you could set your meal or skateboard or whatever. Other side of the bathroom. There was two packs of smokes and three bottles of wine tucked away in somebody's sweater and pants."

"Did you drink the other two already?"

"Naw. I mixed them with water like those old sheepherders in Europe and filled the water bladder on my pack with it. Just for the hell of it. It's pretty tasty."

"You know why they did that?"

"To stay loaded all day?"

"That and because they couldn't get any potable water."

Across the highway and skyward from where Grayson and Ben sat in front of the hotel, geese in formation going back to some warm spot upriver loosed their rubber-necked cries in flight and behind the men at the table in the lawn the ivy hanging like bedsheets from the windows over the batten hotel wall rustled in the wind. The wheels of the world moved again, and it seemed suddenly the sky was near dark. Grayson gestured at the yellow pack of cigarettes on the table and Ben slid it over and set his lighter beside the pack. Grayson shook one out and lit it with his back turned to the wind.

"I guess you didn't find him." Ben seemed worried.

"Nope. But I want you to stay right here. You find any food?"

"Some stiff tortillas and a few cans of black beans."

"That'll last you a few days."

Ben watched Grayson remove the bandage from his thigh and dope a replacement with iodine.

"My mom used to say about our neighbor growing up, Howard. Howard something, I forgot this last name, but he was always bouncing a basketball in the front driveway of his house until after dark. She'd always say to him out the window trying to get him to shut up and stop dribbling, 'Howard you just don't quit do you?'"

"Was she right?"

"I don't know. Probably. But that's the same with you. That's what she'd say, 'You just don't quit do you?'"

Grayson took a pull on the smoke and brought the recon gun up and broke it open to remove the bolt carrier group. He sat wiping the face of the bolt on his shirt before he responded to Ben.

"You quit and it haunts you. You can retreat from something if you have to or you can even take a sabbatical. For years if necessary, as long as the intention to return is genuine."

"I quit shit jobs before, and they didn't haunt me. Quit shit girls before and nothing happened." Ben didn't look like someone bluffing. He gave no tell, and there was a hint of earnest tone to his claim.

Grayson looked at him and tapped the cigarette on his boot. Ben was waiting for the reply but Grayson only silently replaced the bolt and carrier in the receiver.

"I'm referring to your mission. You're thinking you don't have one. And even though you don't see it, you do have a mission because every living man has one. One that you might have never started or even considered. Or maybe you knew all along but got so far from it, so far from home, you couldn't hear anybody or anything calling you back. Without the mission, you're just a phantom out there knocking on doors in the night. Make sense?"

Ben lit another cigarette and took a slug from the bottle. His eyes shone in the moonlight. Past the dark yard and the quiet highway, the wind howled up from the gorge and through the archways on the bridge.

"Yeah, I get it," he said swallowing hard and shaking his head.

* * *

Grayson came in over the desert plateau on a wide parabola in broad daylight, sheer cliff and crevasse. Crumbling post pile and slick rock slide. The last half mile of flatland he moved with the sound of the chainsaw. He crawled through the sage and chaparral and then descended on foot to the cooler canyon behind the house where the tessellated Mojave serpents were coiled at the edge of the sunlight, regulating themselves and licking the air of his passage. Mid-afternoon he came out in the neighbor's yard. From the protective umbra of their gardens, Grayson watched Denny stand in the shade of his apple trees snapping bull flies off stumps with a damp rolled up kitchen towel. There was a 455 Husqvarna chainsaw at his feet. A small red gas can and a white bottle of oil sat on one of the larger stumps beside a blued 9mm Browning Hi-Power with checkered walnut grips. Denny shaped and reshaped his moustache with two fingers as he looked for flies and then set the towel on the stump, fitted his earplugs, and brought up the chainsaw and fired it before he bent to work the pile of cottonwood trunks.

Grayson studied everything: the windows of the houses down the culdesac that were empty, the dried mud on the truck tires, the canyon walls and the willows growing up out of the creek. Always the hunter, he sharpened the focus of his awareness and sought to expand into all before and around him—the reality that comprised his hunting ground. He tried to feel the rate and texture of Denny's breath to calculate when he might tire and when he might need a cool drink from the house. He postulated the declination and the range of the shot if he took that option. Sixty yards, assuming the zero is a hundred and the rounds are match grade, from a cold barrel on a hot day with no humidity. Could be an inch of drift in any direction or it could be dead nuts.

Grayson started talking to himself. You don't want to bleed him out too soon. You don't want to leave him enough range of motion to get to the Hi-Power. You also don't want to flat miss. Pull the trigger when the chainsaw is running, no one takes notice, and no one comes running. If it turns into a gunfight or he has that radio on him somewhere, well, then the problems multiply fast, and killing him flat out gets us nowhere.

Stone still, Grayson observed Denny for another forty-five minutes start and stop the saw and stack the rounds and snap flies at his leisure until he finally dropped the towel on the stump and picked up the handgun. For a moment Denny stood there thinking. Then he set the pistol back and walked the path with his big forearms swinging to the open garage. Grayson heard the door to the kitchen shut. The window in back was open. Sounds of china on countertops and jars jiggling in the shelves of the refrigerator came through and funneled up the cut bank. Not too loud, but go fast, he told himself. And he did. A moment later he eased the door through the garage open and felt cool air running out over in his face. Smells of lunch meat and cola. He crossed the first bit of the nook and looked into the office where Denny was sitting in the rolling chair at his desk. A plate was at his elbow, fork and a crust of sandwich there on the desk and a child's pink sweatshirt lay draped over a leather reading chair. Grayson brought the gun up and went forward. A span of dark sweat lay on the yoke of the blue polo shirt. A loop of the gold chain spilled out over the collar as he slipped a pinched section of photographs from a stack.

"Just going over old times, are you?"

Denny's neck twitched reflexively, and his head snapped halfway around, but it stopped there so Grayson could only see his profile. Through the window and the blinds a purple smoke bush tilted opaline leaves in the wind.

"I hope you have a better plan than you had last time we tried this," Denny said.

"Keep your hands on the table."

"They say it's twenty-one feet."

"I'm gonna wager there is no shortage of handcuffs here so let's start there."

"They say it's twenty-one feet of ground that you can get across and still get to a man before he draws and fires. Heard that from a cop friend of mine. Don't know if it's true or not, but it probably is." It was less than twelve across the room.

Denny spun the chair around with the section of photographs in hand and looked over Grayson and the rifle he was holding. "In the safe," he said.

The safe was in the left side corner of the room. Grayson took two steps inside to let his eyes adjust. Denny chuckled, and his body bounced the hydraulic stem of the chair.

"It's open," he said. "Just swing the bar."

Grayson swung it out slowly never letting his gaze leave Denny. He stepped around with the gun trained and glanced inside. Big stacks of storage DVDs in thin clear cases and rubberbanded photos crammed into gallon Ziploc bags. The short-barreled AR sat muzzle up in a long pocket on one side beside green surplus ammo boxes.

"Johnny was a veritable gook-slaying machine in the day" said Denny. On the top shelf was a Seecamp .32 pistol and a medical examiner's jar of clear viscous liquid where something pink and gray floated inside. Beside the jar were industrial strength zip ties, a ham radio, and two sets of cuffs in a green powercoat finish. Denny was fixated on the top photo in the stack in his hand. Grayson slid the cuffs over the desk.

"To the chair."

Denny attached the cuffs to the runner on one side of the chair. In the corner beside the safe was his 80mm surplus box sitting upright, and he reached over and popped the latch and peered down in the dim.

"You got all the makings for some pretty decent IEDs there don't you? We taught the guerillas to use solidox in the sandbox. Works good. Your gold's gone. Africans took it and tried to say there never was any, but then some of the dumbshits used it to bet on your marathon out there in the mountains and the captains called me. I said let 'em keep it. But I don't think gold was what you ever wanted anyway, was it?"

"Waiting on that cuff" Grayson said.

Denny hiked up in the chair and after of minute of fumbling the sound of ratchets pulled tight.

"Push around here." Grayson said. Denny chuckled, and Grayson slammed the lee end of the desk with his boot sending it spinning into the corner. The stacks of photos went slipping away to the floor like leaves in a gale and there sat Denny in his white jockey shorts.

"Turn that way," Grayson said and gestured with the recon gun to one wall.

Denny made a quarter turn and tensed a bit when the muzzle came to rest along his cervical spine and then lifted his feet as might a child while Grayson rolled the chair out the door and through to the garage. He punched the button beside the jamb and when the big door was down the only light was from the opener blinking overhead. The garage was tidy and smelled like store-bought fertilizer and old canvas.

"Guess you never found your buddy. This must be eye for an eye and all that." Denny said.

"I'm gonna take more than your eye."

Denny snorted.

Grayson added, "You found your sons though, didn't you?"

Denny wove his head back and forth against the light. Grayson watched him.

"I'm going to ask you one time, and then I'm going to proceed to torture you to death. I'll leave this side door open, so your scent draws the coyotes. They'll want to eat your asshole first, core you out, as is their method. So I'll leave you face down to facilitate that. And the parts of you I leave piled in the corner, those can go to the mice. Do you understand me so far?" Grayson rummaged through a toolbox open on the floor.

Denny said, "No, you fucking pussy, I don't. If I answer, do you get to the torturing? Or is it that if I don't answer you get to torturing? You never did this before. You're a shithead amateur. That's clear as day. If you'd even read the manuals much less had proper training, you'd know to establish the alternative, my reward, straight out of the gate. Otherwise your interrogation subject can shut down and you have to wait again for him to reset."

Grayson stepped under the flashing light over their heads and brought the serrated open jaws of a pair of blue channel-lock pliers over the bridge of Denny's nose. He closed with both hands. There was a juicy snapping sound of crushed bone. Denny screamed once and pitched over contorting and sucking air through his teeth.

"You want me to take your sunglasses off, so you can see, or you like it dark?'

Denny tried to control his response. Muscles in his sides quivered as he moaned.

"Take a minute," Grayson said, stepping behind him.

Denny spat blood and coughed. A wormlike pink vessel about six inches long hung from one nostril and he tried to shake it loose. He laughed weakly. Grayson stepped over again and folded Denny's polo around his hand and yanked the vessel away from the oozing cavity and pulled his hand away leaving the vessel stuck there on his polo. Denny breathed through his mouth.

"Ask," he said.

"Where's Phil? His wife and child."

"That's easy."

"Then it's easy to answer."

"Your friend is dead, and you know it. You've known all along. I saw it in your eyes on the mountain. You knew it then. He was rolled up at the first hit.' Denny paused to spit blood. "Surveillance program associated him to you in the advance work we did six months ago or more. You killed him. In essence, you killed him by association."

"Where?"

Denny sighed and Grayson clacked the channel locks.

"Look I'm going to tell you. Alright? Gimme a second. Since you don't know how the fuck this is supposed to go. Let me catch my breath. I know where we're at."

"Catch it and be quick."

"I'm gonna tell you exactly where. But I'm going to ask you a favor for when you go, alright? Alright? It's nothing. You can do it when you see your buddy. My dogs are still in their kennels at the warehouse, okay. The body is behind the warehouse in the open yard. Just at least open the kennels and let them go. There's food and water above them on the shelves."

Grayson paced. The overhead light went out and they sat in the dark a weird moment, each man breathing loudly until Grayson flipped the switch on the standard lights. He squinted at Denny.

"There is no open yard at that warehouse."

"It's beyond the hedges at the back. We own the open lot there too. I was on my way to feed and water them right now. After I finished the woodpile. It's cruelty to leave them in the heat. The jigs won't go back for them."

"Sounds like a set up."

"It's a fucking dead man's request. Don't you know what honor is?"

"It's a dead man's set up."

"You have to honor it."

"You didn't earn any honor from me."

Grayson went back through the door into the office and snapped the lid on the 80mm box and came back in the garage with it and a handful of the zipties and set to binding Denny's ankles together and then binding those to the stem of the chair. "Keys to the warehouse."

Denny said, "Back bedroom on the bedside." He snapped his head around and yelled, "Wait." There was a pause, a moment as if he'd say something to Grayson. The slow drip of blood on the polo shirt caught in the light.

"Aww let it go." He muttered.

Down the hall the bedroom door was closed and quiet. Grayson turned the knob and saw a young girl straight in front of him bunched against the wall on the floor and chained with a dog collar to a stainless handrail. The tiny bare feet were tight together flaking dried dirt. Little blue dress, dark brown hair wet and smeared around her forehead. What was she, nine, ten maybe? Grey duct tape was wound over her mouth and in her hair and zip ties were cranked down on her wrists over more duct tape.

Intelligent, wide blue eyes searching him. Just look at that. She shifted against the unknowing. Something subtle and of absolute purity inside of his chest unmoored like it would fly up his throat and leave forever. What could she think as she looked at him there in the doorway, embattled and rangy? Covered in the blood of a dozen men. She shivered. In the other corner an arm's length away was a small black duffle bag of Denny's paraphernalia.

Grayson managed to blurt out, "I imagine it's hard to believe, but I'm the good guy."

She nodded. He grabbed the keys off the table. "We're gonna move on outta here, okay. I'm gonna cut this off." When he had the tape and ties off her wrists and the dog collar from her neck, he slid the blade deftly behind the tape at her ear leaving a mark of oil from the carbon steel blade on her cheek and then matched the mark on the other side and told her the tape might hurt coming off.

When he had it off, she wiped her face and said, "I'm ready when you are."

There was maturity and sweetness in her voice. He remained silent, waiting a moment as by reflex she straightened the wrinkles in her khaki shorts and the black blouse. On the far wall in front of them hung a walnut-framed mirror that caught a clean triangle of sunlight. The house was quiet. Lined up behind them in the bathroom through the open door hung a large vanity mirror. He stood there a stolen, eerie moment peering into the stepwise recursion of the reflected images framed one inside the other, leading to infinity. Himself—tatterdemalion and raging with war, and she seeming the tiny apotheosis of innocence. All that is good, true, and everlasting: someone's child.

In the truck he told her he had one more thing to do.

"This isn't your truck, is it?" she asked. He looked at her. He waited for her to look at him even a little bit.

"No it's not my truck. But we're going to use it to get out of here, and then we'll get a different one. We're commandeering it. Okay?"

In the house he brought one of the ammo cans of 5.56 from the safe out to the kitchen island and then went to the bedroom for the duffle bag that he dumped out in the hall as he walked. He brought it to the island and filled it with bottles of water and canned food from Denny's pantry. He cracked one of the bottles and drank half and breathed. In his hand were photos from the office floor. One of Johnny in the jungle. Some of different children. Most were of the same woman that was bald in the living room photo. In these she had hair still, and in some of them Denny had his arm around her. As Grayson had known when he'd sat in the diminutive oaks overlooking Johnny's compound, bona fide terror lay somewhere in his near future. He now knew the precise time of that meeting.

For right or wrong, he was about to dim the ever-loving light in his own heart and shoulder full responsibility before for doing so. "God have mercy," he said. God have mercy. In the garage he took a length of red climbing rope from a crate on the shelves and drew the knife and bent behind the chair and slipped it down and through the right Achilles tendon above Denny's top-sider shoe. There was a snap like a plastic fork breaking and Denny gasped. When he cut away the ankle ties and clasped the bracelets one to the other and stood him on the hobbled leg, he was almost tranquil. Grayson put the rifle in his ribs, and they walked through the kitchen.

"Outside," Grayson said.

They walked slowly over the deck in the shade, leaving a sputtered blood trail on the boards and through the garden beds where rosemary and tomato leaves were in the wind and the chainsaw chips from the stump were piled in the short grass as if it were a stall. The desert he had traversed earlier that day was also shaded out past the canyon and then farther, beyond the demarked line of the hillside shadow, the sun baked the swooped red rocks and the tenacious pine shrubs that grew in the rock interstices without mercy.

"Stand up next to that stump," he said. Denny put his back to it. "Other way, face it." And when Denny was positioned how he wanted him, Grayson knotted a loop in the rope like a trucker's hitch and ran the free end around the stump and through the loop to torque it down. He reverse wrapped Denny's legs tight round and round until he tied off the knot again through the hitch. Constricted blue blood stood out in Denny's thighs like sea snakes, and what little blood still ran in the veins oozed from the oblong incision on his ankle.

Grayson walked up the side path and looked across the yard to make sure she was still waiting in the truck. She was. The Hi-Power pistol was hot on the stump in the sun. He stood looking at the cut wood stacked up at the edge of the yard. After he'd figured it all out, he picked up the pistol and walked to the truck and opened the driver's door with the gun obscured behind his leg. She looked out of the corner of her eye at him.

He said, "I'm gonna be one more minute. I'm gonna turn the air conditioning on real high so it cools it down in here, and I'll be right back. And we're gone. Never to return."

She nodded.

When he had the truck started and the air going, he rolled up her window and said, "Keeps the cool air in." Not entirely certain that the flowing air and the sealed doors of the truck would keep from her ears the noise he was about to make he said again, "God have mercy."

He tapped the garage door opener on the visor and shut the door and went through to the house and came back with the two surplus ammunition cans--his with the explosive materials and Denny's, full up with green tip 5.56 rounds. He also grabbed the duffle bag of food and set everything in the bed, and tucked the Hi-Power into a pocket on the side of the bag. A moment later he reemerged from the garage with a framing hammer and a rusted Guatemalan machete swinging at his leg. He coupled these with the gas can in one hand, picked up the chainsaw with other, and brought it all down through the arbor to the side yard.

Denny grimaced when he saw the tools. He was pouring sweat and favoring his good foot. Grayson set the tools and gas can on the deck and primed the pump and ripped the cord on the chainsaw and went walking toward Denny running the gas and testing the slack of the chain. The stump was cut high to about Denny's waist and Grayson eyeballed his angle and dug the saw in and wound it around so close on the sides the he nicked him on each upper thigh. Denny winced and spat out the dust rising in a bloody particulate spewm. Grayson shut the saw off and kicked the loose disc so it broke at the splinters in the rear. Sawdust clung about the sweaty parts of them both.

"What the fuck are you doing?" Denny yelled.

"You're the professional, correct? Tell me if you've seen this one before."

Grayson pulled the thin round away from the stump and dropped it to the side. He walked away and came back with the hammer. He didn't say a thing--just looked him in the eye as in genuine survey, as if he might see what was back there behind the sunglasses and the mask. As he was looking he reached down and unbuttoned and then unzipped Denny's shorts. Denny wriggled and said, "What the fuck?" It was the first note of fear that Grayson had heard. He pulled the shorts down as far as they would go against the rope binding his legs and set the hammer against the stump. Denny flailed against the cuffs and swung his torso against his immobilized limbs. The sawdust plastered on the one side of his body gave him the impression of being some mutant, mange-ridden bear.

From his pocket Grayson brought out three galvanized framing nails, sixteen-penny. There was no good way to do this, so he just leaned in to steady him and reached down for his balls and his cock from underneath and stretched them over to the stump. He brought the nail down as hard as he could keeping his shoulder to the thrashing and he held it there until he got the hammer up and pounded it through. Denny let out a high-pitched wheeze and looked like he might faint. Grayson slapped him hard enough that the sunglasses flew off into the garden boxes. He drove the nail down about halfway and put another one right beside it to the same depth. He turned and came back with the gas can.

Denny's eyes went wide. His teeth bared in a seething grin. Slobber and tears were smeared in the sawdust and then the demonic inner gears synchronized and Denny dropped his mask entirely as his neck bulged, and he half-growled half-shrieked like something possessed. Grayson emptied the gas can over the stump and washed it over Denny's balls and belly and the blood ran from the crosscut wood. Denny groaned and grit his teeth.

"You never caught me. None of you did."

Grayson swallowed standing, straight up and down. "You were caught the instant you took this road. Before your first step had even hit the ground," he said and each of them believed it for that moment. In the flash of belief, as if some transaction between accounts had been made, fear rose to the surface of Denny's uncovered eyes, and Grayson felt the vibrating grip of his own terror simply erased.

The machete was on the ground near the saw. When he brought it up Denny seemed to relax. Grayson swung and stuck the blade into the rough bark at such an angle that the handle was positioned right back to where Denny's hand would hang once he was uncuffed. Denny started to say something unintelligible. He started to break apart, but Grayson just held up two fingers to quiet him.

"You got the idea, right? You get to choose. I get to choose. Everyone gets to choose. And then we live with it. Then here we go."

The lighter sparked at the base of the trunk and the whole area whooshed with flame for a moment and then died down so that just the stump and Denny's balls, belly, and legs were on fire. Patches of white skin emerged as the hair singed away and then the patches blistered pink and sagged. Grayson picked up the rifle from in among the arbor vines and walked around and loosed one hand from the cuffs as the flame billowed sideways and scanted in the wind. Denny's hand shot forward and hung in the air as the fingers and arm hair waved in flame and sizzled a moment before he gripped the machete handle and yanked it loose from the stump. Grayson waved the robust stench from his nose and went around to study Denny's face. Denny hadn't swung the machete yet. Tears and snot raced in the soot accumulating on his neck and he gibbered in a revenant tongue about whether to chop away his equipment and maybe live briefly without it or just continue to immolate and take it with him. Grayson watched his face twist a bit more and then raised the recon gun. A single gunshot emanated out in the canyon and in the culdesac when he put him down, and the girl turned her head in the seat but then turned right back. A few birds picked up from out of the creek willows and set back down up the ridge. At the hose Grayson ducked his head under and washed his hands and face.

Take a minute, he thought. Nothing's over. Cold clear rivulets of the water ran down his back and the stream running strong from the hose splashed into the green grass. He felt transported to childhood—summers spent free and on the run with Jack. Phil was too young to join them. The visceral sense of gratitude for the water cooling him overrode the nausea that he hadn't even noticed settling in his guts. *Take one minute to appreciate these things*, he thought. No more. But no less. And so he turned the faucet so the flowing water slapped the pool in the grass with less noise and drank again knowing for at least that single moment nothing bad would happen. Despite appearances, chaos is a passing phenomenon, not the underlying condition. That's the fact. The translucent wings of tiny insects glittered as they hovered over the wet grass. Green apples swayed heavy on bent boughs in the orchard. The confounding thing is not that the living world wants only strength from a man and nothing more, he thought. But rather that to live in a world so beautiful requires so much strength.

In the truck he rolled his window down and laid the rifle behind the seat and the 1911 next to him on the console. He set a bottle of water in the cup holder for her. She'd been sitting, waiting for him a little over five minutes.

"Sorry that took so long."

When he had the truck rolling she took the water and held it in her hands.

"Did you cut his head off?"

Looking down at the top of her head, he blinked, stunned maybe. He said, "No. I didn't."

"That's what they do in Mexico," she said.

"Is that right. How do you know that?"

"I heard it."

"Where did you hear it?"

"In Mexico."

* * *

They went the empty back ways and side streets around Spanish Valley road where deer nibbled at the tree line of the creek and rested under trees twitching their ears in the shade, following the truck with their coal eyes. She twisted in the passenger seat to watch them. When they made the left up Murphy Lane, she started asking questions.

"Where are we gonna go?" The tape was out of her hair and she was still holding the water bottle in both hands. A hornet crawled along the windowsill, and she touched the button and it flew out.

"We're going to see a doctor," Grayson said. "But we have to wait until night."

"How come?" she asked.

They passed the late arcadia of the desert golf course littered now on the green with discarded peripatetic tents and dingy mattresses and in the sandtraps were the multifarious castoffs of invasion, the tin can and the spent shell. He craned his neck to see the big white house on the hillside.

"Up there. It's safe." he said.

She was looking out the window at tumbleweed piled in the ditch. He kept glancing at her, searching for blood or bruises but there was none. Just a layer of grime and justified suspicion. And while this gave hope, he knew it was a very cursory examination. At the top of the driveway he steered the truck through the turn-around and parked in the shade of cedars where they could look out upon both the red vastness of the public land canyon to the left and the opposite valley where the town and highway wound through.

It was cool and quiet inside. It had that old house smell, lemon oil and myrrh incense of years. Mission-style arched windows framed the sunlight into gold keyholes on the wide floorboards where the leaves of dead plants lay in mummified crescents. He cleared the house up and down and came back to the tiled foyer and found her under the high ceiling and fans of the main room where she'd installed herself in a corner of the white couch, feet tucked away under her seat. In her hands she twirled and caught the light with a cut-glass figurine dancer and sent the prismed afternoon rays out on her dress in a fractured shower of sparks. He went around into the kitchen to inventory the shelves and cupboards while she wandered over looking at artifacts in glass cabinets and on the walls as she went.

"The people who live here are old, aren't they?" she said.

He came back around and said, "Yeah. They were pretty old."

"Who are they?" she asked.

Looking through the cupboards, he stopped and thought about how to answer that. "They were just folks that lived here a long time. Nice folks with kids that had their own kids, so they became grandparents and had big get-togethers in the fall and spring. They also had another home in the north where they could go to escape the heat. That's about all I know."

"Are they your parents?" she asked.

"No," he said. "I just worked for them a few times."

She was lost in her survey of the foyer and living room where treasures of lions and giraffes carved from blonde jungle wood and Russian triptychs of the saints and miniature brass reproductions of the pyramids and the Empire State building were displayed on Scandinavian teak shelves. She came to the hide of ibex stretched out on the wall and a rusted spearhead set between long Javanese masks. She touched the toe cap on a pair of shriveled women's or children's cowboy boots that had to have been eighty years old and were ensconced on the lowboy amid decks of gypsy occult cards and a souvenir replica of the Paris tower cast of silver. A leather-cut mural was stitched on the side of the boots. Green cactus and white and red horses and yellow stars.

Grayson pulled from the cupboards all the bottled water and a good portion of the canned food and set it all on the tiled kitchen counter. He said, "Did you drink enough water, you want some more?"

From far off she said, "Yes, please. I'd like some more water, please."

He poured a bottle into a glass and set it on the side table and stood looking out the back windows over the canyon. After a bit he went to the front porch to look over the town. Small hovering drones that looked like dead pixels on a screen until they moved had been dispersed a few blocks out from the cordoned perimeter core. The drones appeared to float along their points in a grid and shift in concert at some timed interval. He watched and waited five minutes for them to move, but they didn't he came around and sat on the couch. She looked at him and went and sat on one of the white lounge chairs.

"Let's make a plan," he said. "We have five, probably six hours to kill. Our options are to eat, sleep, wash up, or stare out the window at nothing. What do you think?"

"I know for certain I don't want to stare out the window."

"Me neither. I recommend we wash up and eat, then sleep. Wake up and go over to the doctor. Go from there." She thought about it and then nodded her head so her straight blonde hair swung in front and the water in the bottle sloshed where she had it in her lap.

"Sounds good," she said.

"I like eggs and bacon. What do you like?"

"Pancakes."

"Pancakes it will be."

In the basement he found the generator and the panel box where he switched the well pump back on and ran the sink until the water turned clear again. He found some towels and set them on the toilet and came back to the living room to see she had the cowboy boots on. She tried to flex the toes.

"Pretty good fit," he said.

"They're crunchy," she said.

"I know a way to fix that."

"How?"

"I'll show you after we eat."

The pantry was well-stocked. Grayson took what he needed and brought it to the kitchen. The propane burner fired right up. A half hour later she walked around to the table and set the boots on one side and sat down at one of the two place settings. There was butter and syrup in the center and a glass of limeade between the settings. He brought the pancakes out from the oven on a plate and set the plate in the center and slid the glass of limeade over to the edge of her placemat.

She ate and watched him work conditioner into the flamboyant desiccated boots one by one. With some coaxing she told him that she was from San Diego and that with her parents and grandmother had attempted to move to live with an uncle somewhere in Arizona. Before they reached the uncle, she'd gone to sleep in a Phoenix hotel at night and woken up in the daylight moving fast through the flat desert in a car driven by a man she'd never met but who'd smelled like candy and told her over and over they were going to meet her parents in the north. When Grayson asked her how long she'd been at Denny's, she said it had only been a few hours. She said she knew he meant to do bad things to her but she hadn't been scared because her brother was a guardian angel who watched over her.

"Where is your brother," he asked.

"In heaven. My mom said he went to heaven from her stomach. That's why I was only a little bit scared," she said.

She finished the last of the pancakes and thanked him and took the plates to the sink and came back to the living room. From a chair she looked out the window over the golf course, bouncing her feet. The sound of his towel working the dry leather filled the room.

She said, "This is an emergency. And we're taking evasive action."

"That's right."

"My dad said this was a long time coming. It started before I was born even and I'm nine." She thought about that for a second and then asked, "How old are you?"

"I'm a hundred and thirty-seven."

"No way," she said and smiled.

"Oh. Maybe it's thirty-seven. I can never remember."

She slept on the couch and he sat out on the patio watching the road and drinking water and coffee. He put a second treatment of conditioner on the boots and set them on the railing to air. It seemed to him that she had dissociated from whatever had been done to her, and then he reminded himself that he had no idea if anything beyond what he witnessed was done to her. Nor did he know what her history was, if she had only recently been snatched up, or if she'd been in the many pipelines of abuse operated by people such as Denny. His gut told him she hadn't been truly abused. Yet just a few hours in the presence of a predator of Denny's order might be enough to traumatize a child. He wasn't sure. The dissociation could be from the loss of her family or the total instability of the world.

From the truck he brought the 80mm box up to the porch and sat in lastlight and in the twilight wiring and configuring the devices into their housings. In the dark, he took the box back to the truck where he sat on the open tailgate and replenished his magazines from Denny's canister of green tip rounds and smoked one of the cigarettes Ben had given him in the starlight the evening before. He came in once to check on her sleeping in the master bedroom, enfolded deep in the white swells of an enormous down comforter like a fawn curled in snow drift. He came back out with two dry almond butter sandwiches on stale bread that he forced himself to eat. At ten he thought about waking her but waited until eleven-thirty.

Certain events and moments don't actually end. Like a rich purple dye in water altering by degrees everything in the stream ahead, these moments have transfigured some essential substance of the man who lives through them and that substance is carried forward through time for as long as he may walk. Perhaps farther. He thought that it was best to die full saturated in the color. He thought of Denny's claims regarding Phil and wondered. *Just see the promise through.* She heard him moving around and got up and found the boots were by the couch on the floor. She put them on, drank a glass of water from the sink, and they went out the door and crossed the patio into the night.

"We're going to the doctor now?"

"Yes."

She said, "What's your name? I'm Alice."

"That's a good name," he said. "Grayson is my name."

"Grayson is a good name too, I think."

"Thanks."

* * *

It was only a few miles distance but took nearly a half hour as he drove with the headlights off and kept a slow steady pace so that he might hear any other vehicles on adjacent and nearby roads. From their place in the dark neighborhood hills outlying Moab, they saw the small constellation of lights in town where the contractors held their perimeter in aggregate glowing like a fallen loadstar on the dim valley floor. Grayson noticed Alice watching the road ahead as they rolled forward. When they paused at an intersection she craned her neck to listen when he listened. He began to ask her at each such pause if all was quiet and she nodded in the affirmative throughout the rest of the short trip.

When Alejandro the doctor came outside, Grayson was waiting in a deck chair and looking at the stars. The halo and orb of the doctor's wife's flashlight shone in a second story window. The doctor wore an expensive pair of green nylon hiking pants, stained and torn at the knees, and dusty running shoes. In his hands he carried a bottle of Scotch whiskey and two squat square glasses. He sat down in one of the patio chairs and sighed.

"I don't think they got to her." He cupped his hands between his knees. "Psychologically, there's obviously some stuff going on.

Dissociation of some sort, perhaps. But considering the circumstances I could say the same about virtually anyone right now, myself included. And physically, although there might have been some type of, shall we say—." He glanced away and exhaled his disgust and quickly glanced back and continued, "There might have been some kind of activity, but I don't think anything was completed. That's not to minimize anything, it's just the most positive point of view. If you know what I mean."

"I think so," Grayson said.

Grayson didn't look at the doctor but continued gazing at the sky where by virtue of the lightless earth around him he found new depth to the galaxies that could be seen--the stars and the perceived depth of them seeded as they were in three dimensions. He, them, everything--all scaffolded in a tensioned web of nebulas and blackholes. A universe. And somewhere within, or behind, that universe was the mystery of this totality of existence existing at all. The doctor too, having little in the way of leverage or rejoinder, or perhaps just needing a break, was silent as he poured liquor in the two glasses and passed one through the space between them.

"My wife is just putting her, Alice, and my son to bed," the doctor finally said.

Grayson nodded. "Thanks for taking her," he said.

"The money's gone, but I still could really use your help," the doctor admitted.

Grayson shook his head and said, "It didn't matter then. It doesn't matter now."

"I take it you didn't find your friend."

"No," Grayson said. "Not yet."

"This is just supposition on my part, but it's something you might want to consider. I don't think this was a wholesale slaughter type of thing. That money, the six grand I mentioned to you previously, I used it as a bribe, maybe three or four days ago. The helicopters swept through in the morning and by noon or so they shut down the road and seemed to go door to door through this specific neighborhood. I just waited right here in front for them to come. I was quite certain I was going to die. A fellow approached the house, looked African to me, walked up with rifle and body armor, everything, and I held the envelope with the cash and about six gold eagles out, so he could see what it was. I said take it. He took it. He told me to go inside and not come out and so that's what I did."

Grayson looked off in the neighborhood, dark and quiet and yet underlaid with the anxious fact, the vibration of temporality. A soft ceaseless draft sucked up out of the rock canyons behind the neighborhood rustling tall desiccant pod stalks of yucca. The dry seeds encased at the ends of the stalks shook arrhythmic and eerie. The sun would rise and fall again in the darkness, its whirl of nova and globe, and in this darkness and the next, death asks the question: what meaning will you make of your life before I take it from you? Grayson had always answered this question with the sacred notion of fatherhood. God's track laid out for man. To believe there is no inherent meaning in life is to cede the future to those who do and ceding anything at all was flatly not in his nature. He had exiled it, but perhaps now fear returned low-grade. A grim lorry of sour remorse and sorrow. The roving glow of the doctor's wife's flashlight emerged again within the dim house. With an act of faith comes not cessation of doubt but rather its primacy, a dialogue bending certainty to its breaking point. What is faith if it is untested? The evident way is not the way.

Yield to whatever is left that is good, Grayson thought. It's time.

"If your friend had money, then he's probably out there somewhere. If he didn't then maybe he's not. I'm suggesting it's a possibility. That's all. Obviously I have no real way to know anything." The doctor drew the empty glass up beside his face as if to juxtapose it with the conjectural expression of his raised eyebrows. "Did he have money?"

"An inheritance of gold and silver."

"Well then, he's probably out there."

"The problem is, the coins were not in his possession. Not when they came through." But Grayson wasn't thinking about money or schemes. He was thinking about Denny saying the mercenaries had targeted Phil at the outset. Grayson wrestled with the intractable paradox that despite all perceptions, the shadows we disappear in or emerge from are each cast of God's same sheltering hand.

"Well, like I mentioned, there's no evidence to really suggest one way or another. It's a single example of their behavior. No way to guess further into group dynamics much less motivations. I mean to say, I hope you find your friend."

A moment later the doctor's wife emerged at the front door. Though she was silent, Grayson felt the quiver of impending catastrophe upon her as if it had enveloped him bodily. It was a feeling you never, ever forgot. Graceful, she took a chair. It was impossible to go back and untangle events leading up to the unbounded moment, the lever of time, or central contradiction, where Grayson had cradled his own son in his arms but he could recognize when others were feeling similar incongruity hypostatizing around them. A madness lay in that paradox. One lived already. But could he maybe spare her that anguish, even if he could not transfigure his own, he wondered. He finished the drink and poured another.

The doctor's wife, Gia, was Lebanese and had thick dark hair, an intelligent and fiercely open beauty. Her eyes were wet and swollen from crying. She touched the doctor on the knee and nodded to him. They both looked across at Grayson and sighed.

"The way things lay now we'll get you out by going south."

* * *

Up the hill from the unemployment building Grayson waited the hours until he could make a move towards the shop to let Denny's dogs go free. A promise made to a devil was still a promise and perhaps those are some of the most important kind to keep. He sat in the shade of the cut bank overhang and watched the hovering drones configured like latticework on the blue sky. Each a set of roving eyes and the accumulating whir of the small rotors pervaded the central area of Main with an ominous pulsing carrier wave. Across the road in the shade of rhododendron an irregular band of hobos in patched cuts and dilapidated leather stewed some foul meat, cat or other, in a shallow pot made of a crimped bit of quarterpanel and they braised and seasoned the course with pine needles dried and crushed into a powder and steeped in vinegar or something else makeshift and similarly astringent. They guarded their gaunt dogs against one another's jabs and pulled them close on leashes of rent rope, so they'd stay near, and the dogs sat close and sniffed Grayson in the wind over the stew, certain he was near. The corrugated roofline of the warehouse was visible from his hide and he watched it stand unvisited for the better part of the day. When the hobos moved off, one of them went to relieve himself in a provisional cathole on the far side of the rhododendrons. He wiped with some of the leaves and saluted as if he saw Grayson up there and turned and left, otherwise silent.

An hour before dusk, when the sun and moon both sat opposed in the sky he sprinted down the hill and crossed the road and kept sprinting on through the rhododendrons to the neighborhood block where he cut into the alley on the far side of the warehouse lot. A long line of blackberry tangle hung over a sagging wood fence on one side of the gravel strip and on the other were the screened back entrances of a few looted and desolated shops or cafés. A small, galvanized walk-in freezer adjacent to one of the back doors sat dormant and a green dumpster turned over on its end obscured the continuous view down the alley. A squirrel shook in the leaves overhead passing limb from limb. A dairy and ammonia stench emanated from the dumpster as he squeezed his way to the fence amid the blackberry vines. Down a few paces he came to the charcoal and rubble of a pallet fire made to one side of the alley. In the ash lay the charred ribcage and offal bones of a horse that had been seemingly rolled into the fire. Scorched reliquary tires of a car or truck had been stuffed inside the carcass and upon them were chalk letters of some half-written word. For height he stepped onto the creaking ribcage and hiked himself up over the fence and dropped nimbly into the dark lot to find it fully contained and wrung round with shady trees. He raised the recon gun and walked out on the field like some slave gladiator before an audience of the departed.

Across the lot, a chain-link truck gate draped in blackberry was open a few feet. As he traversed the tracked ground and his boots scuffed in the dry ripples of earth a black stray dog started from the shadows and crashed through the trailing vines stretched out over the backlit interstice of the gate. He heard the nails skittering on the aggregate outside the warehouse and a flock of pigeons lifted from their pickings and settled into the high limbs of the contiguous alders.

The black dog had moved too fast to be one of the loping hounds. Grayson believed Denny had told the truth about intending to feed them the day before. He thought he could hear their baleful whining as he got to the gate so he concluded the dog was a stray. The door to the rear loading bay was open. The dogs were pawing a gate or a chain of some sort. It rattled and stopped and then one of them would whine and get the others whining and the chain would rattle again. Crouching in the shadows he watched the lifeless abstract gloss of the parking area for a while. He felt as if he stood on the precipice of some otherworld lookingglass, and he listened to the thrum and chug of the powerplant. He imagined a man who had for a brief slip of an hour centuries prior likewise hunted this ground before twilight and crouched in his battered buckskin outfit on this precise quarter of the valley. It would have been creek woods back then. Of course, that imagined ghost was Grayson himself in some ideal typification. As that realization crossed his mind inevitably it was followed with the casting of his mind into the future where he presumed some next backwoods insurgent in the line, cast in the same rare conglomerate of the same elements, gazed back at him there.

This spot might have been an oasis to the weary and beacon to those in exodus of the east and to the flight of sects. All aspects he figured were much unwound and fading. At the left side of the lot a yellow bulldozer with its dull blade raised on hydraulics rested in dirt, and resting there as well, some few meters separate, sat a wiry black dog of medium size. And then it seemed for a moment that dog and man both tried to see each other but also could not, as if between them lay some lensatic, correlative veil that obscured the light of the eye that meets the eye of another.

Grayson did a double-take but the wiry dog was gone. Through the rifle scope he saw keys in the ignition of the bulldozer, orange foam keychain. The dirt around the burnished steel tracks was dry, but fresh. He stood and went to the open hangar door and crossed the sheened concrete saying soothing things in the direction of the kennels. Denny's dogs saw him and all looked and then got excited. They made little groans and he heard the shuffling of their haunches on their blankets, the thump of tails against their enclosure. Straightaway he rustled the paper food bag on the shelves and they whimpered and then went quiet again as he slung cups of the kibble over the concrete to the far corners of the warehouse and went dipping back in the bag in the fashion of a man bailing water from a sinking dinghy. The coonhounds kept quiet and trotted one by one out of their kennels as he opened the gates down the line and they proceeded to padding and slipping their way over the whole expanse of the square, never leaving the imaginary boundary at the open hangar door. While they ate he filled their bowls from the sink and set them out on the floor where they came eventually and drank for a long time and then went back to scrounging out the last lost nuggets.

The card table and mercenaries, taped bundles of heroin, the bodies and weapons were all displaced somewhere, and a cleaning crew of some skill had redacted the previous night's events. Bolts of dying red sunlight bored through three bullet holes in the hangar door as the solitary trace of yesterday, a signature of fine weaponry. He cast more kibble over the floor and walked back out the hangar door and stood pondering the motel next door and the pool turned lagoon where television sets bobbed on the algae surface and dragonflies patrolled the festering air. Part of him knew or sensed that he was at the psychic door that would not remain closed, the one over which was engraved: *Defeat.* Another part which already knew the defeat of years knew that—until you agreed—no defeat was final. Despair too was negotiable. He spat mist into the horizon light and crossed back over to the gate and looked in upon the field glowing pink and gold now in the shifted sun refracted out of the redrock.

The black dog had returned to his original place along the far line of berry vines and fence to his left where it was still dim. It was digging with its forepaws at something. Under its chest was a small mound of loose, excavated dirt. It would dig and check its progress, head erect, and dig some more. He watched it, trying to see a collar. He looked over his shoulder at the backhoe in the lot and then stepped through the gate and shook his pack down his arm and squatted again. At the rise of fresh earth, the black dog glanced up at him and waited to see what the man would do exactly. Grayson kept watching and when the dog turned back he lit the last cigarette letting most of the smoke spindle off in the lengthening shadows. The incessant hiss of the drones was met and matched on earth by the cicadas waking up. On the backdrop of the sky their diode blue false lights twinkled.

The clicking of the hounds' nails on the warehouse floor echoed over as they sought every last morsel. The black dog would stop digging every now and again to snap at something flying around him and he'd search around for it after he popped his jaws to see if he'd gotten it and then he'd turn back to digging. Grayson could see a few little collections of the insects here and there along the rise of earth, whirling and dispersing. The dog broke through the top layer of earth and tried to pull at whatever was down there. But it wasn't going to move. It would lift in the dog's mouth and he'd tug and drop it back. About the third time this happened he saw that it was a stiffened, dusty human hand attached to the body, still buried. Grayson's head went down toward his chest. He looked at his boots. All he said was, God damn.

Behind him the satiated hounds wanted order. Two of them had hazarded beyond the hangar door and nuzzled the chain link gate by his knee. "Git," Grayson said and they meandered off. He absently wiped his mouth with one hand as if he'd pull away some unspeakable thing before it could coalesce. A deep breath and he let the rifle down by the pack and stood half hoping he'd misread Denny and this was a set-up, an ambush, instead of what it actually was, which was far less manageable and vastly more frightening. He thought for a few minutes then picked up the rifle. At the top of the rise, the black dog was snapping yellow jackets in assault. He waved one away. He looked at the hand stuck up out of the earth. It was the sleeveless and ringed left hand and forearm of a grown white man caked in thin red mud.

The panting dog some four feet to his side watched him with evident certainty they'd work on the problem together. As he crouched, the first one stung him behind the knee. He just swatted it away, muttered. The second and third of them came in at his head in unison. He ducked and swore as he looked for their silhouettes. There were maybe ten or twenty of them, swirling in a mass like dark electrons on the orange backlight of the setting sun. When he went to digging on his hands and knees they seemed to multiply out of nothing. Fifty, a hundred—so thick he could hear their armored bodies colliding, jostling for the orbit around his head and face and neck. He swore again, and the dog barked and snapped and worked one off of his pink tongue. Both man and dog skittered away with him muttering and the black dog yelping.

From the stainless sink in the warehouse bathroom he splashed water on his head and picked a few of the burrowing hornets from folds in his ragged collar. Another was crawling on his arm that he shook off. His face and neck were already swelling in an evil, rosy dough. The black dog had tried to follow him into the hangar but two of the shorthaired hounds growled and the black dog skulked off into the chaparral. Grayson shushed them. A moment later, he walked back through the gate to the hill to look again and see if the swarm would move off in the dark.

* * *

It was past midnight when Grayson shuttled over the luminous gold dashes on 191 and up the driveway to the once fine hotel that now seemed haunted and ruinous. Under his breath he muttered the same few lines of an old song, the name of which he had never known. *Going away to a far distant land, going away for awhile.* His footfall on the earth or pavement had held the motive backbeat and when he stopped at the Jeep and looked in he stopped muttering. Ben wasn't there, so he set the pack and gun on the tailgate and finished his water and soon enough Ben came through the ivy with the .22 crosswise to his hips. The wind caterwauled over the rim crags and through the cracked glass of the upper windows of the hotel rooms. Grayson moved his pack and Ben took a place on the tailgate with the .22 hung down between his knees. He gestured with a thin moonlit finger to the empty water bottle.

"I found some more like that, full ones in the bar." Ben angled back on one arm and switched the rear dome light on and then flopped reaching and came back upright with the bottle. He jolted when he got a full view.

"Jesus. What happened to you?"

In the quarter light Grayson looked cave-born. A bog dweller. The side of his face and head were so swollen that the tension on the skin of his cheek turned white at the peak and the hair over his ear angled out from his scalp. When he twisted to face him Ben winced and gawked as the other side of him was nearly normal.

"I got stung a few times."

"Are you allergic?"

"Slightly. Are you packed?

They crossed the highway with Grayson mumbling the quiet song lines again. *The sun will dry up the ocean, heaven will cease to be, and the world will lose its motion if I prove false to thee.* Ben didn't ask what they meant then nor later. By the time they'd gotten through the marshland and the trailer blocks and back into the western side streets where the Humvees were casting searchlights, the boy was all but mute with capped terror. The lights stretched a block or more, blasting through the boughs of the old trees sending owls down from their hunting rooks and throwing sinister weaving shadows over the bleak wreckage of the neighborhood. The native talk of the Africans, echoing dull from the cabs and from the sidewalks those few times when they got out to investigate some hobo's bivouac, brought Ben to near hyperventilation. They cooled off in the worst of hidden marginal places—the trash strewn and reeking canals or the streets marked by the homeless with white rags where theirs or others nameless dead had been collected-- where rot, ruin and worse, warded even the Eastern Europeans back to their trucks content to fire teargas canisters through windows or under vehicles and wait for their prey to move in the headlights. Grayson and Ben lay cramped under the porch steps of a townhouse, beset on one side with heaping fetid piles of trash and on the other with the sporadic and sluggish grunts of innominate vagabonds coupling under a filthy sleeping bag.

"God damn that drone noise is driving me insane," Ben said, covering his ears against the whirling panopticon above. One of the androgynous tramps took to bludgeoning the other with the bullet-ridden door of a microwave. Grayson and Ben bolted from their hiding place to make the crossing of Main.

* * *

Denny's truck was parked right where Grayson had left it, and as he dropped the tailgate and nodded for Ben to put his pack in the bed, the doctor opened the front door of the house and stepped out carrying travel bags and a suitcase. Ben pushed the 80mm box over the bed when Grayson told him to and he hauled it down onto the pavement. The doctor joined them nodding to Ben and then looking askance at Grayson. Alice was standing in the open doorway with a tiny knapsack and a brown grocery bag of her things, studying the truck glinting in the moonlight against the desert hills. When Grayson turned around for the doctor to see the swelling, Alice saw too and started crying. The doctor's wife, Gia, saw him as well and put her hand over her mouth and bent to console the girl. The doctor adopted a wide stance to accommodate the scarce light and turned Grayson's shoulders gently with both hands.

"Christ almighty," he whispered. "How many times did you get stung?"

Alice was sobbing now in the doorway. Grayson didn't answer the doctor. He was in substantial pain. The swollen feeling obscured the sense of interior and exterior. It seemed that Alice was in his head or perhaps that his pain was in the world. By sheer force of will he moved, taking a few shaky steps as if through psychic water, and then found his equilibrium going back to the truck the gear the mission. Always the mission.

On the tailgate he had laid out the 1911 pistol and Denny's Hi-Power. He took the two spare magazines from his pocket and set them down and took up the gun and ejected the round into his hand. He racked the slide several times and dropped the hammer and seated the magazine again and repeated the operation on the Hi-Power. When Grayson spoke, it sounded like a drunk speaking through his coat.

"Ben you know where you're going, right?" Ben leaned over the side of the bed. He looked at the doctor.

"Arizona I guess."

The doctor stopped gawking and searched through a backpack for his kit. He turned back to his wife and they exchanged a look that said it was time to go. She nodded and spoke to the girl and boy. The doctor brought out an epinephrine syringe and started unpeeling the wrapper.

"Come around to the light so I can get this in you."

"He's not going." Ben sighed.

The doctor swallowed and touched Grayson's arm, cupped it under the biceps gently and pulled. Grayson went along into the light and started rolling up his shirt but couldn't get it over the swelling.

"Just drop your pants down a little bit and I'll put it in your hip," the doctor said. He dropped the automatic plunger on the injection.

Grayson thanked him as he watched Alice and the boy in the yard. Children born in uncertain and degraded times would sometimes grow to be the adults to bring certainty and value to the next generation. He wished that for them. The doctor had an alcohol wipe between his teeth which he tore neatly so it exposed the wipe. He dabbed it over the dot of blood.

"This truck isn't going to set off any alarms or draw the helos. You're still going to keep the headlights off. Take Spanish Valley to Beeman. That's where you stop for ten seconds, and I get out and you keep going. All the way to the old airport road and then wait. Don't hit the highway until you see or hear the guard shack go up."

"Go up?"

"Explode."

"Then what?" Ben asked.

"If you drive through the night you can get through the reservation. Do not stop in the reservation for anything. Pick one of the little towns south, in the forest. Just don't cross the 40 freeway by day."

"Stay in the forest,' Ben said. Fear was evident again in his wide eyes.

The doctor saw that Grayson was leaving and there would be no discussion. "Are you going to say goodbye to her? I don't know what I'd tell her otherwise."

They all three stood there a moment. He had his head down. He tried to say something and stopped and started again. He told them to load up and nodded as he walked off to the bushes. Ben put his hand out for the doctor and they shook, and then he took up the .22 and tucked himself into a corner of the bed as Gia brought the children down and situated them in the rear seats of the truck. Grayson came back to the tailgate. He held Denny's Hi-Power out for Ben to take and he took it and thanked him.

"Remember the frog's egg conversation," Grayson asked.

Ben nodded. "It just gets harder."

"That's right. Every day is training for the next. There's no reprieve. Ever."

"I'll remember."

"Then you'll be fine."

When Grayson opened the rear door, the doctor's boy seemed to look up at him, but they were really on the same level, and it was just that the boy's eyes were wide and unsure. Grayson kept his neck craned to one side to hide himself. In the footlamp he saw Alice had her cowboy boots on. She started coming across the seat to him, but he was already up the running board and he caught the boy's head under his armpit and just pulled him in too and he had them both there in his arms, whispering the world to them, its snares and outs, until she stopped crying and believed him. The boy's arm was around his waist. Gia in the front seat turned back around to see and brought her hands over her mouth, her shoulders shaking a little bit.

All he said was, "It's gonna be okay. It's gonna be okay."

6
The Hell

At four in the morning as the mercenaries occupied them-selves investigating the destruction of the south going guard shack, he was back with the hounds. He closed the hangar door and fed them again in their cages and went out through the foyer and around to the lot. He wondered if the stray black hound would be on the hill, but he was gone. The drones at the perimeter with their blinking lights wavered like close galaxies or simulacra of galaxies as the dawn light diffused on the sky. Their false code was given only to observe the petty crime of mendicants and insurgents and to catalog the bobbing of broken television sets in the green hotel pool that day. He turned the key and started the bulldozer. He worked fast, just making two short runs, where he stuck the great brown blade into the earth and reversed to pull the dirt back before he cut the engine. From his backpack he took two cans of wasp and hornet spray and shook them as he walked back toward the bulldozer. There was no buzzing. They were gone from the area. He set the cans in the dust beside the hole the dog had dug and went back for his gloves.

In the crepuscular hour he worked though the dusty jumble of arms and legs, torsos and dirt until he had enough of them out of the hole that he could get down inside the grave. He puked and had to climb back out and get the bandana around his face. He went over each of the bodies like some crude and toolless archeologist to make sure, absolutely sure. And when he was satisfied, he started the tractor up and pushed the back and packed grave down. He cut the engine again and got down on the fresh earth beside two long bodies, so red with caked mud they were like effigies. He had finally found Phil and his wife Sarah. Beside them lay a small bundle wrapped in a blanket. From the warehouse he took bolt cutters and extension cords, one of which he plugged into the auxiliary panel on the power plant and then unlooped upon the ground through the lot and under the boards of the old fence on the far side.

With the bundle in his arms he processed through the side street and the alley to the freezer behind the coffee shop, bent at each step under a certain quality of intangible weight. The freezer door was padlocked, and he stood there a moment staring at the diamond shapes pressed into the metal door like quilted foil, listening to the sparrow's language weaving amid the drone whir. He cut the padlock and set the dead child inside on a wire shelf. He brought the electrical extension cord through the alley. When he connected it, the freezer lurched to its work. A thin quantity of warm water lay on the steel floor of the freezer but by some grace it was otherwise empty and clean. Oily drops of condensation anointed the baby's blanket.

As the sun came up on the rim, he carried the bodies of Phil and Sarah likewise over the course and set them inside and closed the door on the freezer. With the cutters he trenched a place to bury and hide the extension cord so that it would not be found and disturbed in his absence. For an hour he sat in the alley contained within the cool dim of the thorned vines with his head in hand, replaying decisions and affairs of his life and thinking out lines of logical motion that could have but never did happen. Man's omnipresent option to give up was there for Grayson too, but he gave it no attention. He knew this fight. Just as he'd told Ben: it never ends. He thought now that to live is to fight. In the morning currents vacuuming through the valley, tender green tips of the individual vines dandled about, seeking light and softly sweeping the brown sweat- soaked hair on his head. Shadows of those vines cast on the alley floor wavered over the shadow of his tasseled head and seemed to pull to him as if in that negated dark mirror of the world, where shadow is primary, perhaps the tentacular vines sought not light from the sun as their sustenance rather the green, opaque light of his sorrow. And while the graceful precise purr of the freezer motor tethered him to the material world at hand, the demoniac nexus between planes where planets and deserts collide generated a replete chaos in his heart. He felt driven by a noble madness that fights the day and that chisels at its own vessel of being, like some wicked beak that picks at its shell. But this was the condition of every man and Grayson suffered to contain it in each minute. The secret axiom to unseen warfare is humility at whatever cost, because beyond humility is the fact of being alive which one cannot see in despair, and if one actualizes the fact of being alive he also realizes he will die and thus, gratitude for the stupendous gift of existence floods the desert of the real and waters the barren plains of heartache.

When the hour was up Grayson forced himself to stand and go back to the warehouse. He filled the bowls and set them out in the shade and dumped the rest of the food out on the slab in piles, so the dogs would not contend for it later. He let the faucet outside the hangar trickle. They sniffed him as he stood in the hangar door thinking about them, how their first day out would be full of danger. But they were already a pack and well fed and would fare fine. In time the rangy black dog emerged over the dry lawn of the motel and trotted a line, watching the hunting dogs and looking between Grayson and the gate. "Go on home," he said to the dog. It looked at him with its ears cocked and knowing the man wasn't serious went back to sniffing until one of the hunting dogs walked out and bayed halfheartedly. The black mutt ran off over the hill with his ears and tongue flopping and his beard blown back to the oncoming drafts. When the food was half cleaned from the slab, he slipped away with his gear.

At quarter to three he touched off two IEDs on the perimeter. One on Main and the other on the eastern flank. He was back up on the hill behind the unemployment building when he hit call on the cell phone and the shiver went out through the streets. The first plumes of white smoke were followed by orange sheeted flame and then the black smoke of the conflagration went curling, licking up above the trees. Having run out their timers, two more devices detonated in the trailer and city parks where he had configured them amid the ready tinder of previously scorched wooden houses. The secondary explosions from adjacent propane tanks went off minutes later and redoubled the dark billows rising on the blue sky.

Against the lights, Grayson picked up and ran. By the time he was parallel with the main drag, he heard the Humvees and some trucks powering over the road toward the fire growing from the trailers into pastures and the surrounding neighborhoods. He caught snippets of the men through the spaces between buildings and then the fire trucks were on the strip, and they flashed too, red and silver remainders as in a picture carousel. In the interchange of mercenaries coming and going he slipped over the sandbag wall of the perimeter and crept up to the first island of pumps at the gas station where he popped the sheet metal housing over the guts of the central pump and fitted inside his device and then, on his way to the rim behind the rented room on Joe's property some few winding miles south, he installed more devices on pumps at other stations and on propane tanks in yards and at a hardware store. Thirty minutes passed as he ran and ran and when the last devices timed out they set to burn most of the southeast quarter of town, and a good portion of the southwest caught soon after as it spiked over Main and then horseshoed. He went to walking the rest of the way to the rim and saw in the blasted-out pocket lot, his old room in the A-frame, now ashes. He thought of the mushrooms cajoling him, prodding him to fear under the porch that day of the initial assault: how he'd felt he carried some passenger with him. The sense of freight was returned now and he rose over the rim and went out into the desert like some old seeker of serpents or occult teaching. He walked until nightfall when he crouched and dug a cantaloupe-sized pit in the sand and made his cookfire by which to warm his beans and sardines in the tin cup, and in the way sequences and small patterns of the world are comprised so that micro mirrors in some sense the macro, he observed his small solitary lambency of manzanita coals in the bowl of silica sand and remarked that he had made both fires large and small, one of the valley and this other upon the plateau. He said out loud that while he was not God he was, by God, so constituted with the tiniest mirror of this Being. And he said he was grateful to be in the arena, in the world, fighting.

It seemed to Grayson ten years had been passed in chasing the forerunner of existence. Not to know why his son was taken but rather to know where his son was taken to, and how he could get there to be with him. To check on him would be enough. Time was to give no malleable moment for him, or for any other man. There was only the forward running into that mystery. Running and fighting along the way. Each step and blow landing on the ever-advancing ground of an abiding and absolute conditionality. It's not that man tests his will against the scaffolding of creation, it's rather that man's will, like the composite elements of creation, is all—from quark to consciousness--contained in total within God. And Grayson thought: perhaps then it is the case that in this way that I am essentially and forever contained in what we call God, then my son too is so contained in me. Not merely in sentiment, but in spirit which necessarily must precede matter.

Upon the La Sals, Grayson saw the distant floodlamps of the mercenaries' forward base and said to himself out loud half-screaming, "If this is the doorway through dreams to death, then I was right about the nature of these lives." And then he talked straight to himself, "You better get your shit together. Enough."

He rose, leaving the small fire to burn and reclaim his scalded tins to the earth. Bats wove in multitude of pairs and triplets out from the mountain caves as if among crooked hollows was some-where the uncapped tunnel to hell. He donned his pack and rifle and marched over the nightmare plateau where ahead was death and where behind him the great fire raged, pulsing a pink orb of heat out over the plateau and up to the dark stars, spilling smoke from the Colorado to the Green river. There were orange motes on the mountain in front. Fires where the mercenaries sat out bullshitting.

The wiry black hound was behind him somewhere silhouetted black on black over a rim here and then skipping through an ar-royo and picking up the pebbles with his padding paws. Grayson sensed him. He didn't look back but heard him panting, keeping up. Grayson envisioned the dog veering from the terra cotta scars of slickrock upon the earth, racing through the divine slip into a netherland malpais parallel to him somehow, where in the dark, darkness proper, emanates its ever-fading green and where ideas of creation seduce matter. Grayson, in the envisioning over footfall's hours, travelled in his way that same outland path but toward his quarantania, through the pine foothills and scrabble until at dawn he drew his knife and unseamed the first canvas tent where two mercenaries slept in cots.

There was just a light seesaw of snoring and a pressed wood fire in a box stove at the corner that with the shifting of the logs pushed out twists of smoke between the cracks in the pipe chimney. The tent stank of used rubbers and Turkish cigarettes, and he wrenched down quiet but firm with the spine of the blade against his knee twice in quick succession just as the first birds were chirping in the trees. On one side of the encampment where the workers cavorted, women whispered in Croatian or Russian, some in Spanish. He whispered back, "Start running."

The night guard on duty walking on the needles and cones rounded the approaching bend in the trail saying his last words in yet another language and did it quietly as if muttering them to himself, repudiating their intent. Grayson pulled him trailside amongst the sage and little lodgepoles to send him off. Up the path he saw the valley was hazed out and scanted smoke stretched from the inferno of the town over the plateau and hung on the mountainside like thin fog. The fog concealed him over the raised-up earth and through trails to the work trailers where the workers and mercenaries not at the firefighting still slept and the power plants idled for air conditioning alone. He fit two devices under the tanker and placed the last two in his pack on power plants at random in the maze. Returned to the tanker, he cranked off the spigot cap with the bar key and switched the valve safety in the cab to let the diesel flow out and over the terracing. He waited in the brush for the rivulet to reach him some two hundred yards down the slope and scratched the sparking tab on a road flare from the cab of the tanker and then joined the two as he leapt off and the runner of fire ripped back up the rivulet in a terrible, audible sucking sound.

As he ran through the forest and through the jets of rock dust cascading about them, he was joined on the trails of the foothills by the half-naked whores to whom he'd given warning and were so kept safe but ran shoeless and had nowhere to go but further down the slope to the waiting inferno. He cut out to a spur. They didn't see him in their panic and flight. In the relative after quiet, he stood pounding water from his canteen bottle, and watched them flee.

* * *

That night in the warm dark, an autumn wind blew through to clear the air in the valley. He lay on his side in the dry lawn of a dark condominium watching the candles flicker and glow in the windows of the amalgamated whorehouse. He was two yards down from the spot where he'd set up to wait for Munson, whose body still resided in the madam's minivan and whose bike now lay stripped to the frame in a garbage pile at one end of the yard. Grayson could see the madam silhouetted at the back of the front room, rocking in the old lounge chair and drinking from a glass. Open for business in Gehenna and in Moab. She'd been in there since seven when it had started to cool down, and she had swung the blue door open and latched the screen for some breeze. Smell of lard and beans and toasted flour had carried across the street, and then she'd taken up a position in the living room broken only to visit a bottle and the ice box a few times. The smell caused him to dig out his last provisions and eat them cold as he watched her outline and the lithe outlines of the girls as they came and went from the adjoined quarters relaying their hardships of the day and twirling in experimental outfits composed out of their poor, shared wardrobe. After his meal he climbed the wrought-iron condominium stairs to pilfer and came back down with an infant's plastic bowl and a half box of baking powder that carried on it a hint of curry and he poured a little water in the bowl with the powder and made a paste that he slathered on the stung places which were much reduced but still wholly deformed that side of his face and neck.

Opaque firelight reflected from the smoldering fires in town upon a taut linear cloud of smoke stretching from the river north to the mountains south. Where the cloud met the untainted air just over the proximate rim wall, an inconceivable yellow band like an aurora borealis oscillated, disappeared, and returned. By some chemistry it would not comingle and in this repudiation the yellow emanation arose and held him. He watched it for an hour or more and could invoke no explanation but was reminded of certain places where oceans meet and upon the surface a stark band of divided light and dark water stretches off to the horizon.

Chickens in their roost murmured through the hours. A tree or roof timber somewhere distant in the blocks split and collapsed but nothing moved on the street while he drifted in and out of sleep. Upon waking, he crossed the street and filled his bottle from a faucet beside the coop and with his eyes traced the white plastic pipe back into the whorehouse yard where there was a solar unit rigged to a well pump. Then he wandered back slowly over the pavement and sidewalk where oak leaves were falling upon miniature sand drift dunes, compiling themselves grain by grain on the concrete. Low thin branches of the sidewalk oak trailed on his shoulder. He thought of the dead, his and everyone else's, and knew that though they were not present, they were contained somehow in the same great genius gyre of creation. Somewhere. From far below knowing, a wave of sorrow pounded him.

More sleep, he told himself. *You've gone far enough.* He slept again and when he woke, the madam was still seated in her luminous room, the only light on the street. When he stepped onto the porch boards he made the sign of the cross, right to left. At the creak of the boards, her eyes looked over the rims of her glasses.

"It's open. Just reach in and tip that latch, honey."

The house, where it was in candlelight and he could see, was tidy and dignified. It smelled of menthol, beeswax, and dried chilies. There was a red leather couch across from the dark fireplace where she pointed for him to sit and another white floral chair with brass studs like the one she occupied where a stack of folded bedsheets was placed. More candles in the kitchen backlit her curly head of hair. He could see her thin hips were cocked languid to one side with her feet stacked on the ottoman. She was holding knitting needles while she sat in shadow. From a pack on the side table she lit a long cigarette and set the pack down beside the ashtray. Beside the ashtray was a highball glass sweating onto a paperback and a stainless snub revolver.

He leaned the recon gun between the cushions and sat down.

"I see you never closed."

She tapped the cigarette. "In thirty eight-years, you know I closed for one day. For a funeral. I had to go to Phoenix in January and got caught in a blizzard on the way back. Slept on the bus. Otherwise though, the party never ends."

"Might end this time."

"I know. How are we going to get out of this one? The ash raining down reminds me of Christmas. Don't you think? And now there's no one around. People don't think it snows in Moab and it doesn't that much. Not every year. But when it does, it's gorgeous. With the desert. Good lord. It's kind of like that now, that's how it feels."

From the hall where the trailer was attached he heard the women in their portion of the patchwork house laughing through the sheetrock and wood. Otherwise still, she peered over the rims of her glasses to gauge his reaction. But when he didn't say anything, she took up the drink and ashed her cigarette in the tray.

"What happened to your face?"

"Yellow jackets."

"Little devils."

"Who was the funeral for?"

"The what? Oh. My son."

"I'm terribly sorry."

She nodded her head. "Do you want a drink? Tequila or Southern Comfort, that's all I got."

"Southern Comfort, please."

She took up the ashtray and the glinting revolver and turned to the kitchen. Faint music from a stereo emanated out of the trailer windows where the girls had them open, and it carried through to the house. Grayson rose, leaving the rifle where it lay, and wove around the dining table to stand at the open house window and listen to the young women's voices, their laughter, and the music. He watched the madam in the kitchen quietly making the drinks. She was surrounded by an aura thrown from the glass votives dispatched to the corners and the counter for her work. The kitchen was narrow with a yellow tiled strip on the floor and beige countertops. A black and white print of Lupe Velez in a red frame hung on the back wall. In the picture her face was turned so that it seemed she was looking at the refrigerator. The sink was wet at the rim and clean and some mismatched dishes sat in a drying rack on a bright blue towel.

Her solar unit and auxiliary water pump were arrayed at the threshold of the back door. Battery banks and hand-wired panels with switches retrofitted to the application and a manifold of copper and plastic pipes crimped and cut, soldered and welded all with passable skill and pride of work. The glass stood on the counter half-full of the viscous liquor that undulated in the candlelight aura. As he watched the madam take three limes from a plastic mesh bag and slice them in half with a paring knife, he listened more intently to feel the texture of the Russian words the women spoke between the bars and at the bridge of the song, for he could not imagine knowing their meaning but thought he could feel it somehow just the same.

He could. And as he listened and watched the madam work the knife, he saw her hands for the first time and it began to click for him. The vague incongruity he'd sensed on her dissolved. The madam pressed each of the half limes on an old aluminum juicer and shook out the little seeds between each pressing. When she did this it actualized for him that she had once been, or still was in some way, a man. As if some other conclusion might be reached in looking elsewhere, he peered out into the backyard where it was only austere night staring back at him. The pastel, downy fruit of a peach tree outside the women's open window was cast in the green hue of their stereo display and in the slow breeze dandled like planets suspended in a child's mobile.

"Ice?" the madam asked. "I don't usually put ice in these, but if you want it, I got it."

"That's fine, thank you."

She stirred the juice and the liquor with a long cocktail spoon and held the glass up to thread the light through and satisfied brought it over to him by the window. Now he saw the density of the forehead and noted nicks of tool scars on the wrist. Wide fingernails. It was just a beat or a shade off, little more. He said nothing. He sipped the liquor and looked at the glass and took another and sighed.

"Tell me about it," she said and drank.

They passed a moment in silence and she took another of the long, slender cigarettes from a pack and offered it to him, but he declined. She lit up and looked over her shoulder. Grayson realized she was waiting for him to talk, but he just continued looking at the glass and feeling the liquor warm him.

"Smoky out there," she said.

"Indeed," he said taking his place back on the couch. The ice tinked in her glass as she circled it over the arm of the chair and drew on the cigarette. There was a silent moment where it seemed to Grayson it was two men staring at each other and when she realized, or sensed this too, she sat back in her chair and brushed her chest as if something were there, but there was nothing there.

Speaking of the smoke he said, "It'll clear up in a few days."

One of the Russian women had come down the hall and was standing at the mouth of the hallway poised on one foot as if she would pirouette. To Grayson it felt like she had simply appeared. Blonde straight hair was collected in a hand at her cheek, and she wore only a long black blouse that covered her to the supernal thigh. In the candlelight she smiled slyly and then joking pursed her lips the way one would in awaiting orders from a congenial, familiar field master. Grayson looked at the madam smoking, and then he looked away to the fireplace as if yet another, perhaps more attainable, less devastating vision might appear there in its dark bricks.

The madam saw him do it and said as she exhaled, "On the house tonight. It's on the house."

"I wouldn't know why," Grayson said.

"You don't have to. I know when I know."

The Russian took his hand and led him down the dark hallway and whispered something about watching his step that he didn't properly understand. Behind them she pulled the door tight so all was dim and led him to the left where there was a bathroom and more candles. He smelled potions and rinses and soaps. The tiles were clean. She slipped the blouse off and pulled the knob on the shower and turned and undressed him in the steam saying a few playful words about his scent and then more serious ones about the vast distances and sights he must have gathered to his experience. She went on saying she too knew about distances and also about the ways of men who traveled them in his manner. She acknowledged it was a manner weighted equally with abandon and self- control but this was only reasonable given the tragedy, the carnivals, and the wilderness he had surely encountered and she promised him that to come together and bear faithful witness to the fantastic and the mundane, whichever and however God proffered them, in whatever strange order, this was His greatest gift after life itself. For by this co-witnessing, in this communion, do we go on to construct worlds anew, with His guiding hand.

* * *

Behind the smoke scrim hanging in the near sky, the sun glowed florescent orange. The night wind had carried away the worst of the smoke, but still the air looked powdered. The contractors had commandeered the grocery store at some point. While it mirrored the disaster of the town in most ways, it was unburnt and most of the packaged food remained intact and edible. He sat in the back among stacked boxes of rotting fruit and cases of canned peaches and ate salami slices cut with his knife and wrapped in spongy white bread that he subsequently dipped into open jars of mayonnaise and mustard set between his boots. The loading dock door was open, so the sun came in part way. He drank a warm soda that he found in the employee refrigerator. When he was done, he went out the swinging rubber doors to the main floor with the empty silver propane tank off the forklift in one hand and he came back a minute later with a full tank in a dolly, wheeled through the empty aisles and back through the disarray to the dock. He fitted and clamped the tank and got up and turned the key. He got off to grab the remainder of salami, and he stuck it in his pack and got back on the forklift and revved it and went out through the rubber doors and down the aisles ripping what was left of the shelved goods from their stations and leaving a crinkling multicolored aftermath on the floor. The front doors were jammed open and he rolled right out on the sidewalk and over the faded yellow crosswalk with the rifle situated against his bent knee. It was quiet and still.

On the sidewalk he rammed through shopping carts that went over the curb and others rolled out onto the mayhem of charred and looted vehicles. At the corner he rode the concrete scoop onto the side street pavement and wove slowly amid the wreckage on Main to the westside streets where the trees were grey with ash but intact and swaying in the breeze on either side of him. Turning at the alley, he proceeded over the potholes and the gravel to the back of the coffee shop and stuck the forks under the freezer. The motor groaned, and when the freezer was free floating, he idled the lift and pulled the plug from the socket. The hard tires spun and kicked gravel along the scarred yellow fenders as he powered the lift and swiveled it out from the wall toward the blackberries. When he had it angled properly he reversed to the pavement, and so stabilizing, continued back over Main heading into the neighborhoods behind the grocery where he had emplaced no IEDs and where he remembered just nine months prior the houses had been well kept and the gardens were always grown out to the sidewalks under the old trees that reached over the rooflines. At one such house, where the sunflowers bent out upon the picket fence and lavender stalks grew up to meet them, he stopped and idled the motor.

This is a good place, he thought, and after he'd reversed the lift into the shade along the curb, he turned the keys to off and hopped down. In the shed around back he found a shovel and walking back he peered through the windows powdered in ionized ash and saw there was a piano and books in shelves that lined the walls down to a wood floor that was clean. A pitcher of dead flowers sat on a sofa table. There were coats hung on hooks by the door. There were no bodies. These were nice people.

* * *

At dusk he came up out of the hole between the front beds and his hands were curled up to the exact diameter of the shovel's handle. He flexed them and drank some water. The breeze was up pushing smoke and racing down the rim through the street and back over the desert. A calico cat watched him from across the street and then watched the birds finding their nests. In the base of the hole a basketry of interwoven roots was laid bare where he had worked around them with the spade and trowel going beneath the surface roots and leaving all of them that were bigger than his little finger. The smell of the lavender had hung with him each minute of the digging and did so as he placed the figures of Phil and Sarah and the child into the hollow.

Andrew Edwards 313

It was a long time standing there before he filled back the hole. At some point when it was done, he started the forklift and drove down the street with the freezer still up on the forks and the frost turned to water again within the freezer sloshing back and forth until eventually the lift itself began to teeter as well, and he proceeded like this, pendulating through the lonesome dark like a mad warehouseman at errands in a ghost town.

* * *

In the dream there was a youngish man of slight build with a scraggled wisp of beard talking to him from across a campfire dense with coals and rung in snow. It was cool and dry, and a white hem of powder lay behind the shadows at the edge of the camp. The man was holding two blue enameled mugs that were steaming, and the man was talking saying he had been a disc jockey in a former life. Not the kind on the radio, but in clubs. Grayson thought he knew this man but could not remember his name or how he knew him, and he thought also that this man harbored a secret of central and great importance right then. There was a pair of snow dogs, malamutes or huskies, curled up together on one side of the radiating fire like birds with their muzzles tucked down by their hind legs, steam puffing out of their black glossy noses. The moon was full and vivid in the bright cold and past the trees there were layered ranges of cold bare hills white under the moonlight for miles and miles. And so perfectly could he see the twinkling off the crystals, how each flicker individuated itself amidst an infinity of them, it crossed his mind that they were encased in a snow globe. But where were they? The silence was complete. The man was saying something again now, something about Phil, and he looked back, and the man was Phil. The fire in the circular hollow of snow crackled between them. The dogs groaned in sleep.

There was nothing to say so Grayson just stared. Phil smiled as a man might smile to an apprentice in a trade. He saw that Phil held a bright red mushroom that was spotted white and the size of a saucer plate. The color was overt, all encompassing. Phil's eyes were glistening wet, but it wasn't with proper tears. He was saying something else and the Malamute dogs woke and looked up. The roots moved on the ground below, undulating, and he felt their motion through his thigh bones. Far beneath the snow. Phil smiled and pointed to the moon and said, "Look," and Grayson looked and saw that it was eclipsed by a much smaller planet or negative sun of some kind and that this atramentous body burned in faint ovoid bands of green fire that turned upon the face of the orb like the axis discs of a gyroscope.

A block off Main near the bakery, Grayson woke among his bindles to the sound of tin cans on gravel and then ash shushing in footfalls. He sat up in the grass and listened. It was an animal going through trash. It was pawing at something now in the shadows of desolate houses. He pulled the pack over to him where in the open compartment lay the 1911 and he cocked the hammer with care and relaxed back to listen and accommodate his eyes to the night. There were tamarisks grown up and the branches were swishing the adobe wall of the bakery and catching on a rusted red and white soda sign. He told himself not to start hearing things that weren't there. But then he heard the shushing again and he told himself not to go to sleep with hungry folks traipsing around, itching to rob a foolish traveler of his weapons. He got up from his bedroll and crossed the side lawn of the bakery. There was a dark yard beyond the bakery fence, some trash strewn near the back door. His eyes adjusted further. In the shadows the wiry black dog was wagging its tail in the dust. You. His head cocked up at the man as if he were waiting for him to open the door and help him get into the bakery.

* * *

Two days later, Grayson pulled a battered and requisitioned Dodge 250 off Highway 59 somewhere between Many Farms and Chinle in the center of the Navajo reservation, and he continued on down the red dirt road heading northeast. The morning sun was already blasting away on the wasteland. The windows were open, and he let his hand dangle out against the door. Seven miles down, past the pallet and plywood and cinderblock houses with their roofs of tarp and Tyvek, he slowed and turned off into a steep gravel driveway where, at the base overlooking a white canyon, there was a single trailer set just that side of the cliff's edge. The trailer was banded once around in blue plastic like an old station wagon and there was a single solar panel poised on the roof between a whirligig that was spinning and one each of satellite and radio antennae. A few aluminum and woven plastic lawn chairs were set outside the front door and a small barbeque grill between them exhausted thin puffs of smoke. Behind the chairs a pile of empty beer cans and glass bottles stretched back under the block foundation upholding the trailer, appearing to continue in a snaking line off into the weeds where a lone chicken picked around near a portable water tank. In the dirt beside the tank was the bloated body of a man lying face down. Long black hair tangled up with burrs and twigs spilled out to one side.

When Grayson stepped out it was quiet aside from the wind swirling. The engine settled. There was sage and sour beer on the air wafting up the canyon walls. He walked over to the man lying in the weeds. Huge black ants were marching up one flabby flank and down the other. The line of them rising and falling as the man breathed. Back at the truck he opened the door and turned the key and pushed the buttons to reconfigure the windows, so they were all down about four inches.

"Be cool," he said.

The chicken clucked as he crossed the yard back to the trailer. The little window on one side was slid open and sun-bleached curtains with faint pictures of edible mushrooms and their Latin names under them were pulled back. Dark inside, smell of old meat grease and sorrow. Around the side of the trailer he could see down into the canyon. Great slips of talc powder over white rocks turning to more talc powder. Rounding the corner again into what was the back yard, he watched as dreadlocked Mike from the hostel wiped his bloodshot eyes and stood wobbling up out of a chair, starting to speak. Grayson brought the 1911 up and, as promised, squeezed and put a bullet through his fucking heart.

A bit later when Joe's truck came down the road billowing white dust, Grayson was sitting in one of the chairs at the front of the trailer waiting for him. In the other chair he had Mike's body set up with the limp legs crossed. He'd put his sunglasses back on and placed a half empty jar of corn liquor in his lap as if he might drink at his own wake, such as it was.

The flies were touching down, and Grayson waved them away and stood as Joe crossed the yard with a brown bag of groceries in one arm and a double barrel hammered coach gun swinging in his opposite hand. The fat man who'd been laying in the yard had gotten up some time ago and now he and the woman Joe had attached himself to, who he'd never named to Grayson, stood in the kitchen looking out through the screened window. From a distance Joe said, "God damn Grayson, I can't believe it. I coulda guessed. Ben find you? Did you ever find Phil?"

He had the 1911 alongside his leg. Joe could see it just fine.

Grayson said, "Sit down in that chair."

"Well damn let me put these groceries away and we'll drink a beer," Joe said. But he was looking over at Mike now and the hole in his rainbow Deadhead shirt and the coagulated blood running into the colors. He looked back at Grayson and hollered out the woman's name: Bettina.

"She's inside. With Skins, or Lame Duck, or whatever his damn name is," Grayson said.

"Lake Duck," Joe said.

"What's your Indian name, Joe? Sit down in that fucking chair."

Joe set the bag of groceries on the steps.

He nodded to the shotgun and said, "I know you gotta cock those hammers but leave it there anyway." Joe set the coach gun against the trailer and turned and walked a wide circle around and came back to sit in the chair.

"Surprised there's still a store open," Grayson said.

Joe laughed and said, "They been living like this the whole time, man. For decades. Lard and corn, some potatoes left." He paused and added, "It won't be open much longer. Trucks not rolling anymore." Joe sat. He looked up, stretching his fingers out and brought them into fists. "We're all on one big reservation now."

"Well I'll have to stop by there on my way out."

The introductory moment faded with Joe looking in the dirt and the wind blowing. He brought his head up smiling and he swung the long grey hair back over his shoulders where the veins stood out.

"Hell of a way to treat your landlord, you know it."

"Hell of a way to treat a tenant."

Joe scoffed. "How in the world did you find me?"

Grayson put his hand in his back pocket and brought out a folded-up envelope caked in blood and dirt, and then let if fall.

"That's the mail-in rebate on a solar panel."

The old man shook his head in disbelief.

"Funny thing is, I got that out of Bob's office. Your pal, the pedophile preacher."

Grayson kicked the envelope across the ground. It fluttered and landed by the barbeque.

Joe cleared his throat.

Grayson said, "Maybe you wanted Bob to have the rebate. Maybe you owed a little money."

"Look, man. Shit like this ain't always black and white. Hell, it hardly never is. You think you got all the information but if you get right down to it, you don't. If you really think about it hard enough. You can't be in this place and Mike's place, and hell, my place all at once. You're old enough to know that."

Grayson hadn't pointed the gun at him. It hung in his hand. Joe's eyes behind the spectacles were immense. Not pleading, but watchful rather, and his big scarred hands were loose over the arm rests. He looked up toward the window and at the shotgun.

"It's alright darlin."

There was no face in the window.

"It's alright," Joe said lightly as if maybe she was out there with them. Or as if maybe he were talking to someone else entirely. Someone who wasn't there at all. He looked back up at Grayson standing over him. "It's a damn sight more complicated than you must be making it out to be, man. I don't know. You tell me."

Grayson's eyes were squinted in the sun. His face angled away. The pistol was still loose in his hand and the hammer was back and his thumb slid down and flipped the safety away. He sighed.

"Joe, I guess maybe you have attached yourself to the hope that I just tracked hippie Mike here. Perhaps you would like to pry open a wedge based on confusion or plain obfuscation. Argue relativism. Fog of war and such. Talk your way out."

Joe's fingers went absently to his shirt, padding along the pocket seam for his Zippo.

"But I am certain as a man can be certain."

Joe was silent. The Zippo slipped around in his hand. Grayson went on.

"You owed on a dream that was never going to manifest. The screws of the world were turning. The opportunity to sell men you knew out to other men you knew was simply a mechanical operation at that point."

Behind Joe's ear was a rolled cigarette that he plucked out now. He struck the Zippo and dragged so hard his jaw popped. He exhaled and swallowed.

"Or is that all made up, and it's just that strange things happen sometimes?"

Joe smacked his mouth like it was dry. "No, man, things do happen. Lemme tell you. They do just happen. They don't always add up. It wasn't me. It wasn't you. There's a whole shitload of things, of causes, man."

Grayson shook the 1911 just a bit to hear the slide clack in the frame races. Joe puffed the smoke and glanced around at the coach gun and the hills and at the jar in Mike's lap encircled in his stiffening hands.

"They sold me out too. Just so you know. That's the real truth."

"The real truth now, Joe, is that I came here with justice and mercy. Exile or death. I haven't brought any loopholes, ways out."

Joe threw up his hands. "Well look at me. I'm fucking exiled."

"By avoiding mercy—that is by showing none, you've chosen justice.'

"I gave you a place to lay your head, man. To live."

"The rentier's unique guilt. I'm immune," said Grayson.

"Well help me out, man. Explain this shit."

"Joe, if you believe that any single part of me came out to this shithole to have a substantive philosophical conversation of the sort where we can then both go away in peace, having learned a thing or two, then you are truly blessed in ignorance. That's not in the least why I came out here."

"Then what did you come out here for, Grayson?"

"I came for satisfaction in the ancient sense. I came here to blow your brains out."

He brought the pistol up and leveled it in the space between them. Joe laughed, dry and hard, just as the gun jumped and recoiled in Grayson's hand. The white canyon cupped away the report, carrying it off through the passes. A little falcon alighted from a branch of manzanita and dipped into the chasm as if she'd follow the echo or safeguard its transfer into oblivion. And the blue bands of plastic along the trailer were all the sudden speckled white with bone and matter. Grayson stood for a moment watching the colors slide away and then he turned and crossed the yard to the Dodge.

Coda:
The Wheel

At a state line, Grayson pulled off the highway. The map said there was a lake, and he needed gas. In the parking lot a few dusty cars were abandoned in the shade. No one was around. Evergreens grew up to the road and lined the lot. At the back of the truck he dropped the tailgate and pulled the backpack around for the siphon hose inside and he took it in hand with the pistol and opened the rear passenger door on the double cab and the wiry black dog came stepping over the seat to put his head against the man's chest. He put his arm around the dog, holding him, and they stood there like that for a moment and then the dog lifted his chin and set it back down on the shelf of Grayson's shoulder blinking his brown eyes out at the lot and smelling the air. Watching. When they had gone around and collected the gas and a few items from inside the cars they went back together, and he set the canisters in the bed of the truck and bungeed them to the side panels and the dog observed him and then went around to the passenger side thinking they were driving again.

But Grayson said to him, "No let's go see."

Then the dog was ahead of him on the path trotting and sniffing the edges where the dandelions and ferns were grown up or coiled like green snails. They wound around on the soft black dirt where there were many tracks, old and new, and he saw through the treeline that the lake was placid and misted above and when they declined through the moss and long cedar boughs and the dog saw the water he looked back at the man to take the measure of him. Maybe the dog was inquiring as to the nature of the lake, having never seen one, or the purpose of their walk to its shore.

He pointed at the blue water. "Get in there, boy."

And the dog ran down the rest of the way and crossed the gray sand to the soundless edge and walked a little way in lapping the water but he stayed in the shallows and would look up for the man on the bank and drink and look up again, waiting for him. Always waiting for him.

Made in the USA
Coppell, TX
22 September 2020

38571914R10189